Draft Pick

Season II: Andrei

DARIE McCOY

Edited By

All That's Wright

Edited by: All That's Wright

Cover Art/Design: A.S. McCoy

EBook ISBN: 978-1-961999-10-7

Print ISBN: 978-1-961999-11-4

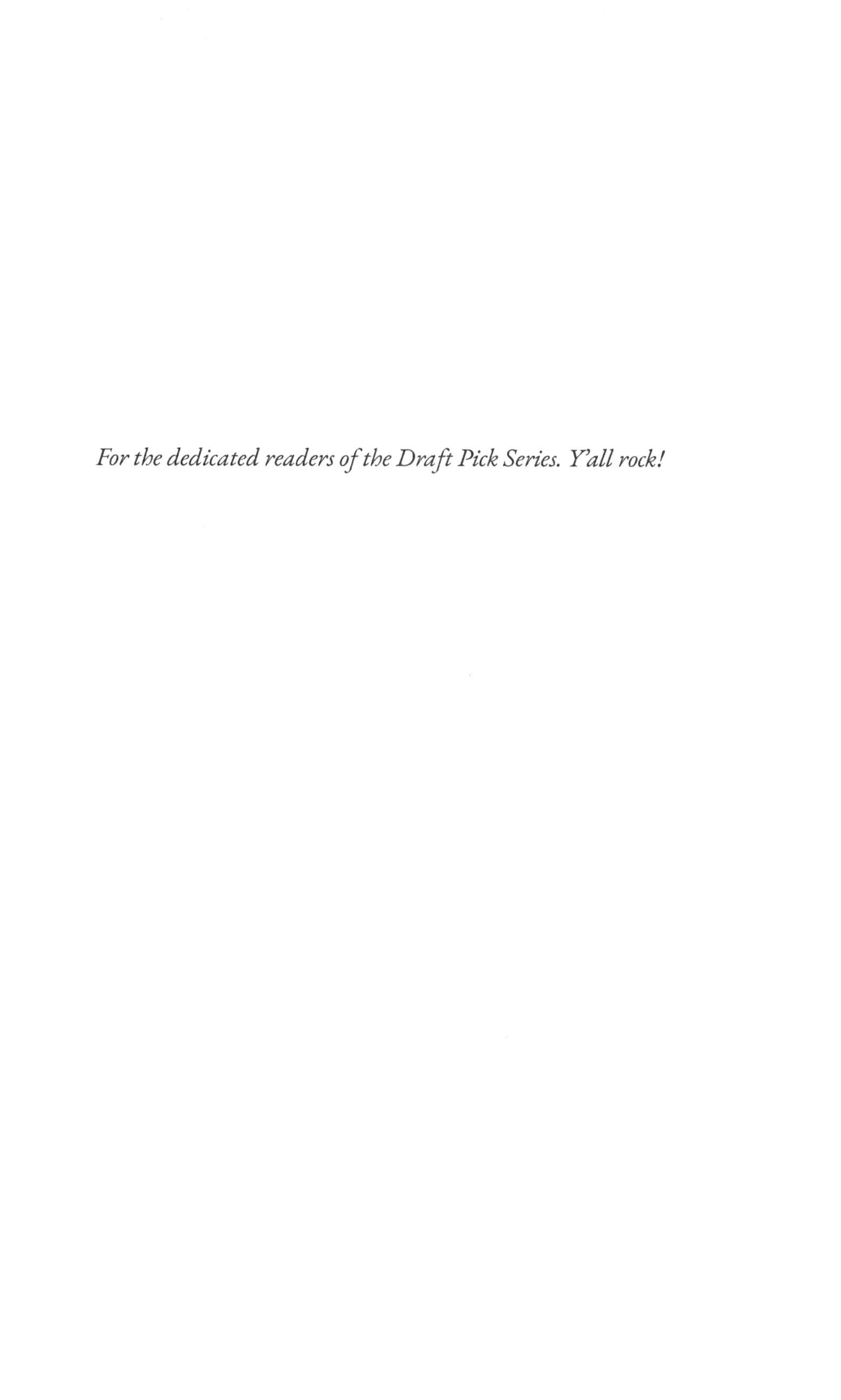

For the dedicated readers of the Draft Pick Series. Y'all rock!

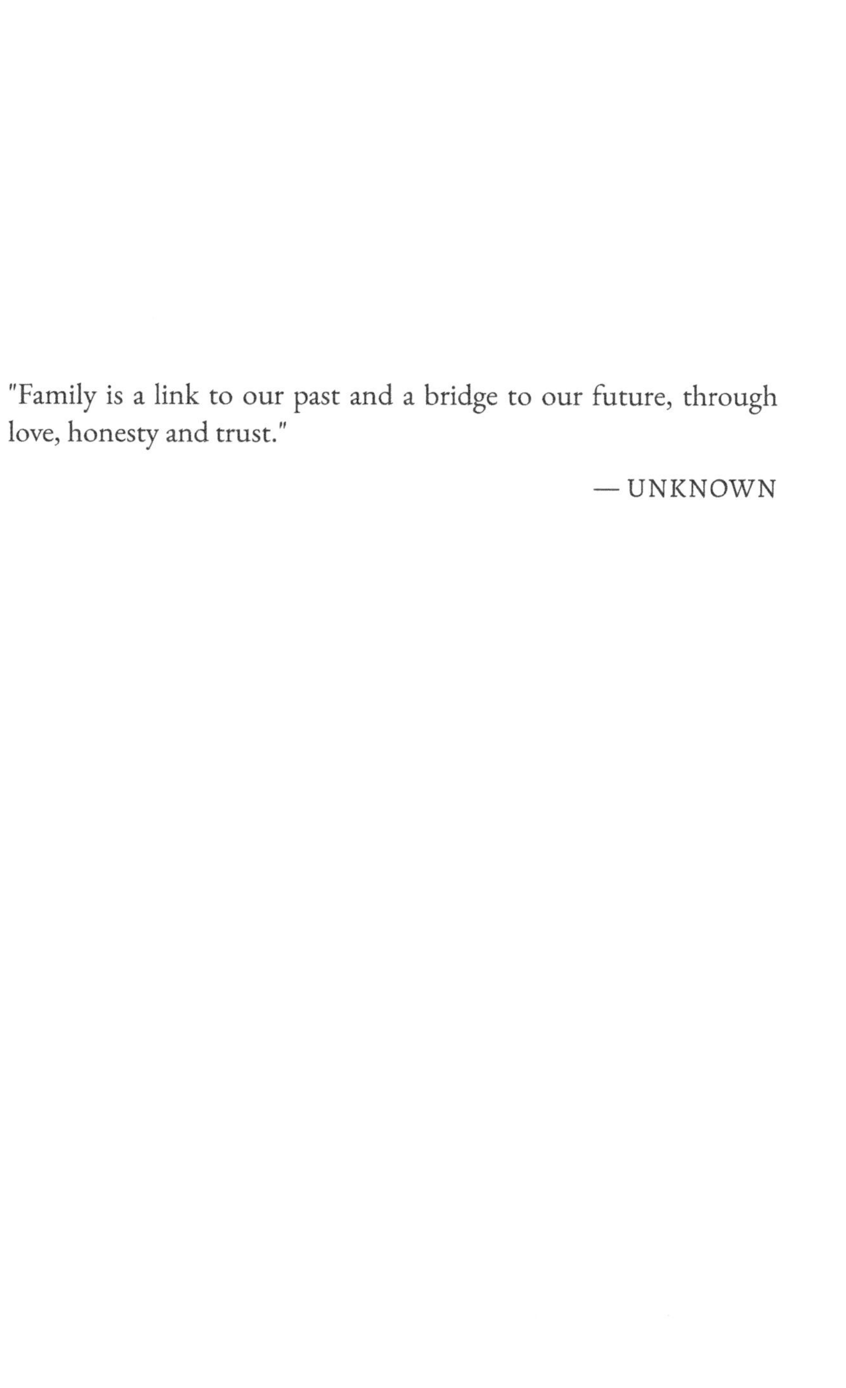

"Family is a link to our past and a bridge to our future, through love, honesty and trust."

— UNKNOWN

Prologue

Beeping brought Andrei Antonov out of dreamland. It was one helluva dream, but the compact plush body of the woman in the dream was better in reality. Blindly reaching out with one arm, he picked up the cellphone making the offensive noise, robotically swiping the screen to end it.

Once the noise was silenced, he put the phone down and rolled to his left. Empty space greeted him. Where there should've been a bronze-skinned beauty, there was nothing except the stark white of his sheets. *Where the fuck was she?*

"Svet!" He called out hoping she was simply in the other room. "Zoyra!" His Russian accent was thicker than usual as he tried again.

Sitting up in the bed, he listened for sounds in the suite. *Nothing.* The previous night, he'd been too eager to plunge into her sweetness to make the drive to his home. So, he'd brought her to his private suite above his casino. The floor was littered with the evidence of the multiple rounds of mind-blowing sex the two had engaged in.

For Andrei to admit, even to himself, that a sexual experience blew his mind, was a feat. In his years as a star on the ice, from his time as an Olympic athlete to his life as a professional, he'd had too many partners to count. But none of them had anywhere close to the level of impact Zaria Coleman had on him. Not one.

He'd planned to start his day between her thick thighs. Andrei needed another taste of her honey before he wrapped up his business to allow him to hop a plane to fly halfway around the world to attend his friend's wedding.

Zaria ruined that plan by not being where she was supposed to be. Only the faint scent of her perfume remained. *Who did she think she was?* No one ghosts Andrei Artyom Antonov. Whipping the sheet away from his body, he got out of bed and stalked into the bathroom. Just wait until he saw the little escape artist again.

Fuming, he turned on the shower and set about getting his day going. Not starting it balls deep in Zaria's pussy wasn't something he let go of easily. He was gonna spank her ass for her disappearing act. A sinister smile stretched his lips as he thought of how great the rounded globes were going to look with his handprint on them.

His shaft hardened between his thighs drawing another curse. Adding this to her list of infractions, Andrei took his length in his hand. Closing his eyes he pictured Zaria's plump lips, imagining them stretched wide to accommodate his girth. She was definitely going to pay for him having to relieve himself.

Although he was in his penthouse and not his home on the outskirts of Las Vegas, Andrei still had everything he needed for his morning routine, including suits in the large walk-in adjacent to the bathroom. Once he completed his shower of frustration, he dressed and went to the kitchen to prepare his morning coffee. Along the way, he picked up his phone from the bedside table.

Filling the small, long handled, Jezve pot with water, he placed it on the stove setting the temperature on low heat. This small task, preparing his own coffee, grinding the beans, was a process which helped him focus his mind. He'd only have the one cup for the day; he never drank any more than that. As he waited for the coffee to heat to the point where he could stir, he swiped through messages on his phone.

Realistically, he didn't expect a call or message from Zaria, but part of him wanted to see something. When he'd given Alyssa his business card all those months ago, he'd held out little hope that she'd actually tell her friend he'd offered to accommodate them at his restaurant in the future.

Andrei had seen them there on occasion and the compact, curvy little lawyer caught his attention.

She was stunning, vivacious, and utterly captivating. The old Andrei. The pussy hound from his days of playing professional hockey would've approached her a long time ago and bedded her quickly before moving on. The person he was now, owner of the most exclusive resort and casino in Las Vegas and part owner of the Las Vegas Chevaliers hockey team, was more reserved in his approach to women—even those he simply wanted to bed.

The issue was, he didn't want to just fuck the feisty little attorney. One night wouldn't be enough to sate him. Having tasted her sweetness and felt the grasp of her honeyed walls, he was certain he'd need more than a single night to get his fill of the luscious Zaria Coleman.

As he brewed the coffee Turkish style, he stirred as he swiped through his phone making decisions about his daily schedule. After dipping out the first foam into his coffee cup, he resumed stirring as he reviewed the preliminary reports from the previous evening. He'd been occupied with Carver and Alyssa's joint Bachelor and Bachelorette party. So, he hadn't walked through as he normally would have when he was still on the premises at night.

By the time the coffee was ready to pour, he'd skimmed enough to have the general idea of how the night went. Besides, the question of where the fuck Zaria went was pressing on his mind. More importantly, when had she slinked away from his bed?

After he'd finished drinking the strong brew, Andrei left the suite heading for his office several floors down. As he stepped into the private elevator, images of the ride up the previous night assailed him. Images of Zaria's ass cradled in his hands as he held her against the wall plundering her lips while she writhed, undulating her hips against the erection tenting his pants. His nostrils flared as the memory of her scent became so prominent he could swear she was standing right next to him.

Once again, his anger blazed. *How dare she rob him?* The elevator doors slid open just outside his office. Standing next to the open doorway was his personal bodyguard, Yeva. Like the rest of the security at Anton's, he was highly trained to be both effective and invisible. Without a word, the man followed Andrei into his inner office.

Walking behind his desk, Andrei pressed his finger against the keypad to wake and login to his computer. When the screen came to life, he looked up at Yeva standing silently just inside the closed door. Folding his arms, Andrei stared at one of the few people from St. Petersburg he still allowed within his orbit.

"When did she leave?" The question was simple, and he knew he didn't have to clarify further.

"At four a.m." Frowning, Yeva tipped his head slightly in question. "Should I have stopped her?"

"No. She was not and is not a prisoner. She can come and go as she pleases."

Andrei sincerely wanted to believe the words weren't just lip service, but heat licked up his neck. She'd left thirty minutes after their last round of hot-as-fuck sex. It was obvious she'd waited for him to fall asleep to sneak away. Oh. He was definitely spanking her ass for that one. Zaria owed him a debt. She'd started this whole thing with her request the previous night. He wasn't nearly done fulfilling it.

Chapter One

THE TRIPLE A EXPRESS

Zaria power walked her way through her office as if it were any other day. Outwardly, she was the picture of professional calm. Inside, she was an absolute mess. As much bravado and rah-rah as she did with Alyssa, Zaria didn't indulge in impulsive acts. That kind of shit had lasting affects for Black women. And, for an attorney with her own practice, she had to play things close to the vest. She lived, but she picked her moments very carefully to let her hair down.

Heads turned as she made her way past the cubicles to reach her executive style suite. They hadn't expected her today. When she'd made the plans for Carver and Alyssa's joint Bachelor/Bachelorette party, she'd considered they may party too hard to work the next day. Besides, she'd intended to be off for the remainder of the week.

She was only at the office for one meeting, then she'd go home and finish packing so she could be ready when the car service picked her up. Carver surprised Alyssa with wedding plans for Bali. They'd fly there on his private plane a few days early allowing them to acclimate to the time difference before the big day.

Zaria was sincerely happy for her friend. Although they hadn't been besties for over half their lives like some people, they shared a strong bond. One Zaria cherished. She was her parent's only child; however, she was raised by her aunt who had two children of her own. So, Zaria valued pure and true friendships like the one she had with Alyssa. They balanced each other and helped one another work through the tough things.

They also called one another out for fuck-shit without ending their friendship over it. That kind of relationship was rare. As she stepped into her office, Zaria's fingers itched to pick up the phone and call her friend, but she didn't. She didn't know what she'd say...*Hey girl. Guess who got her back blown out by Triple A himself?* Nope. Not going to happen.

Besides, Alyssa had enough to do without listening to her talk about how she snuck out of Andrei's suite like a thief in the night after he damn near sucked her soul from her body with that damn mouth of his. The man should teach a cunnilingus master class. It was a good thing Zaria was inside her office by the time the memory of the previous night kicked in.

Her knees nearly buckled remembering Andrei ordering her to sit on his face as he brought her to one of numerous orgasms before he lifted her like she weighed nothing and placed her on his thick shaft. After she was where he wanted her once more, he delivered another order—for her to ride his cock. An order she obeyed like she was a jockey going for a triple crown win at the Kentucky Derby.

Zaria was no stranger to hanging out with wealthy people, heck she had money herself. Not old money or generational wealth, but she wasn't hurting by any means. However, she might not have dropped whatever coin was necessary to close down the Rooftop Bar at Anton's for the night for her bestie's Bachelorette party.

Nevertheless, she took a shot and called the number on the card the big man gave Alyssa a few months ago. After she'd laughed at Alyssa's retelling of the interaction between Carver and Andrei, Zaria simply filed the card away. She really thought he was blowing smoke when he said to call if they needed anything. He surprised her by answering the phone on the second ring.

When his deep lightly accented voice flowed over the line, her core clenched. Brushing off the feeling, she pushed forward, because there was no way she was hot and bothered just from the man speaking. Yet when she met him face to face to discuss the festivities, she had to remind herself to breathe.

He was a man like any other, plain and simple. Only...he wasn't a man like any other. He was six-feet six-inches of brawny sex on two legs. Her initial thought was that it was a good thing he was rich because he couldn't possibly fit anything off the rack. Her second thought was, she wanted to latch onto him and climb his big body like a spider monkey.

While he was nothing but professional in their meeting to work out the details of the party, his gaze appeared to linger on her breasts a little longer than necessary. Zaria chalked it up as the norm. Her girls entered the room first. They got plenty of attention on a regular day. However, the night of the party, his gaze burned her clothing to cinders. Having given herself a pep talk about not treating him any differently than any other man, she had the bright idea to call his bluff.

The party was winding down somewhat, and Andrei stood behind the bar. He was acting as bartender after sending the regular person home for the night. His sleeves were rolled up exposing his thick forearms. Zaria tried and failed not to notice the prominent vein traversing his muscles disappearing beneath the shirt sleeve.

Andrei poured vodka into a glass and slid it down the bar right into the hand of the big Texan who'd crashed the party escorting her legal buddy Ensley Warren. Not sparing Ryker more than a quick glance, Zaria licked her lips and placed her hands palms down on the bar top. Stepping onto the low rail attached to the front of the bar, she hoisted herself onto the tall stool.

After putting the vodka back on the shelf, Andrei strolled to a stop in front of her.

"Is there something you'd like, Svet?"

Her brow wrinkled. She wasn't sure what he'd just called her, but she chalked it up to some common Russian endearment she wasn't familiar with. "I don't think you can pour me what I want from one of those bottles."

Zaria couldn't believe she'd actually said those words aloud, and she hoped her expression and body language didn't give away the nerves making her belly tumble. Ice blue eyes peered into hers as he leaned forward on the bar closing the distance between them.

"I believe I asked you a question. You do not worry about whether I can supply your need. You simply tell me what it is and I will do the rest."

Not backing away from the intensity of his stare or the confidence in his words, her gaze went from his eyes to his lips, then back up to those arctic pools. "Is that so?"

"Da." His voice seemed to drop two octaves with the curt response.

"Well...I want what your eyes have been promising me since I walked in tonight."

A shiver skated down Zaria's spine when she felt the warmth of his touch gliding along the back of her hand tracing a path up her arm before gently wrapping around the back of her neck. His hand was so big, his thumb was able to stroke the front of her neck while his other fingers caressed her nape.

"Is that all you want?" His accent was thicker and his voice was deeper with a gravelly edge to it.

In turn her own voice softened, taking on a breathy tone. "It's a start." When she licked her lips, his eyes tracked the motion.

"We are leaving. Now."

Sweat beaded on her brow and upper lip as Zaria jerked back into the present. Snatching a tissue from the dispenser on her desk, she wiped the moisture away. She had to get herself together before her meeting. She couldn't allow her memories to take her back to the five blissful hours she'd spent being tuned like a piano in the hands of an expert technician. While she'd given herself fully to the experience, Andrei had worked her body in ways she'd only heard about.

If one of her best clients hadn't contacted her with a late request, she would've passed the meeting off to a junior partner and not even come into the office. A girl needed recuperation time after taking a ride on the Triple A express. However, the contract Howard Voss dangled in front of her had the potential to reach eight to nine figures easily within the first year, which meant her firm's cut would be more than hefty.

So, she didn't have time to obsess about Andrei Antonov and his magic hockey player dick. Because she was certain, that wasn't the casino owner Andrei who bent her like a pretzel last night. No, he'd pulled his younger self out of retirement for the naughty hump fest they had in his suite. His stamina was top shelf, just like the liquor he served the night before. The phone on Zaria's desk rang saving her from going farther down the rabbit hole with her lustful thoughts of the broad-shouldered Russian.

"Hello?"

"Miss Coleman, Mr. Voss is here."

"Thank you, Kendra. Can you put him in the main conference room? I'll be there shortly."

Zaria knew she didn't have to ask Kendra to make sure the client was comfortable. She was very proficient at her job, possibly too proficient to still work reception. However, she seemed content with the role. When Zaria called earlier with the last-minute addition to her schedule, Kendra got on top of getting the room ready and securing refreshments for the client.

Grabbing the file and her laptop, Zaria left her office taking a left to join Howard Voss in the conference room. Although Zaria practiced contract law primarily, her firm was full service. Howard had come to her initially by recommendation to have her work on his Prenuptial Agreement with his third wife. That was ten years ago. He was currently on wife number four.

However, she'd moved from drawing up marriage contracts for him to reviewing and negotiating contracts for his business interests as well. As most wealthy people did, Howard had a team for such things. But, after Zaria found a loophole in a contract saving him millions, he didn't make major moves without her putting her eyes on the inked words.

Entering the conference room, Zaria pasted a smile on her face and extended a hand to her client. "Good morning, Howard. What ways are you going to test my skills today? I know this meeting can't be about this simple contract you emailed late last night. Lucky for you I saw the alert."

Releasing his hand, she gestured toward the chair to the right of the head of the table. She sat after he was settled. Flipping her wrist, Zaria made a show of checking her watch.

"I'm on limited time. So unfortunately, I can't indulge in your normal dance of 'hide the lead' today. You'll have to give it to me straight."

Smiling wide beneath the stark white beard outlining his lips, Howard chuckled. "That's what I appreciate about you Coleman. You're straight to the point." Dipping his head, he looked at her under his bushy white eyebrows. "Still, you know I like the dance."

Zaria narrowed her eyes ever so slightly, and Howard lifted his hands. Sitting back in his seat, he released another chuckle. "Alright, alright. I'll get down to brass tacks. The contract I sent you is for a small upstart, but I'm sure you're aware it has potential. If it goes where I think it's going, we could be talking about something which will knock the fruit off the tree."

Even if Howard didn't mention the giant computer company two guys started in their garage, Zaria knew exactly who he was talking about. She also knew he was right. If he could swoop in, he had the financial backing to keep the smaller company from being eaten up then swept into the fold of the titan, becoming a cog in the wheel instead of the revolution that they could be.

Connecting her laptop to the wide screen monitor mounted on the wall, she pulled up the contract. Going directly to the sections she highlighted when she'd reviewed it at home, she launched into her thoughts on the deal. Not one to operate in the gray, she made certain to point out where more clarity was needed to decrease the odds of a civil suit in the future.

Chapter Two

I OWE THAT PERFECT ASS A SPANKING

Although he didn't take many impromptu trips, Andrei always had a flight crew on standby. It took very little effort to get the information on when Carver planned to leave. It took even less to find out Zaria was included on the flight manifest. Taking into consideration the flight time to Bali from Vegas, including refueling, Andrei coordinated to be in the air no more than an hour behind his friend.

True, he'd planned to fly out a day later since he didn't need the same amount of recuperation time they'd built into the schedule. However, since a certain someone thought it was okay to pull a disappearing act, he altered his plans. He could work from the plane. In the event a major decision needed to be made, his assistant knew how to reach him in flight.

Snagging sleep where he felt necessary, Andrei arrived on the island without any discernible feelings of jet lag. Though he knew from experience it could sneak up on a body. Arriving at the villa, he was greeted by the staff who informed him the others had already been assigned their rooms and were taking some rest. That worked out just fine for him. Following the house manager, he accepted his room assignment in the east wing on the second floor.

Andrei took a few moments to shower and change. No sooner had he exited the bathroom than there was a knock on his door. When he opened it, Yeva stood on the other side. Without a word, the man passed him a folded piece of paper. Opening it, Andrei's lips stretched into a grin.

"Spasibo."

Nodding, Yeva stepped away from the door. Slipping his shoes on, then grabbing a small carrying case, Andrei left his well-appointed suite. Less than five minutes later, he stood before a door with plumeria flowers painted on it. The island native flower was a golden yellow at the center with white at the edges. Andrei stared at the intricacy of the design before raising his curled fingers to rap lightly on the door. It only took a few seconds before it swung open.

"Lyssa, I promise. I'm fine..."

Zaria's words trailed off when her eyes met his chest instead of whom he was certain she expected to see on the other side of her door.

"Good afternoon, Svet."

Andrei spoke the words softly, but even he heard the edge of hardness in the greeting. Walking forward slowly, he left her with the options of backing away to allow him entry or allowing her body to be pressed against his. She chose to back away. Although, in his mind, she only delayed, not prevented, the alternative. Her body would definitely be pressed against his.

"Andrei...what are you doing here?"

Looking around her suite, he took in the difference between hers and his. Her room looked more like a cozy apartment—sans kitchen. Returning his gaze to her, he swept over her frame taking her in from her bonnet covered hair, to the silky bathrobe concealing her curves, down to her pretty painted toenails. He didn't bother to address her question; he had a more pressing one of his own.

"Why did you sneak away from my bed?"

Stepping completely over the threshold, he closed the door without looking behind him. Blindly, he located and turned the lock.

"Excuse me?"

"You are not excused."

Andrei continued to advance on her taking note of the way her breathing changed causing her nostrils to flare slightly and her breasts to lift a little higher with each inhale. While a puzzled expression blanketed her face, they both knew she wasn't the least bit confused.

Her soft palms landed on his chest when she stopped retreating and his body was nearly flush with hers. Her head tipped back while his dipped lower. With his gaze locked on hers, he placed his much larger hands on Zaria's relocating them to the small of her back where he gathered both of her hands into one of his. At his touch, Zaria's breathing hitched. She bravely attempted to cover it up.

"Andrei, what do you think you're doing? I didn't invite you inside my room."

Tipping his head, he leaned closer to her face. "Did you not? I seem to recall you asking me to give you the promise you saw in my eyes. What made you think a few measly hours would be the extent of that promise?"

Grasping a handful of her luscious ass, he squeezed the pillowy softness. "You owe me a debt. I am here to collect."

"Andrei—"

Andrei swallowed Zaria's words with a searing kiss. He didn't need to hear her pretend she didn't want him to be exactly where he was. Her body told him everything he needed to know. Releasing her lips, he rained kisses down the column of her neck.

Letting go of her hands, he grabbed two hands full of her delectable bottom and lifted her in his arms. Not one word of protest was murmured as she wound her legs around his waist. As if he'd memorized the way, he walked them through the suite to the king-sized bed. Zaria's head was thrown back and little whimpers escaped her as he continued his campaign on her senses.

When he reached the bed, he dropped one knee onto the soft duvet cover and lowered her, placing her on her back. Following his drugging kisses, she made no attempt to conceal her desire. It was good. They were long past pretense. Beneath the thin barrier of her bathrobe, her nipples pebbled standing out begging for him to take them between his lips.

The gap below where the robe was belted showed her neatly trimmed pussy and Andrei's mouth watered. Rising to his feet, he quickly shucked off his clothing. She didn't move, not even to cover her exposed mons. With her eyelids at half mast, she watched him undress.

Leaning over the bed, his fingers traced the path his gaze had taken, Andrei indulged himself in the softness of her skin. He hadn't forgotten that he owed her a spanking for her *Whodini* act. But first, he needed to satiate his need for her sweetness.

With one jerk, the knot in the sash belting the robe pulled free and the front of her voluptuous body was exposed to him. Licking his lips in anticipation, Andrei dropped to his knees on the floor beside the bed. Slipping his hands beneath her thick thighs, he hooked his arms around them and tugged her to the edge of the bed throwing her legs over his shoulders.

Her sharp inhale was followed by a keening moan when he dipped his head and latched onto her pearl. Andrei didn't play around with teasing her by lapping at her slit or dipping his tongue into her channel. Their previous night together had provided him with a roadmap to her pleasure. So, he bypassed the scenic route and went straight to the main attraction. The place she was most sensitive.

Sliding one finger inside her velvet walls, he groaned at the feel of the slickness clamping down on his digit. He wished it was his cock instead, but they'd get to that. Zaria's hands were on his head with her fingers threading into his hair pulling at the strands. She was close. Andrei could tell. Just before she tipped over into her first orgasm, he lifted away from her fragrant center.

Her digits stiffened in conjunction with the little growl of frustration issuing from her throat.

"What?..." There was a whine entwined with the single word question.

"You do not get to come yet. You have been a bad girl."

Andrei pierced her with a stare as one side of his mouth tipped up in a wicked grin. Since he was a scant few inches from her dripping core as he spoke to her, he knew his breath was teasing her sensitive nub. Maybe he wouldn't have to spank her. There were other ways to deliver punishment. Although he still liked the idea of his handprint on her rounded ass cheek.

"What?" Her confused expression was absolutely adorable, but cuteness wouldn't save Zaria Coleman this time.

"You waited until I was sleeping, and you snuck out like a burglar under the cover of darkness."

Mumbling under her breath, she met his stare with a stubborn tilt of her chin. Tracing a finger along the seam of her pussy, sinking inside, he sought that special spot like a heat seeking missile. Adding another finger, he stimulated the internal nerves. Zaria's hips tilted as she undulated them keeping time with his tunneling digits. Her hold on his hair tightened.

The scent of her arousal was almost too much for him to resist, but he managed. Once he felt the change in her silken walls, he immediately halted his ministrations. This time, Zaria's expression of frustration was a muffled scream. Releasing his hair, she grabbed a pillow placing it over her face to obscure the sound. Snatching it away, Andrei tossed it to the floor.

"No hiding from me, Svet. You were brave enough to plant your sexy ass in front of me and demand I give you what I promised. Now, you will take it. You will take all of it and you won't hide your response from me."

"You're mean."

Zaria's lips pursed into a pout. She wrapped her arms around her middle. Her body twitched and she tried to twist away from his hold as desire heated her satiny smooth skin.

"I am mean?"

One eyebrow quirked as he stared at her. Images of those plump lips wrapped around his thickness skated across his mind. The memory of how they felt devouring his length was fresh. He'd have them again... But, not yet. There were lessons to be learned.

Releasing her thighs, Andrei shouldered her legs open wider as he joined her on the bed. With his arms braced on either side of her head, he settled his hips at the juncture of her thighs. His throbbing cock was poised at the entrance of her leaking walls. Gliding his shaft between her puffy lower lips, he coated it in the slickness. She was more than ready for him.

"We must come to an understanding, Svet. Then, I will give you what you need."

The fire in her stare would've caused a weaker man to wither. However, Andrei wasn't a weak man. He wasn't afraid of the compact beauty whose thighs cradled his hips like they were made specifically for that purpose. He continued to slide his dick between her folds reaching the opening of her channel, but doing nothing more than nudging the head of his cock against the opening before moving on.

Zaria squirmed attempting to tilt her pelvis to capture the hardness being held just outside her reach. Finally, she yielded. *Thank fuck.*

"What kind of understanding?" She asked the question so softly, had he not been staring directly into her face, he wouldn't have known she spoke.

Sliding inside her channel until it engulfed the head of his cock, he pierced her with his gaze.

"You seem to be under the impression you can come into my bed, share your delicious body with me, then leave when you are ready. That is not how this works."

"It isn't?"

Andrei didn't miss the challenge in her response and his removal of the tip of his erection from her channel told her so. Her fingers immediately clutched at his sides and her thighs clamped in an attempt to hold him inside.

"Okay! Okay! It's not." When he didn't seem convinced by her acquiescence, she turned those bottomless dark brown eyes on him looking at him through her lashes. "It's not how this works." She agreed softly.

"Khoroshaya devochka."

Zaria didn't speak more than the basic Russian terms most Americans learned from movies, however the way her gaze turned sultry when he called her a good girl made him wonder if he'd been misinformed. As a reward, he slid inside her honeyed walls until a little more than the head of his shaft was enclosed in her heat.

"You do not leave my bed, until I release you."

A slow thrust took him deeper inside her center.

"You most definitely do not slink away while I am sleeping."

Another thrust took him to the halfway mark. His lower back burned, not from exertion, but from the willpower it took to keep from plunging completely inside her.

"You wanted the promise in my eyes, Svet. Now, you have to accept it. All of it."

With his declaration, Andrei captured her lips as he sank deeper until he could go no farther. His balls rested against the outside of her pussy, drawn up tight with the urge to come. It was then that he realized he hadn't used one of the condoms which lay useless in the pocket of his pants.

As he had the thought, he withdrew from her depths then plunged back inside. A new goal now in his mind. He'd fuck Zaria until she couldn't walk to leave his bed and he'd release his seed in her tight little pussy each and every time. It was an imperative.

Zaria's head tipped back as she let out a throaty moan. It was accompanied by a tightening of her core. To Andrei, it felt like she was using her velvety walls to massage his cock. *This was it*. The control she had over her body to give pleasure as she received it. It was one of the reasons he couldn't let her simply step away. No. She wasn't allowed to take her sweet pussy from him until he was ready to let her go. And, Andrei wasn't close to being ready for that.

Cupping her breasts, he kissed the full globes, each one getting equal attention before he wrapped his lips around one nipple sucking it while holding it captive between his teeth. The corresponding grip of her channel on his shaft almost made him lose control.

Nonsensical words tumbled from her mouth as she rocked her hips riding his cock from below. Her responsiveness was addictive. She wasn't faking it to boost his ego. No, Zaria enjoyed what he did to her body and wasn't shy about letting him know. Transferring his attention to her other breast, he lavished it with the same intensity as the first.

Releasing it with a parting kiss, Andrei maneuvered them farther onto the bed without withdrawing from his personal slice of heaven. Lifting one of her legs against his chest, he straddled the other plumbing her depths from a new angle drawing more unrestrained moans from her lips. Her hands roamed as much of his body as she could reach as if she couldn't not touch him.

"This is what you want, da?" Andrei bared his teeth as he stroked his length inside her to the hilt. Withdrawing, he started the process over again.

"You want me to stretch you, mark you, make sure your sweet pussy gushes anytime you simply hear my name? That is what you want. Da?"

She didn't respond, but he knew it wasn't stubbornness keeping her from admitting the truth of his words. No, his Svet couldn't form coherent answers at the moment. Her skin was flushed appearing to glow in the sunlight streaming through the curtains. Long lashes lay against the apples of her cheeks as her eyes squeezed shut while her mouth stretched open, but no sound issued from her throat.

Her walls gripped his cock so tightly he jerked to a stop mid stroke. Lightning shot down his spine and his release spurted into her grasping channel. Involuntary grunts were wrenched from him. Spasmodic shudders racked him as he flooded her hot quim.

Finally coming down from his orgasmic high, Andrei lowered her leg from his chest and slid down until they were face to face. Bracing himself on his elbows, he watched as she came back to awareness of the world around her. Her hands patted his shoulders, then chest before dropping to her own body as if to assure herself they were both real.

When her hands landed on her head, her movements stilled. Wide eyes shot to his. He lifted one eyebrow nonverbally questioning her look of surprise.

"Oh my God! Don't tell me I had my bonnet on this entire time!"

Since the answer to her question was obvious, he simply stared at her.

"Oh my God...I did..." She moaned trying to turn herself as if to hide from him.

Dropping more of his weight onto her body, he stilled her movements. Cupping her chin, he turned her face back to his.

"No, Andrei. This is embarrassing enough."

"Why?" His gaze on her was steady.

"Why?! I'm wearing a hair bonnet that isn't remotely sexy."

"I do not give a shit about this thing." He plucked at the satin covering, but didn't attempt to remove it—nor did he allow her to remove it.

"It does not cover your sweet pizda keeping me away from it. So, what do I care if it is on your head or not?"

To emphasize his point, he reached between them and strummed the hooded bundle of nerves above the entrance to the sweet pussy he just mentioned. A strangled moan issued from Zaria as her hips swayed into his touch. He'd just come, but Andrei was ready for round two. That was the other thing about being with his feisty little lawyer. She awakened his libido in ways it hadn't been stirred in too long.

In recent years, he'd maybe give two rounds of fucking before he sent the woman on her way. He wasn't a selfish prick. So, he'd make sure she came at least three times in the process. However, with Zaria, he was insatiable. Many men at his age of forty-four, couldn't achieve the type of stamina she inspired without pharmaceutical help.

His Svet was all the stimulant he needed. Even when she looked, what she considered, less than her best, he still wanted to sink inside her and never leave. Wetness from their joint release coated his fingertips as he slipped them into her passage. When she used her internal muscles to grip his digits, he groaned and pulled them out.

Sitting back on his knees, he tapped her outer thigh. "Turn over, Svet. I owe that perfect ass a spanking."

Still somewhat boneless from their last coupling, Zaria was slower to move than he liked, so he gripped her hips assisting her in the task. With her chest pressed into the bed and her ass pointed up to meet him, he bracketed her thighs with his. He gave no warning as he stroked his entire length into her weeping core. Andrei's head fell back onto his shoulders as he took a moment to appreciate the flawlessness of the feeling.

Splaying his fingers against the rounded cheeks of her ass, he remembered his promise spank the plush globes. When the first crack rang out into the room, her core squeezed his length in response as a muffled gasp flew from her lips. Stretching his lips in a rare smile, Andrei set about keeping his word.

It was sometime later, after they showered together, and as Zaria lay with her back pressed against his chest while they lounged in the surprisingly large tub, that they actually held a conversation. Well, at least began a conversation. The woman was wily and more than a little evasive. Having spent a large part of his career as a professional athlete avoiding the trappings of relationships, one would think her reluctance would be welcome. It was not. Not even a little. The reason wasn't something he wanted to delve into at the moment.

Water dripped from Zaria's fingertips as she lifted her arm from the, in his opinion, entirely too hot liquid covered in fluffy bubbles. He tracked the progress with his gaze as she turned her wrist over before plunging her limb beneath the surface once more. His arms were wrapped securely around her with his hands splayed on her rounded tummy just below the breast he could practically taste on his tongue.

"Why did you leave?"

It was the question he really needed an answer to. He wouldn't try to name the reason knowing the answer was so important to him. He simply had to have it. Silence stretched between them, and for a moment, he thought she'd do what she'd done earlier. Deflect.

"I didn't think you'd want me there when you woke up."

"Bullshit."

Turning slightly, she looked up at him over her shoulder. "You don't get to tell me the thoughts in my head, Mr. Antonov."

"Oh...It is Mr. Antonov? Was it Mr. Antonov who had you unable to form real words just now?"

"Cocky much?"

"Very."

"Ugh! You're incorrigible."

Despite her sounds of frustration, Zaria didn't try to move out of his embrace. That was a good thing, because he wouldn't have let her go anyway.

"Now...Tell me the real reason you crept away from my bed."

Chapter Three

I DO NOT DO MESSY

Shit... It was obvious Andrei had no intention of letting her get away with not answering him truthfully. Her normally quick wit was failing her like a motherfucker and she did ***not*** appreciate it. The truth was, she hadn't expected him to reciprocate her attraction. And, she damn sure hadn't expected him to immediately take her to his suite and show her one of the many reasons she should've avoided his big sexy ass to begin with.

Some may say he wasn't traditionally handsome, but Andrei had a masculine beauty about him which was impossible to ignore. Combine that with his tall, thickly muscled frame and net worth north of ten digits, and it made for a man who could take two steps out of his door and fall over coochie. All day. Every day. In no way did she consider other women competition, however a certain subset of the male population didn't seem to appreciate plus sized curves.

That's what she believed. Well...Until Andrei fucked her from across the room with those piercing blue eyes, she thought he was in the same category as his wealthy peers. She should've known better when she found out he and Carver weren't just casual acquaintances. They actually considered each other friends. Carver didn't waste the word friend on superficial elitists.

Apparently, she took too long to answer Andrei's question. Zaria squeaked when he lifted her from the water, turned her around and placed her on his lap. They were now nose to nose with her hands braced against his massive chest. Latching on to the first thing floating to the top of her thoughts she tried to return his intensity with a determination of her own.

"Why is it so important for you to know why I wasn't there when you woke up? It's not possible I'm the first woman you've had sex with who didn't spend the entire night with you. What gives?"

"Do not do that. Do not try to turn this on me. I never told you you had to leave. You decided on your own."

"You never told me I could stay either. It wasn't like you took me to your home. We went to your private suite in the hotel. That in no way gives off, personal vibes. It gives off hook up. Who hangs around for morning after stuff with a hook up?"

Andrei's fingers bit into her sides when they tightened on her hips. The artic blue of his eyes seemed to blaze scorching hot as he stared at her. It was enough to make her wish she'd kept that particular assessment locked behind her teeth. But, it was too late now.

The intimacy of their position, him flying in a day early and immediately coming to her room said a lot more than casual sex. However, they hadn't made any promises to one another. Hell, they'd barely talked before he kissed her the first night they were together. Yet, when she overheard Carver and Denzel talking about Andrei deciding to fly out a day early, her stomach flipped. No matter what she said to herself or to him, it wasn't simply a one off.

"Svet...I do not like to repeat myself. In fact, I *never* repeat myself."

One large hand wrapped around the back of her neck. His fingers clasped her nape as his thumb tipped her chin to keep her face tilted toward his.

"If I tell you to leave. Fine. Go. If I do not tell you to leave, you will not go. I am a man. I have no need to play games. If I wanted to pick up a woman for quick sex, I would not choose the best friend of my friend's fiancée.

It is messy. I do not do messy. So, hear me and hear me well, Svet. That was your one and only pass. You do not get a repeat."

Lifting one eyebrow, Zaria pursed her lips. Part of her wanted to pop off about him thinking he had the right to be so high-handed. The other part was happy she was already in a tub filled with water—the wetness dripping from her core wouldn't be so noticeable. Because, the big dick energy Andrei wielded—along with his *actual* big dick—was what kept the romance industry on top of book sales worldwide.

It was just...Zaria really wasn't the, yes sir, kind of girl.

"You don't tell me what to do. I'm not a little puck bunny from your glory days on the ice. I—"

Zaria's words froze in her throat, snatched away with the breath she needed once Andrei filled her with his thickness in one thrust. *Goddamn!*

His fingers at her nape gripped her hair while the ones on her hip moved to her ass and squeezed.

"Svet...You talk too much. You also think too much. There is nothing else to say or think about. You like taking my cock. I like giving it to you. That is all. Nothing else needs to be said."

His shaft tunneled inside her delicate tissues filling her to the brim. This wasn't supposed to happen. She was supposed to give him a piece of her mind. Let him know she wasn't the one or the two.

Instead, she planted her feet beside his hips. Then, she bounced on his dick like he'd offered her everything she'd ever dreamed of on a platinum platter. It was so very wrong, but it felt so very right. Shit-talking Zaria would have to wait a little while. The sensations skating over her skin and pulsing from her center didn't leave room for anything beyond feeling.

Zaria's head dropped forward and her fingertips scraped across his chest and abdomen leaving streaks of red on his lightly tanned skin. Her lids drifted closed and her lower lip was captured by her teeth. A tug on the bun she'd used to secure her hair made her eyes pop open.

"Do we understand each other now, Svet?"

Zaria's eyes swept over Andrei's face. She noticed the hard set of his jaw and the muscle ticking there. His gaze was fixed and fire blazed from those artic pools. Another upwards thrust from his hips and she forgot the question. Zaria didn't have it in her to try to argue her point. *Did she even have a point*?

No. Zaria couldn't think of even one point beyond Andrei and his magic stick. Whether it was due to the tension of the moment, the position or their location, she reached her peak quickly. Her feminine essence coated his turgid length, moments before he stiffened. Both of his hands were filled with her ass cheeks. Zaria was certain she'd wear his handprints for a couple of days, nonetheless she couldn't bring herself to care.

When they came down from their orgasmic high, the activities of the past forty-eight hours crashed down on her. Limply, she allowed Andrei to cleanse her then place her in bed. Vaguely, she heard him speaking to someone, but couldn't lift her eyelids to investigate. Sleep took her. The last thing she remembered was curling into Andrei's side.

The next time Zaria opened her eyes her suite was cloaked in darkness. She lay on her side facing away from the door. A sliver of moonlight peeked through the lightweight curtains covering the windows. The room was silent, save for the even breathing coming from directly behind her in the king-sized bed.

A tingling sensation in her lower abdomen reminded her of why she'd awakened in the first place. She shifted, lifting the covers. Andrei's strong arm clamped around her tugging her body into the cradle of his.

"Where are you going, Svet?"

"Bathroom."

Mercifully, his tight hold immediately loosened. It had placed unnecessary pressure on her already screaming bladder. He flopped onto his back as she climbed from the bed and made a beeline to the ensuite. Closing the door behind her, she just barely made it into the water closet before the dam burst.

Afterwards, she stood at the sink washing her hands, looking at her reflection in the mirror. Although she had no memory of putting it on, her bonnet was once again secure over her hair. The bonnet was the only thing covering any part of her body. It seemed Andrei had put her to bed completely naked.

And, he'd most definitely put her to bed. Her legs hadn't carried her anywhere since they took her to the door to open it for him. The man seemed to have something against her walking under her own power. Considering what she did the last time she walked in his presence, she guessed he was a little gun shy. Turning out the light, she exited the bathroom.

Using the moonlight to navigate the room, she stopped at her open suitcase. Zaria hadn't unpacked much, but she remembered laying out a nightgown atop her clothes. She never got the chance to put it on. When

Andrei knocked on her door, it was quicker to toss on the robe she held in her hand at the time. Just as she touched the sleepwear, Andrei's voice reached her ears.

"Whatever it is you are thinking of doing over there, stop it. Come back to bed."

Whirling around, Zaria squinted as she raked her gaze over Andrei sitting upright in the bed. The sheet pooled at his waist covering the lower part of his body leaving his chest and arms exposed. Despite the husky, sleep laden, sound of his voice, his eyes were bright as they dared her to do anything other than follow his directive.

Huffing to herself, Zaria cursed his big ass out—in her head. Not a word was said aloud as it took everything in her not to stomp over to the bed like a petulant child. He was lucky she was too tired to argue with him.

It's not like she was self-conscious about him seeing her naked. The things they'd done together made that kind of shyness irrelevant. It was sleeping away from home which drove her to at least put on a nightgown. Sleeping nude in your own house was one thing. If anything were to happen in the middle of the night, finding something to cover yourself with was easier than doing so in an unfamiliar place.

As soon as she planted one knee on the bed, Andrei pulled her across the mattress.

"Excuse you!" Zaria huffed out the word as she pressed against his brick wall of a chest.

"I do not need to be excused."

His matter-of-fact response was followed by him adjusting her body to his liking and covering them both with the sheet. One bicep was slipped beneath her pillow cradling her head, while his other arm wrapped around her clasping one of her wrists in his hand. He was so serious about her staying put.

"You don't have to wrap me up like a burrito. I'm not going anywhere. This is *my* room."

"Shh, Svet. Go to sleep. You need your rest."

It was on the tip of her tongue to tell him again how he wasn't the boss of her, but a jaw cracking yawn erupted from her when she parted her lips. *Fine.* Zaria reasoned she wasn't taking orders from him. She was giving her body what it needed. That's her story and she was sticking to it.

Sunlight bathed Zaria's face turning the backs of her eyelids red. Tossing a hand over them to block out the offensive brightness, Zaria stretched. When she wasn't immediately pulled into Andrei's big hard body, she dropped her hand and looked around. The side of the bed he'd used was empty. Only an indentation in the pillow indicated he'd been there. The state of the sheets didn't count. She'd been known to pull those completely off the bed by herself.

She brushed off the twinge of irritation at his absence. So what if he made a big deal about her skipping out on him while he slept, then turned around and did it to her. Zaria wasn't bothered. Not even a little.

At least that's what she told herself as she went into the bathroom. Her movements were slow out of deference to the ache in her pretty pocket. She'd never tell him to his face, but Andrei really was packing a monster in his pants. If she hadn't been blinded by lust the first night, she might've come up with a reason to jet long before he wielded that weapon.

She didn't regret it though—even if she still felt it with every step. After relieving her bladder again, she hopped in the shower and started her morning routine. Zaria had no idea what time it was. It didn't matter. The sun was up. So, if she wandered outside, at least she wouldn't be traipsing around the property in the dark.

Turning off the water, she pushed against the glass door of the shower and it swung open much wider than she expected. Before she recognized him, Zaria's hand flew out defensively making contact with Andrei's chest. He had the decency to grunt at the blow which would've caught a shorter man in the throat and stolen his ability to breathe.

"Easy, Svet. No need to abuse me because I was not there to kiss you awake with the sun."

Holding onto her hand, he stepped back helping her from the shower. Once she was standing on the plush bathmat, he motioned for her to raise her arms. After he patted her skin dry, he wrapped a fluffy bath sheet around her securing it by tucking the folds between her breasts.

On the one hand, she wanted to tell him she was a big girl and perfectly capable of drying herself off after a shower. On the other hand, she appreciated his desire to take care of her in such a small way. Once he was done, he dropped a kiss on her lips and tangled his fingers with hers tugging her through the bedroom into the small sitting area.

Before she saw it, the smell of food caused her mouth to water and stomach to grumble. Zaria couldn't remember the last time she'd eaten. Andrei led her to a seat at a small table situated in front of the garden doors leading out onto the terrace.

The small table and chairs weren't there when she went to bed. So, she assumed he brought them in. Initially, she wondered why the table was set up inside the room instead of the terrace, but she told herself to let it go. Whatever this was she was doing with him, she wasn't ready for everyone to know about it. Not until she figured it out herself.

They'd all come to the island to celebrate Alyssa and Carver's wedding. Zaria didn't want anything to take away from her friend's big day—which included announcing a situationship with Andrei Antonov.

Once he was seated across from her, Andrei removed the covers from the serving dishes. Beneath them were Belgian waffles, an egg scramble and breakfast potatoes. In a separate bowl was mixed fruit. She recognized the Java plum and Pomelo in the mixture. Both were native to the area. She'd seen them in her research and was happy to get the chance to try them.

Looking up, she found him simply watching her. "What?"

"Nothing. Are you not hungry? Did I not hear your stomach rumble?" He gestured to her empty plate. "Or do you not like these things?"

"Oh! No." Holding her hand in front of her, she reassured him. "I like them. And, I am hungry. Thank you for this."

Tilting his head toward the food, he nonverbally prompted her to fill her plate. Once she'd taken something from each dish, he served himself and re-covered the remainder to keep them warm.

"Is it actually breakfast time or are you one of those people who will eat breakfast whenever?"

"It is mid-morning. So, technically, still the time of day for breakfast. But, I am not opposed to breakfast at whatever time of day I want to have it." He waved a hand above his plate. "It is food. Why does it matter what time of day you eat it?"

"Good point."

Zaria poured syrup on her waffles, taking care to fill each little pocket. When she was done, she glanced up to see Andrei watching her. Thinking he was waiting for the syrup dispenser, she offered it to him. He declined. Using his knife, he scraped a pat of butter from a separate small plate and put it on his waffle.

The entire scene was very domestic, but also very intimate. Much like the bath they'd shared the previous evening. If anyone had asked her before today if she thought Andrei Antonov was the kind of guy who'd be content with such things, she'd have replied with a resounding no. And she would've done so without any proof to back up her claim.

Unlike some current and former superstar athletes and high-profile business owners, Andrei wasn't regularly the subject of tabloid or gossip news. The business section of legitimate publications, sure. In the conversation between sports analysts about the best to ever play the game, absolutely. Yet, there wasn't one morsel of information available about his personal life. Not that she'd been trying to dig anything up, of course.

"You said it's mid-morning. Like nine-thirty? Ten o'clock?"

Zaria looked around the room. No clocks were visible and she'd left her cellphone on the night stand next to the bed. Andrei flipped his wrist over and the face of his watch lit up brightly.

"It is nine forty-five."

Returning to his meal, he speared a potato on the tines of his fork. Zaria's shoulders relaxed when she heard the hour. Nine forty-five meant she still had some free time before she had to be on.

"Is there somewhere you need to be?"

"No. Not yet anyway."

Taking one of the purple java plums from the bowl, she popped it into her mouth. The sweet, slightly sour taste burst on her tongue. She considered the flavor was what candy makers tried to reproduce with limited success.

"Not yet...but you *do* have plans for today." Although he phrased it as a statement, Zaria heard the question in his voice.

"Yes. Of course. We're here for a wedding remember? I'm the maid of honor. There's pre-wedding stuff to do."

"Such as?"

Andrei's sharp eyes speared her with their intensity as he waited for her to answer. *Why did she feel compelled to tell him every detail? Why couldn't he be satisfied with the general reply she'd already given?*

"Such as... pre-wedding stuff. Spa treatments, manicures, pedicures. Activities designed to keep the bride calm and relaxed while pampering her in advance of her big day."

"Hm."

While it sounded like his curiosity had been satisfied, something told Zaria he was simply acknowledging the fact that she'd spoken. However, he didn't dig any further. They spent the rest of the meal in companionable silence. When they were done, he inquired as to the time the activities started.

"Our first appointment is at two p.m."

"Which is in..." checking his watch again, he added, "four hours. Plenty of time."

Quirking an eyebrow at him, Zaria tipped her head to the side. "Plenty of time for what?"

Andrei leaned forward with his forearm on the table between them. "Time for you to make another payment on your debt."

Chapter Four

WHAT'S GOTTEN INTO YOU?

Andrei sat at the desk in his suite with his laptop open in front of him. On the screen was the comprehensive report he received daily from the casino. The numbers were standard for the season, but he knew they'd pick up once the weather turned cold.

He huffed when he thought about what Americans considered cold weather. Where he was from, in St. Petersburg, Russia, at least five months of the year were spent at or below freezing temperatures. Yet, at the first flake of snow, his casino and resort would be bursting at the seams with reservations from those fleeing colder climates.

Some used it as a stopover on their way to their winter homes. However, others would reserve a suite of rooms for more than a month. They'd spend the time gambling or partaking in the many concierge services available at Anton's.

Checking his watch for the hundredth time, Andrei saw that only two hours had passed since he'd left Zaria's room. She was off with the other ladies doing 'pre-wedding stuff', as she called it. He was certain he could have taken part in whatever Denzel had planned for Carver and the other guys. Except, in addition to looking over the casino reports, he needed to give some attention to the Chevaliers.

As part owner of the hockey team, he was more hands on than the others. From his first buy-in, he'd been increasing his stake in the team each year. It had taken some time, but he was now the majority owner.

The league draft had occurred in July, but Andrei already had his eye on next year. There was a kid in Miami with some real skill. He was already better at reading the ice than some veterans of the sport.

Andrei pulled up the file on Francisco Truman. Then, instead of focusing on the stats and game footage his scouts compiled for him, his thoughts were on the curvy little lawyer. Zaria had left her suite wearing a flowing maxi dress which skimmed her figure in all the right places. The information on the screen was nothing but a blur as Andrei imagined pulling said dress up over her rounded hips and taking her from behind.

This is fucking ridiculous! Andrei chastised himself for losing focus. It wasn't like he wouldn't see her again. A group dinner was planned for the evening and there was always later that night. If he didn't spend it in her suite, she was damn well spending it in his.

An electronic ring emanated from his laptop and the video chat icon pulsed in the corner of the screen, drawing his attention. His brother's name was displayed at the top of the little box. Selecting the icon, he adjusted the volume. Soon his younger brother, Vitaly's face replaced the player file.

"Privet, brat." Andrei naturally lapsed into his native tongue when speaking with his brother.

"Hello yourself, brother. What are you doing? I came to your hotel to surprise you, but they said you are on vacation. Since when do you take vacations?"

Crossing his arms over his chest, Andrei stared at the younger man. "Since when do I answer to you or tell you my whereabouts?"

"Since we are all we have left, brother."

Vitaly's comment was below the belt. Yet, Andrei couldn't fault his brother for it. They were all each other had in the way of family. Their parents were gone. They had no extended family that they were aware of, with exception of an uncle with whom they'd cut ties around the same time their parents died. Actually...it was because of their parents' deaths.

Scrubbing a hand over his face, Andrei propped his elbow on the desk and leaned his head on his curled fingers. Ignoring Vitaly's smug look, he reminded him of their previous conversation.

"If you were not so busy with your face in someone's pussy, you would have heard me. Then, you would have remembered me telling you I would be traveling this week."

In the background, beyond Vitaly's shoulder, Andrei saw his brother had made himself comfortable in Andrei's personal suite of rooms at the hotel. He wasn't bothered, seeing as it was their usual arrangement when Vitaly visited Las Vegas.

"Was that before or after the Chicago game?"

"After."

"Oh..." Vitaly's eyes lit up. "Brother, you can't expect me to remember anything you tell me when I have a woman like Nina waiting for me. She was extremely talented. If you get my meaning."

Rolling his eyes, Andrei cocked an eyebrow at his brother. Of course he got his meaning. Andrei didn't begrudge him the enjoyment of his youth. He'd be a hypocrite to do so. He simply wanted Vitaly to recognize that the fast-paced life he lived, couldn't be sustained long term. But, Andrei didn't push. He was positive his brother's day of reckoning was swiftly approaching.

Vitaly would be thirty-one on his next birthday. Thirty was around the time Andrei started looking at life after hockey. Although, he hadn't really ever been able to live his life with the carefree abandon of his younger sibling.

"Anyway, where are you on this not-vacation you're taking?"

"Nusa Dua."

Vitaly's brow furrowed and he looked away as if physically scanning his memory banks. "Nusa Dua?..."

When it finally hit him, the dip in his brow deepened as he scowled at Andrei. "You're in Bali? You went to Bali without me?"

"You were not invited."

"You could've invited me."

Huffing out an irritated breath, Andrei pinned his brother with the patented expression he'd used countless times over the years to end unwanted conversations.

"No. I could not invite you to a place when I am a guest myself. That is not how it works."

"How many times have you told me things work however you want them to work?"

Andrei hated it when the brat threw his words back in his face. "Vitaly, I am at a private wedding for a close friend. There is no pussy for you to chase here. You would be bored out of your mind. Besides, your season just started."

The thought popping to the forefront of his mind, caused Andrei to narrow his eyes, peering at the computer screen.

"Speaking of which, why the fuck are you in my hotel suite when you should be in Denver getting ready for your next game?"

Before he could catch it, Vitaly's façade slipped and Andrei caught the frustration with a hint of sadness in his expression. Reverting to the same behavior he exhibited as a pernicious child, Vitaly scratched the hair at his nape loosening the bun holding the long strands away from his face.

"I'm on suspension for the next five games."

"You are ***what?***"

Andrei's voice deepened and he wished he were on the other side of the world so Vitaly wouldn't be able to turn his head away to hide from him.

"Why am I just now hearing of this? What reason did they give you?"

"Don't worry about it. My agent is working on it. It'll be overturned."

"If you are so confident it will be overturned, why are you in Vegas? Should you not be home, putting in time on the ice so you can be ready when they call?"

"I don't have to be home to put in time on the ice. I can use the rink at your place."

Andrei's frown deepened at Vitaly's flip assessment. While it was true, there was a rink on the property at his mansion, it wasn't the same as being where the team management could see him still putting in the work.

The chime of the doorbell at Andrei's Las Vegas suite pulled Vitaly's attention.

"Gotta go, brother. That's probably the massage I ordered."

"Vitaly. I'm sure I do not need to tell you not to fuck the masseuse."

Vitaly's mouth stretched into a wide smile. "Andrei...brother...what kind of man do you take me for? I would never abuse my position."

"True, except you don't often turn down offers from the willing once they make the first move."

Winking, Vitaly walked toward the door. "You may have a point."

Andrei glared at the screen. "I am serious, Vitaly. Do. Not. Fuck anyone on my staff. Leave the hotel if you want to chase pussy."

"I can agree to no staff, but you haven't seen the Hollywood starlets walking around downstairs. There must be a movie set nearby."

Andrei pressed a hand to his forehead as he tapped the screen to end the call. It was pointless to try to dissuade Vitaly from flirting with a willing female not on his staff. So, he didn't try. He also didn't bother to say goodbye before ending the chat.

For a brief moment, he considered that maybe he'd been too lenient with Vitaly as he finished the job his parents began. They'd wanted him to not have the same worries they had as children. Andrei hadn't escaped those worries. His success as an athlete meant Vitaly had a different childhood than him. One without the same burdens or concerns. To honor his parents, when Andrei took over as guardian when Vitaly was fourteen, he attempted to follow their playbook. Some days, he thought he got it wrong.

Sliding his phone closer to him on the desk, Andrei woke the screen. Speaking to the automated voice, he instructed it to make a call. Calculating the time difference in his head, Andrei figured he'd have no issues reaching Gregor since it was only ten p.m. in Las Vegas.

"Hallo."

Gregor answered on the second ring. He'd been in America more than ten years, yet his deep voice still held hints of his Norwegian accent and he clung to his commonly used slang.

"Gregor, I need you to look into something for me." Andrei didn't waste time with small talk. It wasn't the nature of their association. He heard light rustling in the background before Gregor responded.

"Dritt. What did Vitaly do this time?"

"Shit is right, and I do not know. That is what I want you to find out. He called me from my suite saying he has been suspended, but would not say why. I have heard nothing about it. I have been...occupied for the past twenty-four hours.

Vitaly claims his agent is working on getting it overturned, however I want to know what was so serious to warrant a five-game suspension."

"If he did not tell you, maybe he does not want you to know. He is fully grown, you know."

"I am aware."

As much as Andrei tried to be hands off with Vitaly, old habits die hard. Besides, he promised his parents he'd always look out for his little brother. Sometimes, keeping his word meant protecting him from himself. Andrei's silence following his reply to Gregor's statement was an indicator he wouldn't be dissuaded from his request.

"I will call you when I know something."

"Good."

Ending the call, Andrei checked his watch. He'd lost count of how often he'd done that. It wasn't like him, but he'd done more than a few out of character things since he'd met Zaria Coleman. The woman was wreaking havoc on his life and she had no idea. As they had done often since he first laid a finger on her silky skin, his thoughts veered to her turning the tables on him.

When she asked him why it was so important for him to know why she left, his thoughts scattered for a moment before he brought the conversation back to where he wanted it. On her motives. Not his. He still wasn't ready to delve into why it bothered him so much that she'd left him.

She was right. It wasn't the first time he had sex with a woman and awakened to an empty bed. The difference was, it was the first time he'd gone to sleep next to a woman and wanted to wake up next to the same woman. The reason it bothered him wasn't up for debate.

Seeing as his mind wasn't on work, and knowing he wouldn't get another round of reports for at least eight hours, Andrei closed his laptop and changed into workout clothes. When he arrived at the villa, the concierge told him there was a fitness center onsite. So, Andrei went in search of it.

Maybe some exercise would help clear his mind and keep him from following behind Zaria like a lost puppy. When he reached the room, there were already a couple of people inside. Nineties hip-hop met him when he opened the door.

Carver was seated on a bench with a fifty-pound weight in one hand, while Denzel was running on one of the three treadmills. Carver set the weight down on the mat when Andrei approached. When he tapped his cellphone, the music stopped.

"Hey! I didn't expect to see you today. I figured you'd be working or something."

Andrei nodded as he considered where he'd like to start. "I was. There is not much for me to do since I worked on the flight. I reviewed a few reports. Everything else is under control."

The sound of Denzel's footfalls on the treadmill halted, and the whirring sound of the machine ceased. When Andrei turned to look at him, the other man looked stunned.

"What?" Andrei prodded.

"That was like...four whole sentences."

Rolling his eyes, Andrei stared at him. "What is your point?"

"I don't know if I've ever heard you speak four consecutive sentences outside of giving an interview. On top of that, you gave up personal information. What's gotten into you?"

Darkness dropped over Andrei's face as his brow furrowed. "Fuck you. I talk."

"Nah...not fuck me, but you must've fucked somebody." Denzel waved his hand in a circular motion in Andrei's direction. "Because all of this is downright mellow. It's either sex or good drugs, and I know you well enough to know you don't fuck with narcotics."

"Den, leave the man alone. It's like my daddy says. If you don't want a man in your bed, stay out of his." Carver chuckled. Picking up the discarded weight in his other hand, he resumed his curls.

"I'm just saying...You didn't have to pull the Pop Jamieson country wisdom out on me." Denzel huffed and started pressing buttons on the treadmill.

Andrei sat at the multi-purpose workout machine, set it to the desired weight and configuration before he began stretching. He didn't bother looking toward the treadmill when he heard it restart. Shortly after, the thrumming baseline of the music filled the space again.

They worked out in companionable silence. As if they'd done it a thousand times, they rotated using each station, although there was enough equipment to allow them all to do the same thing simultaneously if they wanted. There was no pressure to fill the space with chit chat. Andrei appreciated that about these two.

While they could converse on any number of subjects and talk shit with the best of them, Carver and Denzel didn't put on false pretenses. It was one reason he counted them amongst his small circle of friends. The three had met during a charity event. It was one of the few all of the professional sports were united in sponsoring.

Andrei attended out of obligation to the team, but once he was there, he became interested in the charity's work. Denzel and Carver were regular participants, despite it being pretty early in both of their careers. So, mutual philanthropic interests brought them into a loose friendship and they'd stayed connected all these years later.

Denzel's crack about Andrei speaking four consecutive sentences was their normal thing. Andrei wasn't particularly loquacious; however, he could hold up his end of a conversation. When he was done with his last set, he hopped on the treadmill to cool down.

"So, what are you up to today, big guy? We were thinking of going out to look around the island since the ladies are doing their own thing."

Denzel stood a few feet away with a towel draped around his neck. Carver was putting away the free weights.

"I had no plans other than to work and eat." Andrei also planned to spend some time wrapped around Zaria, but he wouldn't tell Denzel that. It would only feed into the other man's theory about good pussy making Andrei mellow.

"Pssh! Work? Come on, man. We're in a tropical paradise and you wanna work? I think you should come hang out with us. The dads are off doing stuff together, the ladies are doing bridal stuff. So, it's just the three of us until the rest of the guests arrive."

"Sounds like a good idea to me. We have a boat parked at the dock. I can get the captain to take us out, maybe do a little fishing." Carver chimed in.

Andrei started to say no. Then he thought about how long it had been since he'd had any type of break which extended beyond twenty-four hours. With his business interests, the casino, and the hockey team, free time wasn't something he typically had in abundance. He'd already deviated from his normal routine by exercising so late in the day. He'd missed his morning routine the past few mornings...for...reasons...

"Sure. Why not?"

Andrei surprised himself. For almost three solid hours, he didn't check his watch. That's not to say he didn't think about Zaria, but he wasn't obsessing about the time like he was when he first left her. He guessed there was something to be said about *hanging out* with one's friends.

Chapter Five

THIS IS NOT PRIMARY SCHOOL

Zaria eased her way onto the massage table before arranging the sheet covering her intimate areas. On the table next to her, Alyssa was already stretched out. Both were waiting for their masseuse. Alyssa's and Carver's mothers were in the room next to theirs, undergoing the same treatment.

When Zaria looked over at Alyssa, her friend quirked a questioning eyebrow at her.

"What?"

"What do you mean what? I'm not the one moving around like an old lady"

"Old lady? I take offense. Besides, it's just soreness from the flight, then not sleeping as much as I needed for the past two days. The time difference might be messing with me."

Zaria tried to keep her voice upbeat. Alyssa knew her too well, and she wasn't ready to share about Andrei. Alyssa's expression said she didn't one hundred percent believe Zaria, but she let it slide. They were there to enjoy themselves, pampering, and to relax in advance of Alyssa's wedding.

Under normal circumstances, Zaria would've told her bestie something by now. However, she was playing this one close to the vest. Their interconnected friendships could be a recipe for things to blow up in her face.

You really should've thought of how the two of you were connected before you put your pretty pocket in that Russian's mouth. Zaria really didn't appreciate the snarky commentary from her inner voice. Thank you very much. Furthermore, she'd let him put his face in the place again. If she wanted. She was an adult. A liberated woman, if you will. She could indulge in his expertise whenever she pleased.

Zaria was saved from further conversation when the massage therapists entered the room. After introducing themselves, they rehashed the instructions, being certain Alyssa would receive her massage from the petite, dark-haired, woman; while Zaria's masseur was a muscular Balinese man.

It turned out having Ketut rub the tightness in her thighs away was exactly what Zaria needed. At the end of the massage, she was practically boneless, and she no longer felt like she was astride a really large horse every time she moved. Andrei wasn't a horse, but he was damn sure hung like one. And, his larger than average frame meant she should probably stretch before she attempted to ride that ride again.

"What are you smirking about over there?" Alyssa interrupted Zaria's trip down recent memory lane.

"Who me? I'm just enjoying how good my body feels. I might have to kidnap Ketut and take him back to Vegas with me." After a few moment's thought, Zaria shook her head.

"Nah...the first time he put those magic hands on one of those rich women, they'd use their money to lure him away from me. I don't have pockets deeper than those casino wives. I guess I'll just have to keep my appointment with my regular guy."

Alyssa giggled. "Speaking of which, I'm gonna tell Manuel you cheated on him."

Giving her side-eye, Zaria sucked her teeth. "You know what? You're being messy, but I'm not worried. You'll probably never see Manuel again if Carver has anything to say about it."

Alyssa fiddled with the sash on her robe. They'd both donned the plush garments provided by the spa to continue with the remainder of their treatments. Tilting her chin defiantly, she squinted her eyes at Zaria.

"I'll have you know Carver doesn't run me. If I want to make an appointment with Manuel when I get home, I will."

Zaria patted Alyssa's shoulder. "Sure...whatever you have to tell yourself to make it through, babe."

"I'm serious."

"I know you are. That's what makes this so cute. You really believe it."

Alyssa's bottom lip poked out, sending Zaria into a fit of giggles. "Poor baby. It's okay. I'm sure Carver listens to what you want."

With zero guile, Alyssa's head bobbed as she agreed with Zaria. "He does listen when I tell him what I want."

"Mm-hmm...and you listen to what he wants. Because the two of you have a healthy relationship."

Alyssa folded her arms across her waist and tipped her head to the side, looking at Zaria. "We do. We've worked really hard at respecting one another's boundaries."

"I know you have. It's how I know you'll never see Manuel again. When Carver expresses that he doesn't want another man's hands on you, you'll respect his boundary and look for someone else."

As they exited the room, Alyssa's face was scrunched in concentration to the point the mothers noticed immediately.

"Uh-oh...What has your thinking face on?" Anna Ripley stroked Alyssa's arm as she looked up at her.

"Nothing to worry about, Mama Ripley. Alyssa's just coming to terms with some re-arranging she's gonna have to do in her life. No biggie."

Zaria was happy to keep the focus on Alyssa. After all, the entire trip was for Alyssa and Carver. There was no need to put a spotlight on anyone or anything aside from that goal.

"And what might those arrangements be?" Carol Jamieson walked to the other side of Alyssa and rubbed her other arm.

As they followed the attendant to their next appointment, Alyssa and Zaria filled them in on their discussion regarding their regular masseuse in Las Vegas. Both women found it hilarious that it never occurred to Alyssa her use of Manuel's services would meet a quick end as soon as Carver realized she'd been seeing a male massage therapist this whole time.

The ladies had a late lunch, then spent the rest of the afternoon getting facials, manicures and pedicures. Zaria had specifically asked each of them to hold off on getting the services because she'd planned this activity for them to do together. She may be Alyssa's only bridesmaid, but she would make damn sure her friend got the pre-wedding treatment whenever possible.

By the time dinner rolled around, they were all glowing. If Zaria wasn't mistaken, she heard one of the mothers hinting to her husband about getting some special therapy tonight. Politely turning a deaf ear to the comment, Zaria struck up a conversation with Alyssa to drown out the words and imagery they evoked.

For dinner, the staff set up a long table on the patio on the west side of the villa. They arranged lanterns and other hanging lights, putting a soft glow on the area. By the time they arrived, the men were already milling around with drinks in their hands. Their good-natured banter continued as the ladies entered the discussion.

Thankfully, it wasn't as awkward as Zaria feared it might be for her to be so close to Andrei. His gaze raked over her in the breezy floral print dress she wore, and her eyes devoured his physique in his linen pants with a coordinating button down. He looked more tanned than he had when they'd parted ways earlier, letting her know how he'd spent the hours they'd been apart.

"Zee, are you going to sit?"

Alyssa's question jerked Zaria into the moment. Her face heated with the knowledge she'd been eye-fucking Andrei in front of the entire group. She had to get ahold of herself. That kind of behavior wouldn't do.

"Here, let me help you."

Denzel pulled out a chair. Unconsciously, her eyes flew to Andrei's as she accepted the offered seat and thanked Denzel for his assistance. The heat in Andrei's responding stare differed from what she'd seen just moments before. She wasn't delusional enough to think she didn't understand exactly what that look meant. Zaria simply hoped they were on the same page and he would contain whatever it was in front of the others.

A single eyebrow lifted before he took a seat directly across from her. Although she caught the censure in the expression, Zaria's shoulders relaxed in relief. Once Denzel pushed her chair under the table, he resumed his conversation with Mr. Ripley. Zaria vaguely heard something about Tech and their chances to make a good bowl game at the end of the season.

When the meal arrived, the conversation shifted to the array of traditional Balinese foods they'd prepared. It was served family style, so Zaria had small portions of each dish. Flavors burst on her tongue and she closed her eyes occasionally to savor particularly delicious items.

As they were finishing up, Alyssa's cousin, Candy, arrived with her husband and baby in tow. Zaria and Candy were acquainted from one of the previous times Zaria had visited Georgia with Alyssa. Candy had also hung out with them a few times when she'd had clients request her services in Las Vegas.

"Oh my goodness, I didn't expect to see you guys until in the morning!"

Alyssa went to stand from the table on her own, but Carver was quickly at her side to help her to her feet. She rushed to hug her cousin. After brief introductions to the rest of the group, Candy admitted they couldn't stay long.

"I know you guys and little Alexanderia are probably still adjusting to the time difference. If I had known you'd be up and about, I would've invited you to come down for dinner instead of having it sent to your room."

"We are adjusting—just walked out on the beach to get her some fresh air. We heard y'all talking, and decided to come say 'hey' before heading back up."

The conversation continued as Alyssa's parents joined the discussion. Zaria barely had a chance to do more than say hello and tell Candy how cute the baby was before everyone was going their separate ways.

She'd just crossed the threshold to her suite and removed her shoes when there was a knock at the door. Stooping, she scooped the sandals into one hand and turned the knob. An unsmiling Andrei stood on the other side of the open doorway. Without a word, Zaria released the doorknob and stepped back. Responding to the silent invitation, he came inside, turning the lock behind him.

Andrei's presence filled the room. Zaria stared at him, trying to read his expression, searching for anything to indicate his mood. He was a freaking vault. The only place he showed the slightest hint of his thoughts was in the depths of those ice blue eyes.

Removing his shoes, he placed the loafers to the left of the closed door. Tracking his movements, Zaria noticed how large they were. *What size were those things?* They had to be at least a fifteen. Her fascination with his shoes caused her to miss his advance.

Strong arms slipped around her, pulling her body flush with his. His fingers threaded into the hair at her nape as he tipped her chin up with his thumb.

"Did you enjoy yourself today?"

The mundaneness of the question caught Zaria off guard. She'd fully expected him to have something to say about the interaction between her and Denzel earlier. Maybe she'd misread his look.

"I did. It was relaxing. We got the deluxe spa treatment with facials and the whole nine."

Andrei's other hand rubbed in large circles, dipping to the small of her back where his fingertips barely grazed the top of her ass before he moved his palm to the area between her shoulder blades. He pressed a soft kiss on her lips, then gathered her lower lip between his. Giving it a quick suck, he released it with a slight pop.

"Is the treatment the reason your skin is glowing? You are shining like a bronze statue."

Who knew Andrei Antonov could be so poetic with his words? Momentarily dazed, Zaria stared at him blankly.

"I guess..." Her words were slow as she remained locked in his gaze. "They had some really wonderful products which felt great, and the massage therapist was excellent. He really worked out the soreness in my thighs."

If Zaria hadn't seen the fire blaze to life in his eyes, the way his body turned to stone around her would've clued her in that she'd stepped on a landmine. Internally, she replayed the words she'd just spoken. *Shit...* She'd been so busy trying to hip Alyssa to her new life, her situation with Andrei hadn't crossed her mind.

Should it have? Sure, they'd had sex, but they had made no promises to one another. *Zee...that's dumb bitch shit. We don't do dumb bitch shit.* She didn't have more than a millisecond to give to her internal thoughts, because Andrei's lips were moving.

"Svet, did you just say some man had his hands on your body while you were naked?"

"Ummm...not exactly. I said the massage therapist worked out the soreness in my thighs."

The fingers in her hair had gone from resting against her scalp to curling. The tug at her strands wasn't painful, however it definitely got her attention. Her brow dipped as she warred internally about why the shit felt so good that her pretty pocket clenched with his fist.

"Do not twist words with me. The *massage therapist* was male. Correct?"

"Yes."

"While you received this massage, you were naked, correct?"

"Technically, but I was covered by a sheet."

His left eyebrow lifted as his grip on her tightened. "Is that the way you want to play this? With technicalities? Ok, Svet. We can do that."

Zaria didn't care for the lightness of his last two sentences. It was deceptive considering the fire still blazed from his artic blue eyes. She found herself being maneuvered to the sofa, where he placed her on his lap. Her lightweight sundress was hitched halfway up her thighs as she sat astride him.

"Question, Svet..." Andrei's fingers trailed up her legs, traveling from the outside to her inner thighs stretched wide to accommodate her position.

"Did this male masseuse also massage your back?"

Zaria's breath hitched when his fingers paused just shy of her center. His warm digits rested less than an inch from where they'd bring her the most pleasure.

"Answer me, Svet."

Finding her breath again, she replied. "Yes..."

"Tell me. How did he effectively perform that task with a sheet covering your body?"

She'd walked right into that one. Zaria leaned back slightly and frowned. "Well, of course the sheet was tucked around my waist then. I was lying on my stomach. So, it's not like he could see anything."

"True, however it means some strange man placed his hands on your skin. I do not like it."

"Well, that's too bad."

If Zaria thought he looked fierce before, she'd been mistaken. The thunderous expression on his face was enough to make her consider taking the words back. However, she simply straightened her back and looked at him head on.

"Why is it too bad, as you said?"

The question was a set-up. Zaria couldn't bring herself to care. Andrei was acting like they had some kind of agreement. She'd never agreed to anything, and she'd be damned if she let him run over her or ply her with good dick. It's not like she couldn't find sex whenever she wanted.

Okay. The *sex whenever she wanted* wasn't exactly true. She could find sex, but she'd never encountered a man who worked her over like Andrei Antonov. The man used his entire body to give pleasure. It was addictive. Still, she couldn't let him think he could control her just because he gave immaculate head and laid amazing pipe.

"It's too bad, because you don't have a say in who touches me. I'm an adult and very much single."

"Is that what you really think, Svet?"

Ignoring how his voice deepened with the question, and how his accent thickened, Zaria tipped her chin up.

"It's what I know. We had sex, Andrei. Sex does not a relationship make."

For all of her bravado, Zaria gasped when Andrei's fingers tightened against her thighs. Once again, she was caught between wanting to be angry and enjoying his dominant tendencies.

"Svet, you seem to be under the impression that I am some little boy playing at being a man. This is not primary school. I will not pass you a little letter asking you to be my girlfriend.

Also, we did not simply have sex. Do not cheapen it by saying such things. I will not allow you to pretend you did not give yourself to me as I gave myself to you. You accepted my seed. Multiple times. I have *never* given it to anyone until now."

Why? Why couldn't she just stop while she was behind? Zaria had no answers. Purposely skimming over what he said about them giving themselves to one another, she latched onto what he said about his seed. In the numerous times they'd come together in the past day and a half, he'd not used a condom and she hadn't demanded it. It was completely out of character for her.

"Speaking of which, next time—if there is a next time—we need to use a condom. We're too old to be out here playing roulette with our health. This is real life, and I don't live my life playing casino odds."

A ripping sound rent the air, and Zaria squeaked at Andrei's sudden movement. Who knew someone so large could move so quickly?

"You are mouthy, Svet."

His lips crashed into hers as he used two fingers to tunnel into her passage. Her pretty pocket completely contradicted her sassy words by gushing at his exploration coating his digits in her juices. *Hussy.*

He flipped their position on the sofa without breaking their connection. His big body loomed over hers while his kiss devoured her and his fingers drove her closer to climax. When he released her lips, it was only to inform her that she was sorely mistaken about who he was and what they were to one another.

"I see now. You need all the words, Svet. Fine. I will give them to you."

With a skill which should be illegal, he located the special spot in her channel and pressed against the pleasure center. His eyes dared hers to look away.

"You are *my* woman. I am *your* man. I am the *only* man who gets to put his hands on you in any capacity."

Belying her internal battle, Zaria's head began to shake in denial. Because...what? How did this even happen? She was just supposed to call his bluff, maybe have a quick romp. Now she had at least three hundred pounds of Russian in her face staking his claim on her.

"Not no, Svet. Do not lie to me or yourself. You feel it. You know it is true. You can be as adult as you like, but you will remember at all times that you are also *mine*."

Andrei followed his words with action, tossing her over the edge into an orgasm. Involuntarily, Zaria's back arched and the pitch of her scream was so high it left human hearing range. *Where the fuck did he learn how to do that?*

She was given little time to ponder the thought and even less time to recover before Andrei replaced his questing digits with his hard length. Her dress had been discarded at some point in the process. Her bra lay in parts unknown somewhere in the room, allowing him access to her rounded peaks.

His tugging at her nipples combined with the way his cock stretched her walls was too much and not enough at the same time. Zaria's bold words were lost and quickly forgotten as she tilted her hips to capture more of his length. Andrei issued a muttered curse and a short spurt of Russian before lifting her from the couch and stalking into the bedroom.

When her back met the soft duvet cover, she understood his grumbles. His body was entirely too long for them to do what they'd started on the average sized furniture. Her mind only had half a second to consider anything before she was once again surrounded by Andrei—inside and out.

Chapter Six

THE HOUSE ALWAYS WINS

Even to his own ears, Andrei sounded completely unhinged as he declared to Zaria that she was his woman. Whether she was right in her assessment of their status didn't matter. The insane quickness of it all wasn't allowed a foothold in his mind. He wouldn't permit social norms or limits when it came to the two of them.

His arms were wrapped around Zaria's thick thighs, holding them to his chest as he swiveled his hips, tunnelling his thickness into her slick channel. Determination to prove to her they were more than she said motivated him. Her moans mingled with his as he delved into her sweet haven.

Insanity was quite possibly the correct word to describe his irrational behavior, but Andrei couldn't be bothered to consider anything beyond driving Zaria over the edge into her next orgasm. That she thought it was okay to look him in the eye and say they had no claim to no one another sent him down a path he wasn't familiar with.

Andrei draped her legs over his thighs as he leaned forward. Zaria's face was flushed. Long lashes rested against the tops of her cheeks, and her lips parted slightly, releasing her satisfied whimpers. When he stopped the rhythm of his strokes, her brow dipped in a frown. Taking care to avoid her coily mass of hair, he braced himself with his elbows on either side of her head.

"Open your eyes, Svet. I want to see you."

Andrei impatiently waited the half a second it took her to comply. The fog of lust clouded her expression, and he held still until he was certain he had her complete focus.

"I do not just want your body to agree with me. There is no question. Our bodies play very well together."

Soft hands skimmed his sides before she brought her palms to rest on his chest.

"What do you want, Andrei?"

Her voice already held a scratchy quality filled with strain from having her pleasure denied. As if she couldn't control them, her hips tilted away then toward him, gliding on his shaft as much as their tight embrace allowed. To stop the torment, he dropped himself more into the cradle of her thighs, pinning her to the bed.

"Do not try to distract me."

"I'm not..." The frustration in her tone, as she released those two words, contradicted her.

He didn't argue his point; he simply stared at her. His cock was still buried in her velvet center. The hardness was to the point of aching, but he refused to move until they reached an understanding.

"You needed the words, Svet. So do I." Holding her gaze, he waited for understanding to dawn on her.

"What words?" This time, her tone didn't call her a liar.

Searching her gaze, he allowed his resolve to show. "The words that say you understand this thing between us is not some fling or game which is played."

"Andrei..."

"No, Svet. Do not do that. Do not lie to yourself or to me." He saw the hesitation in the dark depths of her eyes and he didn't like it.

He ignored the way her fingers stroked his chest in an almost absent manner. Instead, he watched Zaria's thoughts play out across her face.

"Andrei, how can you say that? How can you expect it? You don't really know me."

With a swiveling thrust of his hips, he reminded her of their current position as he lowered his head until the tips of their noses touched.

"I do not know you? That is what you think?"

She attempted to turn her head. The move was halted when he wrapped his fingers around her chin to hold her in place.

"I do not know you? Zaria Marie Coleman, born in Jackson, Mississippi on November twenty-fourth, nineteen eighty-five. Graduated high school in two thousand two, with honors. Went to college on a full scholarship before attending law school.

You are a member of both the California and Nevada State Bar. You are the managing partner of your law firm, Z. Coleman and Associates. You have no siblings, but you were raised with two cousins whom you consider your brother and sister. Do you need more, Svet?"

Zaria's eyes widened and her jaw dropped. The hands resting on his chest pressed against his skin, however he could tell she wasn't pushing him away.

"Andrei? How did you?"

"Svet, you said before that you do not play roulette with your life." Andrei stroked his length in her tight sheath a few times before he continued. "Neither do I. The difference is...I ***am*** the casino, and we both know the house always wins."

Capturing her lips, he swallowed her shock and coaxed her back into the moment with a drugging kiss. His hips acted with a mind of their own, and his buttocks clenched as he guided his length inside her slick walls.

He wanted. No. He needed her words, but once he'd unleashed his desire again, he couldn't stop. And he didn't. Not until they both tipped over into nirvana. Andrei's body jerked as he spilled his seed again, without an ounce of remorse.

Once he regained control, he pressed a chaste kiss to Zaria's plump lips as he left the bed. Giving himself a quick wipe down in the bathroom, he went back into the bedroom. Zaria was exactly as he left her. Gently, he cleaned her folds. After he was done, he tucked her into his side as they lie beneath the covers.

"Svet?"

"Hmm?" Since her head was tucked beneath his chin, Zaria's languid reply sent a slight puff of air across the base of his neck.

"This is not a game for me. I have not, nor would I ever, treat you like a one-off or a dalliance. Do you understand?"

Although he was reluctant to release her, Andrei loosened his hold as Zaria sat up in the bed. She held the sheet to her chest with one hand and pushed her hair away from her face with the other. He suppressed the urge to tug at the linens covering her plush curves from his gaze.

"Andrei...don't you think this it's kind of soon to say things like that? We've barely had real conversations with each other. And I'm not going to get into all the things you seem to know about me."

"Are you telling me a woman in your line of work does not investigate the people who come into your life even peripherally?"

"Of course."

"Then it should be no surprise that I know things about you. Most of which is public record, by the way."

Unable to withstand their small separation any longer, he tugged until she once again lay cuddled into his side. As if drawn by a magnet, his fingertips traced the hairline at her neck before delving into the springy coils.

"Do you require more convincing?" He asked after a few moments of silence.

Zaria gave a light chuckle. "No. I don't think my pretty pocket can take more of anything from that anaconda you call a penis."

"Do you want me to kiss it and make it better?" Andrei licked his lips at the thought.

"Uh...No. We both know where those kinds of kisses lead."

Lifting her hand from where it lay on his chest, Andrei tangled their fingers together. The low light in the room cast them in shadow, but it was bright enough for him to marvel at the contrast between their skin tones. They were stunning together.

"I have never been one to let time be the deciding factor on whether I pursued something. I will not start now." Andrei lightly tugged her hair until she looked up at him.

"We are consenting adults. No one gets to tell us what pace is best for us to move. If you do not want to be with me, then say so. I am a man. I can handle the truth."

Even as he said it, he knew it was only partially true. If she said she didn't want to be with him, he'd simply convince her she was wrong. Because it was obvious that she wasn't immune to him. When his statement was met with more silence, he continued.

"Whatever you fear you will lose, by admitting what you truly want, will not happen. I will make certain of it."

After what seemed like an eternity, Zaria threw one lush thigh over his waist as she settled herself astride his hips.

"I'm going to hold you to that Andrei Antonov. Trust and believe, the minute you start slipping, I ***will*** tell you."

The warmth spreading through his chest had little to do with their position. Those feelings. The ones he didn't want to define were the cause. Still, he pressed her for clarity.

"The words, Svet. Say the actual words."

Lifting one eyebrow, she stared into his eyes. "You're mine Andrei."

Grabbing two hands full of her lush hips, he squeezed. "And?"

Leaning forward, she braced herself with her hands on his chest. "And...I'm yours."

Andrei's growl was accompanied by Zaria's giggles as he rolled them over, placing her beneath him. Despite what she'd said earlier, he made good on his offer to kiss her pretty pussy. Of course, exactly as she predicted, it led to another round of explosive sex.

Andrei awakened the next morning to the sounds of Zaria moving around in the bathroom. When he heard the spray of water turn on, he left the bed to join her. She put up a modicum of resistance to him sharing the shower with her, but eventually conceded after he promised to be good.

And he was. Mostly. He gave her morning kisses—above and below. Then he took over the task of cleansing her body. He didn't know how he managed to sit through the entire meal the previous night without touching her. Andrei felt he deserved a reward for the restraint he'd shown.

Begging off from breakfast, Zaria said something about going to Alyssa's suite to help her get ready. The wedding was hours away, but Andrei didn't argue the point. He'd been involved in very few weddings. So, he had no clue what women did all day to prepare for the occasion.

Parting with a kiss at her door, he went to his room to get in a few hours of work. When he arrived, there was a message from Denzel giving a time for them to meet in Carver's suite. Andrei grunted and continued on with his morning plan. He could get in a good three hours of work before he indulged his friend in wedding day activities.

There was no need for him to set a clock to remind himself. Exactly three hours later, he stood from the desk. Before Andrei stepped out of his doorway, the concierge arrived with the coffee he'd requested.

Although Denzel was the only official groomsman in the wedding party, Andrei noticed Jasper Hunt was present in Carver's suite. They spent the morning and part of the afternoon conversing amicably and alternately being groomed by the team of barbers Denzel hired.

Andrei watched Carver as the day progressed. His normally unflappable demeanor was slightly off. Nervousness or anxiousness had him unable to settle. Andrei found it interesting since it was obvious to anyone with eyes that Alyssa loved Carver. There was absolutely no reason for him to be nervous. Yet, he checked his watch every few minutes until it was time for them to move outside the villa where the wedding would take place.

The ceremony was small and didn't last overly long. While Andrei was happy for his friend, the majority of his focus was on the vision Zaria presented in the lavender dress she wore. The vee of the neckline dipped low enough to put her bountiful breast on display. Uncaring if anyone noticed, Andrei consumed her with his gaze.

When the minister announced Carver and Alyssa as husband and wife, Andrei wanted to kiss the man out of gratitude. A slight breeze flirted with the edge of Zaria's dress, giving him glimpses of one curvy leg via the split in the material. Andrei stood and clapped at the appropriate time, but his mind wasn't on the couple walking back down the aisle arm-in-arm.

His gaze zoomed in on where Zaria's hand was wrapped around Denzel's bicep as they followed Carver and Alyssa back down the flower covered path. Reminding himself that the gesture was a part of the custom, Andrei stopped himself from shooting his friend a glare for daring to touch Zaria—even though the contact wasn't skin to skin.

Immediately following the nuptials, everyone convened on the west side patio again. With the sunset as a backdrop, they toasted the happy couple. Zaria had expressed to him that she didn't want to do anything to overshadow Alyssa's big day. So, Andrei had mentally prepared himself to once again spend an evening not touching her the way he wanted in front of the others.

Andrei's thoughts of giving Zaria space and not crowding her vanished when he looked over at her standing near the dessert table. In her arms was the baby he'd glimpsed the previous evening. Next to her was Denzel standing entirely too close. It irritated him that they actually looked like a little family. What bothered him more was the earnest way Denzel was speaking to her. Zaria didn't help the situation by looking up at him with a smile on her face.

The little green monster on his shoulder tapped the side of his head and Andrei had seen enough. Not bothering to excuse himself from whatever Jasper was going on about, Andrei strode across the terrace. As he approached, he watched as the plump-cheeked infant tried to take a bite out of one of Zaria's breast. What happened next made him quicken his steps.

Not caring how it looked, Andrei snatched the cloth napkin Denzel extended in Zaria's direction.

"What the hell?" Denzel stared at Andrei in confusion.

"Exactly. What the hell are you doing?" Andrei replied. He made no attempt to disguise the growl in his voice.

"Andrei, don't." The baby began to fuss and Zaria bounced her while making shushing noises. Candy immediately came over and lifted her from Zaria's arms.

"I'll take her. I'm so sorry she drooled on you! Her belly clock is still on Georgia time. She's ready to eat." As Candy turned away, her husband appeared at her side.

Using the napkin he'd taken from Denzel, Andrei dabbed at the drool the infant left behind. Ignoring Zaria's gasp, he focused on his task.

"Oh...So, it's like that?" Denzel stated knowingly.

Lifting his eyes from Zaria's bosom, Andrei pierced him with a glare. "Yes. It is." Returning his gaze to her chest, he inspected his work. "Because you are my friend, I will consider this discussion closed. Da?"

"Andrei...A word."

Zaria spoke through gritted teeth as she tipped her head toward the arched opening leading away from the terrace. It was obvious to Andrei the sparkle in her eyes wasn't merriment. Internally, he considered that he may have taken things too far, but the thought was quickly discarded. Denzel should know better, and so should she.

It had been less than twenty-four hours since he told her how he felt about having another man's hands on her. Yet, there she was chumming it up with his friend with complete disregard for their conversation. As she strode ahead of him, her back was straight and stiff. Casting a glance at Denzel, Andrei noted the perceptive expression on his face.

As soon as they were relatively out of earshot, Zaria whirled on him. The flowing material of her dress fluttered briefly, exposing her thigh before she covered it.

"Andrei, what was that? One day. We didn't even make it a whole day before I have to tell you you're being an asshole. Grr!"

Zaria put her hands up to the sides of her head like she wanted to pull her hair, but decided against it and simply pressed her fingertips to her temples.

"Svet—"

"Don't, svet, me! What does that mean, anyway? You know what? It doesn't matter. Just answer the question. What possessed you to make a scene just now?"

"I did not make a scene." Andrei narrowed his eyes. "I should ask you what you were doing out there."

"What I was doing? ***Me***?" Zaria placed a hand against her chest, then looked over one shoulder then the other. Other than his bodyguards in the shadows, nothing was there, and he was certain she didn't even know the men were posted in the corridor.

"It is only us here, Svet. Yes. You."

Andrei would've thought the way she sucked her teeth and quirked her lips was cute if he wasn't on the receiving end of her ire. He thought he caught a snatch of a muttered, "*This muthafucka*," before she crossed her arms under her bosom and leveled him with a withering stare.

"***I*** was enjoying my friend's wedding reception and talking to someone who you claim is ***your*** friend. I finally got a chance to hold that sweet little baby, and you messed it up barging over, acting like you don't have any home training."

"And why was he standing so close?" Even as he asked, Andrei's internal voice was advising him to fall back, assess the ice, see the whole rink. Instead of following his own sage advice, he stood firm.

"For your information, I dropped my phone while it was ringing. When Denzel picked it up, he saw my cousin's picture on the screen. All he was doing was asking me about her and trying to get me to put in a good word for him since she won't give him the time of day."

Her gaze traveled over him from head to toe, then back up to his face. "You know what? This isn't going to work. If you're jealous of an innocent conversation between me and *your friend*, we won't make it together."

Before the words completely left her mouth, Andrei wrapped an arm around her, pulling her into his hard frame. It sounded a great deal like she was trying to end things between them. That wouldn't do. Her body wasn't as softly compliant as it was when he left her earlier, but she didn't push him away.

"Nyet. We are having a disagreement. It does not mean you get to use it as an excuse to put up barriers between us."

"I don't need excuses, Andrei. Caveman behavior doesn't fly with me. I don't have the time nor inclination to deal with someone questioning my loyalty at every turn."

"I did not question your loyalty."

Andrei took offense until he finally followed the advice from the coach living in his head. He was fucking this up. Royally.

Chapter Seven

EVERYTHING'S FINE

Zaria fumed as Andrei held her body close to his. Her libido wasn't remotely stimulated because she was sincerely offended that he'd question her faithfulness. *It took all of a day for him to act a fool.* Part of her knew she should've seen something like this coming considering the way he responded to hearing her masseuse was male.

Under any other circumstance, she'd give any other couple severe side eye for demanding exclusivity so soon in the relationship. But, like Andrei said, they were adults. Time for playing games was long past. There wasn't anyone on her roster to call into question her decision to give it a go with Andrei.

"If what you just said wasn't calling my loyalty into question, exactly what was it? Because what I don't need, is you pissing around me to mark your territory."

"Svet—" Andrei's statement was interrupted by the photographer.

"Excuse me, would you mind if I snap a few pics? I told the happy couple I'd get some candid shots of their guests and you two are posed perfectly."

Zaria's eyebrow quirked as she looked from the man to Andrei's face. She and Andrei were practically glaring at each other. What exactly about that pose was so cute?

"I am okay with it, if you are willing."

Zaria sucked the inside of her cheek at Andrei putting the decision on her. Of course, she would take the pictures. After all, she'd said she didn't want to do anything to take away from Alyssa and Carver's big day. Zaria had no doubt her refusal would get back to the two of them causing questions. Questions she didn't want to answer right now.

Play the show. The words were on a loop in her head. They were the ones she used on herself when she was in a situation where she couldn't display the depth of her feelings. The guarded way she became, following the choices her parents made which led her to be raised by her aunt and uncle, was her go-to mask.

Allowing her body to relax in Andrei's hold, she smiled for the camera as Jack clicked away. When Andrei's fingers flexed against her lower back, she looked up at him. The sound of the camera's shutter faded as she read the expression on his face.

How, she didn't know, but he seemed to recognize she was phoning it in. When his left hand cradled her face, she unconsciously leaned into it. In the moment, no one existed except the two of them. Her focus shifted so completely that when Jack spoke again, it startled her.

"I think that last one is the money shot. Thanks!"

Either he was oblivious to the tension between them, or he didn't care. With his head bent reviewing the images on the small viewscreen, he walked away. Once again, Zaria and Andrei were alone. Well mostly alone. At least one member of Andrei's personal security was nearby. Whoever it was, did an excellent job of hanging in the shadows, but she spotted him when Jack approached to take the pictures.

"Now. Back to our discussion."

"No."

Andrei's frown would probably scare a normal person shitless, yet Zaria had no fear of him harming her physically. She'd decided she was done with this conversation—at least in this arena. There wasn't a doubt in her mind ending the discussion wouldn't be as simple as saying 'no', however she was determined not to participate in even the slightest blemish on her friend's day.

"We are not done talking, Svet."

"I am. This was a bad idea and we've been gone too long."

Andrei's hold on her tightened, as he shot daggers at her. "I do not care what it looks like for us to be gone together. I am not ashamed of you. Of ***us***. Who cares if someone notices?"

Releasing an exasperated huff, Zaria stopped trying to extricate herself from his hold. "It's not about anyone seeing us. I should've waited to have this conversation. I let my anger get the best of me for a minute."

His grip on her loosened and he clasped her hand tucking it into the curve of his elbow. "Fine, we will go back to the party. We will say our goodbyes politely. Then, we are going to have this discussion, Svet. This cannot be allowed to fester. It's not healthy."

Zaria blinked slowly. Did he really just say something wasn't healthy as if any of the things they'd said and done up to this point could be considered remotely in that realm? Shaking her head to keep herself from going down the rabbit hole, she attempted to slide her hand from his grasp.

"I think I can find my own way."

"Are you trying to make me angry?"

The steel laced into each word gave Zaria a second of pause. She didn't think she was purposely trying to anger him; although she could objectively see how her actions could be taken that way. Grudgingly, she searched her motivation for attempting to pull away from him.

Was it really because she didn't want anything to overshadow the day's events? She wanted to believe that's what it was, but in reality, it was starting to feel like an excuse to keep what was between her and Andrei private. If no one knew, and things went sideways, there'd be nothing to tell.

Considering the way he'd behaved following an innocent interaction with his friend, she really didn't see how they'd make it to anything deeper than what they had at the moment. A man prone to jealous fits wasn't someone she'd ever considered being in a relationship with.

"I'm not trying to make you angry, Andrei...Fine. Let's go say goodnight to our friends."

Responding with a curt nod, he led them back onto the terrace. Scanning the area, she located Alyssa and Carver on the small space slated as the dance floor. A love song played softly from the hidden speakers and the two swayed to the music.

They looked so happy and in love, Zaria temporarily forgot her own dilemma. Not far from them, Alyssa's parents were in a similar embrace with Mrs. Ripley's head and one hand resting on her husband's chest.

Their image simultaneously warmed Zaria's heart and clamped it in a vice. It reminded her of her aunt and uncle. The ones who raised her like she was their own child. They were loving and affectionate to their children as well as each other. Too much time had passed since she'd last been home. She probably should look at clearing some time on her calendar and making the trip to see them.

Andrei guided her to the low wall bordering the patio in an unspoken directive for them to wait until the song ended before approaching the happy couple. A server came by offering beverages, but they both declined. In a blessed reprieve, the song ended shortly after. Andrei wasted no time escorting her over to intercept Carver and Alyssa before they could retake their seats.

Alyssa's smile froze on her face and her eyes widened when she looked at Zaria essentially plastered to Andrei's side. He'd released Zaria's hand from his elbow only to wrap one arm around her with his hand resting at her hip. With her eyes, Zaria silently pleaded with Alyssa not to give voice to whatever thoughts she had. Fortunately, or at least Zaria hoped it was fortunate, Carver was the first to speak.

"Hey, Andrei. I take it you've reached your social limit."

"Da. We wanted to come over and say goodnight. It would be rude to leave otherwise."

"Okay..." Alyssa said the word while still looking at Zaria. A million and one questions were painted across her face.

Carver shook Andrei's hand and thanked him for the courtesy. Concern hovered in Alyssa's eyes. So, Zaria pasted a bright smile on her face. Andrei offered no resistance when she stepped forward to give her friend a hug. Once Alyssa leaned into the embrace, Zaria whispered in her ear.

"Everything's fine. Don't worry about me. Enjoy your new husband. Don't scandalize my niece or nephew with your wedding night antics though."

Her last statement drew a giggle from Alyssa. Giving her a reassuring squeeze, Zaria stepped back. The warmth of Andrei's palm on the small of her back sent an automatic ping of desire to her core. Except Zaria was done listening to that trollop. She'd put on a pleasant face in front of others. However, once they were behind closed doors, all bets were off.

The walk through the halls of the massive villa was done in silence. When they reached the door of her suite, Zaria pressed her thumb to the keypad to unlock it. Reaching past her, Andrei pushed it open. Briefly, she considered them always being in her suite and never his, but she didn't dwell on it.

She liked being on home turf as it was. The only significant drawback was she couldn't storm out if she didn't want to continue the discussion. There was little hope that Andrei's obstinate ass would even consider leaving until he was good and damn ready.

"Now, Svet. Shall we continue our conversation where you thought you could put an end to our relationship over a simple misunderstanding?"

Zaria tipped her head from one side to the other as she stared at him in disbelief. It only took her a few seconds to realize he fully believed what had just happened was a *simple misunderstanding*.

"Wow...You're serious right now."

"Of course."

Stepping out of the heeled sandals, Zaria allowed them to dangle from the fingertips of one hand. *Why was good dick always attached to crazy bastards?* She watched silently as he took his shoes off as well. Part of her wanted to tell him he shouldn't bother, since he wouldn't be there for very long.

"Andrei...You obviously ran a background check on me, but your investigator missed some things."

"Such as?"

"Such as, the only time I do messy is when I'm scrolling through videos online. Not in my personal life. You said you didn't do messy either. Somehow, that didn't stop you from showing your ass just now."

Andrei closed the distance between them, stopping when the tips of his toes were just inches from hers. His proximity meant she had to tilt her head farther back to look him in the eyes. Prepared for him to try his manhandling routine, she was surprised when silence stretched between them as he simply watched her.

"I cannot explain why it bothered me to see my friend be so...friendly with you." Andrei finally breached the quiet.

"Can't or won't?" Zaria arched one eyebrow; skepticism painted her expression.

After a few beats, a look flit across his face before he quickly replaced it with a blank one. Zaria wasn't sure if she saw it because she studied him so closely or because she was learning his tells. Although she couldn't identify what it meant, she recognized that he wasn't as confident as he projected.

"I cannot."

"He's your friend. Are you saying you don't trust him?"

"No one can be trusted completely, Svet."

Stunned was the only way to describe how she felt in response to Andrei's statement. Logically, she saw the truth in his words, but it was such a lonely way to live. It meant he never let his guard down.

"Does that mean you operate under the assumption everyone will betray you? It's not a matter of if, simply when?"

Andrei lifted and lowered one shoulder in an unspoken response. Zaria took a few steps back, creating physical space, mimicking the emotional gap growing between them.

"Ok...Well it says a lot about how you see the people in your life. But, since we're talking about us. I won't go there."

Extending her hand, she gestured back and forth. "This. Any relationship, for that matter, is doomed without trust. My earliest memories in life are of watching people who claimed to love each other do some pretty fucked up shit in the name of so-called love.

And they did it because of their lack of trust in one another. Granted it was rooted in fact, since he couldn't seem to remain faithful to her, yet was constantly accusing her of infidelity. I r*efuse* to live that kind of life. I've managed to make it thirty-eight years on this giant rock without tying myself to someone like that. I'll be damned if I start now."

Turning on her heel, she strode toward the bedroom. As she walked away, she tossed over her shoulder, "you can show yourself out."

Not looking back, Zaria entered the bedroom; then closed and locked the door behind her. She didn't stop walking until she was standing in front of the glass-enclosed shower. Robotically, she stripped off her clothes, leaving them in a pile on the floor. Without further thought, she twisted the knobs to start the water. Once it was hot enough, she stepped inside.

It didn't start immediately, however the longer she stood beneath the spray pelting against her skin, the more difficult it became to ignore. Mixing in with the wetness on her face, the tears streamed. *How had she gotten so deep so quickly that it hurt this badly to walk away?*

Zaria didn't try to answer the question; she simply stood there and waited for the hot water to work its magic. She had no concept of how long she imitated a statue in the shower, but eventually, she grabbed her exfoliating towel and began actually bathing.

Steam preceded her into the bedroom when she opened the door. In a small corner of her being, she expected to see Andrei there waiting for her. However, her quick scan of the bed and the chaise longue disabused her of the notion.

Straining her ears, she listened to the noises of the suite. She heard nothing except the sound of her own breathing. Dropping the towel into the bin for housekeeping, she slipped on one of the nightgowns she'd yet to use. Sliding beneath the covers, she grabbed a pillow from the other side of the bed. Hugging the inadequate, but fluffy, replacement, she attempted to sleep.

It was a good thing there were no group activities planned for the next day, because Zaria slept very little. Everyone was left to their own devices until it was time to board the plane. She had less than twenty-four hours remaining on the island before Carver's private plane took them back to the real world.

Debating on what to do for breakfast, she unlocked and opened the bedroom door. When she stepped over the threshold, she stopped in her tracks. Andrei was seated. Actually, it was more like slouched on the sofa. His eyes were closed, and his head was thrown back against the top with his arms crossed over his chest.

Between her next two breaths, his eyes popped open and his head lifted from the cushion. His bleary gaze was laser focused on her as she stood stock still in the doorway.

"Good Morning, Svet."

Taking tentative steps into the room, Zaria walked to the small bar on the other side . Leaning against the countertop, she folded her arms over her stomach.

"Andrei, what are you doing here?"

"We did not finish our discussion."

Bracing his fisted hands on the cushion to either side of him, he sat up straighter on the woefully small sofa. The thing was probably normal-sized, and Andrei's big body simply made it look tiny.

"What else is there to say?"

"Many things."

Leaning forward, he braced his elbows on his knees with his hands clasped together loosely.

"Tell me. The people who showed you the poor example of love. The ones who made it so you will try to end things at even the slightest hint you are not trusted in a relationship. Were those people your birth parents?"

Zaria stiffened. The countertop she leaned against held her upright because the perceptiveness of Andrei's question almost tipped her over. That was exactly her M.O. If a guy displayed a jealous streak or acted as if he didn't trust her, she showed him the door. Expeditiously.

"I let you have your say without interruption last night, Svet. However, you gave me no chance to respond to your declaration before you closed me out."

His eyes raked over her from the top of her bonnet covered head to her slipper enclosed feet before he returned his gaze to her face.

"I would like an answer. Now."

"I'm not one of your employees, Andrei. You don't get to order me around."

The speed at which he left the couch and entered her space should've been impossible, considering the distance and his size. For Andrei, those details apparently meant nothing. Scant millimeters separated them as he probed her with his stare.

"Do you think I do not see what you are doing?"

Zaria stared mutely in response to his question. She refused to volunteer an answer to his far too perceptive query.

"No savvy words for me? Fine. Just know I will not fall for such obvious tricks to anger me or push me away."

Had he not been staring directly at her, he probably would've missed her stiff nod in response to his question. Except, he did see it and his corresponding nod said he understood she was answering his original question.

With far more gentleness than she expected, Andrei wrapped her in his embrace. In slow increments, he pulled her closer to him until her head rested against him as his fingers massaged her neck and back.

"I am not your father, Svet. And you are not your mother."

Zaria remained silent, allowing his words and the entirety of the situation to sink in. He was dead ass wrong for the way he came at her about Denzel. Nevertheless, in the light of day, she could see it from a different angle. They'd told no one about their relationship.

With Denzel's handsome face and the reputation many star athletes carried, one would easily assume he was shooting his shot. From the outside looking in, Zaria could see how one would think that. Even though he wasn't trying to get with her.

Zaria was blunt—to a fault. She was full of opinions and had no issue expressing herself. Flying off the handle and making snap decisions wasn't a normal part of her package though. That's exactly what she'd done with Andrei. She'd stepped completely outside of her character. Yet another thing to add to the list of topics to go over during her next appointment with her therapist.

Tired of holding herself apart from him, Zaria allowed her body to melt against Andrei's. Her previously listless digits gripped the sides of his dress shirt. He'd discarded the jacket at some point during the night. The relaxation of his muscles beneath her hands was unmistakable.

As much as he was within his right to prod her into an admission, Andrei said nothing. He simply held her until she was ready to speak.

"Maybe I jumped the gun a little last night."

"Maybe? A little?"

Swatting his chest, Zaria squinted at him. Her expression held no real heat. So, his response was a raised eyebrow.

"As I was saying...Maybe I jumped the gun when I ended things."

"When you tried to end things."

"Do you mind?"

"By all means, continue."

"We have some things to work out, because I don't like where my head went when you said no one can be trusted completely."

Holding up a hand to ward off his attempt to explain, Zaria continued.

"That is a longer discussion we need to have, but not right now. Right now, I'm hungry and tired. I want to eat and try to get a few hours of rest. Then I want to see some of the island before I hop on a plane and fly to the other side of the world."

Zaria's eyelids fluttered closed involuntarily as Andrei massaged the base of her neck. She released a sigh when he lightly kissed her closed lids, then the tip of her nose, before landing on her lips.

"I will get you fed, Svet. Then, you can get some rest. However, if you would like to really see the island, I can arrange for us to stay longer. My jet can fly us back to Las Vegas whenever we would like. We do not have to leave tonight with the others."

Zaria's eyes popped open. "Are you for real?"

Chapter Eight

YOU DON'T PLAY FAIR

It turned out time alone on the island was exactly what he and Zaria needed. They spent the morning as planned. Rather than bother the newlyweds with a visit, messages were sent to both Alyssa and Carver regarding their change in plans.

Carver's responding message contained a few expletives and threats while Zaria's phone rang and she stepped away to speak with Alyssa privately. It was a short conversation, which was followed by another message from Carver containing a few more choice threats.

This one time, Andrei would give him some latitude. Carver was naturally on high alert when it came to Alyssa. With them expecting their first child, he was well beyond his normal levels of protectiveness. Andrei knew causing stress to Zaria would equate to stressing Alyssa in Carver's eyes.

His friend needn't worry, but Andrei didn't tell him that. Zaria was equally protective of Alyssa. She would do her level best to keep anything potentially distressing from her friend. He was positive she hadn't uttered a word about their disagreement to anyone. Neither had he. It wasn't anyone else's concern.

For the first time in recent memory, Andrei actually turned the reins over to the various section VPs at Anton's. If they couldn't handle their respective areas for a few days without him, they should look for new jobs.

He'd received a call from Gregor about Vitaly, but he pushed that aside as well. His Svet deserved his full attention. He also had some making up to do.

Andrei was aware how close they'd come to ending while they were still at their beginning. Just thinking of her attempt to walk away gave him ideas, which were most likely unreasonable, and if he followed through, definitely illegal in most civilized countries.

"What's the frown about?"

Andrei shifted his gaze from the plush landscape drifting by the window to Zaria seated at his side. Bringing their clasped hands to his lips, he kissed the back of hers.

"I was frowning?"

"I'm sure most people can't tell; since your, *not smiling,* face looks almost the same as when you frown just a little. But yeah. You were frowning just now."

"It is nothing. I did not realize I was doing that."

"Are you sure you're going to be okay being away from the Casino and your other work for so long?"

Using their joined hands to draw her closer, he dropped a chaste kiss on her lips. "I am sure, Svet. If the people I hired cannot handle the responsibilities they are paid to handle, then they will be replaced."

"As simple as that?"

"Yes. It is that simple."

Shrugging, Zaria ended her visual inspection of his expression and leaned her head against his forearm. Andrei went back to staring at the landscape. They'd done the tourist thing all day and would cap off the evening by watching the sunset at the Uluwatu Temple.

Zaria had a keen interest in learning about other cultures, so the addition of the temple to their activities was an immediate hit. When he simply mentioned it as a possibility, the way she lit up inspired him to make sure she had the best experience available. Andrei made a few calls to ensure the normal crowds weren't in attendance on this particular evening. He was certain the organizer thought he'd balk at the price, but it didn't deter Andrei in the least.

It was all worth it when the men entered the small outdoor area with their arms raised as they chanted. Zaria's entire being became incandescent. While her eyes tracked the shirtless men forming a four rowed circle around a dark statue with multiple arms, Andrei's gaze was focused on her. When she turned her excited face to his, a warmth spread through him at the purity in her expression.

For the entirety of the show, Andrei divided his attention between watching the dancers, in ornate gold costumes, and observing the stages of Zaria's emotions as the performative drama unfolded. He was only mildly curious as to the origin of the routine. However, Zaria seemed entranced by all of it.

He wasn't a man given to poetic prose, but there was something almost magical about the experience. The ride back to the villa he'd secured for them was spent with her excitedly recounting her favorite parts of the enactment. Andrei wished he could bottle the moment and reference it in the future so he'd have a clear memory of their time together on the beautiful island.

Later, as they sat across from one another on the patio outside their bedroom, he admired the way the lights of the lanterns put a glow on her skin. Slightly more dark bronze than usual due to their time on the beach, his fingers itched to get reacquainted with the smoothness. Although, technically, the times when he wasn't touching her in some capacity were rare. Tugging his next thought directly from his head, Zaria sighed.

"Aw man...What am I gonna do when we go back to the real world tomorrow?"

Absently stroking his fingers from her shoulder to her fingertips, Andrei inclined his head. "We will do what we must."

"Yeah...I know...It's just the past week has been so great." Turning her hand over, she tangled her fingers with his. "Thank you for this. I didn't realize how much I needed a break."

"You are more than welcome. I have enjoyed our time together here as well."

Andrei left unsaid the discussions they had about the future of their relationship. After the close call following the wedding, they spent more time talking. He wasn't fond of the word *boundaries*, but agreed some basic ground rules needed to be set. While the make-up sex was phenomenal, he'd prefer they eliminate obvious sources of strife between them.

Of course, that meant he had to agree to tone down his inclinations to rip off limbs when other men thought to get too close to her orbit. He didn't like it. *At all.* Still, he relented. There was absolutely no way he'd have another night like the one he spent on the Lilliputian couch in Zaria's suite.

Even thinking about the little brick furniture made his back ache. Thoughts of the uncomfortable little sofa brought him back to the many ways they'd apologized to one another using their bodies. Which led him to what he was eager to do as soon as they completed their meal.

"What are you thinking?" Zaria's question cut across his recollections about their argument and the aftermath.

"That is a dangerous question, Svet."

"Well, I don't ask questions I don't want an answer to."

He pierced her with a loaded stare. "I am thinking of all the ways I am going to bend your body as I devour every inch of you."

Zaria's eyes widened slightly, and she sat up straighter in her chair. Her lips formed a perfect 'O' around the word.

"Oh. Well, don't hold back. Tell me how you really feel."

"As you wish."

Andrei stood and rounded the table. His eyes never left hers as he pulled her from the seat and into his arms.

"First, I am going to devour these lips."

He tugged her full bottom lip between his, giving it a suckling kiss before delving his tongue into her mouth. When he grasped two hands full of her voluptuous ass and lifted, her legs wound around his waist. As they kissed, he walked them into the suite and over to the large duvet covered bed.

Placing Zaria on the soft bed coverings, he reluctantly released her. Her dress was a wrap style belted on one side. It had fallen open, exposing one thick thigh. Andrei brushed both halves apart. Pressing his fingers against her panty clad center, he looked up to see her staring at him.

"Next, I am going to kiss ***these*** lips. It has been almost twelve hours. I am sure she misses me."

As he rid her of the cock-blocking undergarments, Andrei smirked internally at the way her hips rocked—as if seeking the fulfillment of his promise. When it seemed he took too long in the process to suit her, she prodded him.

"Don't talk about it, be about it. You won't know if she missed you if you don't give her a proper greeting."

One side of Andrei's mouth tipped up in a devilish smirk. "As you wish."

Not wasting another moment, he licked the folds of her fragrant pussy, coaxing her pearl from its hood. Zaria's sharp inhale was followed by her fingertips digging into his scalp while she tried to grip the short strands of his hair. Smiling against her center, Andrei redoubled his efforts—not stopping until her voice gave out as she screamed from one climax to the next.

Zaria's breath came out in heaving puffs as Andrei stood from the bed and discarded his clothing. His cock throbbed, demanding to go where his tongue had the pleasure of being just moments before.

Zaria did nothing more than stare at him languidly until he tugged her up to finish removing her dress and bra. Andrei maneuvered her nearly boneless body until she was completely nude and stretched out atop the pristine sheets.

He lay on his side with his head propped on one hand while lightly running the fingers of the other along her silky skin. His gentleness belied what he ached to do next. When he nudged at the juncture of her thighs, both of her hands grasped his.

"Uh-uh. Wait. I'm too sensitive."

Allowing her to move him away from her center, he guided their hands to his thickness.

"You would deny him his prize after he has been so patient, Svet? I did not think you were a cruel woman."

Her soft digits glided along the length of his shaft, and her tongue swiped across her lips. Andrei tracked the movement before his eyes closed briefly, savoring the feeling of her hands on him.

"You don't play fair."

Zaria moaned the words and followed them with a kiss to his chest. Rolling onto his back, he took her with him, adjusting her until her slick folds encased his length.

"There is no such thing as fair, Svet. I play to win."

Punctuating his statement with a thrust of his hips, he slipped into her velvet walls. Regardless of her claims of sensitivity, Zaria rocked against him, taking over the rhythm of their joining. This time, it was his voice snatched away when he reached his pinnacle.

The light hum of the plane engine was the only noise in the cabin as Zaria slept beside him. Since there was such a dramatic time difference between Bali and Las Vegas, Andrei encouraged her to sleep to help get her body back on the correct cycle more easily. While they'd left the island during morning hours, it was nighttime in Sin City.

He'd like to say his reason for keeping her up until the wee hours was to aid in getting her to sleep on the flight, but it was nothing so altruistic. Andrei knew once they hit the city, they wouldn't be with one another as much as they had been over the past week. They each had busy lives and businesses to run.

While Zaria slept, Andrei went over files and reviewed information from his head of security. There hadn't been any issues at the casino, however he needed to evaluate who could be rotated to Zaria's service. He was aware she had security at her firm, however she didn't have a personal team. That would have to change.

He hadn't discussed it with her yet, but he would. Andrei wanted a team and a plan in place before he brought it up. In spite of her flippant way of speaking, Zaria was a woman who appreciated a plan. He'd present her with one she couldn't refuse.

The woman at the center of his thoughts shifted beside him as she snuggled closer.

"Are you working?" Sitting up, she rearranged the pillows to support her back against the headboard. "You said it was better to sleep so we could be ready to stay up all day when we landed. Or was that advice just for me?"

Closing the lid of the laptop, Andrei placed it on the bedside table. "I slept. I simply woke before you did."

One eyebrow lifted as Zaria stared at him. They'd only been in flight for five hours. They hadn't even reached their refuel point yet.

"Besides. I did not say we needed to sleep the entire time. I said we should try to switch our bodies back to the correct time zone before we landed by sleeping on our normal schedules."

Zaria pursed her lips. "Mmhmm. Should I remind you that I make my living off words, meaning, and intent?"

Sliding down in the bed and tugging her with him, Andrei kissed those pretty pouty lips of hers. "No, Svet. It is not necessary."

The lights were already low in the room. So, once he had her back pressed against his front, he kissed her shoulder. Then, he wrapped one arm around her holding her in place.

"Try to sleep for a few more hours."

Andrei already had plans for their non-sleeping time spent on the flight. He intended to continue his campaign to have her as addicted to being next to him as he was to having her there. The prospect of returning to waking up alone had zero appeal. However, he knew Zaria would need convincing.

Keeping to his plan, they spent their non-sleeping hours with Andrei *entertaining* Zaria in various ways. They took their meals in the bedroom and didn't exit until there were less than two hours left in the flight.

Andrei had his laptop open while Zaria scrolled social media on her cellphone. Service was excellent since he'd made certain the new jet had updated onboard wi-fi installed.

"Aww...Look Andrei...Alyssa and Carver posted some of the pictures from the wedding and reception."

Lifting his eyes from the computer screen, he leaned over to see the images on the phone better. Like most people, Andrei had social media accounts, but he rarely posted on them. His PR team handled the business-related accounts and his personal accounts gave very little information.

He dutifully looked at each picture as Zaria scrolled. She moved slowly enough to give them both time to fully see one image before she moved on to the next. They perused amidst Zaria's occasional soft exclamations until they reached one Andrei didn't expect, although it didn't bother him. It was the photo Jack had taken of the two of them after he interrupted their disagreement.

Zaria stiffened beside him, and Andrei shifted his gaze from the phone to her face. "Is something wrong, Svet?"

"No...I just didn't expect to see any pictures of only the two of us."

"Is that a problem?" He stared at her so intently, he was certain she felt the weight of it. Her dark eyes regarded him.

"Not for me."

"Did you not give them permission to post photos of you?"

Andrei had received the literal consent forms prior to attending the wedding. It was something he'd grown accustomed to since he attended private functions regularly. The social media age had changed things in those circles.

"Of course. Did you?"

"Yes. I did. Yet, you are the only one of us who seems unpleasantly surprised to see the photo."

Andrei's eyes drifted to the phone again, and he made a mental note to visit the page later.

"Oh, I'm surprised, but not upset."

Zaria stroked his arm. Andrei wasn't sure if it was to reassure him or herself since she hadn't scrolled past the picture of them yet to show him the rest. When she finally resumed, the remaining few images went by quickly.

Once she was done, she mentioned something about catching up on Messytok—whatever that was. She put in her earbuds and switched to watching videos. He returned to his work while she alternately tsked and giggled. They continued this way until the flight attendant informed them it was time to prepare for landing.

When the wheels touched down, everyone operated like a well-oiled machine. The flight and ground crew secured the plane, and by the time Andrei assisted Zaria into the blacked-out SUV, their luggage was already in the cargo area.

As they drove away from the private air strip, Zaria's eyes were glued to the passing scenery. He should have, but Andrei hadn't told her he had no intentions of taking her home just yet. Once she figured out they were traveling farther away from the city, she turned from the window.

"Andrei, where are we going?"

"To my place."

She crossed her arms. The action pushed the tops of her breasts up more in the vee of the blouse she wore. Andrei steeled himself to focus and not be distracted by the tempting picture they presented.

"Who said I wanted to go to your place?"

"You do not want to go home with me?"

"I didn't say that either, but you could've asked. You need to work on your manners, sir."

Sliding his hand into the hair at her nape, he closed the small distance between them.

"You do not get to lecture me about manners, Svet. Also, do not call me sir unless you want those delicious cheeks spanked red."

Zaria's eyes slid closed at his implication. Andrei smirked and waited until she opened them again.

"Now...I am not ready for us to go back to the real world just yet. I want us to spend the weekend together at my home." He studied her face intently as he waited for her response.

"Do you understand that wasn't a question?" Zaria lifted one sculpted eyebrow.

"Is that a no?" Andrei countered.

"Andrei, I have things to do. I've been gone more than a week."

Pulling away, he went to press the intercom to speak to the driver, Victor.

"Wait! What are you doing?"

"I am going to tell Victor where to take us, if we are not going to my place."

"Wait. What?" Zaria's face scrunched in confusion.

Andrei looked at her and spoke slowly. Only the slightest hint of his accent was detectable. "If you do not want to go home with me, I will tell Victor to take us to your place. It is fine. We will work from home tomorrow. You have wi-fi correct?"

"So...basically what you're saying is we're either sleeping over at your place or you and your hidden entourage are camping out in my house for the next few days. Do I have that right?"

Kissing the tip of her nose, Andrei actually smiled at her. "I am so glad we understand each other."

When he reached out to push the button again, Zaria laid her hand on top of his. "Fine. You win. I do need to go by my place to get my laptop though. I really do have to look over a few things. I have court next week."

Andrei hid the self-satisfied grin threatening to take over his face as he rattled off Zaria's address to Victor. They made a quick detour to stop at her modest bungalow style house. Andrei accompanied her inside.

She didn't bat an eye when Yeva preceded them into the house and swept the premises before they entered. Instead, she waited for him to give the all clear, then she grabbed what she needed from her office. They were back in the vehicle, driving toward his home, in less than ten minutes.

Chapter Nine

BIG AND BIGGER

As they drove farther away from her Coryville home, Zaria watched the passing landscape as if she'd never seen it before. She had, but it hadn't been while on the way to the home of her new...*Lover? Boyfriend? Man?* What was the correct term to use for who Andrei was to her? Shaking her head to loosen the thought, she resolved not to think about it for now.

Either way, she'd never driven through the upscale community which still considered itself part of Las Vegas but was too far out to actually be a part of the city proper. Unlike other neighborhoods with similar sized houses—well, mansions—Andrei's home and the others surrounding it were set on very large lots. She didn't bother mentally calculating the millions involved in securing that kind of space. She'd seen multi-million-dollar homes in the city, which were still situated insanely close to the mansion next to it.

Unlike the area Carver and Alyssa had chosen, there wasn't a gate at the entrance to the community. Instead, each individual property had their own entries. From the homogenous look of things, there was an ordinance or covenant in place limiting the design choices. When they rolled to a stop, Zaria switched her gaze to the structure barely visible behind the large double gate.

When the barrier was removed, her eyes widened as the Spanish style mansion came into view. She was mildly surprised he'd chosen a house on such a romantic style, but the size of it appeared on brand with the way he seemed to do things on a larger-than-life scale. Still, she was fixated on the exterior of the mansion with the towering palm trees which would provide sparse shade in the light of day. In the fading light of the late evening, they cast a short shadow.

Seeing all of it up close made the descent into reality sudden. Zaria knew Andrei was attempting to keep them inside the bubble they'd created on the island. However, it wasn't possible to pretend the outside world didn't exist when the front door of his mansion was in view and his normally hidden security detail was standing at the ready for his next instructions.

After offering her his non-choice-choice, Andrei hadn't said much, allowing her to sit with her thoughts for the duration of the drive. Once Yeva opened the door and she made no moves to follow Andrei from the vehicle, he leaned back inside and extended his hand.

"Is something wrong, Svet? Did you forget something?"

Shaking off her hesitancy, Zaria refocused her attention on Andrei's concerned face. "No. Nothing's wrong. Just lost in my thoughts for a second."

Accepting his hand, Zaria stepped out. Keeping their fingers entwined, he introduced her to a few more members of his staff and security as they entered the house. She vaguely wondered if he had some kind of height and weight requirement for his security personnel because she hadn't seen one less than six feet. Their considerable bulk meant they all tipped the scale at well over two hundred and fifty pounds.

"Would you like a tour?"

Andrei stopped inside the foyer. His icy blue stare was intense in his focus on her. *Was he offering her a tour of the massive house or a* ***tour****?*

Taking the decision out of her hands, he set the bag containing her laptop on the chair next to a sofa table along the wall, and tugged her into the room on the left. When he actually began talking about the space, she realized he was very serious about the whole 'tour' thing.

By the time they made it to the ice rink he'd installed in a building connected to the house by a covered walkway, she was ready to beg off and climb into bed. However, seeing the ice seemed to rejuvenate Andrei.

"Do you ice skate, Svet?"

Giggles, either from exhaustion or actual humor, burst from Zaria's lips. They tapered off when he simply watched her, waiting for a response. Clearing her throat to smother the remaining chuckles, she gripped the edge of the low wall with her free hand.

"I've been on the ice a few times, but it's not something I've done regularly."

"Would you like to skate with me?"

"I would love to; however, I don't know if my legs will support me tonight. Between the trip and your energetic *entertainment* during the flight, I might fall flat on my face."

Andrei released her fingers to wrap his arm around her waist, tugging her closer to him. "I will take care of you. If you were to fall, I'll be there to catch you."

"Is that so?"

"Always, Svet."

Ok, that was entirely too sweet. Dragging her gaze from his stare, she looked at the well-maintained rink. When she turned back, his eyes were waiting for hers. Trying not to get sucked into his thrall, she lightly tapped his chest.

"Maybe tomorrow. I'm not up to it tonight."

"Okay. Tomorrow then."

He said it with such finality, Zaria was certain she would have to put up or shut up the next day. Andrei led her back toward the main house continuing a discussion.

"It will give me time to get skates in the correct size for you."

"If I'd known you wanted to skate, I could've brought mine from home."

Andrei stopped in his tracks. "You have your own skates?"

Quirking an eyebrow, she looked up at him. "Yes...Why is that surprising?"

She'd never gotten any weird vibes from Andrei, so the response was more of a reflex than her actually thinking he was implying she wouldn't have ice skates due to her race.

"We live in a desert city. Most people here never see snow, let alone own ice skates. Even when we open the arena for free skate activities, we have to set up stations for people to rent them."

"Oh. Well, I was forced to buy multiple pairs years ago."

Andrei tugged her gently, and they began their trek once more. "Who would force you to get ice skates? It does not sound normal."

"That's because it's not. My cousin Cisco plays hockey at a college in Florida. When he first got started, we all tried to support him by getting skates and joining him on the ice during free skates in Memphis.

Whenever I'd go home to visit, he wanted to head to the rink to show me what he'd learned. I couldn't simply watch him from the side lines, he wanted me out there with him...So, I own multiple pairs of skates. I keep one pair here with me and the others are with my family."

As they walked back to the main house Zaria brought the topic back around to his request.

"Is that what you normally do? Like after a trip? Or work? You skate?"

"You could say that. I get on the ice once or twice a week. I find it helps me unwind or clear my thoughts."

They came to a stop in the massive kitchen where Andrei seated her in front of a long island. Once she was perched on the tall chair, he rolled up his sleeves as he went to the sink. After washing his hands, he walked over to the industrial, steel, double-door refrigerator.

"Are you hungry, Svet?"

On cue, a rumble issued from Zaria's belly.

"I guess I could eat."

Zaria watched Andrei as he moved around the kitchen, which looked like it was designed for a professional chef. If she considered him possibly entertaining due to his life as a casino owner and his affiliation with the Las Vegas Chevaliers, then it stood to reason he'd have his home equipped for entertaining.

As he prepared the meal, their stream of conversation was steady, but not every second was filled. There were moments of comfortable silence as he diced mushrooms and onions on the butcher block. Zaria's seat at the counter gave her a perfect view of the entire process.

Propping her chin on her fist, she marveled at the simplicity. Who would've thought Andrei had such a nurturing side to his personality?

Admittedly, he'd begun exposing it while they were in Bali. It was in such stark contrast to the dominance he exhibited in other arenas.

Before long, Andrei set a steaming plate of Beef Stroganoff in front of Zaria, along with a glass of port wine. Fixing himself a portion, he sat in the chair next to her.

"This smells amazing."

Zaria leaned over the plate inhaling the delicious aroma of the beef, mushrooms, onions and gravy poured over the wide egg noodles. When she looked up, Andrei's eyes were on her, displaying an entirely different hunger.

"Eat up, Svet. You will need your energy."

A zing shot through Zaria's center at his obvious implication. Without a word, she picked up her fork. Her first bite caused her eyes to drift closed as she savored the flavors dancing on her tongue, and she released an involuntary moan. When she lifted her eyelids, Andrei was still staring at her.

"What?"

"I am trying to determine if I should be jealous of food which causes you to make such noises—even if I did prepare it."

A heated blush crept into her cheeks from the bold desire clearly projected in his gaze. She would've never thought Andrei Antonov would be so expressive about his feelings. Although she was certain he wasn't revealing everything to her, what he did reveal spoke volumes. Beyond his physical attraction to her.

"I don't think you need to be jealous of food."

Behind lashes lowered halfway, she stared at him before returning to the delicious pasta dish. As tired as she thought she was when he asked if she wanted to skate, Andrei simply implying that they'd be tangled together again shortly gave her a surge of energy.

One would think her pretty pocket would be signing up for disability with the way they'd been going at it since that first night in Bali. But no... The little trollop was leaking from only a mention of playtime with her new best friend.

Determined to remain focused on the meal and not the activities waiting in the near future, Zaria turned her eyes down to her plate as she stabbed another bite onto the tines of her fork. Shortly after, she heard the clink of Andrei's silverware as he finally began to eat as well. Unlike her, there were no moans or sighs of appreciation for the well-cooked meal coming from him.

They ate in relative silence; however, it wasn't uncomfortable. One of the things she'd come to enjoy when spending time with Andrei was that she didn't always have to be 'on'. She could quietly enjoy moments without feeling the need to fill it with conversation—especially when nothing needed to be said.

When they were done eating, he took their plates and glasses and loaded them into the dishwasher before filling the sink with water to wash the cookware he'd used. He waved off her offer to help.

Considering the size of the place, she was certain he had staff, yet he performed the small household tasks as if he did it regularly. Even the way he moved around the kitchen while he cooked signaled it was something he'd done often.

"What is it, Svet?"

Sitting up straighter at his question, Zaria's eyebrows dipped. "What is what?"

"You look as if you would like to say something."

Shaking her head, Zaria rubbed her hands on her jean-clad thighs. "No. I was just watching you be all domestic."

Strolling toward her, he didn't stop until he turned her in the chair and spread her legs. Stepping into the space he created, he tangled his fingers in the hair at her nape. He seemed quite fond of doing that.

"Does seeing me do dishes turn you on?"

Andrei's voice seemed deeper, as his eyes roamed over her face. His gaze left a heated trail in its wake.

"I didn't say all that."

"You did not, but *they* did. Unless there is a chill in the air I did not feel."

His stare moved from her eyes to the pointed peaks of her breasts, then back to her face. It was just her luck that she wore one of her lacy bras and a thin top which hid nothing when her nipples decided to perk up and insert themselves into the conversation. The fire in his arctic blue eyes was more than enough incentive for the other part of her body which craved his touch most.

When the hand on her waist moved to her ass, giving one cheek a firm squeeze, Zaria knew it was pointless to pretend she wasn't interested in what he was offering. Gliding her hands up the front of his shirt, she fisted two hands full of the material, tugging until he leaned closer. Lifting her face, she presented her lips for his taking. He needed very little encouragement.

As usual, he preferred carrying her to allowing her to walk to their destination. It was a good thing he'd already given her a tour. She had very little time to take in the décor of the massive bedroom before he stripped her bare. They dissolved into a puddle of arms and legs, exploring one another until they were too spent to move.

Zaria looked at the two men standing before her. It was Sunday morning and she and Andrei were seated at a table beside his infinity pool, enjoying a late breakfast. They'd spent the weekend much like they had the previous few days in Bali—completely cut off from the rest of the world.

Or at least that's what she thought until big and bigger walked out onto the patio and stood a few feet away from them. If she hadn't seen them approach, she wouldn't have known they were standing there. Men that big shouldn't be able to move so quietly. Part of her wanted to ask how they did it, but she didn't.

Instead, she looked from the obvious bodyguards to Andrei as he leaned back in his chair. One hand rested on the glass tabletop, the other was on her thigh.

"Svet, meet Logan and Dakota. They will alternate with Grace and Bianca."

The two men nodded in acknowledgement as Zaria said hello. Where Dakota was dark haired with lightly bronzed skin, Logan's locks were so blond they almost looked white in the low man bun at his nape. Andrei didn't follow the introductions with an explanation quickly enough for Zaria, so she placed her hand atop his on her thigh. Squeezing his thick digits, she got his attention.

"They will alternate with Grace and Bianca doing what?" She was sure she knew the answer, but she wanted him to say it aloud.

"Providing your personal security."

Zaria stared at him for a beat. Logically, she knew it was coming. She also understood why it was necessary. Having given Alyssa two tons of shit for bucking against Carver for doing the same thing, she couldn't even throw a proper fit about him taking the initiative. It came with the package of being with a powerful man.

"Okay... Can I speak with you a moment? Alone?"

Nodding, Andrei directed the men back inside. Zaria had no hope that they were simply there for the introductions. It was more likely they'd resume a post on the property and wait. Which meant, she'd have to figure out how to accommodate having a detail at her home. It wasn't nearly the size of Andrei's mansion. Once they were out of hearing range, she turned to him.

"Were we going to discuss this at all?"

"Of course. I wanted you to meet them first. Unfortunately, Grace and Bianca couldn't be here until later. They each worked their last rotation on night shift on Friday. I gave them the rest of the weekend off so they could transition to their new duties."

"Their new duties being?"

"I just told you. Protecting you, Svet."

Pushing back his chair, Andrei tugged at her hand until she left her seat and was perched on his lap.

"You are important to me. That fact will soon become obvious to others. While I may not have the crazed fans of some of my contemporaries, my business interests make me and anyone close to me a potential target.

I will not have your safety compromised. Since it is not possible for me to be with you twenty-four hours a day, the next best solution is for you to have your own security team. They will not get in your way or disrupt your daily life.

When you are not with me, some combination of the four will be with you in groups of two. I have spoken with Yeva about any upgrades he thinks you may need on your property as well. We can go over that plan together once it is complete. We will discuss how the nights will work once you have an opportunity to meet the ladies later today."

His admission of her importance to him took the wind right out of Zaria's sails. She'd been ready to concede to the detail, but not having them inside her office building—which was already secured by an agency. However, each potential question or concern she had was answered by Andrei.

"You've thought this out, haven't you?"

"Every facet. I would not have mentioned it otherwise."

Zaria's heart rate picked up as the implications of all that Andrei was saying, without saying it, filtered into her brain. This man was setting up a whole future with her and she wasn't sure what to do with the knowledge she possessed. Whether she was ready or not, this was happening. She'd conceded as much on the island.

What was developing between them now was the next logical path for the fast-moving train of their relationship. It was barreling down the tracks, and she had no idea where the pull cord was to initiate the brakes. But...Did she really want to stop it? It was scary as hell, yet it was equally exhilarating for someone to put her first.

It filled her heart near to bursting. Which led to a different type of fear. *What the hell had she gotten herself into?*

Chapter Ten

DID YOU JUST GROWL AT ME?

Andrei sat behind his desk closely regarding Gregor seated in one of the two tufted visitors' chairs on the opposite side. The dark mahogany desk was custom made to accommodate his height. Although he rarely spent extended time in his office, he didn't want to spend it hunched over something that looked like it belonged in a child's play set.

"As I told you on the phone, Vitaly's agent was able to get him reinstated earlier than expected and the fine was waived. For a change, your brother was thinking with the head above his shoulders instead of the one between his legs."

Andrei didn't take offense to Gregor's assessment of Vitaly. He was one of the few people who could speak with such honesty about Andrei's younger sibling without repercussions—regardless of the truth of the statement.

"Were you able to uncover anything else?" Andrei rolled a pen across his knuckles while staring at Gregor.

"I was. You already know how this began, but I was able to uncover video of the inciting incident."

Pulling a tablet from the bag at his feet, Gregor tapped the screen a few times before sliding it across the desk to Andrei. Accepting the device, Andrei pressed the play icon. The frozen image became exonerating evidence for Vitaly and damning for the man who took his fit of jealousy too far.

Andrei watched as a petite brunette repeatedly attempted to get Vitaly's attention. The footage was from an event which was teaming with players, owners and various sponsors.

To his brother's credit, he remained polite but decidedly aloof—giving the woman no indication he was interested in her in the slightest. With each advance she made, he either side stepped or completely removed himself. Pausing the video, Andrei pointed at the woman.

"This woman, she is at the center of all of this. Da?"

"She is. Her name is Angelica Marsden. She is the wife of Bellamy Marsden, the majority owner of the Torrent."

"If I am understanding this situation correctly, Marsden suspended my brother because his wife tried to fuck Vitaly? Unsuccessfully. The official report from the league stated he'd violated the code of conduct clause in his contract. I do not see that in this video."

Leaning back in the chair, Gregor waved one hand in the universal sign for 'kind of'.

"It was not entirely because of her failed attempt to bed him. Keep watching."

Andrei resumed the playback. The sound wasn't clear enough for him to hear exactly what was said. At least not until Marsden approached Vitaly red-faced. Using one gnarled finger, he poked Vitaly in the chest.

"You! You empty-headed hoser! You stay away from my wife."

Remaining remarkably composed, Vitaly stepped back from the man and put his hands up. "I haven't gone near your wife, sir. Perhaps you should tell your wife to stay away from me."

"You think because you get a few saves on goal a game and you have groupies following you that you have the right to anyone you want? Think again."

Andrei's jaw hardened, watching as no one else seemed to have the balls to intervene. Yes, Vitaly was an adult, but the power dynamic between an owner and a player wasn't equal.

Once again, Vitaly attempted to de-escalate the situation—or at least his statement began that way.

"Mr. Marsden. I assure you. I have no interest in your wife. As I said, you should tell her to stay away from me. I haven't approached her, not once—ever. Yet, every time I've turned around tonight, she has been trying to press the breasts you bought her into some part of my body."

Angelica Marsden gasped and pressed her hand against the surgically altered bosom, which probably ***were*** a gift from her rich husband. Bellamy looked from his wife's now tear-filled eyes to Vitaly.

"You immigrant piece of shit. Did you just insult my wife?"

"Is it an insult if it's true?" Vitaly's eyes sparkled in an expression Andrei knew well. His brother had reached his bullshit limit. "I am going to leave now before this goes too far. If you keep an eye on your wife, you will notice she's not leaving with me."

When Vitaly was turned partially away from the irate man, Marsden grabbed him by the arm. Using the quick hands that got him the job as the starting goalie for the Colorado Torrent, Vitaly slapped away the man's hand and lifted him from the floor. His fists were clenched around the expensive designer suit Marsden wore as the other man's feet dangled inches off the surface.

"Let's get one thing straight. You **do not** put your hands on me! I am not your lapdog nor your punching bag. Maybe if you satisfied your wife, she wouldn't be throwing her pussy at every hockey player in the room. Or is it that you've tried to satisfy her and have come up...short?"

The snarl on Vitaly's face reminded Andrei of his own, although Vitaly took more of their mother's looks. Marsden's jaw dropped, but no sound escaped his mouth.

Vitaly shook the smaller man slightly. "Get yourself together, man. I really don't give a shit when, if, or how you do or don't fuck your wife. All I care about is that you leave me out of your dysfunctional bullshit."

A few of Vitaly's teammates finally stepped in, prying his fingers from Marsden's lapels and separating the two. As they did, Marsden rediscovered his voice.

"That's it, Antonov! You're finished! You just flushed your career down the toilet. I'll ruin you."

A normal man would've been worried about such a declaration from a person who was essentially their boss. His brother, on the other hand, smiled at Marsden.

"You will ruin me? Are you sure about that?" Not even struggling against his teammates holding each of his arms, Vitaly raked a disdainful gaze over the team owner. "Let's see what happens when you tell the board about this little incident."

"You're suspended! Without pay! Get the hell out!"

The video wasn't the best quality, but Andrei saw the sweat dripping off of Marsden's reddened face.

Backing away, Vitaly smiled again. "My representation will be in touch."

The video ended with Vitaly moving through the crowd of elegantly clad people. Six of his teammates trailed behind him.

Laying the tablet down flat on his desk, Andrei looked up at Gregor. "So, his agent and his lawyer got him reinstated. However, something tells me this is not over."

"Because you are a smart man." Gregor tapped the arm of his chair. "Marsden is beyond pissed that the board forced his hand. It seems he hadn't considered Vitaly being able to file a Complaint against him and his wife for harassment."

"Has he?"

"No, but it didn't stop his lawyer from saying he would."

Andrei grunted. He guessed Carlson was worth the obnoxious rate he charged for his services. He'd kept his brother's career afloat. Although something told him the idea to make such a threat came from Jamie Shannon, Vitaly's agent.

"Who recorded this?"

"One of his teammates."

Andrei cocked an eyebrow at that bit of information. Gregor held up a hand, sitting up taller to answer Andrei's unspoken question.

"It started as a joke. He saw how uncomfortable Vitaly was with the attention and wanted to use it as fodder to chirp at him. Once he realized what was going on, he thought the footage might come in handy. It's a good thing he did. Although he probably put himself on Marsden's radar."

"Are there any others?" Although things worked out in Vitaly's favor, Andrei knew the slant of the video could be used against him if someone chose.

"No. This is the only copy. Any others were wiped, including cloud storage."

Nodding, Andrei slid the device forward to Gregor, then leaned back in his seat. He was relieved Vitaly's situation had been mostly resolved, but he would keep his eye on it. As yet, Vitaly still hadn't told him about it. However, he was certain his younger brother knew Andrei was aware.

Andrei and Gregor wrapped up their meeting shortly after. Gregor left to parts unknown. He wasn't an employee. He worked for Andrei on a case-by-case basis, and he was the best at what he did.

Once Gregor was gone, Andrei had difficulty focusing on the reports on his computer screen. Without a person physically in the room to distract him, his thoughts drifted back to Zaria. They'd parted ways earlier when he'd left her with her security team on her doorstep. He'd managed to convince her to stay over the previous night, but duty called for them both bright and early on Monday morning.

He was about to give up on being productive when he opened the file from human resources. Unless it was on the executive level or the security team, he didn't get involved with the hiring process. He found it curious that he'd receive anything for someone seeking employment at *The Rooftop*.

When he read the information, he got an idea of why he was informed. The person seeking employment was someone who'd previously been employed as a server. Katelyn Norris. The same Katelyn Norris who'd violated the privacy of one of the few people he considered a friend.

Quickly scanning the information, Andrei lifted the phone from its cradle. Pressing a few buttons, he called the restaurant hiring manager, Delancy Morgan.

"Hello, Mr. Antonov."

"Ms. Morgan, I received your email regarding Katelyn Norris. I am curious as to why you felt the need to bother me with her application."

Muffled shifting came over the line, and he heard her clearing her throat. It was uncommon for him to call personally, but he wanted there to be no potential for miscommunication via email.

"Well, sir. I wasn't privy to the exact reasons she was let go. There is simply a notation that she is ineligible for re-hire. However, I've not seen anything in the company policy stating we make a practice of barring people from future employment. I was hoping to get more clarification."

Andrei bristled under the hint of accusation in Delancy's voice. In turn, the tone of his reply brooked no argument. "Ms. Morgan. As you are aware, Nevada is an at-will employment state. We do not have to give a reason for terminating an employee. However, Antonov Enterprises does have guidelines which must be followed.

Failure to do so can result in termination and barring from future employment in any branch. You do recall that from your review of the documents you mentioned, correct?"

"Yes, sir. I've just not seen it applied to anyone—especially not waitstaff."

"No one is exempt from adhering to the standards set in the employee guidelines. Including the waitstaff. Since you are well versed in the policies and you have seen the notation in her file, there is no need for further discussion. Katelyn Norris is ineligible for employment in any form by any business under the Antonov Enterprises' umbrella."

Andrei left the question of clarity hanging between them. He'd already done more explaining than he deemed strictly necessary.

"Good day, Ms. Morgan."

"Good day, sir."

Andrei replaced the phone in the handset. Clicking around on his computer, he accessed the personnel information for Delancy Morgan. He wanted to know why she was so keen to get Katelyn re-hired. Andrei clenched his jaw in memory of the events which led to the young woman's termination.

One of the reasons his establishments were so popular was his commitment to the privacy of his patrons. His employees, from housekeeping to the senior executives, were paid well above industry standard. There were waiting lists for every position within the organization.

Each person in his employ signed an ironclad Non-Disclosure Agreement to safeguard the privacy of the patrons. Which meant they were not to take photos, video, or relay to anyone information regarding customers. Not only had Katelyn violated the policy, she'd been party to a deliberate plot to try to make it appear that Carver was cheating on Alyssa.

While Andrei didn't peruse social media often, he had people who monitored various sites for any signs of unauthorized information being shared. Paparazzi weren't allowed on the premises for a reason.

Considering the waitstaff at *The Rooftop* was paid better than managers at many restaurants, before tips, it didn't make sense for Katelyn to jump at the opportunity to sell photos of patrons for extra cash. It turned out Carver and Alyssa weren't the only ones to be victimized, but Andrei made damn sure they were the last. Katelyn was lucky she was simply terminated and barred from re-hire. He could've done so much more.

When he didn't find anything in Delancy's file which pointed to a reason for why she'd be so determined to dig into the situation with Katelyn, he closed the file and turned away from the computer. He didn't think it warranted a call to Gregor, but he made a mental note to keep an eye on the situation.

Leaving his desk, he went over to the conference table on the opposite side of his office. Multiple monitors were mounted on the wall, each surveilling different places on the property, including Anton's and the common areas of the office space.

Ignoring the office feeds, he focused on the ones displaying various areas of the casino. Many people wondered why he named it Anton's. Those people didn't understand Vegas history the way he did. It wouldn't have been in his best interest to use Antonov despite his popularity as a professional hockey player. Calling the place Anton's was a nod to the families who originally built Las Vegas from a rancher's town into the booming gambling destination it had become.

Andrei's morning had been filled with meetings and catching up on the few things he didn't address while he was away. His meeting with Gregor hadn't taken up very much of his afternoon. Other than arriving early and leaving late, he had no set hours. In the past, his long hours hadn't been an issue. However, now that he had Zaria in his life, lengthy work days had little appeal—despite him genuinely enjoying the business aspects of his life.

Zaria had told him, when they parted, she expected her first few days back to be long ones. While he wouldn't even consider dissuading her from putting in extra effort in her practice, Andrei didn't particularly care for the prospect of their alone time being cut short by work commitments.

His only consolation was knowing she'd agreed to the security detail without much complaint. Andrei's lips twisted into a slight grin as he recalled their discussion following his introduction of Dakota and Logan.

With Zaria at the forefront of his mind, Andrei slipped his phone from his pocket. He wasn't big on texting, so he tapped the icon to place the call. Although he didn't make a habit of calling women during the work day, Zaria was different. She was *his* woman.

If he wanted to speak to his woman, he would call when he desired. After her initial disappearing act, he made sure he had a means to contact her aside from her business number. The first time she'd called him, she'd done so from her office and not her personal line.

The electronic ring sounded in his ear as he waited for her to answer. With a quick flick of his wrist, he checked the time. Two p.m. After the second ring, the naturally sultry timbre of Zaria's voice came through the device in his hand.

"Good afternoon, Andrei."

"Good afternoon, Svet."

"To what do I owe the pleasure of this call?"

His brow wrinkled and Andrei leaned backwards against the soft leather of the executive chair.

"I need a reason to want to speak to you?"

Zaria chuckled lightly. "No... I guess you don't. It's just, considering your day was probably more jammed packed than mine, I'm surprised to hear from you."

"No matter how busy I am, I will always make time for you, Svet."

Andrei stiffened after the words left his lips. He meant them, but he felt exposed once he heard them said aloud. He'd become a different man in a very short amount of time. No. That wasn't true. He'd wanted something different, to be different, for a while.

The first time he saw Zaria, the feeling intensified. Given the opportunity to spend time with her, talk to her, touch her, feel her, and connect with her in a way he'd never done with anyone else...It was too intoxicating to resist.

"That's good to know."

Zaria's response pulled him from his internal debate about his infatuated behavior. He had no specific plan when he placed the call, other than wanting to hear her voice. Now that he'd heard her voice, his desire to have her next to him was stronger.

"Speaking of busy days...when are you leaving the office?"

Andrei never thought he'd be the kind of man who asked such things of his partner. Hell, he wasn't sure he'd even have a partner. Yet, he'd just done it, and was anxiously awaiting her reply.

"Umm..." He heard rustling noises before Zaria spoke again.

"I'm not sure. I had the paralegals pull some briefs looking for precedence for the case I'm working on. I'm only halfway through the second one, and I have three more to go."

"Hmm...What day do you have court?"

"If it doesn't get delayed, we're on the docket for nine a.m. Thursday morning."

"Okay. It means you have ample time to prepare."

"In theory, but I can't spend the entirety of the next two days working on this one case. I have other clients."

Andrei had dealt with lawyers for various reasons over the years, however, he hadn't given much thought to the time they put in beyond how many hours he was billed for the services they provided.

"So, what is your plan, Svet? Spend the night in your office?"

"Not all night, just later than usual. I'll be here to at least ten or ten thirty."

Andrei didn't like the sound of that. At all.

"No."

"Excuse me?"

"No." Andrei repeated, despite his dislike for doing so.

"No, what?" Zaria asked slowly. Much slower than necessary.

"No, you will not work yourself into the night this way. I do not see how exhausting yourself helps you or your client."

Andrei heard the unmistakable sound of Zaria sucking her teeth. He'd heard it only a few times since they started seeing each other, nevertheless he recognized it.

"Listen, I don't know what you're used to, but this ain't that. The only place you get to boss me is in bed, and not entirely there."

"Svet, what do you think this is? A game?" Andrei's neck heated. He wasn't necessarily angry; however, he was well on his way to being frustrated.

"No. I don't. You're used to ordering people around and they do what you say. Like I said. ***This*** ain't ***that***. You can express your feelings about a subject, but you don't get to ***tell*** me what I will and will not do—especially when it comes to my career.

I'm the one who built this firm. I say how much or how little effort I put into each case. No one else gets to do that. Not even you."

Andrei made no effort to suppress his growl of frustration. It wasn't entirely directed at her, since it was his big ass foot he'd stuck into his mouth. He was well aware of what kind of woman he had, yet he couldn't stop himself.

He was already struggling with the idea of them possibly sleeping apart; then she casually mentioned working into the night as if seeing him wasn't even a thought in her head.

"Did you just growl at me? Like some kind of neanderthal?"

Scrubbing his hand over his face, Andrei released a huffing sigh. "I did not growl at you. Simply the situation. I do not like it when we argue. It was not my intention when I called you."

"What was your intention?"

"I missed you, Svet. And wanted to hear your voice."

Chapter Eleven

WHAT DOES THAT MEAN?

Zaria's breath caught in her throat. Andrei's admission played on a loop in her head. *"I missed you, Svet."*

How the fuck was she supposed to respond to such blatant honesty? Who the hell told that big ass, mean looking, head-cracking, Russian to take her breath away by being all fucking sweet? What was she supposed to do now?

He was still wrong as hell for thinking he could simply tell her what to do about her work life. But knowing he probably had a million and one things he should be doing, and he stopped it all to call her for no other reason than he missed her, did something to her insides. That was the shit which simultaneously scared her and made her stomach tremble with excitement.

"You missed me?" She finally managed to eke out. "It's been less than eight hours since the last time we saw each other."

"What does time have to do with it?"

There it was again. That fluttering feeling in her stomach. The giddiness which should've worn off by now was present and pulsing like it was its own entity. *How the hell did she end up here?* Andrei's frankness was chipping away at her resolve.

Zaria wasn't one of those women. The kind who got a man and

allowed everything in her life to become about him. What he liked. What he wanted. What he needed. Pushing her wants, needs and desires to the back burner. In her estimation, it never ended well. She was the living product of it.

"Andrei..."

Zaria searched for the right words. She needed to convey her boundaries clearly. However, she didn't want to give him the impression she was brushing off his feelings. Whether he'd intended to or not, he'd shown a vulnerability many men ran from—until it was useful as a manipulation tactic. She didn't get that vibe from Andrei.

"Yes, Svet?"

"I will concede it's possible for you to miss me in less than eight hours."

"As I was simply stating a fact, that is generous of you."

"Anyway... I will also admit hearing your voice isn't entirely unpleasant."

"I have been told it is a nice voice."

Zaria rolled her eyes. "I am *not* feeding your ego, sir. It's big enough."

His already deep voice dropped an octave. "What did I tell you about calling me 'sir'? Do not think I will not come to your office and spank your plump ass red, Svet. You test me unnecessarily."

Zaria's lips snapped shut, along with her thighs. The heat flooding her core had her wishing they weren't talking on the phone. She was almost tempted to push to see if he'd truly follow through with his threat. Then, her eyes landed on the printouts stacked neatly on her desk and reality returned with the shock of an ice bath.

"Andrei, this has been..." *Nice* wasn't exactly the word she'd use for the conversation after the twists and turns it had taken. "I don't want to rush you off, but I really need to get back to work. I have a lot to get through before I'm comfortable calling it a night.

Speaking of which. Although I don't appreciate the way you said it, I did hear you. You aren't a fan of my late hours. It's part of the job. As I'm sure there will be times when you work late."

Zaria heard Andrei take a heaving breath. She hoped he wasn't about to start his bullshit again. Despite her profession, she really didn't want to argue. However, no amount of sweet talk would allow her to accept him trying to dictate to her.

"I can respect your desire to do your job well. Yet I stand by what I said, Svet. It does not benefit you or your client for you to exhaust yourself. You cannot tell me you are at your best when you do not get adequate rest."

Oooo! She couldn't stand him! He did ***not*** have to go and insert logic into this situation. She was already tired and re-reading sections of the brief open in front of her. It was why it was taking her so long to get through the information to begin with.

If she wasn't so fucking stubborn, she would've accepted a different court date when it was offered. But no... She had to get the first available slot to get it off her plate sooner. Her client even told her they were okay with a later appearance. They weren't hurting for the funds in question.

"Andrei...I don't want to argue."

"Neither do I. So, how will we resolve this?"

Zaria bit her bottom lip. On top of throwing out saccharine sweet truth bombs, he was now acting like a real grown up and seeking a compromise. Her inner brat stomped her foot at being denied her opportunity to attempt to force his hand. The woman, still on her healing journey, pushed the brat to the back and actually considered his question.

If she moved some things around, she could still leave at her normal time each day. She didn't actually need the briefs she was poring over. The case was a done deal. She simply wanted to leave no stone unturned. Winning could set a new precedent. What attorney worth their salt didn't want to set precedent which shaped future laws?

"Let me look at my schedule and see if I can move a few things around."

"If you are able to do that, what would it mean?"

"It would mean I'm able to leave the office close to my normal time."

"Which is?"

"Five-thirty-ish. Six at the latest."

Andrei asked the question, but Zaria had no doubt he already knew the answer. While Dakota and Grace were assigned to protect her, they worked for Andrei. She was certain he received reports of their movements and projected movements.

Heck, he likely knew what she had for lunch. Especially since they inspected it prior to allowing the delivery to continue. The two of them had caused quite a stir in the office. For a person who liked to keep her private life separate from her professional one, it was an adjustment.

Walking in with Grace in front of her and Dakota bringing up the rear, had all eyes on them. They'd started out with Dakota leading, but not being able to see where she was going didn't sit well with Zaria. The bodyguard's large frame made seeing over or around him impossible for someone of her five-foot-four-inch height. It was at such times when she was most intensely jealous of taller women.

It was easier with Grace. While she was still taller than Zaria, she wasn't as broadly built as Dakota. So, it made the situation bearable. Zaria would still wonder if there was a height requirement if she hadn't met Bianca, who was barely Zaria's height and slight in build. However, Zaria was one hundred percent certain the woman was just as competent as the big burly men in Andrei's employ.

Zaria heard tapping sounds and wondered what Andrei was doing.

"Six sounds good. I should be home by then. We can have dinner by seven."

"Wait. What?"

Zaria pulled the phone away from her ear to look at the screen, then put it back. And just like that, Andrei was back on his bullshit.

"When did we decide I was coming to your place again tonight?"

"You do not have to, Svet. I am willing to compromise. I can come to you. It would be a nice change of scenery. Although, I do not know what you have stocked that I can use to cook dinner. Do not worry. I will make a list and have some items delivered."

Zaria covered her face with her other hand. This man was impossible. It didn't take much to see he fully expected they would spend their nights together going forward. It was in complete contradiction to the agreement she thought they'd come to over the weekend.

"Andrei... You do understand that we don't have to spend every night together, right?"

"I am not...as you Americans say...slow, Svet."

His thickened accent was an indicator of his irritation at her question. It had happened earlier in their conversation; however, it lessened when they began discussing a compromise. The return said his hackles were up again.

"I'm aware you are quite intelligent, Andrei. But you are also stubborn."

Releasing a sigh, Zaria leaned back into the buttery softness of her leather chair. "You're taking me too fast."

"What does that mean? I am taking you too fast?"

"This relationship. Don't get me wrong. I know what I said to you in Bali and I meant it. I'm starting to think it meant something different to you than it did to me."

"You tell me, Svet. What did it mean to you?"

Although they weren't on video chat, Zaria scrunched her face as if he could see her giving him stink eye. He *would* beat her to the punch and ask her to explain first.

"When I said you were mine and I'm yours. I meant that I agreed to be in an exclusive relationship with you."

"How is what you said different from what you think it means to me?"

Since turnabout was fair play, Zaria flipped the question on him. "Why don't you tell me? From where I'm sitting, it seems like you heard my words and took them to mean we'd be moving in together once the plane touched down in Nevada."

The silence was thicker than Andrei's Russian accent when he was irritated. It grew uncomfortable, but Zaria didn't breach it. The ball was in his court.

"As I have said before, Svet. We are adults. If we want to be together each night and wake up beside one another in the morning, what is the issue? We do not have to yield to what other people consider normal."

"True. We don't. But, if your goal is me moving into that big ass mansion with you, just come out and say it."

"If I said it, you would try to end things before the words left my mouth."

"You don't know that."

"Fine. Will you move in with me?"

Why? Why did she feel the need to test a man who gave zero fucks what the rest of the world thought of him? Rule one was to never ask a question you didn't already know the answer to or didn't want to know the answer to. While she hadn't technically asked a question, she had challenged him to state his case. Which he did. Without hesitation.

"Andrei... You know I can't. And you think that's what you want, but it's not."

"One. I do not see why you cannot. Two. Please do not presume to tell me what I want when it comes to being with you."

"Do you hear yourself? We've officially been a couple for less than ten days and you're talking cohabitation. That sounds like three bags of crazy and an ice rink full of red flags."

"I hear myself quite clearly."

"No. You couldn't possibly hear the things you're saying." Shoving her fingers into her hair, Zaria tugged at the coily strands. "How about this? What if Vitaly came to you and said he and the woman he'd just started seeing last week were moving in together? What would you say to him?"

"I am not Vitaly and you are not some random woman. Now, answer my question. Please."

The addition of the 'please' at the end sounded strained to Zaria's ears. "I already answered your question, Andrei. I can't move in with you. At least not now."

"Why not?"

"I need time, Andrei. We're still getting to know each other. Sharing space is a huge step. I won't be rushed into making it. And honestly, the more you push, the more I think there's something you're hiding from me. Like you want to lock me down before the bubble bursts."

"I am not hiding anything from you. There is no hidden agenda. I simply do not see the need to bend to what others think."

"Even me?"

"Of course I care what you think, Svet."

"Then hear me when I say I'm not ready. I need time." Before he could ask, Zaria quickly added. "And I can't tell you how much time. I just know it's not today and it won't be tomorrow either."

After another short period of heavy silence, he finally responded. "Fine. We will do it your way. For now."

Releasing the tension in her shoulders, Zaria breathed a little easier. "Thank you."

"Da. I will have dinner ready by seven. Dakota knows how to avoid heavy traffic. So, I expect you by then. I know you will need to stop by your place to get more clothing. Although if you do not want to stop, I can ask one of the ladies in the shops downstairs to pick out a few things for you."

"Andrei. Artyom. Antonov." Zaria gritted her teeth.

"Talk to you later, Svet. I do not want to keep you from your work any longer."

With that being said, Andrei ended the call. Zaria stared at the device in her hand in disbelief.

"I know he didn't just hang up on me."

There was no one in her office to hear her or respond. Yet, she looked around the space as if seeking clarification from an unseen audience.

"He hung up on me. No. Correction. He completely ignored me, then hung up on me."

Just as she was building up a full head of steam at Andrei's audacity, her phone dinged with an incoming message.

AAA: I heard you, Svet. But I need to see you tonight. We can discuss tomorrow on tomorrow.

Zaria stared at the message for a solid two minutes before she tapped her reply. Prior to moving her fingers, she already knew she would cave. She consoled herself with the fact that she'd be able to talk to him face to face. Then, she could get him to see things her way.

I have to go home first, then I'll be there.

AAA: Good. Now, get back to work.

An unwilling smile stretched her lips. She didn't know who he thought he was talking to.

I'm not one of your employees, sir.

AAA: I see someone wants a spanking. That is fine with me, Svet. Work now. Sass later.

You're not the boss of me.

AAA: We shall see about that.

Zaria's bits tingled at the promise in those five little words. She had no idea how she was going to focus. Before Andrei's call, she was having a hard time. After his call, and the ensuing texts, she would have trouble spelling her own name.

In the minutes which followed Andrei's last text, Zaria worked to get her mind back on the task at hand. No matter how open and shut the case appeared to her, she still wanted to be prepared. However, in the recesses of her thoughts, she was turning over ways she could maintain her usual level of proficiency while not neglecting her budding relationship.

Such considerations were part of the package when trying to be a real partner in a relationship without allowing your career goals to fall by the wayside. Doing that was a complete non-starter for Zaria. She did wonder how some of the other female attorneys she knew managed it. She'd missed her last Black Lady Lawyer group meeting, and the next one was a few weeks away. But she brushed off the idea of asking any of them.

There were only a few who she knew well enough to broach the subject with and, of those three, only one was married. Of the two others, one was engaged and the other single with the intention to remain that way indefinitely. Talia, the married one, was pregnant with her first child. It appeared she had one of those uber-active husbands who had his own thing going. He didn't expect her to be a 'traditional wife'.

The fact Zaria even knew that about them was a surprise because Talia was very private. However, she seemed happy with her husband and her practice was thriving. Zaria knew she couldn't turn to Ensley because she was newly engaged herself. If the way her fiancé behaved, crashing the bachelor/bachelorette party, was any indication, she was in the same conundrum as Zaria.

She hadn't realized she was staring off into space until her phone rang again, pulling her out of her reverie. Checking the display, she was surprised to see Alyssa's face.

"Hey, what's wrong?" Zaria immediately launched into the question when she answered.

"Hello...and nothing's wrong. I haven't talked to you since last week when you said you were staying on the island with Andrei. Other than a quick text to let me know you were back, you've been silent. I was just checking to see if you were alive and Andrei hadn't swallowed you whole."

While Zaria detected an edge of concern in Alyssa's tone, she also heard the mirth in her voice.

"Ha-ha. Very funny."

"I try," Alyssa said airily.

"Well, let me put your mind at ease. I'm very much alive and haven't been eaten by the big, scary Russian."

As soon as she said it, Zaria knew the ways it could be taken. Her lips slanted into a smirk.

"Correction. I haven't been eaten in the bad way."

"Ma'am!" Alyssa gasped in fake outrage before dissolving into giggles. "You're a mess!"

"Don't act like you didn't think it. Besides, I don't need the details to know you've experienced being a culinary delight to a big ravenous man. Don't play."

Alyssa's giggles tapered off. "I plead the fifth."

"You know that typically means you're guilty, right?"

"Yes, Counselor. I'm aware. Be quiet and get back on topic."

"Mhmm. I thought we were on topic."

"Zee..."

Leaning back in her chair, Zaria considered how much she wanted to reveal. Alyssa was her bestie. A friend unlike any other she'd ever had. They could actually trust one another. If anyone knew how to deal with a man like Andrei, it would be Alyssa. Before she could talk herself out of it, Zaria launched into a recounting of the events with Andrei since they'd been back from Bali.

"How do you do it?" Zaria finally asked.

"How do I do what?"

"Navigate Carver's crazy."

"I know you didn't just call my husband crazy."

"Come on Lyss. You know what I mean."

She was met with silence which seemed to go on forever before Alyssa's giggles filled it.

"Of course, I know what you meant. Listen, just like all I could do was set boundaries with Carver and hope for the best, that's all you can do with Andrei."

"That's just it. I set boundaries. He talks to me like a whole adult; then stomps right over them like we didn't just agree."

Zaria and Alyssa talked a little while longer, but no additional sage advice was given from her newly married friend. On a positive note, after they ended their call, Zaria was able to focus and make good progress before wrapping up for the day somewhere near the time she'd given Andrei.

Chapter Twelve

BE A GOOD GIRL

Andrei flipped his wrist, checking the time, although he'd just checked it on his phone not two minutes prior. It was seven p.m. and Zaria hadn't made it home yet. He'd received Dakota's message when they left her office. So, he knew they were stopping at her house first for her to pack a few things.

He still felt it was prudent to have a stylist select some garments from the shops and send them to the mansion. It simply made sense to him. The casino shops were high-end with quality selections. Although, he noticed Zaria didn't seem to care about the brand name of something, if she liked it.

Andrei walked down the hallway connecting the kitchen to the additional rooms on the first floor. Stopping in the doorway of the small conference room he rarely used, an idea formed. He was one hundred percent certain Zaria wouldn't immediately agree, but he tapped out an email to his assistant. She'd see it in the morning and get the ball rolling.

Every time he told himself he was going to relax and let things progress naturally, he ended up going against the very thought. Over the weekend, he and Zaria had discussed what things would look like since they were back home and had to resume their normal responsibilities. Outwardly, he'd seemed open to them not necessarily spending every night together.

Internally, he revolted at the very thought of her resting her head anywhere without him.

Considering they were at the very beginning of their relationship, it didn't seem like the smartest play to make. However, Andrei couldn't see how they'd be able to progress their relationship by relegating their time together to a few hours during the week and a night or two on the weekends.

It wasn't even about the sex. That was an entirely different discussion, since he'd grown addicted to her nectar the more he tasted it. Even a passing thought of her sweetness stimulated his salivary glands. No. Sex wasn't the primary reason he couldn't stomach spending unwarranted hours apart.

Returning to his laptop on the counter, he sat in front of it and lifted the lid. He'd spent the remainder of his day walking the casino floors. There were a few correspondences from the Chevaliers he needed to address. He liked to stay current on what was happening. The team had a series of home games coming up and he considered which he might attend.

He didn't make a habit of going to every game, but he was there often enough for people to know he could be in attendance any time during the regular season. During the playoffs, he attended more frequently—whether they played at home or on the road.

An electronic ding alerted him to a notification on his phone. Looking at the message, he hit send on his final email and closed the laptop. Just as he entered the foyer, Dietrich opened the front door. On the other side was Zaria. Dakota stood behind her with a satchel in one hand and a small rolling bag in the other. Even if it wasn't big enough to hold more than a few days' worth of clothing, the fact that Zaria brought anything at all made his heart smile.

Andrei met her in the foyer, enfolding her in his arms and dropping a kiss on her forehead.

"I have kept dinner warm for you."

Zaria's fingers curled into his sides, grabbing onto the starched fabric of his button-down shirt. For a moment, she seemed to breathe him in.

"Mmm...Thank you. Dinner sounds lovely. I haven't eaten since lunch."

Removing her purse from her shoulder, he told Dakota to leave the bags at the bottom of the stairs, and led Zaria into the kitchen. Andrei ignored the expressions on Dietrich's and Dakota's faces. He was aware of how he looked and sounded and didn't give a shit. Zaria appeared genuinely tired.

So, what they thought of his current behavior didn't matter—even though it varied drastically from the stoic person most of them encountered during their time working for him. It was definitely a departure from the defenseman he'd been for almost two decades as a professional hockey player.

Their state of confusion made no difference to Andrei. Taking care of his woman was the priority. When they entered the kitchen, her stomach grumbled on cue. Once they washed up, Andrei seated her at the smaller table in the breakfast nook and went back to the stove to plate their food.

"Not that I don't appreciate it, but you know you don't have to wait on me hand and foot, right?"

"I am aware."

Using his peripheral vision, he watched her cross one leg over the other and prop her chin on her open palm. She studied him so intently he had the undeniable urge to ask the question men hated to be asked.

"What are you thinking, Svet?"

Without missing a beat, she answered. "I'm trying to figure out if your base setting is to feed people, or if it's just me. Or...are you trying to get brownie points to keep me from bringing up our unfinished discussion from earlier today?"

Andrei opted to address her list in order since he didn't particularly want to re-hash their disagreement from earlier. Placing one plate before her, he put the other in front of the empty seat he'd planned for himself. He answered as he filled each of their glasses with water. He'd learned Zaria preferred water with her meals.

"I enjoy cooking. It is something I did with my mother growing up." Setting the pitcher aside, he picked up his fork and gestured for her to do the same.

"She did not care for hockey. She did not understand it, although she came to every game and cheered for me. When we were home, Mama was always in the kitchen. She would shoo Papa away, but she would let me stay. When Vitaly was born, I helped her take care of him. In the early days, while Papa was away with his work."

Once she picked up her fork and dipped the tines into the creamy mashed potatoes, he took a bite of his own.

"So, you and your mom cooked together. That's sweet."

Andrei huffed. "It was not born of sweetness."

"It doesn't have to be." Silence reigned for a few moments as they each ate the brazed chicken cutlets, mashed potatoes and mixed vegetables.

"Why did you say that your mom teaching you to cook wasn't born of sweetness?"

Lowering his utensils, Andrei took a sip of water. He normally didn't share so much about his childhood or his life in general. But, if he wanted Zaria to be open with him, he would have to do the same. *Right?*

Without his consent, his accent thickened as he spoke. "When I was a child, we were very poor. Papa could not always find work near home, so it was me and Mama most of the time. Mama had to work as well, so she taught me how to make certain meals so I could feed myself when she was not home in time to start dinner."

Softness and warmth brushed the back of his knuckles as Zaria tried to enclose his much larger hand inside her own.

"Andrei...I had no idea."

He heard the sympathy in her voice. The caring pouring from her expressive eyes made her concern not feel like the pitying stares he'd felt on him daily as he'd walked home from school alone.

"It is fine. How would you know about it? It was not a bad life. It simply was not an easy one. Besides, everything changed when my talents on the ice were discovered.

I received sponsors and was able to help my family move into a better home and have a better life. It allowed for Papa to return to living with us full time and he helped me practice to get better. So, it worked out for the best."

Although he'd revealed a lot, there was more that he hadn't said. Andrei hoped Zaria would leave it where he stopped and didn't press him for more. It had taken him years to get to a point where he could look at certain moments in his childhood fondly. The memories he held closest were when he was in his mama's kitchen while she taught him recipes from *her* mama.

The hours on the ice with his father and his uncle taking him through drills even after he'd spent half of the day practicing with his coach and teammates weren't memories he cherished. He did not want to rehash those days when all he could do at the end of them was spoon food into his mouth and crash across his bed, only to wake and do the same thing again the next day.

"Andrei...Baby, I didn't mean to bring up sad memories for you. I'm sorry."

Andrei ignored the reasons for her apology and instead focused on her calling him 'baby' outside of the bedroom. It sent a different kind of warmth through him for her to use the endearment.

"It is not sad. I miss my Mama sometimes, and my Papa. But thinking of them no longer makes me sad."

When he said it, Andrei meant every word. Later, after he'd settled Zaria into the bath he'd run for her, he stood before the kitchen sink. Instead of going upstairs and climbing into the tub with his woman, he allowed the memories to wash over him.

Andrei entered his bedroom tugging the ringing cellphone from his pocket. The thumping baseline of the music from the party raging below could still be heard through the closed door.

"Hallo Mama!"

"Plemyannik."

Andrei pulled the phone from his ear to look at the tiny display. The caller identification said the call was from his mama. The deep voice did not belong to Polina Antonov. The tortured way his uncle said 'nephew' filtered in and the smile on Andrei's face melted away.

"Uncle?"

His Uncle Ruslan's muffled whimpers were the only sound coming through the earpiece. ***Was he crying?***

Easily slipping into Russian, Andrei dropped into the chair beside his bed.

"What is it Uncle? Why are you calling me from Mama's phone?"

"They're gone, Andrei. I didn't think he'd do it, but he did. And now my sister is dead!"

His uncle's wails barely penetrated Andrei's ears as the words reverberated. ***'My sister is dead!'***

"What do you mean, dead? I spoke to Mama and Papa this morning. They called to congratulate me on winning the championship. This must be some kind of mistake."

"It's no mistake, Voin. I saw them with my own eyes. Gavrill made sure I saw them."

Tears laced every word his uncle spoke, and each syllable ripped a hole in Andrei's heart. This couldn't be happening. He couldn't have just experienced one of the greatest victories of his hockey career and lost his parents within twenty-four hours.

Time meant nothing, and Andrei didn't know how long he sat there trying to get his mind to compute the words he'd heard. His uncle's blubbering was the backdrop to Andrei's mental spiral. Numb fingers gripped the phone close to his face.

"...in one week and if I don't, they will be back to do worse."

Andrei dropped back into the conversation in the middle of his uncle's sentence. He wanted to know what happened and who his uncle was talking about, but Andrei had pulled himself together enough to think about his baby brother.

"Where is Vitaly?" Gravel coated Andrei's voice, making his words come out even more harshly.

"What will we do now, Voin? He'll kill me for sure."

Andrei wanted to feel sympathy for his mother's only sibling, but he needed to know about his own.

"Uncle Ruslan! ***Where is Vitaly?!****"*

Finally, his uncle heard him. "He's safe. He's away at that school in Switzerland."

Relief flooded Andrei's body; however, he couldn't completely relax. Whoever went after his parents could very well know about Vitaly and the boarding school. For all he knew, they could be on their way right now.

"Uncle, I have to go."

Not waiting to hear the other man's reply, Andrei hung up the phone. For once, he was happy he'd agreed to buying Vitaly the expensive smart phone. Uncaring about the early hour in Zurich, Andrei pressed the button pre-programmed with Vitaly's number.

Standing from the chair, he paced the room in agitated strides as he willed his brother to answer the phone. When the call finally connected, Andrei took a deep breath before speaking.

"Andrei, baby are you okay?"

Zaria's voice pulled him from the waking nightmare. Her softness leaned into his side as she maneuvered until she was between him and the sink he'd yet to fill to clean the cookware he'd used earlier. He took a step back to give her space. Her skin smelled of the lavender oil he'd added to her bath.

"I am fine, Svet."

Wrapping his arms around her, he dipped to nuzzle the space where her neck joined with her shoulder. Andrei tightened his hold on her plush frame as he pushed away the memories. His life was forever changed that night. He'd thought winning the championship would be the best thing to ever happened to him. It's quite possible it was the worst.

Zaria leaned away from him, causing him to grumble in protest. He wanted her exactly where she was. The softness of her palms pressed against the sides of his face until he lifted his head. The depth of compassion swimming in her dark eyes was something he was unaccustomed to seeing directed at him.

"Hey... You don't have to put on a brave face for me. It's okay to not be okay."

While he appreciated her willingness to allow him to lean on her, he wasn't about to unearth that landmine of emotions again. He wasn't quite ready to relive the night he called in every favor he could to get him to the other side of the earth to get to his brother. Andrei had to work fast before whatever monster his uncle had angered tried to visit the same fate on his sibling which had befallen his parents.

"How about this?" Zaria's touch left his face as she threaded her fingers into his hair. "We'll go to get you showered and into something more comfortable. Then we'll hit the media room and watch a movie to decompress from our day."

Andrei's brow wrinkled. "What do you mean, something more comfortable? I have already showered and changed."

Reluctantly, he released her from his hold and stepped back, gesturing to his white button-down shirt and tan slacks. His attire was a sharp departure from the suit he wore each day.

"Are you saying I look uncomfortable in these clothes?"

Zaria held up one hand. She stared at him skeptically. "Wait. Are *you* saying *those* are your relaxing clothes? You don't have t-shirts or sweatpants?"

"Of course, but they are for exercise."

"Yes, exercise and lounging around the house. You look like you could hop onto a conference call at any minute."

When he simply shrugged at her assessment, her mouth dropped open.

"Are you freaking kidding me?"

Once again, Andrei's brow dipped in confusion. "What is it?"

With no real venom, Zaria tapped one hand against his chest. "You have the nerve to give me crap about working late and you never really stop working. I'd bet a pair of red bottoms that you worked right up until I made it to the front door."

"Technically, I was not working. I prepared dinner and read a few late emails. I have not had any meetings or taken any calls from the casino. So, you lose."

Snaking his arms around her waist, he kissed the tip of her nose. "I wear a size fourteen and I prefer the lace up style, nothing gaudy, in dark brown or black."

Shaking her head, Zaria stared up at him. "Number one. I didn't lose. So, I'm not buying your rich ass shoes you probably already own. Number two. I can tell you're dead serious. You really think you weren't working."

"I was not working. It was a few emails—no meetings or phone calls."

"Wow...If that's really what you think, I'm surprised you didn't break out into hives while we were away and you weren't glued to your computer or phone."

Ignoring her jab at him for his work ethic, Andrei chose to address her refusal to honor his win.

"Are you saying you are not a woman of your word, Svet? You wagered a pair of red bottoms."

"Excuse me, sir. I believe my exact words were, 'I'd bet a pair of red bottoms…' It wasn't a true wager. Besides, you never accepted. You just started talking about the work you don't consider work. I—ah!"

Zaria's shriek was muffled as he swung her over his shoulder in a fireman's carry before she finished her statement. Delivering a swat to one cheek of her rounded ass, he marched out of the kitchen—the dishes in the sink forgotten for the moment.

"What did I tell you about that word, Svet? Now, there is no running from the consequences."

"What word? I didn't say any—ooh! Andrei, listen. I think you're blowing this out of proportion."

Another smack was delivered to the other cheek, followed by a soothing rub to the area.

"I believe my response is in perfect proportion. You have been very sassy today, Svet. I think you have forgotten who I am. It seems you need a reminder."

Lowering Zaria onto her feet, he turned her away from him and whipped the long nightshirt she wore over her head before she could protest. The silken expanse of her naked bronzed body was almost his undoing. She was perfection.

When she tried to face him, he delivered another stinging swat to her ass. "I did not say you could move. Stay there, until I tell you differently."

Gripping the globes in both hands, he rubbed the affected areas. He reveled in the feel of her beneath his fingertips. Unable to resist, he rained a few more stinging taps to her rear.

Leaning down, he kissed her shoulder. Each gasp of pleasure Zaria released went straight to his cock, causing his length to thicken. She liked it when he spanked her plump cheeks. And he liked anything that brought her pleasure.

Dropping to his knees behind her, he groaned at the beauty of her lush posterior before kissing each slightly reddened place on her skin. Zaria's body swayed. Andrei smiled knowingly as he continued to literally kiss her ass. Finally, he tapped each cheek.

"Be a good girl and get on the bed."

Chapter Thirteen

YOU ASKED FOR SIR

Zaria's entire body was humming with anticipation. It never failed; Andrei could take her to the brink of orgasm without ever touching her pretty pocket. On trembling legs, she tried to climb onto the bed. However, lethargy prevented her limbs from cooperating with the hoisting herself onto the mattress.

She was temporarily weightless as Andrei lifted her. Before Zaria could crawl to the center, he flipped her onto her back and dragged her to the edge. Thick thighs were thrown over his shoulders.

Her core leaked at the thought of what he'd do next. Gazing down her body, her channel clenched when she saw the way he was staring at her pussy. He looked like a man who'd been deprived of partaking in her sweetness for decades instead of hours.

His tongue slipped out, wetting his bottom lip and Zaria twisted her fingers into the sheets to keep from grabbing his head and shoving his face into her slickening center. The slight breeze created by him breathing on her exposed mons made goosebumps pebble on her skin.

"Andrei..."

Zaria was unable to keep the pleading note from her voice when she said his name. When she looked down, his eyes stared back at her. Fire banked behind his icy blue gaze.

"No, Svet. Downstairs, you asked for Sir. So, *'sir'* is what you call me."

What the hell? Her eyebrows dipped as she tried to figure out when and how she'd flipped his switch. Andrei was naturally dominant, but the heat in his gaze was hotter than the night he confronted her for ghosting him.

He was seriously on some dominant shit and the way her insides quaked at his declaration said she liked it. A lot. Still, she couldn't keep herself from pressing his buttons.

"I already told you. You aren't the boss of me." The words didn't come out nearly as defiant as she'd intended. Instead, it sounded more like a whispering whimper to her ears.

"Is that what you think? We shall see."

Andrei's voice was thick as molasses and darker than sin. Strong fingers gripped her thighs, holding them firmly to his shoulders. At the first suckling kiss he placed on her folds, her back bowed. Once he coaxed her clit from its hood, she was a babbling mess.

The man had to be a pussy genie or something. If Zaria had the extra brain power, she would've laughed when the thought flit across her mind. However, Andrei was weaving his magic and she was caught in his thrall. He seemed to know exactly when to apply pressure, when to kiss gently and when to tug the sensitive bundle of nerves between his lips.

"Oh shit!"

Zaria's eyes slammed shut with a gasp. She gifted Andrei with thigh shaped earmuffs as she clamped down on the verge of an orgasm. Just as she was about to tip over into bliss, all stimulation was removed. *What the fuck?*

Opening her eyes, confusion blanketed her expression. However, Andrei's face told a different story. *Was he smirking?* Zaria wanted to be mad. To fight fire with fire. But, hovering on the edge of a release left little room for her to think about anything else. Feel anything else. Including shame. Hers was completely absent when her fingers curled around his forearms while he held her thighs apart.

"Andrei...please..."

The throbbing in her core felt like an erratic heartbeat at the apex of her legs. However, she could do nothing to ease it. He crowded the space between her legs so that she couldn't touch herself to relieve the ache. Even if she could, Andrei harshly reminded her it wasn't allowed. Writhing around, she tried to slip a few nimble digits into the gap between his face and her core.

"Ow! You bit me!" Zaria snatched her hand back.

"Calm, Svet. It was only a nibble." Bringing her fingers back to his lips, he kissed them reverently. "It is no more than you deserve for trying to touch my pussy."

Twisting her lips into a pout, she tugged her hand away. "Well, I had to do something. If you aren't going to get me there, I'll do it myself."

That was a mistake. A big one. Andrei's grip on her thighs tightened. Her lower limbs were now surrounded by his steely grip with his shoulders beneath them, his muscular arms encompassing them, and his strong hands palming the insides.

The ferocity of his expression was her only indication of his intent before he dropped his head back to her leaking folds. He didn't say a word to refute her. No. Andrei spoke with action, driving her to the brink, but never letting her tip over.

It was torture. It was also pleasure. Pleasure so intense, tears streamed from her eyes and her voice became hoarse. Just when she thought she couldn't take anymore, a stinging swat to her swollen mons tossed her into the raging ocean of orgasmic release.

Fuck! When did she start liking that? Actually, like was too mild a term to describe how she felt about it. Lying languidly against the sheets, she watched as Andrei peeled off the now sweaty button-down shirt and rid himself of the remainder of his clothes.

The thick length of this cock slapped against his stomach after it was freed from the confines of his underwear. Despite the erotic torment she'd just experienced, Zaria licked her lips and her core clenched at the sight.

Approaching the bed, Andrei grasped her legs, tugging her until her ass nearly hung off the side. With no preamble, he notched the head of his shaft at her entrance and plunged into her channel. Two strokes and Zaria's back was arched deeply with her head tilted into the mattress. Her voice was snatched away, leaving only pants issuing from her lips.

"What is that? I cannot hear you, Svet." Andrei's words were accompanied by a swiveling thrust. "Where is the sass? I am not the boss of you, remember? Where are your sharp words?"

"Mmmm!"

The strangled moan was all Zaria could muster. She wanted to talk shit. She really did, but the way Andrei pushed her thighs toward her chest as he pounded into her, erased her ability to do more than hold on and feel. She couldn't even get a proper hold on him due to the sheen of sweat on his skin.

The force of their movements slid her farther onto the bed. Andrei didn't miss a stroke. Their new position with his knees planted on the mattress gave him the perfect angle to target that special place inside her. It was too much.

Zaria was barely holding onto consciousness. Her eyes fluttered open and she was greeted by the view of Andrei's hulking frame above her. The veins on his forearms were prominent as he braced them on either side of her.

Andrei's shoulders were the resting place for her calves. His muscles flexed as he worked every inch of his body to bring her pleasure. Although his lips were moving, Zaria had no idea what he said since he'd lapsed into Russian.

It didn't matter. Nothing mattered. She was one big nerve ending as she was thrust into a blinding orgasm. Her walls pulsed against Andrei's thickness tunneling inside. His words transformed into growls and his movements became erratic before he stiffened with his length buried in her channel to the hilt.

Damn. That was hot. Maybe she should call him *sir* more often. Zaria lay limply as Andrei lowered her legs. He didn't immediately roll away from her prone form. Instead, he lowered himself to his forearms, dropping his face into the crook of her neck.

She wasn't sure where she found the strength, but Zaria wrapped her arms around him as far as she could reach, stroking along his sides and back. They both breathed heavily into the otherwise quiet of the room. Once he finally pulled away, she missed the warmth of his body blanketing hers.

Beneath lowered lashes, she watched as he walked across the room and disappeared into the ensuite bathroom. She was never more grateful Andrei was an attentive lover than when she heard water turn on. Zaria wasn't sure she would've had the energy to do more than roll to one side and pull the covers over her sated body.

Moments later, Andrei returned. He scooped her from the bed and deposited her into the tub. She wasn't the least bit fazed at having her second bath of the night. Andrei lowered himself into the water behind her, and Zaria leaned back with a contented sigh.

"Now, Svet... What were you saying about me not being the boss of you?"

Zaria moaned as her pussy betrayed her tired limbs. Her walls tightened reflexively. Her pretty pocket knew a challenge when it was issued. The question was whether the rest of her would get on board for another ride on the Triple A express.

Zaria shifted in her seat, seeking a comfortable position. Normally, the buttery soft leather of her executive chair was the height of comfort. However, after a night of Andrei bending her body like she was a Cirque du Soleil cast member, she was more than a little sore.

Her lips twisted into a smile at the memory—despite her discomfort. There was no way in hell she would complain for a second about her man blowing her back out. Although they had work to do to navigate the balance of their relationship, her and Andrei's sex life was spectacular. She considered it a reward for the duds she'd dated in her past who were not the most generous of lovers. They never lasted long, because Zaria didn't do selfish.

Two taps on the door of her office were followed by the appearance of one of her paralegals, Falana.

"Hey, I just got a call from Judge Lander's office. They want to know if you have time this afternoon for a quick meeting with opposing counsel on the Thompson Industries case."

"Did they say what it was about?"

"I'm guessing they're trying to file for a continuance. I looked at your calendar and you have an opening right after lunch, but I didn't tell them that. What do you want me to tell them?"

Propping her chin on her hand, Zaria strummed her fingers against her cheek. "Go ahead and have Tika get back with them to set something up for this afternoon."

"Yes, ma'am." Falana turned to walk away.

"Oh, and Falana."

"Yes, ma'am?"

"If they should contact you directly again, remind them that you aren't my executive assistant and forward the call to Tika. I appreciate everything you do; however, you aren't here to schedule my meetings."

"Yes, ma'am." Falana closed the door behind her as she left.

Zaria was understanding of how busy a judge's docket could be—especially in civil court—but Judge Lander's office was well aware Tika was her assistant and not Falana. How had the call even been routed to her office?

Zaria put her head down and got back to work. Other than fitting in the last-minute meeting, her day was uneventful. Just as they suspected, defense counsel wanted a Continuance. Since she and her client were okay with a later court date, Zaria didn't throw up any road blocks. With the reprieve, she was able to re-organize and plan the rest of the week in order to finish no later than five p.m. each day.

Andrei should be happy with the change. He made no secrets about his stance on her working late. Although Zaria considered his objections to her schedule more than a little hypocritical. He barely seemed to stop working himself.

She hadn't missed the looks some of his staff exchanged with one another. His being home, the way he'd been after their return from the island, wasn't his norm. Zaria would be willing to bet he spent more than a few nights a week at his suite at the casino to make sure he was close and available to the gaming and the Chevaliers' office. He wasn't fooling anybody—least of all her.

Just as Zaria closed the last file and clicked the screen to lock her computer, her phone rang with an interoffice call. Checking the display, she saw Tika's name. A quick glance at the clock showed the time was five fifteen.

"Hey Tika, what are you still doing here?" Zaria asked, in lieu of a greeting.

"I'm on my way out. I was packing up when a call came in for you."

"You should've let it go to voicemail. The work day is officially over."

"I would have, only the number had a Hollywood area code. I thought it might be important, so I answered."

The only person Zaria knew who might call her from Hollywood was her cousin Domonique. But Dom had her cell number. Why would she call the office instead of calling her directly?

"It's your cousin—the movie star. I figure you'd want to talk to her."

"I do. Thank you. Put her through and you get out of here."

"Yes, ma'am! See you tomorrow."

Tika's cheerful voice was soon replaced by the familiar tone of her cousin Dominique.

"Hey, Dom. What's up? Why didn't you call my cell?"

"I did. It went straight to voice mail."

"What?"

Frowning, Zaria picked up the phone and looked at the screen. *Crap!* She'd turned it off earlier and forgot to turn it back on. Pressing the button on the side, she put it back on the desk while it powered up.

"My bad. I turned it off earlier. I don't even remember why now, but I forgot to turn it back on."

"Oh. Okay." Dom sounded relieved. "I was starting to get worried. Your phone is never off."

"I didn't mean to worry you."

As she apologized to her cousin, the device in question started to vibrate and ding, alerting Zaria to the missed calls and messages. *Damnit*! She'd missed a call and two messages from Andrei. Scanning the messages quickly, she shot off a quick apology and assured him she was okay. The last text was a few minutes prior.

She had no doubt the only reason he hadn't tried again was because he knew exactly where she was. *Nowadays, he always knew where she was.* Zaria pushed the edge of resentment aside. In her heart of hearts, she knew Andrei wasn't keeping tabs on her. The security detail was for her protection.

"So, what's up? You normally call on the third Sunday of the month. Today's Tuesday."

"Am I really so predictable?" Dominique sounded as if it never occurred to her that she communicated with family members on a specific schedule.

"Yes." Zaria's response was immediate.

"You didn't have to answer so quickly."

"It's true though." Softening her voice, Zaria reassured the woman who was essentially her younger sister. "It's okay to be consistent when it comes to staying in touch with your family. I like knowing I'm going to hear from you regularly. It helps me stay connected with you guys."

"Yeah, but when you said the thing about third Sunday, it made me think of the Missionaries leading the service on the third Sunday of the month. Which sent me down a whole different rabbit whole."

Giggles tumbled from Zaria's lips. Lord...she dreaded third Sundays. Miss Susie was a talker and when she got the chance to lead the service everything went longer than it should. Longer than first Sunday—which was saying something since that was usually their longest day.

Wiping the tears of laughter from the corners of her eyes, Zaria got herself under control.

"Okay, so what's going on? I thought you were working nights on the show you're doing. Shouldn't you be asleep?"

"I was asleep. Then Cisco called. He's all excited. Some big-time sports agent has been putting out feelers like he's interested in signing him to a contract."

Instantly alert, Zaria sat up taller in her chair. "Have they made contact with him? Or is it just rumors?"

"You know they can't actually talk to him right now without messing with his eligibility. So, it technically came from one of the coaches.

There have been some scouts hanging around and the buzz in the college hockey world is saying Cisco could go high in the first round."

She already knew why Dom was calling, but Zaria asked anyway. "So did you call me, when you should be sleeping, to share the *maybe* good news? Or is there another reason?"

"Don't play crazy Zee. You know why I'm calling."

Although her cousin couldn't see her, Zaria rolled her eyes and sat back. "How many times do I have to tell y'all? I'm ***not*** a Sports and Entertainment lawyer? I'm primarily a contract attorney.

Sports and Entertainment is just as niche as contract law. You need someone well versed in the nuances to look out for your best interests when it comes to that stuff."

"Who's going to look out for our best interest better than you? You say it's not your thing, but you're the reason I have an agent who hasn't tried to rob me blind."

"It's because I have your best interest at heart that I'm recommending you find someone who is more competent in than I am in the area of Sports Law."

"Zee, stop being modest. You could've been an entertainment attorney if you wanted. It's not that you *can't* do it. You just didn't *want* to do it."

Twisting her lips, Zaria looked at the phone as if Dom could see her. "Flattery won't work. I'll make some calls and try to find him someone good. I know a guy who played professionally. I'll see who he recommends."

"And by you know a guy, do you mean the sexy Russian I saw you hugged up with in the pictures from Carver and Alyssa's wedding?"

Zaria reverted to her twelve-year-old self, squinting her eyes and making a face. "You don't know my life. I know people. I live in a large city. I meet people."

"Girl please. If you think your boo thang knows some people, go on and ask him."

"My boo thang? Whatever, Dom."

"Do they not say that anymore? I need to ask somebody what the new lingo is."

"***Whatever***, Dom."

Zaria's phone dinged with an incoming message. Andrei. Again.

"Listen, I need to go. I'll let you know what I come up with."

"Mhm... I heard that ping. Tell Mr. Antonov I said hello."

"*Bye, Dom!*" Zaria ended the call and scooped her cellphone from her desk.

AAA: Svet...

So much was said with the one word on the screen. He was close to his limit. Andrei wasn't necessarily a needy guy, but too many attempts to contact her had gone unanswered. And apparently her quick text earlier hadn't done the trick to appease him. Biting the bullet, Zaria tapped the icon on the display.

"Good afternoon, Svet."

Chapter Fourteen

WE HAVE A PROBLEM?

If Andrei had been having a better day, he was certain he would've let it go that Zaria hadn't replied to his messages or taken his calls in the past eight hours. But, he'd had a kind of crap day and to top it off, he hadn't been able to at least hear her voice for a few minutes.

They were both busy people, so he didn't expect a long conversation. However, he was at least willing to admit to himself, that talking to her for even a moment had a positive effect on him. He'd begun to crave the feeling. Although feeding his hunger was part of the reason he'd tried to contact her, it wasn't the only one.

"Hey Andrei, sorry about earlier. I turned my phone off and forgot to turn it back on. I didn't realize it until Dom called my office line to get in touch with me. I should be leaving for the day soon."

Andrei wasn't sure how he felt about the way she rushed to reassure him. He didn't actually call her to give her grief about not responding to him. He knew where she was and what she was doing. However, he guessed he couldn't blame her. He'd been far more demanding of her time and attention than he'd ever been in the past. Maybe she thought he required such stroking.

"It is not a problem, Svet. There is no need to rush. You explained as much in your text. However, you did not give me an answer in regard to my dinner invitation."

"Dinner?"

"Yes, dinner." After a moment of silence stretched between them, Andrei realized she'd seen his messages, but hadn't actually read them. The light tapping he heard was confirmation. He gave her time to view the messages he sent after his call went unanswered.

"Oh. Okay. Sorry. Dinner at *The Rooftop* is fine. I guess I can hang around here a while longer. It doesn't make sense to drive out to my place or yours, then turn right around and come back."

Andrei's jaw tightened at her reference to *his place*. No matter how illogical it was, he'd begun to consider it their home—not just his.

"That is not necessary. I will have Grace and Dakota bring you to the suites here at the casino. If you would like to continue working, you can. Or you can rest for a couple of hours."

"Mm... A nap does sound good. *Someone* kept me up way past my bedtime last night."

A self-satisfied smirk lifted one corner of Andrei's mouth. That someone had been him and he had no regrets. Simply thinking about the way her sweet heat accepted him was enough to make him consider canceling his remaining meetings and foregoing their dinner plans. However, the meeting was necessary.

"We will have to endeavor to put you to bed at a decent hour tonight." His voice deepened with an unspoken pledge.

"Getting into bed isn't our problem, Mr. Antonov."

"We have a problem?" Andrei didn't find their enjoyment of one another to be problematic.

"Knowing you, you don't think it's a problem. But, I'm a person who's accustomed to a certain amount of sleep. I'm not complaining about the reason I haven't gotten my usual six to eight hours. Still, it's an adjustment."

A sliver of guilt shot through Andrei. He'd long ago learned to manage on four hours of sleep. It wasn't unheard of for him to walk the Casino floor until well after midnight, only to get up before the sun to work out and start his day.

"I will keep that in mind for future reference, Svet. I would not want you unfocused due to lack of sleep."

"Listen...Considering the all-nighters I've pulled over the years, a few nights where I get less than eight hours won't matter."

Andrei didn't bother to continue to belabor the subject. He simply made a mental note. If Zaria did not get enough sleep, it wouldn't be due to him keeping her up until the wee hours of the morning. He was certain they could work their...activities...around a decent rest schedule.

Smoothly transitioning the topic to her being brought to the casino, he allowed the previous subject to drop. The notification on his laptop alerted him to the time. He had to leave to avoid being late. So, Andrei brought the call to an end.

Stopping at his assistant's desk to dispense a few instructions, Andrei continued to the private elevator and the waiting SUV in the underground parking area. There was a Chevaliers owner's meeting. It was last minute, but it wasn't projected to be long.

He was almost correct. While the meeting wasn't as lengthy as those regularly scheduled, it took more time than Andrei felt was necessary. Bertrand Van Cleef held the third largest share of the team, but it was tiny in comparison to Andrei's stake.

Had he known then what he knew now, Andrei would've found a way to keep the pompous blowhard from buying into the team to begin with. The man knew less about running a hockey team than he did about running a business. It was shocking he'd managed to retain any of the generational wealth he'd inherited.

There'd been recent rumblings surrounding another increase to the minimum player salary. It had only been a couple of years since the previous increase. It was rumored that there could be another bid to renegotiate the number. Andrei kept abreast of the situation, so he wasn't concerned. No legitimate source had confirmed the information. He didn't feel it warranted the attention Van Cleef was giving it.

The man was convinced the players were conspiring to drive him into the poor house. Andrei knew the team and the league were profitable enough to absorb another increase without feeling much of a pinch. If Van Cleef was so worried, it likely meant he'd put himself into a financial bind in other areas of his professional life. Andrei filed that information away as well. The time may have come for him to offer Van Cleef a buy-out he'd accept.

While the other man worked himself into a frenzy and the other franchise owners chimed in via video call, Andrei sent messages to the appropriate persons to find out the root of this sudden paranoia. If his suspicions were correct, he might yet be able to rid himself of the pretentious asshole.

By the time they left the Chevaliers headquarters, less than an hour remained before his date with Zaria. He chuffed ruefully at the thought of him actually going on a date. Andrei could admit, if only to himself, he'd essentially sworn off dating—opting for hook ups with women who knew the score. Which meant they wouldn't pressure him for more, because he wasn't giving it.

His attraction to Zaria, for more than a quick round or two in bed, caught him unawares. It was the reason it took him so long to act on it. He was woefully unprepared for feelings, but one night with Zaria Coleman could never be enough.

When he entered the suite fifteen minutes later, he was surprised to see Zaria snuggled under a blanket. She was fast asleep on the couch. He half expected to find her seated on the sofa with her computer on her lap, working away. She looked so comfortable with her hands tucked beneath the pillow cushioning her head, he hesitated to wake her.

As he stood at the edge of the room debating, the display on Zaria's cellphone lit up and hip-hop music began playing as it vibrated. Without opening her eyes, Zaria reached above her head and plucked the phone from the arm of the couch.

She didn't open her eyes until she held the device up to her face. The music stopped. Zaria rolled onto her back and dropped the phone onto her stomach.

"If you need more rest, I can have our food brought to us here."

"Oh shit!" Zaria's head whipped toward him with one hand clutching her chest. Her eyes were wide as she stared at him—accusation painted her expression. "Make some noise or something. You're too damn big to be so silent."

Chuckling, Andrei placed his satchel on the nearest chair and closed the distance between them. Bracing one arm on the back of the sofa and the other above her head, Andrei leaned in. Taking her lips in a chaste, but thorough, kiss he offered apologies.

"I did not mean to startle you, Svet. I arrived moments before your alarm went off. You were sleeping so peacefully that I did not want to wake you."

"So, in other words, you were staring at me like some creeper."

"Is it creepy to admire your peaceful rest?"

Zaria's soft hands cupped the sides of his face. Something in his statement seemed to flip a switch on her demeanor. Dark, intelligent eyes probed him.

"Do you need some peace?"

Clasping one of her hands in his, he kissed the palm. "I have all the peace I need." His gaze bore into hers. After a moment, he kissed her other palm and tugged until she was sitting upright.

"Come, Svet. Our reservation is in twenty minutes."

Zaria searched his face a moment more before she conceded. Standing from the couch, she walked toward the bedroom.

"Fine. I'll go freshen up. But, you're not off the hook. We'll talk later."

Something in her tone told Andrei she planned to follow through on her promise.

Andrei's private table at *The Rooftop* was positioned to offer the best view of the restaurant as well as the Las Vegas skyline. The bright lights against the dark sky did most of the work to set the mood. Although Andrei wasn't specifically going for romantic. He simply wanted to enjoy Zaria's company.

He'd cooked dinner for her more than once since they returned from Bali. The amount of time he'd spent preparing meals took him back to the days when he'd first brought Vitaly to America to live with him. While he made a good salary and had a few endorsement deals, he wasn't earning money the way he was currently.

He didn't have a large staff. The condo he'd purchased in Chicago was big enough for the two of them. It was located in a gated community giving him some semblance of privacy. At the time, they were both missing their parents.

Cooking was the way Andrei felt closest to their mother. Eating meals prepared from her recipes seemed to help them both. Hockey was their connection to their father. So, they each threw themselves into being the best they could be at the sport.

Andrei's eyes swept the room in a cursory manner, but he still saw everything. Zaria was seated to his right perusing the menu. No matter where his gaze went, it always came back to her. Without trying, she garnered all of his attention.

"Have you decided what you would like?"

Andrei hadn't bothered to look at the menu. He wasn't a picky eater. He'd already decided on the chef's special—it didn't matter what it was. The executive chef at *The Rooftop* was excellent. Any meal she prepared would more than suffice.

"Umm... I think so."

"Do you not see anything you want, or do you need help deciding between multiple things?" Andrei shifted closer to view the menu with her.

"I actually know what I want, it just seems like too much food for one person."

Tipping the menu toward him, she pointed to the herb roasted chicken and vegetables. The chicken was served spatchcock, so he understood her hesitance. It was an entire chicken.

"Do not worry. It is not as large as you think." Andrei's reassurance was countered with a pinched look on Zaria's face.

"It's not Cornish Hen is it?"

From her facial expression, she considered the possibility repugnant. Andrei almost laughed at her look of disgust.

"No, Svet. It is not Cornish Hen. It is simply not a family-sized bird. You should be fine."

Zaria pulled the menu back. "I don't know...small chickens are suspect. Maybe I should look for something else."

Andrei covered her hand. "I promise. You will love it. It is a regular chicken. It is simply cooked to perfection."

Lifting a single eyebrow, Zaria appeared to study him to gauge the truth of his words. "Okay...I'll give it a try. But only because this menu is completely different from the last time I was here. Also, the herb encrusted chicken is the meal I kept coming back to."

Lifting the menu from her fingers, Andrei signaled for the server.

"Yes, Chef Yarrow changes the menu every few months. It is part of what keeps the patrons returning. By the time they work their way through one menu, it is replaced with a new one."

He placed their order with the server and asked for the sommelier to recommend appropriate wines to accompany each of their meals. Zaria's stare tracked the entire interaction, but she didn't speak until the server left their table.

"That is just part of who you are isn't it?"

"What is?"

Andrei leaned away from the table. The support from the chair, hit him just below his shoulder blades, so he didn't stay pressed against it for more than a second.

"Taking charge. Giving orders."

"Someone has to be in charge, Svet."

"True...So why not you, huh?"

Andrei shrugged in response. It had been him for so long, he didn't know how to be any other way. Even on the ice, before he'd gained veteran athlete status, he was a leader. Despite the fact that he didn't speak much. When he did, it seemed to carry a lot of weight amongst his teammates.

"So, do you want to tell me what had you so tense earlier? Meeting went sideways? Bad day?"

"Went sideways?"

Andrei had gotten better with American colloquialisms over the years; however, Zaria was introducing him to variations on slang he hadn't encountered. Unlike some people, she didn't seem bothered when she had to rephrase something which he didn't immediately understand.

"It went off topic into something that you didn't expect."

Andrei nodded in agreement. "Yes, more than one of them did. But, everything is fine. It is handled."

"Are you sure? If you want to talk it out or bounce some ideas, I'm open. I may not be well versed on running a casino or a hockey team, but I know about the trials of being at the helm of a successful business."

Lifting her hand, Andrei kissed the back. “Thank you, Svet. It was simply one of those days when multiple things required my direct attention. It does not happen often. I am fine.”

“If you say so.” Zaria’s expression said she’d let the matter drop even if she didn’t really want to do it.

“I do.” Andrei squeezed her hand gently. “I also appreciate you offering to listen.”

Zaria shrugged and flipped one hand at him. Shifting gears, Andrei inquired about her day. She was the one who was so tired she needed a nap. Her recap of the day’s events was light on the details for obvious reasons, but she did share. They talked amicably through the Shrimp Ceviche appetizer.

As the plates were cleared between courses, Zaria snapped her fingers.

“I almost forgot. There is something I wanted to ask you about.”

Andrei gave her his full attention as he waited for the question.

“First I need to give you a little back story. Well, you know part of it. We won’t go into how.”

She stared at him with a pointed look. He didn’t feel the least bit of remorse for having her investigated. So, he simply stared back.

“I was raised by my aunt and uncle. They have two kids of their own. Both are younger than me, so I’m kinda like their big sister. Anyway, one of my cousins plays hockey for his university in Florida. Cisco’s a senior this year.

So, the scouts, lawyers and agents are hovering. I don’t have any sports and entertainment lawyers on my friend’s list. Also, I attend Bar Association meetings, but I haven’t befriended anyone in that specialty. I was wondering if there is a firm or someone you could recommend to represent him?”

Andrei thought carefully about how to respond. He knew great attorneys in the field. However, he also did business with them. As a team owner, he had to make certain he wasn’t seen as exerting undue influence. Especially since Zaria had just confirmed the Right Winger he’d been watching footage of for the past month was her blood relative.

This situation had to be handled very delicately. He wanted to help her, but he also had to make certain his help couldn’t be seen as manipulation.

"You're awfully quiet, Andrei. Is it that you don't know anyone you'd recommend or you want to keep them to yourself?"

Zaria's face held a slight smile; however, her eyes were full of questions.

"I am sure I can get you a list of fine attorneys to vet and choose who would work best with your cousin."

"But..."

Zaria's stare seemed to peel back the layers of his skin to peek directly into his brain. Already she seemed to know him better than people he'd been acquainted with for years.

"I do not want to appear biased, or as if I am setting him up in some way."

Zaria's brow wrinkled. "Setting him up? For what?"

Andrei released his pent-up breath slowly. "My association with the Chevaliers is not a secret. I have been scouting a player from Florida named Francisco Truman. That is your cousin. Correct?"

Zaria sat back in her chair. He couldn't accurately read her expression. So, he simply waited for her to respond to his question. His mind didn't sit idle while he waited. His brain ran scenarios of what she was possibly thinking. One of which was her making the incorrect assumption that his pursuit of her was somehow linked to her cousin.

Andrei didn't even know who Zaria was the first time he noticed her at *The Rooftop* with Alyssa. He'd only had a surface level investigation done after the second time he spotted her. When he realized he was so far gone he was offering his friend's woman his personal card he did a deeper dive. He couldn't fault Gregor. The information on her cousin was probably in the report he compiled, but Andrei gave anything peripheral to her only a cursory glance.

It was unlike his normal thorough assessments. He was more than a little distracted by the vivacious beauty. After a loaded silence, she spoke.

Chapter Fifteen

PENIS PROMISES

Zaria sat next to Andrei processing what she'd learned. Around them the conversational lull of the restaurant continued as if she hadn't just been given information which made her question his motives. She knew he was a competitive, savvy businessman. She had no doubt, when the situation called for it, he could be ruthless. He had to be in order to not only survive, but thrive in the casino sector as well as navigate the world of professional hockey as a player and team owner.

Was he so cutthroat and competitive he'd string her along for a chance to snag a possible first round draft pick? Was she simply a means to an end?

Once her world stopped spinning internally, Zaria was more than a little disappointed in herself for allowing the thought to have a foothold. Her inner Bad Bitch gave her hell for even considering that Andrei wouldn't be the luckiest man walking to have her undivided attention.

Besides, keeping it real, Cisco was good. But he wasn't *spend millions on an impromptu vacation* good. Not when it would have been much easier to grease a few palms and start back door trade negotiations to get him on the Chevaliers.

The team was doing too well for them to get a pick in the range Cisco was projected to be drafted. So, the only way they'd get him would be through trades on draft day. That last bit of knowledge sealed it for her.

"You know y'all are doing too good to get a selection so high in the first round, right?"

Zaria was more observant than people gave her credit for. Sure, she was prone to say something flip or audacious, nonetheless she paid attention. She was really good at reading body language. Once she got out of her own head, she noted the tension Andrei held even though he probably thought he didn't give anything away.

His posture was typically erect and could come off kind of rigid, but she knew the difference between the normal way he held himself and the tightness in his frame leading up to his revelation about scouting Cisco. When she commented about their draft order, she watched the tension fade from the corners of his eyes and his fingers relaxed where his hands lay on the table between the two of them.

"The season is just beginning. Many things could happen between now and Draft day."

Shaking her head, she chuckled. "Not enough could happen to lift your chances. You guys have gone to the playoffs three times in the last five years. With consistent winning seasons, it's unlikely you'd be able to select anywhere within the top ten.

Of the twenty-three players on your active roster, almost fifty percent are routinely in the running for the all-star game. The league MVP has come from the Chevaliers for the past three years and y'all weren't even in the finals all of those years. There's no way in hell you're making it lower than fifteen."

Andrei's eyes sparkled in the low lighting as he leaned closer to her. "I must say, Svet. I find your display of hockey knowledge very sexy. Maybe we should take our dessert to the suite."

Zaria tried to tamp down the tell-tale tingle in her core brought on by his suggestion. She was positive if they went to the suite, the dessert that would be eaten was her. Which wasn't strictly a bad thing. Reining in her Andrei addicted libido, she tried to steer the conversation back on course.

"Don't try to distract me with penis promises. We were discussing Sports and Entertainment attorneys. I understand if you can't recommend anyone because of conflict of interest. Don't worry about it. I can just ask Carver."

"Nyet."

Waving him off, Zaria picked up her phone to make herself a note to get with Alyssa the next day. "Don't worry about it. I should've considered the potential conflict. No need to put you in a bad spot over this."

"I said no, Svet." Andrei's hand covered hers stopping her thumbs from flying across the cellphone display.

Zaria stiffened. Looking from where his hand lay atop hers to his face, she pursed her lips. It was on the tip of her tongue to remind him she wasn't one of his employees. Then, she remembered how he responded to challenges worded that way. She wasn't sure her pretty pocket could take another session like the one they had last night any time soon.

Picking her words carefully, Zaria tried to avoid any verbal landmines.

"Andrei… We discussed you unilaterally making decisions for me."

"I am not allowed to object after you unilaterally made a decision for me?"

Zaria's jaw slackened at his accusation. He kept going before she could interject. His strong digits squeezed her fingers slightly. It was a firm grip, but not painful.

"I never said I would not help you with a list of potential candidates. I simply did not want to give the impression I was exerting undue influence over him."

"That's why I can just ask Carver. We can avoid the appearance of a conflict of interest."

"Do you intend to stop seeing me as well?"

Zaria was taken aback by the question. "Why would you ask such a thing?"

"You want to avoid the appearance of a conflict of interest, yet you are dating one of the owners of a professional hockey team. Even if he isn't selected by the Chevaliers, anything he receives which is perceived as above what Rookies normally get will be scrutinized because of our association. Maybe not in the media, but by his teammates. That is unless your plan was to try to keep our relationship a secret."

"Aren't you taking it a little far?"

While Zaria conceded there may be someone willing to do those kinds of mental gymnastics, it wasn't realistic. She couldn't and wouldn't structure her personal life to keep someone from being jealous of Cisco. Essentially, avoiding potential jealousy is what it boiled down to. They had no indication anything of the such would actually happen.

"I am simply pointing out possibilities and asking how far you are willing to go to protect your cousin from scrutiny."

The very thought of giving up Andrei made Zaria's stomach clench—and not in a good way. *When had that happened? When had she gotten so attached that simply thinking of not being with him caused physical reactions?*

"Slow your roll, Mr. Antonov." Zaria attempted to keep her tone light. Flipping her hands over, she tangled her fingers with his.

"I believe we can find a happy medium. Some sort of...compromise?" Wiggling her fingers, she smiled triumphantly when his digits squeezed hers in reassurance.

"Of course, Svet. As long as we both understand no compromise will involve you going to another man for help—even if it is a man I consider a friend."

"A man who is also madly in love with his *wife*. My *best friend*."

Andrei's response was a shrug. His stance brought back a snatch of a conversation they had in her suite in Bali. He was deadass about no one being trusted completely. The memory made her briefly wonder where she stood with him. He and Carver had a far longer history.

"Fine. If you could get me a list at some point this week, I'd appreciate it. I need to vet them before sending suggestions to my family."

Andrei nodded and kissed the back of her hand. Apparently, that was his way of agreeing. Although they talked, he wasn't a huge talker.

She'd seen clips of him when he played and it tracked that he was more a man of action than words. He played with intensity. While his head didn't whip back and forth to follow the puck, he had an eerie awareness of what happened on the ice. He regularly appeared to come out of nowhere to defend the goal. It would seem like the other team should've expected him to show up instead of being blindsided every time.

Zaria was learning his intensity and focus wasn't confined to the rink. She had no doubt he had a short list and a more thorough background check on the options than what she could get on her own.

When their server came with dessert choices, she smirked at Andrei when he renewed the suggestion for them take it back to the suite.

"You aren't slick, S—"

She caught herself before the rest of the word left her lips. But, of course, Andrei heard her. The muscle worked beneath his jaw and those arctic blue eyes bore into her.

"What was that, Svet?"

"I said you aren't slick. I know why you are trying to talk me into cutting dinner short. I've peeped your game."

Zaria smiled cheekily trying to cover her slip. Andrei's single lifted eyebrow said he wouldn't be so easily deterred.

Tossing her hair, she shifted in her seat. "Come on, man! You mean to say I can't use that word *at all* without you going all Incredible Fucking Russian on me?"

Andrei frowned. "What is an *incredible fucking Russian*?"

He genuinely looked so confused Zaria burst into laughter. His expression sent her into fits each time she thought she had the giggles under control. Wiping tears from the corners of her eyes, she got herself together.

"Explain." Andrei prompted.

With her voice filled with mirth, Zaria let him in on the joke only she found amusing. "So, it's like the Incredible Hulk, but with sex and being Russian."

Andrei simply stared at her for a moment. He was so stoic, Zaria started to doubt the brilliance of her mashup. Personally, she thought it was pretty damn funny.

"I am a United States citizen born in Russia."

Zaria studied him trying to determine if he was pulling her leg or serious with his literal statement. She knew he'd become a citizen years ago. He'd completed the process while he was still playing professionally. He was one of the few athletes who could lay claim to having participated in the Olympic games for two separate nations.

"Andrei...I was joking. I didn't mean to be offensive."

One side of Andrei's lips tipped up. It was the first crack in his armor before a full grin spread across his face. Seeing him smile so big wasn't a regular occurrence. So, Zaria was temporarily spellbound. Andrei took advantage of her silence to call the server back and have their dessert packaged to go. Squeezing her thighs together, she didn't object. She knew what was up, and her lady bits were ready to report for duty.

~

By Thursday, Zaria saw herself slipping into a routine with Andrei. They'd spent every night together for the majority of the month. She had to put a stop to it. In the early days of a relationship, people wanted to be together all the time. It was understandable.

However, the swiftness of the lifestyle adjustment she made by agreeing to be exclusive with Andrei was giving her whiplash. She wasn't super eager to sleep alone in her own bed, but she wasn't trying to be totally dickmatized either—no matter how spectacular the dick was.

Andrei wasn't being as circumspect as he thought. During at least one of their calls or texts throughout the day, he'd make plans with her which required her to meet him at his penthouse suite in the casino hotel or drive out to his mansion immediately after the workday was done.

Zaria looked down at the phone on her desk with a wry grin. She had his number, and she could show him better than she could tell him. He'd sent her a message asking if she wanted to attend the Chevaliers game on Friday night.

Dinner for Thursday had already been discussed. He was cooking for her again. It was a late game on Friday. She was actually looking forward to it, since it was against Nashville. That was the closest she came to having a hometown team.

Briefly, she wondered what Andrei would think if she wore her Colton James Jersey. He was her favorite player on the *Marauders*. She ditched the idea almost as soon as it formed. Not because she thought Andrei would blow a gasket or dispense pleasurably intense punishment.

No, she considered the environment. The hockey match was an opportunity for them to spend time together, but it was also work for him. She wouldn't embarrass him publicly by showing loyalty to a player from another team. Especially not during their first such outing. She could reserve her jersey for the nights she watched on television.

The more Zaria thought of the implications of being in the owner's box with Andrei, the more she understood the gravity of the appearance. Confidence wasn't something she lacked. She had it in spades. As the leader of her own successful firm, she was accustomed to working a room and networking.

However, she wouldn't mind another friendly face in the place besides Andrei's. Drumming her fingers against her desk, she had an idea. Tapping the screen, she made a call. Alyssa answered on the second ring.

"Hey Zee. What's wrong?"

"Don't be trying to use my lines on me, Miss Smarty Pants." Zaria groused.

She knew it wasn't a normal time of day for her to call her friend. Alyssa thought she was funny turning Zaria's words back on her. Giggles were the response to her complaints.

"Okay fine. Hey Zee. How are you this morning?"

"That's better. I'm well thank you. How are you doing? You treating my nephew-niece good?"

"You are so wrong for your hybrid nickname."

"What? You won't tell me the gender, so I'm covering my bases." Zaria pulled a face and leaned closer to the phone. "Now...if you want to slide me some info, I can start calling the little peanut by the correct title."

"Stop, Zee. You know it's hard enough for me to keep Carver from telling the world without you adding on."

"I don't understand what you're waiting on."

"I told you. We're going home. We're having another wedding reception. We'll do the gender reveal that weekend."

Zaria leaned into the cushioning support of her chair. "I never would've figured you for the gender reveal party type. I guess there's always something to learn about your friends though."

"I guess. So... Did you really call to talk about me and ask me about the baby?"

Alyssa was another person who was far more perceptive than she was given credit for. Zaria wasn't keeping her reason for calling a secret. She just considered it rude to ask for a favor the moment someone answered the phone.

"No, ma'am. I didn't. I was wondering if you and Carver had plans for tomorrow. Wait, is he even in town this weekend?"

"Yes. He's home. They got back Tuesday morning. We haven't planned anything since he's coming off the road and has to leave again soon."

"Good. You wanna come hang out with me in the owner's box at the Chevaliers game tomorrow?"

"You know I'm not a big hockey fan, right?"

"I know..." Zaria couldn't keep the hint of whine from seeping out.

"Oohh... This is your first time out with Andrei in his element isn't it?"

"Yes, and I thought it would be nice if there was someone else I knew besides him. I've seen the Chevaliers games on TV and the Owner's box is normally filled with the Who's Who of Vegas. You know I'm not a fan of the hoity and toity."

"I know, but since when do you need an emotional support person? You work a room as easily as you breathe."

Alyssa's statement was correct. It didn't stop Zaria from being a little disappointed that she didn't immediately agree. The legal field was slightly more diverse than STEM, from what Alyssa told her, however Zaria was still often the only woman of color in many of the spaces she found herself in. It's part of the reason she was so active with the AAWA. Being around other Black women who had shared experiences helped.

The Who's Who, she referenced were ***not*** people of color. While not as monochromatic as in the past, hockey was still a sport played and enjoyed by the non-melanated population in larger numbers.

"It's cool if you can't come. I just thought I'd ask." Zaria tried and failed to keep the disappointment from her voice.

"Zee...I didn't say no. I have to check with Carver, but I don't have anything planned."

"Ok. Well, let me know as soon as you can. I'll get the big guy to put your names on the list."

"I'm sending him a text now. He's at the practice facility until later today."

"So, what are you up to? When are you going back to work?" Alyssa had taken off a few weeks for the wedding even though she and Carver didn't have a traditional honeymoon.

"I'm not sure. I'm taking time to decide if I even want to go back."

Zaria propped her elbow on her desk and rested her chin on her fist. "Why? Because of the whole Ballard thing? Or is it the, *my husband bought the company because they hurt my feelings*, thing?"

"You know what?...I would feel some kind of way about how you said that last part, if it wasn't true. But...it's a combination. I enjoy my career. I just didn't like the way they handled my HR complaint. However, Harrison, my direct manager, did step up.

He reprimanded the guys in the group chat and he was the one who went to bat for me working from home indefinitely. That being said, things are awkward now."

"Because Carver owns it?"

"Because, technically, I'm the majority owner now."

Zaria sat up ramrod straight in her chair. Her jaw dropped so low, it felt like it unhinged.

"What?!! You've been holding out on me! When did this happen?"

"Carver said it was always his plan to turn it over to me. He's calling it a wedding present."

"That's a helluva wedding present."

"Tell me about it."

"So... you really do have a lot to consider. Would it even be possible for you to be able to work your projects as usual?"

"I doubt it, but there are a few clients who only want to work with me. So, we'll have to figure something out."

"Good luck with that."

The two chatted for a little while longer. Zaria had a meeting; however, Alyssa confirmed she heard from Carver before the call ended. He was fine with coming to the game on Friday. Knowing she'd have at least one other person there eased a lot of Zaria's anxiety about the outing.

She'd have Alyssa and if Andrei didn't want to press palms with the Vegas elite, he'd have Carver. *Wait. Could this be considered a double date?* Zaria shuddered at the thought, then tapped out a message to Andrei about the newlyweds joining them in the box.

As expected, he didn't push back. For all of his fierce outward appearance, Andrei was a teddy bear with her—most of the time. She hadn't asked him for much, but when she asked, he delivered. Except for the matter of her going home and sleeping in her own bed. She'd get to that though.

By the end of the day, Zaria was more than ready to power down her computer and let Logan and Bianca escort her to the mansion. She'd adjusted to her security detail relatively easily. It was likely due to their uncanny ability to only be seen when it was required.

Riding in the back of the SUV, Zaria stared out the window without actually seeing. She was looking forward to another evening with Andrei. It was nice having someone to go home to. But part of her was waiting for the other shoe to drop.

Chapter Sixteen
MORNING KISSES

Andrei looked around the suite. As usual, the Chevaliers owners' box was buzzing with people who wanted to see and be seen. He didn't make an appearance at every game. Occasional showings were necessary to keep them on their toes. It was also rare for him to use his guest list allowance. He did tonight.

Zaria asked if Carver and Alyssa could join them for the game. So, he added their names to his guest list. It was no big feat, but the gratitude his Svet displayed made him want to find other things she desired.

With his hand on Zaria's lower back, Andrei led her to one of the sectional sofas which had a good view of the rink. There were a few other similar pieces of furniture lining the walls or in conversational groupings. Not all were occupied. Some people gravitated toward the plush stadium seats closer to the ice.

Typically, Andrei made it a point to know who he was sharing space with, even for short amounts of time. So, he recognized the majority of those present. Those he didn't were with people he was acquainted with. Thankfully, no one had the expectation of him to smile and press palms.

He'd long ago set a standard of engaging in minimal conversation. His involvement in various business interests required him to occasionally engage, but the majority of the time, he actually watched the game.

The players were on the ice going through warmups when Andrei and his group entered. Once they were seated, Andrei and Carver left the ladies to get them drinks and something to nibble on. The food in the suite was catered, so there was more than the ordinary stadium fare. However, popcorn, peanuts and the like were available for those who wanted them.

Since Alyssa couldn't drink, Zaria was having a non-alcoholic cocktail in solidarity with her friend. While Andrei and Carver were waiting for the bartender to finish making the mocktail daquiris, they were approached by Hiriam Baxter. Baxter was the CEO of a solar energy company based in Las Vegas and longtime friends with Bertrand Van Cleef.

"Antonov, I didn't expect to see you this evening. I catch a few games a year with Bertrand and this is the first time I recall you being here."

Andrei looked at the man, only giving him a slight nod to acknowledge he'd heard him. He owed him no explanation and there wasn't a question asked in that rambling segue.

"I don't believe we've had the pleasure of meeting, but who doesn't know Carver Jamieson? Hiriam Baxter."

Baxter extended a hand toward Carver. The two shook briefly and Baxter turned his attention back to Andrei. With a lowball drink in one hand Baxter stepped closer to him and lowered his voice.

"It's not my business, but I know no one else has the balls to tell you."

Andrei lifted an eyebrow and continued to stare at the man. They weren't friends or even friendly acquaintances. So, he was curious as to what Baxter had to say that he thought Andrei would care to hear. Apparently, his silence was all the encouragement Baxter needed.

"You should really be careful who you're seen spending time with. A man like you can't give off the wrong impression."

On the outside, Andrei looked neutral. Internally, a fire erupted in his chest. However, he didn't allow it to have control. Not yet.

"What exactly do you mean?"

He took no pride in how calm he sounded. He'd practiced keeping a cool head when necessary. Rheumy grey eyes widened as Baxter glanced at the sectional where Zaria was seated before looking back at Andrei.

"That woman. Her kind can ruin a good man's reputation."

Cool head be damned, the words had barely left Baxter's mouth before Andrei had him by the collar. Carver moved just as quickly. Standing behind Baxter, he blocked anyone's view of what occurred between Andrei and the older man.

"What exactly do you mean by *her kind*?" Andrei growled.

"That's what the fuck I wanna know." Carver added.

Andrei didn't spare him a glance, but he was certain their expressions matched. In his hand, Hiriam Baxter began to shake—and not because Andrei shook his lanky frame.

The drink glass tumbled from his fingers as he clutched at Andrei's forearm. His eyes were wide as understanding fell over him. "Wait, wait, wait. Not like that. It's not a race thing. I was talking about lawyers."

Andrei studied the other man's face for a few moments before he released him. They were starting to attract attention. And while Carver blocked any roving camera from the ice rink from seeing what was happening, there were people in the suite who might have a clear view.

"I am not sure who gave you the impression you could speak on who I allow in my life, but it was not me. I will say this once and only once. Keep Zaria Coleman's name out of your mouth and your thoughts. From this moment forward, she does not exist to you. If I should hear of you offering this same *advice* to anyone else..."

Andrei allowed the rest of the sentence to trail off as his eyes blazed angrily. "Do I make myself clear?"

Baxter visibly gulped and his head bobbed on his thin neck. Andrei had zero remorse for his handling of the much older, slighter man. He'd attempted to malign Zaria's reputation. That couldn't stand.

"I cannot hear you, Baxter. Do you understand."

"Ye—" His voice cracked. Baxter cleared his throat and tried again. "Yes. I understand. I meant no disrespect."

"Actually, you meant a great deal of disrespect." Andrei collected Zaria's drink from the bartender. "Consider this your lucky day. Do not test said luck again with me."

Brushing by him, Andrei left the other man wringing his hands behind him. From his periphery, he saw Carver fall into step with him. As they drew closer to the ladies, Zaria's eyes raked over his face then looked past him.

Accepting the fruity concoction, she returned her stare to him. Once he was seated, she leaned into him.

"What did you do to hyena Hiriam?"

Andrei almost laughed at the nickname, but he managed to keep it to a slight uptick of his lips.

"I did not *do* anything, Svet."

"Then why does he look like he needs to change his diaper?"

Andrei looked over his shoulder and sure enough, Baxter's pants seemed to sag a little. Shrugging instead of shaking with laughter as he wanted to, Andrei turned back to Zaria.

"I have no idea. I have heard some people become incontinent when they get older."

When her perfect lips set into a grim line, he stopped joking. Once she placed her drink on the nearby table, he knew she wasn't going to let it go.

"Fine, Svet. I simply informed him it would be in his best interest not to speak of you. Ever. To me or anyone else."

Zaria folded her arms across her middle and tilted her head. "Why was it necessary for you to tell him that?"

"It was necessary because he came to me trying to warn me about being seen with women like you—lawyers who could ruin my reputation."

"The fuck?" Zaria's brow creased. Then, she waved a hand in Baxter's general direction. "He's just salty the shady shit he did got exposed, and he had to pay my client an eight-figure payout for breach of contract."

Zaria's explanation solved the mystery of how Baxter knew her and thought to warn Andrei against her. As if what some stranger said would make a difference to Andrei. Simply being a rich person didn't make Baxter's opinion matter more to him. He was yet another elitist asshole.

He'd better enjoy the night, because Andrei would make certain it was the last time he'd be allowed inside the owner's suite. Van Cleef would likely object, but Andrei didn't give a fuck. No one would get away with trying to undermine his woman.

Andrei had almost forgotten Alyssa and Carver were there until she spoke up.

"And what did *you* do?" Her gaze was aimed squarely at her husband.

"I didn't do nothin', Bit-baby. I was moral support. That's all."

Alyssa pursed her lips. "Mhm. That's why you were standing behind him and not Andrei...right..."

The horn blew breaking across their conversation. "Look, baby. The game's about to start." Carver smiled at Alyssa as he pointed toward the rink.

The rest of the evening progressed without much fanfare. They eventually moved to the stadium seating. While their friends seemed mildly interested in the game, Andrei and Zaria were more involved. Occasionally, she would comment on a good play—from either team. Although, he noticed she was disappointed when the Chevaliers won by a one goal margin late in the final period. Until then, he thought the game would end in a shootout to determine the winner.

They ended the night with a late dinner before parting ways. Knowing Zaria had an enjoyable evening was enough for him, but Andrei had a good time as well. It was a change of pace. For a moment, he considered that he hadn't been doing nearly as much living as he had existing. Having Zaria in his life was resulting in far more bonuses than he anticipated.

Sunday night, Andrei rolled over in the massive bed and looked at the clock for the fifth time in what had apparently only been fifteen minutes. It was 11:30 p.m. and he was in bed. Alone. At his suite in the casino hotel. With every fiber of his being objecting, he'd watched Zaria roll her bag into her house and closed the door five hours earlier.

It wasn't what he wanted; however, short of holding her against her will, he couldn't stop her. It didn't matter that she was correct in stating she hadn't slept in her own bed in almost a month. *Why did it matter? Was a bed capable of missing someone?*

He couldn't answer for the bed, but his body missed Zaria's next to his. It hadn't even been a full night. *Fuck it.* Why did he have to be without her simply because she wanted to sleep in the 'house she paid for'? Tossing off the covers, he stalked into his closet. While he dressed, he tapped out a message asking for his car to be brought around to his private entrance.

He didn't worry about waking anyone on his security team, there was always someone at the ready when he stayed over onsite—even if he rarely utilized the option. By the time he had a valise packed and opened the door to exit the suite, a member of his night detail was there waiting.

Twenty-five minutes later, he was standing on Zaria's doorstep ringing the bell. The heavy oak door swung open to reveal his Svet dressed in a gold satin robe which stopped just above her knees. The color brought out the golden undertones of her skin and made Andrei's fingers itch to touch her.

"Andrei, I thought we agreed..."

Zaria's sentence trailed off as Andrei stepped into the house. Closing the door behind him, he locked it, dropped his valise and tugged her into his arms.

"We agreed to you sleeping in your own bed. Why should that mean we sleep apart?"

A single raised eyebrow was her response. "So, that's the logic you're going with? You want to split hairs?"

"Are you turning me away, Svet?"

"You know I'm not."

Zaria's fingers plucked at the buttons on his shirt as her body told him what she hadn't given voice to. She missed him as well.

"Come on."

Tangling their fingers together, she led him through the front room, down the hallway and into her bedroom. Andrei didn't spend any time studying the décor. He immediately began to shed his clothing, dropping the pieces onto a nearby chair.

He had no expectation of sex. It wasn't about that. The past few weeks spent going to sleep and waking beside her each night had fostered an addiction and Andrei had no desire to be cured.

She took off her robe and slid naked beneath the covers. He climbed in on the other side and they met in the middle. Once she was tucked beneath his arm, he was able to fully relax. Having her softness pressed into him was what he needed. It wasn't long before sleep claimed him.

Andrei woke before his alarm went off at five thirty a.m. the next morning. He swiped his cellphone screen to cancel the alert before it could wake Zaria.

They'd shifted positions during the night and they now lay on their sides. Zaria was the little spoon and her plush ass pressing against his morning erection was an excruciating pleasure. He lay there contemplating if he should take advantage of the lack of a clothing barrier between them.

His cock jerked in agreement, but the greedy member was always ready to sink into Zaria's heated core. One would think they hadn't started the previous morning pleasuring one another with the way he ached to be inside her. She didn't make it easy for him to let her sleep.

Her posterior rubbed against him as she snuggled into his embrace. The movement and her modified breathing alerted him to her change of status. She was awake as well.

"If you continue to wiggle, Svet. I won't be able to resist having your pussy for breakfast."

Shifting, she rolled onto her back. Long lashes partially hid her dark eyes as her gaze met his.

"You say that like you think I'll object to morning kisses." Looking at the clock on her nightstand, she murmured. "My first meeting is in three hours. I'm sure you can work with that."

Andrei didn't waste time on words. He tossed off the covers and began kissing a trail down Zaria's body. Taking time to pay homage to her ample bosom, his shaft stiffened even more as he teased the turgid peaks.

Her moans were the soundtrack to the morning and her fingers tapped out a rhythm against his scalp as she tugged at his hair. He loved how responsive she was. Zaria never held back, or pretended she wasn't as into the moment as he was. She took pleasure in giving as well as receiving sexual gratification. Her enthusiasm ratcheted up his desire.

By the time he reached the apex of her legs, she was panting and squirming. Her longing to be filled was verbal and nonverbal, but she'd have to wait a little longer. His mouth watered for the flavor of his morning treat. Andrei's eyes slammed closed at the first taste of her ambrosia.

Prepared for Zaria's normal reaction to him kissing her pretty pussy, he gripped her legs to keep her from clamping his head in a vise. While he'd go a happy man if she smothered him with her thick thighs, he had more pleasure to dispense before he went.

Her juices covered his tongue and dripped into the scruff of his beard, but Andrei didn't care. He wouldn't stop until he heard the tell-tale sound of her reaching her climax. Andrei always wanted her to come at least once before he allowed his dick to become reacquainted with her velvet heat.

"Oh shit! Andrei!!" Zaria's wail pierced the morning quiet.

Smiling against her mons, Andrei lapped up his reward. When there was none left to be had, he placed parting kisses on her folds before lowering her legs from his shoulders. His return trip up her body was made with the same reverence as his descent.

Notching the head of his cock at the opening of her channel, he closed his eyes at the feeling of her slickness engulfing him. Their height difference was insignificant as he maneuvered to devour her lips while simultaneously working his length into her heated core.

Andrei swore her pussy was magical. There was no other way to explain how instantly he'd become addicted to being joined with her this way. Nothing had ever felt so amazing. The connection had never been as deep with anyone else.

Zaria had mentioned the time she had left before her meeting, but Andrei didn't care about staying within a limit. Dispensing orgasms was his only concern as he pulled out long enough to flip Zaria to her stomach and shove pillows beneath her hips. He paused for a brief moment to plant kisses on the plush cheeks of her ass before angling her hips and plunging back within her depths.

As entertaining as it was to watch her ass jiggle with every thrust, in this position, Andrei was prompted to stroke more forcefully bringing them both to the precipice of climax quickly. His movements became almost erratic as Zaria's moans grew louder.

"Fuck, Svet. You take my cock so well."

Leaning over her back, Andrei spoke directly into Zaria's ear. Her hair bonnet was barely hanging on, so he snatched it off, tossing it to the side. Pressing kisses behind her ear, Andrei swiveled his hips to stimulate the sweet spot inside her that he knew would take her over the top.

"You like that don't you, Svet?"

Slipping his arms beneath her, he clamped his hands around the tops of her shoulders pulling her into his thrusts. He didn't hear a response beyond Zaria's moans, but he didn't wait for one.

"You want to wake up to this every morning, da?"

"Mmmm!" Zaria's reply was moaned into the pillow.

Lapsing into Russian, Andrei praised Zaria more. In his native tongue, he revealed the depth of his feelings for her physically and emotionally. Even as far gone as he was in the moment, he knew she wasn't ready to hear the words, but he needed to say them.

The revelation was a catalyst as his strokes became shorter and harder. Zaria's moans turned to keening wails as she reached nirvana. Andrei's hips jerked to a stop as he joined her in bliss—spilling his seed into her tight channel.

After a few moments, he rolled away tugging Zaria into the cradle of his arms. His front was plastered to her back. Giving her a few minutes to recover, Andrei dropped a kiss onto her shoulder before he rose from the bed. Once he had his valise, he went into the bathroom. Turning on the shower, he prepared a towel for Zaria. However, she entered behind him making it unnecessary for him to come back to clean her up.

Andrei watched as she slid open the glass shower door and stuck her hand inside. Apparently satisfied with the water temperature, she gathered her hair with a thick elastic. Taking the towel from his hand, she tangled their fingers together and led him to the shower. Wanting to know where this was going, Andrei silently followed.

Once they were enclosed inside, she maneuvered him beneath the warm spray. Andrei's eyes closed in agonizingly slow increments as Zaria's soft fingers encircled his cock. His length thickened with her touch. Torn between wanting to enjoy the feeling as well as see her beautiful face, Andrei's head fell forward.

Behind half closed eyelids, he watched as she lowered herself to her haunches. When her pink tongue left her lips and swiped the helmet of his shaft, Andrei's hands flattened against the walls. Once she pulled him completely inside the warmth of her mouth, he released a string of curses. This time, he hadn't purposely slipped into Russian, he simply couldn't form the words in English.

Andrei decided then and there he would do whatever was necessary to ensure they had the opportunity to start every day exactly like that. No matter whose bed they awakened in.

Chapter Seventeen

WA. WA-WAMP-WAMP-WAMP

Zaria looked up from her computer when there was a knock on her door.

"Come in."

Tika poked her head through the opening, but didn't come inside the office.

"Hey, I'm just reminding you about your appointment in an hour. You asked me not to let the time get away from you."

"Thank you for the reminder. I'm almost done with this and you can type it up and get it ready to file."

"Good deal."

Tika disappeared closing the door behind her. Zaria looked at the time. The morning had flown by. Putting the finishing touches on the document, she sent it to her assistant. Her phone pinged on her desk. Lifting it, a smile tugged at the corners of her mouth. Andrei.

It had been almost two months since she'd agreed to be exclusive with him. As much as she never thought she would be the kind of person who jumped headlong into a relationship, she was all in with him. After the first night she tried to sleep in her own bed, they'd established a routine of sorts. They moved between households, but most of the time, they were at the mansion right outside of the city.

Andrei made her reasons for wanting to be in her own space less and less by making room for her in his. She now had clothes in her own closet at both the mansion and the suites at the casino hotel. He'd also converted one of the conference rooms into an office for her. So, on days when she worked from home, she had an environment similar to the one she was accustomed to using.

AAA: The arrangements have been made.

Zaria smiled at Andrei's directness. There were times he texted simply to check in on her. Although, when he wanted something, he got right to the point. Him even utilizing text was growth, because he didn't much care for it. He preferred to hear her voice. That knowledge put a tingle in her belly every time she thought about it. *When does the new relationship giddiness wear off?*

Ok. Sounds good. I'm done for the day at 5-ish. I'll see you then.

AAA: I have a late meeting. However, I will be home before seven.

Zaria twisted her lips at his reference to being home. It was *his* home, but he'd started referring to it as *their* home weeks ago. He made no attempt to camouflage his intentions. Andrei wanted them together in one place, and he used whatever tools available to him to make it happen.

The arrangements he referred to were for their trip over the Thanksgiving holiday. Her family didn't celebrate a traditional Thanksgiving, but it was a time when they were more easily able to come together, so they tended to gather around that time or at Christmas.

Zaria usually made one date or the other. She wasn't often able to get away for both. There had been years where her aunt, uncle, and cousins came to visit her instead. Meeting in Coryville was sometimes easier since Dom was able to drive over from California.

Well, drive was a stretch, she used a personal security service called *Ryd* when she needed to go out in public. It was actually pretty cool. It was similar to a rideshare, except they only catered to clients with specialized needs.

Dom had offered to get Zaria one of their exclusive invitations, but she didn't think she needed it at the time. Funny how things changed. Zaria now had her own full-time security detail.

Zaria was nervous as hell about her decision. She'd invited Andrei to go back to Mississippi with her to spend part of the holiday with her family. It would only be the second time she brought a man to meet them. While she was anxious, Andrei seemed unfazed. That didn't surprise Zaria since not much appeared to worry him.

They'd also discussed flying out the day after Thanksgiving to catch Vitaly's game in New York. Since his brother was Andrei's only family, he wanted her to meet him—make it a whole meet-the-family weekend.

Before Zaria knew it, it was time to leave. She didn't want to be late for her appointment. Dr. Zora Kent had been Zaria's doctor for years. Until they showed up on the same day early in their friendship, Zaria and Alyssa had no idea they were seeing the same physician.

The appointment went along as usual—except for the part where the nurse asks about sexual activity and Zaria had to adjust her standard answer. She shifted in the seat even though her pretty pocket wasn't sore from her and Andrei's extra-curricular activities.

The nurse was professional as ever. She didn't bat an eye. She simply placed the items needed to collect samples nearby and continued on with the appointment.

Then came the part Zaria could do without. She was escorted to a room. On one side was an examination table and an area separated by a floor to ceiling curtain. On the other was a sink and cabinets set up similar to a kitchen without the stove.

"The doctor will be in with you shortly. You can go ahead and disrobe."

Nodding in response, Zaria went behind the curtain to get ready for the doctor. By the time she was seated on the table with the paper sheet draped around her middle, Dr. Kent breezed into the room accompanied by her nurse.

"Good afternoon, Miss Zee!"

"Hey, Dr. Kent."

Grabbing a stool, Dr. Kent rolled it closer to the examination table. Zaria sat up straighter. That wasn't their normal routine. By now, the nurse would be pulling things out of the drawers and the doctor would be sitting next to the little desk going over her test results with her before performing the pelvic exam.

The hairs on Zaria's arms stood up. And it wasn't from the chill of the room. Dr. Kent swiped at the electronic tablet in her hand. Looking at Zaria, she started going through the standard battery of tests performed annually. Midway through, Zaria's hearing seemed to go out.

She saw the pretty doctor's mouth moving, but she wasn't able to comprehend the words being said. All Zaria heard was the *Wa. Wa-wamp-wamp-wamp-wamp* of the fictional school teacher from the famous comic strip. *What the hell did she just say?* Blinking hard, Zaria snapped out of the daze.

"Do you want to run that by me again?"

Dr. Kent didn't seem bothered that Zaria had interrupted her mid-sentence. She simply looked back down at her tablet and repeated herself.

"Based on your hCG level, I'd say you are approximately six to eight weeks into your first trimester."

Zaria's head shook vigorously. "Nope. Uh-uh. I'm on the shot. I need you to run the test again. I'm sure I can muster up another urine sample. Or do you need blood? Was what I gave earlier enough for two tests, or do you need to draw more?"

Zaria didn't care for the indulgent look on the doctor's face when she held up a hand to stop her from volunteering bodily fluids.

"There's no need for more samples. The test results are accurate. You're pregnant. I'll have to examine you further to pinpoint how far along, but there hasn't been a mistake."

Crossing her arms across her middle, Zaria slowly shook her head. "No. I take my shot religiously. How did this happen?"

Dr. Kent tipped her head to the side. One eyebrow lifted as she stared at Zaria. Sighing, she leaned forward. "Well...when a man and a woman engage in sexual intercourse—"

"You don't have to be a smart ass about it, Doc." Zaria gave her the stink eye.

Dr. Kent's lips twitched in a grin Zaria was certain was suppressed laughter. Absolutely nothing was funny, in her opinion. She'd made it thirty-eight years on the earth without so much as a pregnancy scare. Until now.

Zaria closed her eyes. Taking a deep breath, she counted in her head trying to keep herself from replaying all the times she'd not even considered using a condom with Andrei. Other than the first night they were together, they hadn't bothered with any contraception.

They, or at least she, relied completely on the potency of the shot. Apparently, Andrei had some kind of super sperm. *Of course he did.* He excelled at everything he touched. Evidently, his swimmers were no exception.

Zaria wasn't sad so much as shocked. Yes, she was aware of the possibility of pregnancy, but she thought she had time to plan for it. Now, she only had time to figure out how her life was about to change yet again. A baby so soon in a relationship could have things going two ways. It could draw her and Andrei closer, or it could tear them apart.

She had no idea how she was going to tell him about it. They were on the precipice of one relationship milestone already with them meeting each other's families.

When she opened her eyes, Dr. Kent was still sitting on the stool with her tablet in her hand. Waiting. Squaring her shoulders, Zaria gave her a nod. Outwardly, she looked more composed. Internally, her stomach flipped with nervousness at this abrupt change.

"Okay. First, let's get you ready for a preliminary examination. We can set up an obstetrics appointment at the end of this one."

Zaria's mind spun with the information Dr. Kent had given her. Tucked in her purse were folded pamphlets, prescriptions and samples of vitamins she was instructed to begin immediately. Andrei, and what this would mean for them, was heavy on her mind. But other things were pressing as well.

She needed to talk to Dr. Fleming. Zaria's next appointment with her therapist was a week away. She couldn't wait that long. Her racing pulse indicated the start of an emotional spiral. In the SUV, she studied the back of the seat in front of her without actually seeing it.

The moment she was back in her office, Zaria was on the phone trying to get a last-minute appointment. She didn't ask Tika to do it for her, she needed to speak to someone firsthand—not relay messages. Fingers drumming against the wooden surface of her desk, Zaria listened as Dr. Fleming's nurse proceeded to tell her securing an appointment before the end of the day was unlikely.

"What about after her last appointment? I *really* need to talk to her today. It doesn't have to be a full hour. I'm willing to come and wait until she's done with her last appointment."

"Hold on just a moment, Ms Coleman."

Soft pop music drifted over the line as Zaria was placed on hold. It had taken numerous sessions with Dr. Fleming for Zaria to make peace with her early childhood and how it shaped who she was. However, sometimes those insecurities crept up and nothing short of talking it out with the therapist helped.

"Ms Coleman?"

Zaria sat up straighter in her seat. "Yes?"

"Dr. Fleming says she can see you at five p.m. today."

Relief flooded Zaria. Her shoulders relaxed allowing the chair to fully support her.

"I'll be there. Thank you so much."

"You're welcome. See you soon."

After disconnecting the call with the doctor's office, Zaria was hard pressed to concentrate on work. Pulling out the pamphlets and other information, from Dr. Kent, she began reading through everything.

While she was perusing the documents, her phone vibrated. The screen lit up displaying a message from Andrei. Zaria's stomach flipped for an entirely different reason than usual. On one hand, it felt wrong to talk to someone else about her pregnancy before she told him. On the other, she knew she needed some help processing so she didn't say or do something that could be misconstrued and she couldn't take it back.

The text was what had become his normal afternoon check in to touch base with her. Shooting off a quick response, she let him know she would be later than usual coming home. Even as she typed it, she realized it was how she'd begun to feel. No matter how much she'd fought admitting it—wherever Andrei was, was now her home.

Five o'clock couldn't get there soon enough for Zaria. The office complex Dr. Fleming worked from was a short drive from the firm, but Zaria was still in the car by four-fifteen on the way to her appointment. Bless Grace and Dakota. They didn't bat an eye at the last-minute schedule addition.

When her name was called, Zaria hopped up from the straight back chair and quickly walked into the doctor's office. Dr. Fleming was standing next to her desk when Zaria entered the room.

"Good afternoon, Zaria."

Waving toward the plush chairs to the right of her desk, the doctor invited her to sit. Dropping her purse onto the side table, Zaria sat and folded her hands together in her lap. Dr. Fleming settled into the opposite seat.

Crossing her legs, she gave Zaria a look that asked the question she never said aloud. *What brings you here today?*

"I'm pregnant." Zaria said in a rush. Immediately capturing one corner of her bottom lip between her teeth, she waited for the doctor's response.

"Is this not good news?" Dr. Fleming's brow dipped slightly behind the black square framed glasses perched on her nose.

Zaria looked down at her fingers twisted together in her lap trying to figure out how to answer the doctor's question honestly. She wasn't *sad* about the news, but she wasn't exactly jumping for joy. A baby hadn't been a part of her plan.

"Zaria?" Dr. Fleming prompted. Zaria knew she wouldn't rush to answer, but avoiding giving a response wouldn't be allowed either.

"It's... a surprise. I didn't plan this." Zaria studied her fingers for a moment more before she looked up at the other woman.

"Ok. It's understandable not to be immediately happy. Having a child requires large changes in one's life. Even if you'd planned to have a baby, it's natural to be a little nervous and apprehensive. So, what's bothering you about it?"

Her question was the one Zaria had been asking herself ever since Dr. Kent said those two fateful words. *You're pregnant*. What bothered her is that she was terrified of becoming her mother. Whether her concern was based in fact didn't matter—it weighed on her heavily.

However, now, she was being asked to verbalize her fear. Dr. Fleming's office was a safe place. One where Zaria had exorcised many a demon and faced some hard truths. Apparently she wasn't done fighting.

"I want to be a good mom."

"Zaria, I have no doubt you'll be an excellent mother."

"How can you say that?"

"Because you're here." The doctor spread her hands and looked around her office. "You've been here, regularly, working on yourself and trying to become the best possible version of Zaria Coleman you can be. That's how I know."

Leaning forward, Dr. Fleming placed a hand on top of Zaria's. "You didn't come here for me to give you that pep talk though. Who you are as a person won't allow you to do anything other than your best. What's really bothering you?"

"What if my best still turns out to be a shitty mom?" Tears welled in Zaria's eyes. They spilled over onto her cheeks. Accepting the tissues offered by the doctor, she dabbed at the wetness.

"What does Andrei think?" Dr. Fleming knew about Andrei from their discussions during previous appointments.

"He doesn't know yet."

"Is there a reason you haven't told him?"

"I just found out today. A few hours ago. He and I haven't talked."

Leaning into the cushions of the seat, the doctor softened her voice. "Are you considering termination?"

Reflexively, Zaria's hand flew to her abdomen. "No! It never crossed my mind."

"Okay. So, why haven't you told the father of your child he's about to be a father?"

Zaria's response was barely above a whisper. She was loathe to verbalize her fear, even if she knew it was necessary.

"What if I'm like her?"

"Your mother?"

"Yes."

"In what way?"

"What if I'm so caught up in him that I don't have any room for the child we created together?"

The doctor's face was a mask of empathy which caused more tears to fall from Zaria's eyes. Her own mother had been so busy trying to please her father, his mood swings and insane jealousy that Zaria was simply an afterthought. She wondered if she was even wanted or simply used as a way to *show* her mother's commitment to him.

Zaria nervously twisted the tissue between her fingers before Dr. Fleming placed a hand on top of hers.

"Zaria, the fact that you're even concerned about how you'll mother your child puts you miles ahead of your own. But, let's talk apples to apples here. In what way do you think your current relationship mirrors the one your parents had?"

Zaria didn't have to search long for an answer to the doctor's question. "I don't seem to be able to hold to my boundaries when it comes to him."

"Okay. We've touched on this before. So, let's talk about it. Which boundaries are you unable to stand firm in?"

"I haven't slept alone in over a month. Since the second night of my trip for my friend's wedding. I tried, but he showed up on my doorstep and I caved. I let him in. We're practically living together because I can't seem to tell him no."

"Okay. Why is that a problem? Do you feel like your space is being crowded and you don't have enough room to be yourself in your relationship dynamic? Are you being smothered?"

Zaria's brow dipped and she jerked away from the doctor. "No. He's not smothering me."

"So, what is it?"

"Since we've committed to be together exclusively, we haven't slept apart."

"That's not uncommon."

"We committed to each other after what I thought was a one-night stand." Zaria gave the doctor side eye because they'd discussed this before. "Most people who go to the living together stage have been a couple for much longer."

Sighing, Dr. Fleming straightened in her seat. "Zaria, as I said before, I'm not a relationship counselor. That being said, you also know you can't place your situation into someone else's box. The timetable you and

Andrei have as consenting adults in a mature relationship, is what the *two of you* decide is the one which works for you. Not what anyone else thinks."

The doctor's words mirrored the ones Zaria had said to herself as well as what Andrei said weeks ago. However, her formative years made her wary of having such a deep connection to someone so quickly.

"Now, other than the not sleeping apart thing, in what other ways do you think you're lacking in boundaries for him?"

Zaria bit the corner of her lip. When she started telling the doctor of other ways she'd allowed Andrei to push or obliterate her boundaries, she realized that none of it was earth shattering and all of it was a part of the development of an adult relationship. Most of the time, it came back to him not wanting to be apart from her. Since, despite her protests, she wanted the same thing, were her boundaries really pushed?

"Zaria, again, I'm not a relationship counselor. I can recommend one to you. However, what I'm hearing is two people learning one another's personalities and deciding how they're going to proceed in their relationship dynamic. None of which is a threat to you being good parents to a child."

Squeezing Zaria's fingers, Dr. Fleming looked at her over the top of black framed glasses. "You are mentally healthier, more emotionally available and more financially secure than your birth mother. Any child you have will be loved and will feel that love daily."

Giving Zaria's hands a few quick pats, the doctor stood. "Unfortunately, I can't stay any later. However, I will have my assistant give you a call tomorrow to set up another session. That's if you need one before your next scheduled appointment. In the meantime, I suggest you go home and talk to Andrei. Don't bottle this up and try to navigate it alone."

Nodding in agreement, Zaria thanked the doctor, gathered her purse and left. Stopping in the ladies' room, she fixed her face before she walked out into the waiting area where Dakota and Grace waited for her. Neither spoke as they left the office. The ride home was done to the backdrop of old school R&B from the satellite radio station they knew Zaria liked.

Girding herself for the unknown, Zaria entered the house. When Andrei wasn't waiting for her in the foyer, she knew where to find him.

So, she changed her shoes and walked out of the side door heading toward the ice rink. As soon as she opened the door she heard the tell-tale sounds of him cutting across the surface on his blades.

Taking a deep breath, she walked over to the barrier separating the ice from the seats and waited. *Here goes nothing.*

Chapter Eighteen

SAY THAT AGAIN, SVET

Andrei glided around the rink with a stick in his hands. Although during his days actively playing he was a defensemen, he'd lined pucks up along the center and went down the line slapping them toward the goal. Without a defender at the net, the black discs sailed in effortlessly.

If Vitaly were there, he'd bat away each attempt with ease and goad Andrei to give him some real competition. But, his brother was safely in Denver. For all intents and purposes, he was flying under the radar and staying out of trouble.

Andrei relished the feel of the air on his face as he skated over to retrieve the pucks and line them up again. It had been almost a week since he'd laced up and it felt good. The chef had left a meal warming for him and Zaria. He'd forgone cooking dinner for the two of them himself tonight. Andrei had the chef prepare something because he didn't want his Svet to get the impression he expected traditional domesticity from her.

He enjoyed cooking for her and making sure she was cared for. Pampering her pleased him. She was appreciative, and she also did things for him. Things he hadn't realized no one else had done—aside from people he paid to perform those tasks. Andrei smiled when he thought of the change he'd noticed in the arrangement of his closet that morning.

It was nothing drastic, but it made a world of difference. His ties, pocket squares and tie pins had been rearranged in proximity to the suits which color-matched those items best. Now, Andrei could essentially pick up anything along a particular line and be coordinated without worrying if he clashed. He also noticed a few, more colorful additions to his ties and pocket squares.

He'd just reset the last puck when the rink door opened and closed again. Looking toward the sound, he watched as Zaria approached the barrier separating the ice from the seating area. Her pensive expression put Andrei on alert.

He wondered if her reason for being home late was why she appeared so contemplative. Instead of continuing with his light workout, Andrei skated over to where she stood with her hands on the low wall. She stared at him as he approached, but he couldn't accurately read her expression.

Without the added height of his skates, Andrei stood a foot taller than Zaria. With them, he felt hulkish towering over her. Her head tilted back to maintain eye contact and a slight smile curled her full lips. Leaning in, he kissed their pillowy softness.

"Good evening, Svet. Did you have a good day?"

Andrei's gaze marked every nuance of her expression. While her lips were still tipped up, her eyes projected a hint of anxiety. Shucking off his gloves, he laid them along the top of the wall and cupped her face. She leaned into his touch, closing her eyes briefly. When she opened them, she still didn't answer his question.

His previous alertness cranked up another few notches. Zaria wasn't the type to mince words—even with him. Her lack of response did nothing to stop him from wondering if there was someone he needed to remind to leave her the fuck alone. Before he entered a complete spiral, he prompted her.

"Did you have a good day? Is something wrong?"

Touching the back of his hand, she kept it pressed to her face as she shook her head. "Nothing's wrong. At least I hope there's not."

"What does that mean, Svet?"

Zaria inhaled deeply, then released the breath in a rush accompanied by words Andrei wasn't sure he'd heard correctly. Slowly, Andrei maneuvered her to the side to allow him to exit the rink. Once he stepped off the ice, he methodically unlaced and removed his skates. Setting them to the side, he approached her again. Tugging until her front was pressed against his, he cupped both sides of her face staring into her eyes.

"Say that again, Svet."

Andrei tracked the movement of Zaria's tongue as it swiped across her bottom lip, wetting it. His heartbeat thundered in his ears so loudly, he hoped he'd be able to hear her voice. Her lips moved again. Despite the thundering of his heart, Andrei was certain he heard her correctly.

"I'm pregnant, Andrei."

Andrei's heart soared in his chest. He hadn't misheard or misunderstood. A baby. His Svet was having his baby. He was going to be a Papa. Of all his accomplishments, he'd never felt happier than he did at this moment.

Lifting Zaria in his arms he hugged her to him raining kisses on her face and neck. For a few minutes, the English language eluded him as he praised her, thanking her, admitting he'd never thought he'd get the chance to be with someone he could start a family with. In that brief moment, Andrei was the most verbose he'd been in his life.

Zaria's arms wound around his neck and her fingers stroked into the hair at his nape. A hint of amusement coated her words.

"I can't understand ninety-nine percent of what you're saying, but I'll take it to mean you're happy."

Finally remembering how to express himself in a tongue she understood, Andrei beamed. "Happy does not begin to cover it, Svet. You are giving me a most precious gift."

Walking them over to the cushioned bench against the wall, he sat arranging her legs to straddled him on the seat. Reverently, he placed a hand on her middle even while knowing the roundness of her belly couldn't be attributed to his child growing in her womb. Silence pulsed between them as Andrei caressed her stomach and began mentally planning their next steps.

When his gaze returned to Zaria's she regarded him with one raised eyebrow. "If I were a more suspicious woman, I'd wonder if this was intentional." Her hands smoothed along his shoulders as she continued.

"However, there was no way anyone could know for certain birth control would be no match for your super sperm."

Andrei didn't mask anything about his feelings when he looked at her. He wanted to be certain his expression matched his words. "I did not plan it. But I am not upset that we are going to be parents together."

One corner of Zaria's plump bottom lip disappeared between her teeth. Using his thumb, Andrei pressed her chin until she released her hostage. Giving her a gentle kiss, he rubbed his forehead against hers.

"Talk to me, Svet. Are you not happy about our baby?"

Unconsciously, Andrei held his breath waiting for her response. *What if she didn't want his baby? What would that mean?*

"I didn't say I wasn't happy..."

"You did not say you *were,* either."

"I'm just...surprised. I guess I need time to process."

"What is there to process?"

Andrei tried not to be disappointed she wasn't as ecstatic as he was. It was a difficult feat. He'd known long before they ever spoke to one another that she would be special to him. When he actually had the opportunity to touch, taste and feel her, it solidified their connection for him.

Zaria needed a moment, but Andrei was ready to make everything about their relationship official. If it meant marriage, he was okay with it. Although, he wouldn't demand it. As long as she was with him, with their child, in their home, he was more than satisfied.

"Andrei, we've barely been together two months. Actually. Not even two months. Having a child is a major decision. For this to happen so soon in our relationship is more than a little daunting for me."

Andrei stared at her, watching the emotions play across her face. Rather than wonder if he'd read the situation correctly, he asked.

"You are worried about what others will think?"

Zaria's shoulder lifted in a shrug. Her gaze drifted past his shoulder for a second before her eyes returned to his.

"What people think stopped mattering to me a long time ago. This is about me...us...having a child can be difficult for couples who've been together for years. Like I said, we haven't even been together two solid months."

Andrei wrapped his arms around her pulling her as close as humanly possible given their position. Tilting her face to his, he fixed her with a stern expression.

"You are very focused on timing, Svet. But, time does not matter. We are not other couples."

Cupping her face, he allowed his fingertips to slip into her soft coils.

"Many of those couples are stressed because they do not have the financial means to provide for their child the way they would like. We do not have such issues. Between the two of us, it would take several generations of unproductive offspring to render them poor.

With that major concern eliminated, all we have to worry with is providing the right environment for our child. I am confident we can do so without issue. Will we make mistakes? Quite likely. We will simply make them together, Svet."

Zaria's head tipped to the side as she returned his stare. "It's that simple?"

"For me it is." Andrei didn't see a need to panic. They were full adults. Of means. There may be things he wasn't aware of, but they lived in the information age. Any question they had could be answered with the tap of the finger and click of the mouse.

He sat, silently watching her as she cycled through her thoughts and emotions. Not speaking, she plucked absently at the generic jersey he wore. Finally, she seemed to come to an internal conclusion. Lifting her eyes to his, Zaria's lips tipped up in a tentative smile. Just as they did, a low rumble cut through the silence.

Patting her thighs, he lifted until she stood in front of him. "Come, Svet. Chef made dinner for us. We must keep our little *businka* well fed."

Andrei made quick work of storing his skates and getting them both back to the main house for dinner. Inside, his mind was working overtime. While he hadn't consciously set out to create a life with Zaria, he knew he hadn't been ***not*** trying to create a life. He'd never gone without protection with a woman.

For the entirety of his hockey career, there was never a legitimate pregnancy scare. He'd always shown up with his own protection and only used condoms he'd personally purchased and opened. After some of the wild things he'd heard about other athletes and celebrities dealing with, he even went so far as to take the discarded condoms with him when he left an encounter.

No matter how normal a woman seemed, he didn't fully trust them. It was understandable since they weren't in a relationship—they were hookups. With Zaria, things were entirely different. He had a primal need to claim her in all ways possible. And, he had no will nor desire to curb the impulse.

While they had dinner, Zaria shared the information she'd received from her gynecologist. Andrei had many questions. She answered what she could. What she couldn't, they resolved to look up after dinner. Thumbing through the paperwork Andrei pointed to a phrase that seemed odd to him.

"Svet, what do they mean by this?"

Zaria brought the paper closer. Then, she shrugged and pushed it back toward him. "Advanced Maternal Age is how they refer to any woman over thirty-five having a baby."

"You are only thirty-eight. Neither thirty-five nor thirty-eight are advanced age. I do not understand."

"Hey, at least they don't call it Geriatric Pregnancy anymore."

Andrei's brow furrowed. He was genuinely offended on her behalf. Was Zaria mature? Yes. But she was also youthful and vibrant. Advanced Age made him think of a nearly one hundred-year-old person wearing adult diapers for incontinence.

Zaria regarded his expression and released a light chuckle. "You look as offended as I was when I first read through it. I get it though. Pregnancy and childbirth are dangerous, and can be more so as a woman gets older."

Andrei looked down at the information and back up at Zaria. His brain keyed in on one word. *Dangerous.*

"Are you at risk? Is that what the doctor said?"

His head swirled with possibilities as his emotions waffled between happiness and concern. Tension coiled his muscles although there was no one he could fight but himself if his Svet was in harm's way.

"No. According to Dr. Kent, I'm in good health. She simply wanted me to be aware of the possibilities, and understand why starting the vitamins and making a few slight changes would be best."

Relief flooded Andrei's body. Nodding, he refolded the papers and set them aside.

"I will have Frederick add your next appointment to my schedule so I can go with you."

Zaria's mouth opened, then snapped closed. She breathed evenly for a brief moment before nodding. "Okay. Dr. Kent's next opening is in about three weeks. It's a mid-morning appointment. Because of the holiday, it was the earliest she could fit me in."

Andrei frowned. He didn't like the idea of them having to wait so long. However, he didn't personally know any obstetricians to call around and get someone else. Fleetingly, he considered asking Carver about Alyssa's doctor. But, he quickly discarded the idea. Instinct told him Zaria wouldn't appreciate it. Besides, the pamphlet said something about not announcing the pregnancy until they were safely out of the first trimester.

He had no idea how ignorant he was when it came to pregnancy. Andrei hadn't even made it through all of the pamphlets and brochures the doctor provided and he felt woefully uneducated on the subject. He didn't like it. His aversion to being ill-prepared had him making a mental note to find books and other available study materials.

As part of their now established routine—especially on difficult or tiring days—Andrei ran Zaria a bath. He opted for a shower. So, he was sitting up in bed when she left the bathroom. The television was on, tuned to the sports channel, but his attention was on the tablet in his hand.

"What are you looking at? I thought we had a no work in bed rule? Are you trying to get in trouble?"

Andrei lowered the device and looked at her. Zaria was resting on her knees wearing the gold satin robe which played off her skin so well. For a second he was distracted by knowing she was completely nude beneath it. His eyes drifted over her breasts watching as her nipples pebbled beneath the shimmering material.

"What trouble might that be, Svet? Are you suggesting you would dispense punishment if I...misbehaved?" Andrei's gaze returned to hers as he considered the possibilities of such punishment and if he'd like it.

Lifting the tablet from his limp fingers, Zaria straddled his lap. "You sound like you don't think I have the means to discipline bad behavior. We had a deal, Mr. Antonov. No work in bed."

Ignoring his growl when she addressed him as Mr. Antonov, she looked at the display.

"What's all this?" A line appeared between her perfectly arched eyebrows as she used her fingertip to scroll back up the page filled with images.

"It is a database of security experts. It is not work related."

"And how is it not work related? I can tell providing excellent security at your businesses is important to you."

"These people also specialize in child care."

"Child care? Seriously?"

Taking the device back, he tapped on an image. The dossier expanded displaying the person's photo as well as a brief synopsis of their education and experience. Zaria focused on the screen for a few moments before she returned her gaze to him—staring in disbelief.

"Andrei...this is a Security Nanny. Like a bodyguard who also takes care of children."

"Yes. I know."

"Why are you looking at potential nannies?"

Laying the tablet on the bedside table, Andrei rested his hands on her hips. His thumbs stroked the sides drifting toward her belly.

"Svet, have you already forgotten that we're having a baby?"

"No. But said baby is literally not even the size of a peach yet. We have time."

"Yes, however it could take several months to find the right candidate."

Andrei seriously didn't see an issue with being proactive, but Zaria's expression said she thought he was being over the top. Or, as she liked to say *#TeamTooMuch*.

"Andrei...We have plenty of time to think about security and nannies. We don't have to do it all today. Can we just have a little time where we don't make everything about preparing for parenthood? Is this what I have to look forward to the better part of the next year?"

"I can agree to stop looking for a nanny tonight. Since I am pausing the search, can you be more specific with your question? My first instinct will always be to protect my family. You are my family, Svet. I have not met the life growing inside you, but little *businka* is also my family. A man in my position has to think ahead."

Zaria swept her gaze over his face. "You are so fucking intense, Andrei Antonov."

Skimming his digits along her sides, he brought them to rest cupping the sides of her face. Leaning forward, he pressed gentle kisses on her lips.

"That may be true, Svet. It still does not mean I am wrong."

"I'm not saying you're wrong." Zaria murmured between kisses. "I'm simply asking you to hold off until we at least see the doctor for the first official obstetrics appointment."

Andrei didn't want to argue or cause her to worry, so he nodded. He felt not one twinge of guilt for resolving to conduct his search when it was less likely she'd walk in on him. Not one care was given to if he was technically going overboard. He sincerely believed there was no such thing when it came to making certain his family was safe.

He hadn't amassed a fortune to simply sit on his hands and not do whatever he could to protect and provide. Zaria would eventually come to see things his way. Andrei was sure of it.

In the meantime, he slipped the knot, holding her robe together loose, and delighted in the smooth softness of her skin. Abandoning her lips, he skimmed kisses down her neck and over her collarbone before latching onto one turgid nipple.

Zaria gasped and her fingers delved into his hair alternately tugging at the strands and gripping his head to pull him closer. Rolling them until she lay on her back, Andrei continued to trail kisses down her body. He knew exactly how to get her mind off his preparations.

Chapter Nineteen

YOU'RE A BIGGUN

Zaria looked around the mini mansion Andrei rented for their visit south. It had been over a week since Dr. Kent tilted their world's axis with Zaria's test results. Now, after another session with Dr. Fleming, she was in a better headspace. Mostly.

Not staying with her aunt and uncle had caused a mini-stir. Zaria had to sooth her aunt, explaining that it wasn't a slight against her for them to stay in their own space since they would still spend most of their time with the family. They simply needed more rooms considering the literal entourage traveling with them.

Nerves caused a fluttering in her belly as she thought about when they'd load into the SUVs which looked suspiciously like the ones the security teams used to drive them around Vegas. With the size of Andrei's plane, it wouldn't surprise her if they were the same.

This was only the second time she'd brought a man home, and the first time that the man hadn't been of the same race. Interracial relationships were more common now, but her family still primarily lived in Mississippi—where it wasn't as prevalent as in states with larger metropolitan populations. Although Southhaven was larger than many cities in the northern part of the state, it was still considerably smaller, population wise, than a city like Las Vegas.

Anxiety had Zaria reaching out to Dom and offering to swing by and pick her up for the trip home, however her cousin had already chartered a flight. She'd plan to come in the day before Zaria and Andrei. She wouldn't begrudge Dom the extra time with her parents and little brother. Her cousin didn't get to visit often after her career took off a couple of years ago.

Since acting careers could ebb and flow, Dom said she had to strike while the iron was hot. The roles were pouring in. While she was careful what she accepted, she couldn't turn too many down. Zaria understood. It wasn't the Hollywood norm for a plus sized black woman to be sought after for leading roles—unless she was in a *Magical Black Woman* savior role. So, Dom had to keep pushing to keep the opportunities flowing for herself and those just beginning their careers.

"Are you ready, Svet?"

Andrei stopped behind her. He slid his arm around her waist resting a palm on her abdomen. The past thirty minutes had been spent with him directing the staff and getting the place set up for them to use. Zaria hadn't even realized people rented these homes for short stays. It wasn't the typical vacation rental.

"Sure." Zaria inhaled deeply. Tapping his fingers lying against her belly, she looked up at him.

"It's okay when we're alone, I just want you to remember we aren't telling people about the baby yet."

Andrei quirked an eyebrow, causing her to huff and turn in his arms.

"Don't give me that look. We both know a man resting his hand on a woman's belly is tantamount to sending out a birth announcement."

He remained silent, but his silence spoke volumes.

"Andrei, I'm not worried about what people will say or think. I'm thinking about the statistics. Even women who are younger and healthier can experience a miscarriage this early on. I just want to err on the side of caution."

They were having an entire conversation—even if she was the only one speaking. He didn't like the idea of hiding her pregnancy—at all. Despite knowing waiting was what the doctor and experts recommended.

"According to Dr. Kent, we only have four weeks, maybe five before we can tell them. So, before the new year." Rubbing his chest in soothing circles, Zaria continued. "So around Christmas, we'll be able to share the news with our family and friends."

"I will do my best." The words he didn't say hung in the air between them. He wouldn't promise he would keep his hands to himself.

It was quite likely the only way she'd be able to keep his hands off her belly would be to maintain her distance when they were around others or up her handholding game significantly. They were an affectionate couple, but they didn't normally do a great deal of that kind of thing.

Since they were leaving Friday morning, they'd arrived on Monday, to give her more time with her family. Zaria's office was closed for the week, although she knew Andrei would likely work part of the time. Hence another reason they needed their own space.

His staff probably had no idea who the guy was walking around wearing their boss's face. She was certain he didn't regularly take time away from being physically present at the casino or the *Chevalier* offices. Andrei didn't complain though. He simply had Frederick work his schedule for his meetings to take place via video conference or moved to the following week.

When they arrived at her aunt and uncle's house, only two cars were parked in the circular drive. Zaria's brow dipped trying figure out who might be the owners. Both Dom and Cisco would've flown in. Dom hated to drive, so she wouldn't have gotten a rental. Although Cisco might have picked one up in Memphis.

As she stepped onto the porch, the heavy oak door swung open and her aunt came out in a streak of red and gold, her favorite colors.

"Hey, my baby!"

Zaria was swept into a huge hug. With her aunt being more than a few inches taller, the exuberant greeting meant she had a face full or her aunt's ample bosom. Returning the hug, Zaria just went with it until she was released.

"Hey, Aunt Belinda. It's good to see you too."

Her aunt held her at arm's length for a moment with her sharp eyes raking over Zaria from head to toe. Zaria unconsciously held her breath. She didn't know how, but older black women seemed to have this innate way of knowing when something was up.

Zaria felt like she was wearing a blazing neon sign reading, *I'm preg-*

nant by this big Russian guy standing behind me. Finally, her aunt completed her inspection and turned her attention to Andrei.

"Hey! You must be Andrei."

"Hello, Mrs. Truman."

Andrei extended his hand only to have it slapped away. Zaria's aunt gave him an almost identical greeting to the one she gave her niece. The difference being Aunt Belinda's face was in Andrei's chest.

"Goodness! You're a biggun."

Zaria wasn't remotely surprised at her aunt's words or the greeting she gave Andrei. She simply smiled indulgently and offered silent thanks to him for going along with the program. Belinda Truman had a big heart and if her kids accepted you, then she accepted you. Period.

Pulling away from Andrei, she ushered them into the house. Looking over her shoulder, she looked at the two men standing beside the SUV they'd arrived in.

"Aren't they coming inside? It's a little chilly out here."

Zaria looked at Andrei, who shook his head. Taking her aunt's hand she kept them moving into the house.

"They'll be fine, Aunt Belinda. It's part of the job. They're used to it."

"Well, do they need to do a sweep of the house or something?"

Zaria couldn't contain the giggles. "Auntie, they aren't the Secret Service. Unless you or Uncle Neal broke bad, there shouldn't be anyone here who's a threat to either of us."

Andrei closed the door behind them, but her aunt's eyes watched Dakota and Yeva until she could no longer see them.

"If you say so."

"I do." Looping her arm through her aunt's, they left the foyer and entered the family room. "Where's Uncle Neal anyway? And whose cars are those in the driveway?"

"Child, he and Cisco are in the basement watching some game. You know they are in sports lover's heaven with all of the televised games on this week.

Cisco rented a car in Memphis since he flew home instead of driving, and the other is your Aunt Maryann's. She decided to join us this year. Actually, the car belongs to her new boyfriend."

Looking at the empty family room, Zaria frowned. "Aunt Maryann is here? I didn't know she was coming." Leaning in, she dropped her voice. "You know you're gonna have to tell me about this new boyfriend, right?"

Her aunt smirked, nodding slyly. "They got in really early this morning. They drove all night. So, they're still in bed."

Zaria quirked her eyebrow. Aunt Belinda was very accepting, but she could be little rigid about the unmarried couples sharing a bed thing. She'd never say it aloud, nevertheless Zaria was thinking many things about Aunt Maryann and her boo thang *laying up* in Aunt Belinda's house. Instead of commenting, she took Andrei's hand in hers and changed the subject.

"I thought Dom was here already? Where's she?"

"She's in her room. She said something about a last-minute meeting with her agent and a producer who wanted to pitch a new series to her."

"Oh. Okay."

"I don't know much about it, but I hope she takes it. It'll mean she'll be closer for a little while. They film in Atlanta, so she'd only be a short flight or car ride away."

As much as her aunt and uncle encouraged them to pursue their dreams and walk their own path, her aunt also wanted them where she could see them on a regular basis. All three had disbursed to cities hours away by flight, and in her and Dom's case, days by car.

"That would be nice, Auntie. I hope it's a good opportunity for her." Looking to the doorway leading to the basement stairs, Zaria tugged on Andrei's hand.

"I'm going to take Andrei downstairs to meet Uncle Neal and Cisco. Then, I'll come back up. Okay?"

"Sure, Zee-baby. I'll be in the kitchen doing a little prep." Her aunt started to pivot away, then stopped. "Are y'all sure they don't want to come inside? It doesn't feel right to leave them outside like that."

"I assure you, Mrs. Truman. They are fine."

Andrei dipped his head giving her aunt his version of a smile. The one where his lips quirked up on one side, but no teeth were seen. It was apparently enough for her to continue on into the kitchen. Blushing.

Zaria tilted her chin up, smirking. He'd said less than fifteen words, none of them flirtatious, yet her aunt was blushing like a teenager because he *almost* smiled at her.

Leading Andrei to the basement stairs, Zaria shook her head at her aunt's antics. She should tell Uncle Neal his wife was flirting. Not that it would matter. He knew Aunt Belinda was crazy about him—as much as he was about her. Uncle Neal wouldn't bat an eye unless someone acted like they were going to disrespect her aunt. Then, her mild-mannered uncle turned into a completely different person.

Although he was her uncle by marriage, he was more of a father to Zaria than the man who provided the sperm to create her. He was in attendance at all of her major life achievements. Wearing a huge smile, he cheered her on and encouraged her to do her very best. As far as situations where a child was taken in by family members, Zaria knew she hit the jackpot with her aunt and uncle. They poured into her the same as they did the children born of their union.

As Zaria placed her fingers on the rail to descend the stairs, Andrei's hand clasped her elbow.

"Be careful, Svet."

Looking up at him, her lips tipped up in a wry grin. "I'm fine, big guy." Pointing to her hold on the railing, she continued. "See. I'm holding on to the rail and everything."

"It is better to be safe." Andrei huffed. His grip tightened marginally as she took the first step down.

Before they reached the landing at the bottom, she heard the television. The voices of the sportscasters mingled with the earnest banter between Cisco and his father.

"I'm telling you, Pops. Second half, the Defenders are going to wipe the floor with the Red Birds."

"Boy, you don't know what you're talking about. You play hockey. I know football. The Defenders are gonna tuck their tails between their legs and whimper home. You mark my words."

Cisco's rebuttal died on his lips when he noticed Zaria and Andrei standing at the entrance to her uncle's man cave. Well, more like when he noticed Andrei. Zaria's presence was inconsequential. Cisco's mouth opened and closed like a fish on land gulping for air.

"Boy, close your mouth." Uncle Neal stood from the leather sectional, meeting Zaria as she stepped fully into the room.

"Hey, Zee-baby." Wrapping her in a hug, he brushed the top of her head with his knuckles as he'd done since she was a little girl.

"Hey Uncle Neal." Returning his affection, she released him and held out a hand to Andrei.

"I'd like you to meet Andrei Antonov. Andrei, this is my Uncle Neal."

Shaking Andrei's hand, her uncle regarded him with an assessing gaze. Unconsciously, Zaria held her breath as the two men stared at one another. Her uncle Neal was normally a fair person, but he was protective by nature.

"So, you're the hockey player turned business mogul, huh?"

"I guess you could phrase it that way."

"Pops, he's not just a hockey player. He was inducted into the Hall of Fame two years ago. He holds Olympic records and distinctions from the US and Russia. He's a legend."

Without looking at him, Zaria felt Andrei's demeanor change. Robotically, he accepted Cisco's enthusiastic handshake. When she glanced at Andrei, his face remained neutral, but she knew he wasn't comfortable with Cisco's star-struck recounting of his achievements.

It wasn't about modesty. It was about the environment. This wasn't a business setting, game, arena or networking event. Her family home was a place he shouldn't have to wear a mask.

"Cisco, that's enough. I'm sure Uncle Neal is aware and since Andrei was there, he doesn't need to hear the list."

"It is fine, Svet."

Cisco's light brown eyes bounced between the two of them. He was so obviously torn between continuing with his fanboy routine and backing off, as Zaria implied. She almost felt bad for him. Cisco loved hockey and had been glued to the TV anytime Andrei hit the ice with the *Midnight Eagles*. His little six-year-old self would put on his Antonov Jersey, grab his stick and stand in front of the screen like he was lining up alongside the players.

It was cute. *Then*. It would still be cute now if she and Andrei weren't a couple, and if she didn't care whether he was comfortable in an unknown setting. She'd thought by letting her family know who she was bringing home, she could give them time to get it out of their system before they actually met him. And by they, she meant Cisco.

One would think, after all the celebrities and professional athletes he'd met through Dominique, he'd be past freaking out. Apparently, he wasn't. The warmth from Andrei's arm wrapped around Zaria and she caught his fingers before he could lay his hand on her belly. She had no doubt he was trying to soothe her while she was trying to run interference for him. They were so in tune with one another, it freaked her out sometimes.

Excitement won out over heeding Zaria's warning and Cisco launched into what ended up being a solid twenty minutes of him recounting various games from Andrei's career with a few Vitaly references sprinkled in for good measure. When he took off upstairs to his bedroom to grab his jersey, Zaria leaned into Andrei.

They were seated at one end of the sectional. Her uncle sat on the other. The middle was vacant after Cisco's departure. Stretching his arm along the back of the sofa, her uncle shook his head and grinned.

"Don't worry about him. It'll take him at least another twenty minutes to find what he's looking for. He doesn't know his mama's been quietly packing his stuff away. That jersey isn't where he thinks it is. He'll have to ask her to find it."

Andrei simply nodded, acknowledging he heard, but not voicing anything further.

"So... are you staying down here because you missed us or is there another reason you haven't gone upstairs to gossip with Belinda? You know Maryann will be up and about soon. If I know you and Belinda, y'all wanna get your heads together about it before the house fills up."

"Uncle Neal. I don't know what you're implying." Zaria tipped her nose in the air, looking highly offended. It lasted all of five seconds before a smile cracked her lips.

"Zee-baby, go on upstairs. You know the rules about my space."

The light brown eyes he'd gifted his son probed Zaria. Unspoken was his assurance that he wouldn't attempt to grill Andrei or make him feel unwelcome.

"Yes, sir."

Zaria closed her eyes briefly when Andrei's fingers tightened around hers. She was certain it had nothing to do with her attempt to leave and everything to do with her word choice. They were going to have to talk about his obsession with that word. In her family, manners dictated she referred to her male elders as 'sir' and the female elders as 'ma'am'.

Andrei couldn't get riled up every time she used the word this week. If he did...Well...she really didn't want to think about it too long. Images of the way he worked her over the last time she'd said the 's' word were very fresh in her mind. She couldn't walk around her family in a constant state of arousal.

Tapping the back of his hand, she moved to stand. "I'll be upstairs helping Aunt Belinda with prep. Do y'all want anything before I go?"

Andrei's eyebrow lifted. Although they'd fallen into doing little things for one another, her request wasn't their norm. Aunt Belinda was old school in many ways. Zaria had reverted to being back in their house. If she went into the kitchen, the first thing her aunt would ask was if she'd checked to see if the men wanted something before she left.

"Don't worry about us." Her uncle made a shooing motion. "Belinda left plenty to eat and drink down here earlier."

"I am fine, Svet. Go. Spend time with your aunt."

Kissing her temple, Andrei stood helping her stand beside him. Looking from his face to her uncle's, she slowly left. Just as she made it to the top of the stairs, she heard Cisco calling for his mother as he stalked across the living room.

"Boy! Stop all that hollerin'! You know your auntie is sleeping and your sister is on an important call."

Sheepishly, Cisco ducked his head. "Sorry, Ma. But, Ma! I can't find my jersey. I need you to help me."

Drying her hands on a kitchen towel, his mother stared at him. "What jersey? You have eighty million jerseys. You'll have to be more specific."

"The one you and pops got me when we went to the *Midnight Eagles* game in Chicago that time. The number six, Antonov."

Zaria hid her grin behind her hand. Although it hadn't taken him as long as her uncle said, he'd been right. Cisco would need his mother's help to find it.

"No."

Zaria's head whipped around to her aunt so fast, she almost made herself dizzy.

"What do you mean, Ma? Andrei said he'd sign it for me."

"And I told you not to be in that man's face asking for autographs and carrying on like you've never been anywhere and met anybody."

Cisco bounced on the balls of his feet like he was an actual child instead of a six-foot two young adult. His eyes rolled and his face scrunched.

"Come on, Ma..."

"No. Not come on Ma. We talked about this. Andrei is here with Zaria. He's not here for all of the stuff he normally gets around strangers. So, no. I'm not going to help you find your jersey so you can keep doing the...what do y'all call it now?... Fanboying. That's it. You can fanboy some other time. This week. Andrei is a man like any other man."

Zaria struggled to hold her giggles after Cisco crossed his arms over his chest and poked out his bottom lip. Aunt Belinda gave zero fucks.

"Now, fix your face and go on back downstairs. And don't be down there badgering that man about every game he ever played."

Dragging his feet, Cisco turned toward the basement.

"And pick up your feet when you walk." His mother called out to him as she turned to walk back into the kitchen.

"Come on in the kitchen, Zee-baby. I've been waiting for you. You know Maryann can't take long naps."

Hustling behind her aunt, Zaria went to the sink to wash her hands. Once she had her assignment, she listened attentively to her auntie giving her all the tea on Aunt Maryann and her new beau. Zaria allowed the warmth of being home to wash over her. She tried not to focus on what was going on in the basement with the men.

Chapter Twenty

WHY WOULD I DO THAT?

Andrei watched Zaria walk away before turning his attention to her uncle. While he wasn't as tall and thick as Andrei, her Uncle Neal was an imposing man standing over six feet with broad shoulders and a physique which suggested he still got regular exercise. Nodding at the other man, Andrei retook his seat at the opposite end of the sectional.

He'd talk to Zaria later about her attempts to run interference. He appreciated her desire to make sure he was comfortable, but it wasn't necessary. When Cisco started rattling off his stats, Andrei wasn't thrilled. He didn't want to present that person to Zaria's family. On the one hand, this time would be the perfect opportunity to find out who's been in Cisco's ear about his pending professional hockey career.

Had the circumstances been different, Andrei would've put on his business face and started building the kind of relationship that would have the young man talking to his representation about finding some way to make sure he ended up playing with the Chevaliers at the end of the Draft. However, Andrei was in town to meet his woman's family. His goal was to make a good impression and connect with the people who mattered most to her.

Zaria was very independent; however, Andrei knew part of her still sought the validation of the people who raised her. In more ways than one, they were her point of reference when measuring if she was doing well, and making the right decisions. Knowing that, Andrei didn't want the focus on his hockey career and accomplishments. Those conversations could be had. But first, he wanted her Uncle Neal to know him as a man. The man who would protect, provide and care for Zaria no matter what.

Andrei sat, unmoving, as Neal Truman stared at him silently. A lesser man may have begun to fidget or look away. Andrei's life didn't lend to him being the type of man who was easily rattled. He simply waited for the other man to voice the thoughts etched across his face.

"When's the wedding?"

"Excuse me?" Andrei wasn't often surprised, but Mr. Truman's question wasn't exactly what he expected.

"I'm guessing this visit south isn't a run of the mill meet the parents situation. From the way you look at Zee and the way she looks at you, the two of you are long past casual. I haven't seen anything like it since I met my Belinda almost forty years ago."

"Mr. Truman... I will not say I have not considered marriage to Zaria. It would be a lie. As of yet, she and I have not discussed it. So, I do not have an answer to your question."

"You can call me Neal." Rubbing his hand over his neatly trimmed beard, Neal chuckled. "You can tell me whatever you like, just be honest with yourself and with Zee. She deserves it." Andrei nodded in agreement.

"You're nodding, but I wonder if you really hear me. Has she told you anything about her childhood?"

Andrei searched the other man's face. He had the basics from the initial background check from Gregor, however it felt like her uncle was asking him far more than what could be found in an internet search or public record information.

"I am aware it was not ideal. If it were, I would be sitting here with her birth father." The unspoken, *instead of you*, hung between them.

"It was more than just *not ideal*. From the time she was born, she was with us, in some capacity, on and off until she was almost four. That's when things got really bad and we brought her to live with us full time. If she hasn't given you all the details, it's not my place to tell you."

Clasping his hands together, he dangled them between his knees. "What I will say is this. If what you're offering her isn't real, permanent, and given with one hundred percent of yourself, don't fuck around. If you can't be all in, then you need to get ghost."

Andrei's jaw clenched at the mere suggestion he'd leave Zaria. He held his words behind his teeth, because he was on the verge of cursing the man for even hinting he'd walk away from her and their child. Andrei couldn't say any of the first five things he considered because it would've all included mentioning the baby only he, Zaria, and her doctor knew existed.

"You do not know me. And you wish to protect Zaria. I respect and understand the desire to keep her safe. I have the same goal. Anything within my power and means will be done to achieve that goal."

"See.. You're talking money and influence. Being able to take care of her financially is great, but she can do that herself. I'm proud of the woman we've raised. She won't fall prey to bad men with fat wallets."

Matching the other man's pose, Andrei leaned forward, placing his elbows on his knees, clasping his fingers together between them.

"If we are not speaking of the same things, what are you implying? That I am a potential danger to her in other ways?"

"Yes. Exactly. Even if she hasn't expressed how she feels aloud, it's written in her eyes when she looks at you. Are you the kind of man who can handle being loved the way she loves you and reciprocate? Not just allowing her to lavish love and affection on you, but to do the same. Protect her heart, mind, and spirit? Are you capable of that?"

It was a good thing Andrei was sitting. Otherwise, he'd have folded into a heap on the floor. He knew how he felt about his Svet, however to know the affection, possible love, she felt for him was obvious to others...he was figuratively knocked on his ass. Not only from his new knowledge, also from the gravity of her uncle's question.

Was he capable of the emotional depth needed? Was it something he could learn if he wasn't? Realizing he couldn't immediately respond in the affirmative did something to him. He didn't like it. Andrei was all in when it came to Zaria, but he had scars which made him keep himself somewhat apart from others emotionally. In some cases, even those he was closest to only knew him to a certain degree.

"Yeah...I know...That shit is scary." Neal's lips tipped into a rueful half grin.

"Men aren't taught to be vulnerable and introspective. We'll fight and kick the shit out of anyone who even looks like they want to hurt the people we consider ours. But when it comes down to expressing our feelings or being a true leaning post to our partners, we're stuck like a deer in headlights. Unsure of what to do, so we simply stand and stare.

It took me almost losing my wife to realize I had to be more than her physical protector. What I need to know is, can I trust you with my little girl? You don't have to tell me if you have the tools to be the man she needs right this second. If you don't have them, I need to be confident that you'll bust your ass trying to get them. For her."

Andrei was saved from the introspection Neal's words required by the heavy footfalls on the stairs followed by Cisco's reappearance in the doorway. If the way he trudged into the room wasn't a clue, the scowl he wore was a clear indicator. He hadn't found his coveted jersey.

"I thought you were going to get your jersey for Andrei to sign it."

Plopping back into his seat at the center of the sofa, Cisco shook his head. "Nah...I changed my mind. I'll get it another time. He'll be here all week. Right?"

Cisco looked at Andrei with so much hope, he almost smiled. "We plan to leave Friday morning. So, there is time."

"Cool."

Cisco drummed his fingers against his jeans before grabbing the remote from the coffee table style ottoman in front of the couch. His adjustment of the television volume didn't drown out his father's chuckles.

"You ain't right, Pops."

"I didn't say anything."

"You didn't have to."

Andrei watched the interchange with a mixture of amusement and curiosity. He and his father had a decent relationship, but the affection, even in teasing, that the Trumans showed their children was foreign to him.

"Don't be mad at me because your mama shut you down."

Cisco's eyes cut between Andrei and his father. "Come on, Pops. Not in front of company."

All out laughter was his father's response. Andrei didn't join in, but he leaned back against the buttery softness of the leather, enjoying the show.

"Company? Who? Him?" Neal pointed at Andrei and dissolved into laughter again. "You might as well get the stars out of your eyes now, son. He ain't company. Company is folks who aren't gonna be around all the time. His big ass ain't going nowhere."

~

Andrei walked beside Zaria, trying to determine how he'd let her talk him into going inside a bargain discount store. If anything, he could only say that there really were no limits on what he'd do for her. He couldn't recall the last time he'd personally gone inside any retail outlet, let alone one with low, low prices as their major selling point.

Tugging his hand, Zaria pulled him down yet another, far too cluttered, aisle.

"Come this way. Maybe I'll see something over here."

"Svet, why can we not simply look online and have what you want delivered?"

Stopping, she turned to face him. "Because. I want to pick it myself, and make it pretty on my own."

After her Aunt Belinda said she had a theme for dinner on Thursday, Zaria had been on a mission to find something she could contribute. Everyone had an assignment. The only rule was their offering had to be of their own creation. Where Zaria was excited, he just wanted to order an easily assembled item and be done with it. Crafting wasn't high on his list of desirable activities.

"Zaria Marie? Is that you?"

Before the man speaking could move one step closer to Zaria, Yeva stepped into his path.

"What the hell?" The older black man took a step back, looking at Yeva warily before attempting to peer around him to where Zaria and Andrei stood.

Zaria's smile melted, and Andrei watched as her entire demeanor shifted. Gone was the eagerness and excitement from just seconds before.

"Zaria Marie? Are you really gone stand there and let this big white dude keep me from saying hey to my niece? It's like that?"

Sighing, Zaria looked at Andrei. "It's fine. He's my uncle."

Her tone and body language contradicted her words, still Andrei gave Yeva the okay to let him pass. Watching him closely, Andrei assessed the other man's mannerisms. His protective instincts wouldn't allow him to be at ease. The man may very well be related to Zaria, but it was obvious she didn't share the same affection for him that she did for the Trumans.

"Hey there, girl. When I saw you a few minutes ago, I thought my old eyes were playing tricks on me. But, it's really you. You not gone give your uncle a hug? What's it been ten, twelve years?"

"Fifteen." Zaria responded. She made no move to step into the man's embrace.

"Really? It seems like yesterday. You still look the same. Just as pretty as your mama. God rest her soul."

If it were possible, Zaria stiffened even more. Slipping an arm around her waist, Andrei gently pulled until she was tucked in closer to him. He was certain something was off when she allowed him to rest his hand on her belly without tangling their fingers together.

"You not gonna introduce me to your friend?"

Andrei had seen Zaria under a variety of circumstances; however, he'd never seen her behave as she did with the man claiming to be her uncle. Pointing between him and Andrei, she mumbled introductions.

"Andrei, this is Vincent Coleman. Vince, this is Andrei Antonov."

Vincent proffered a hand, but Andrei simply nodded in greeting. Dropping his arm to his side, Vincent released a nervous sounding chuckle.

"Uh. Well, okay. Zaria Marie. I didn't want anything. Just haven't seen or heard from you. So, I wanted to say, hey."

"Hey." Zaria's voice held no trace of affection.

"You know. If you're gonna be in the state for a while. You should drive down and see your daddy."

"Why would I do that?"

Zaria's question was laced with shock and what sounded like anger. Andrei tensed. He didn't give a fuck if Vincent was her relative; he wouldn't stand for him upsetting her.

"He's your daddy, Zaria Marie. And he's proud of you. He's not doing well. I think it would do him some good to see you or hear from you."

"I really don't care if he's not doing well. My mother isn't doing well either. Does he care about her?"

The man dropped his head. His eyes closed briefly before he looked up again. Sadness was his base expression, but Andrei saw the anger banked behind his eyes. It was the anger he watched carefully.

"You still haven't forgiven him."

"Is my mother still dead?" Zaria waited a few beats. When he didn't respond, she gave a jerky nod. "That's what I thought."

Her fingers finally landed on Andrei's as they lay on her stomach. Giving his digits a squeeze, she pulled his gaze from the stranger in front of them to her face.

"I'm ready to go. You're right. We can order something."

Dipping his head in acknowledgment, Andrei released her enough for her to turn away. When Vincent reached out as if to touch her, Andrei grabbed his wrist and stepped between the two of them.

"No. She is done. You may go." Looking toward the other end of the aisle, he motioned, "That way."

"Man. Get your hands off me!" Using one hand, Andrei moved Zaria farther behind him. Releasing Vincent's wrist as he jerked away, Andrei allowed Vincent's momentum to take him backwards.

Catching himself before he fell, Vincent snarled at Andrei.

"Who the fuck are you supposed to be? Think you can just put your hands on me because I want to talk to my niece."

"It does not matter who I am." Andrei stood with his arms hanging at his side. He shook his head at Yeva to stop him from intervening. "What matters is, Zaria no longer wants to speak to you. She is done. You may go now. *That way.*"

Andrei felt Zaria's fingers latch onto the back of his shirt, but he didn't turn to look at her.

"Andrei. Let's just go."

"In a moment, Svet. *Vincent* is leaving first. Correct, Vincent?"

Andrei used every ounce of intimidation his size allowed as he stared daggers at the older man. It took Vincent a moment to realize he'd been surrounded while he was ranting at Andrei. Yeva stood behind him, with Dakota on his left. Andrei was in front of him, with Logan standing to Andrei's right.

Andrei didn't have to look behind him to know Grace was there. The loosening of Zaria's fingers was enough for him to know Grace was moving her away.

"Andrei... Please. Let's just go."

Faintly, he heard Grace speaking to Zaria. Their voices faded to a whisper, and he was certain his woman was a safe distance away.

Andrei stared daggers at Vincent. "I am not fond of repeating myself."

And he didn't. Vincent's situation had finally become clear to him. Mumbling about disrespect and family, he retreated in the direction Andrei indicated. Yeva and Dakota separated to allow him to pass, then Dakota followed him. Andrei noted a few other patrons had stopped to watch the interchange. Surprisingly, no one had pulled out their phones to record the incident.

Once Vincent turned the corner, Andre went to Zaria. Gathering her into his arms, he kissed her forehead and nuzzled the side of her neck.

"Are you okay, Svet?"

"I will be."

With a brisk nod, Andrei led her from the store. By the time they made it back to the rental house, Zaria was a little more herself. She scrolled through online shops until she found what she was looking for; then, she placed an order. When they entered the house, she went straight to the bedroom. Andrei trailed behind her silently.

"Why are you following me?"

Zaria looked over her shoulder as she shrugged off her coat before removing her shoes. Lifting the jacket from her fingers, Andrei draped it across the chair in one corner of the room as he stepped out of his own shoes.

"Am I following you, or are we simply going to the same place?"

"Don't be a smart ass, Andrei."

Snagging her around the waist as she walked toward the bathroom, Andrei guided them to the bed. Sitting, he pulled her between his legs. With one hand cupping the side of her face, he captured her gaze.

"Are you ready to tell me about it?"

Zaria's eyes skittered away from his probing stare. Andrei waited patiently. In a few moments, she returned.

"Vincent is my birth father's twin brother. *Identical* twin brother."

Sliding back farther onto the bed, Andrei arranged Zaria on his lap. She tucked her head beneath his chin and the words began to tumble out.

"You already know Aunt Belinda and Uncle Neal raised me from when I was really small. My mother is her younger sister by five years. She was barely eighteen when I was born. So, I was with my aunt and uncle a lot. Even though they were newly married, and really young themselves.

From all that I recall and what I've heard over the years, Stacey, my birth mother, was fool crazy in love with Lawrence. Supposedly, the same was true about him. Except he had a jealous streak, and he thought every man who looked Stacey's way was trying to steal her from him. It led to a lot of arguments, breakups and makeups in a toxic cycle. That is until Lawrence couldn't be convinced she wasn't cheating on him. So, he made sure she could never leave him for another man. He ended her life."

Zaria sniffled and burrowed closer to him. "While I watched from across the room."

Andrei's arms tightened as he held Zaria to his chest. He'd known things weren't good, but he had no idea she'd witnessed her mother's murder. Hearing the details, and how she'd observed her father's jealous, controlling behavior, Andrei now understood why she was so adamant about him pushing her boundaries. Or her response to his own bouts of jealousy.

Fuck. He wanted to kick his own ass. Then, he wanted to drive to the prison where Lawrence was housed and punish him for the unspeakable trauma his Svet endured. Andrei's own history was rough. That being said, at least he hadn't been present when his parents were taken from him. His father had given his life trying to protect his mother. He couldn't imagine how he'd feel if his father had been the one to snuff out his mother's light.

Chapter Twenty-One

I THINK THE FUCK NOT

Zaria had known the day would come when she had to confide in Andrei about the darkest part of her childhood, but she hadn't expected it to be today. She hadn't even considered she'd run into anyone from Lawrence's family. The last she heard, they still lived in Rankin County and the Jackson area.

Seeing Vincent, knowing that it was likely how Lawrence would look if he hadn't spent the last thirty plus years in the state penitentiary, was a shock to Zaria's system. Lawrence probably would've been out in twenty-five, but he had additional charges added on when the police searched the house and property when he was arrested.

Cuddled against Andrei, she allowed his comfort to be a balm to her spirit as she navigated the feelings her four-year-old self couldn't process. Knowing she was the one who made the emergency call which brought the police to their home was a lot for a small child to handle. Testifying in the judge's chambers two years later was no easier.

Following her revelation, Andrei didn't offer empty words. Although she was certain he had questions, he didn't press. He just held her. It allowed her to draw on his strength and comfort. It was what she needed. If he'd pressed or said one word, she would've bawled—until her ducts could no longer produce tears.

After a long stretch of silence, Andrei finally asked one of the questions she was sure weighed on his mind.

"Is it always like that? When you see one of your father's relatives?"

Idly tracing circles on his shirt, Zaria nodded. "Unfortunately, yes. Catholics don't have shit on Black Christians when it comes to religious guilt. Them preaching forgiveness to me and saying how I shouldn't turn my back on my only living parent, is why I had to completely remove myself from them.

It wasn't always that way. Initially, my aunt and uncle would let me visit with certain family members. The visits came to an end after my grandmother took me to the prison to visit Lawrence. I wasn't allowed to go back.

In my early twenties I tried to reconnect—which was when I last saw Vincent. I'd somehow convinced myself I could be a part of the family, but they couldn't get past me not wanting to mend my relationship with Lawrence. Nor would I recant my testimony to help in his appeals."

Zaria twisted her lips as she said his name. She never called him dad, daddy, pops or anything other than his name. He'd never been that person for her. Not in her few memories from her early years, nor in those which followed.

"So, I haven't seen or spoken to anyone from Lawrence's family for more than a decade. And I'm okay with that."

Andrei's stubble tickled her skin as he placed a kiss on her forehead. It conveyed his sympathy for the situation and his support of her decision. He didn't have to say it. She felt it.

"Hey. You up?"

Zaria knocked on her cousin's bedroom door, bouncing from foot to foot. She'd finally gotten all the tea from Aunt Belinda and she wanted to dish with Dominique. Aunt Maryann had interrupted the previous day, so they had to cut their talk short.

The door swung open, revealing a clean-faced Dominique wearing baggy sweats with an elastic attempting to contain her riotous curls.

Undeterred by Dom's mildly grumpy expression, Zaria entered the room and motioned for her cousin to close the door behind her.

"Girl!" She whisper-screamed. "Did Auntie tell you about Auntie Em and her new man?"

Dominique lifted one perfectly arched eyebrow and pursed her lips. "You know mama's mouth can't hold water when she's talking to one of us."

Picking up a discarded fuzzy sock, Zaria swatted at Dominique. "You knew, and you didn't tell me?! I came looking for you the first chance I could when I found out."

"I've been a little busy, Zee." Dominique dodged the sock, then snatched it from Zaria's hand, holding it aloft out of her reach when she tried to take it back.

Giving up, Zaria stalked to the bench seat at the foot of the bed. Sitting, she crossed her arms over her middle, grumbling about tall people using their height against her. It was rude.

Dominique chuckled as she joined Zaria. A wide grin displayed straight white teeth. Straightened courtesy of three years of braces and a permanent retainer. Zaria returned the smile at the memory of her offering Dom comfort following teasing about the braces. Zaria had endured the same thing when she'd worn them in high school. She taught her younger cousin how to effectively shut that shit down.

"Mama is all in a tizzy about Auntie Em not telling her in advance she was bringing her boyfriend. She knows how Mama is about unmarried folks sharing a bedroom."

"Auntie is gonna have to get over that one. Auntie Em is fifty-five. I know she's her baby sister, but she's long past grown. Besides, after she dropped that dead weight, Auntie Em deserves to spread her wings a little."

"Yeah…I think it's only messing with Mama because her man, Tim, just turned forty. She kept hissing, *'She's old enough to be his mama!'*"

"I know right?!"

They giggled. Dominique's shoulders shook, and she bumped into Zaria lightly.

"Technically, it's true, but only if Auntie Em was a teen mother. Which she wasn't. He's still more than a decade older than all of her kids.

Auntie should just let it go. It could be so much worse. She could be dating one of her son's college friends."

Dominique's jaw dropped. "No, ma'am! Do not put that out into the universe. Mama would flip completely out. You should've seen her face when Aunt Maryann started talking about the way *those lil boys* keep sliding into her DMs on social media."

"Auntie Em ***is*** fine, though. She could pull a young dude if she wanted. She might not mind the smell of breast milk."

Dominique pointed at Zaria with a barely suppressed smile. "You stop it."

Sitting sideways on the bench, Zaria propped her elbow on the bed and rested her head on her fist. "What do you think bothers Auntie more? That they aren't married or he used to be one of her students? She gave both equal weight when she was telling me about it."

"What? He was one of her students?" Dom's jaw dropped in shock and she pushed Zaria's shoulder.

"You said she told you everything" Zaria returned the playful shove.

"She didn't tell me that!"

"Yep. It's not as scandalous as she makes it sound. It was ten years ago, and he was in the master's program, taking her class as an elective. It's not like he was a teenager and she was his thesis advisor or anything."

"Yeah... but you know how Mama is about the teacher-student dividing line."

"Mhmm. Anyway. We didn't get to talk yesterday. Catch me up on this series you're thinking about doing in Atlanta."

The two spent some time catching up on life and laughing. Occasionally, Zaria felt the pull of the secret she was keeping from her family, but she didn't yield to the pressure. She knew they'd be ecstatic.

Neither she nor Dominique had been in a relationship serious enough for children to be a consideration before now. Dominique still wasn't. She was focusing on building her career. Zaria had been doing the same—until she climbed that big Russian. Now...

Knocking on the door interrupted their session. Cisco walked in while still tapping on the door with one hand over his eyes.

"Are you decent?"

"If you'd waited until you were actually invited inside, you wouldn't have to ask." Dominique quipped. "What do you want, Cisco?"

"Have you seen Zee? Mama said she came up here. She's not in her room."

"I'm right here. And take your hand off of your eyes."

Dropping his hand, Cisco's face split in a broad smile. Zaria immediately began shaking her head.

"No."

"Come on, Zee. I haven't actually said anything."

"I don't care. I know that look and the answer is no."

Fully entering the room, Cisco dropped into a crouch beside Zaria with his hands folded together under his chin.

"Please, Zee. I promise it won't take long. I just need you to look over this contract real quick."

"Number one, I'm on vacation. Number two, what happened to your lawyer? He was highly recommended."

"I know it's vacation, and me and Winstead couldn't see eye to eye. So, I let him go."

"Excuse me?" Zaria sat up straighter. "What do you mean you couldn't see eye to eye? About what?"

"I have some agents who want to sign me. Of course, I can't officially do anything until after the season is over, but they sent contracts to Winstead. When we talked, he was trying to get me to commit to signing with someone associated with his firm. I didn't get a good vibe from the guy, so I talked it over with Pops and Ma, and they agreed with me. After that, Winstead was taking longer to get back to me.

Coach had people reaching out to him again because they weren't hearing back from my representation. It was like he was salty that I didn't want to go with the person he handpicked. I also got the feeling he didn't think I was very bright."

"Idiot obviously doesn't like money." Zaria shifted, pulling her phone from her pocket. "Fine. I'll make some calls. Check with some other people to see if they recommend someone who might be a better fit."

Covering the phone display with his larger hand, Cisco stopped Zaria's flying fingers. "Before you interrupt someone's holiday break. Can you just look at the contract? I can get another lawyer, but in the meantime, I need to respond to some of these agents."

Zaria narrowed her eyes as Cisco tilted his head and went full puppy-dog stare on her. *Ooo! He got on her nerves!* After a full minute of the stand-off, Zaria caved. Not wasting a second, Cisco bolted from the room to get the paperwork.

Thirty minutes later, Zaria was seated on the sofa in her uncle's office with a highlighter, an ink pen and a copy of a contract from an agent representing a large, well-known sports agency. Lips pursed, she circled one section of the contract, shaking her head.

"I think the fuck not." She muttered to the unseen author of the agreement. No one was around to hear her ranting. Andrei was working back at the rental house so he could be free for the Guy's Night her uncle planned for the men. The rest of the family was spread out in different parts of the house. Other than to bring her a bottle of water and a snack, her aunt left her alone.

For the most part, the contract was standard, however there was a section that concerned Zaria. Cisco wasn't officially her client. If he were, she'd advise him against signing without some modifications. When Cisco poked his head into the office, she told him as much. She then repeated it to her aunt and uncle when they gathered at the conference table in her uncle's office to discuss it.

"Zee-baby. I know you aren't Cisco's lawyer, but could you just speak for him on this?"

"Uncle Neal..." Zaria hesitated. The agency was out of California and she *was* a member of the California bar. So, briefly representing him wasn't an issue as far as her eligibility was concerned.

"Fine. This one time."

Her aunt squealed, Cisco whooped and her uncle squeezed her fingers.

"Don't get too excited. This is temporary." Looking at them pointedly, she spoke clearly. "I'll sit in on one meeting. Then, we'll find you a Sports and Entertainment attorney who will *really* act in your best interest."

"Thank you, Zee-Zee." Cisco beamed.

"Don't thank me yet. Also, you're gonna pay me. I have staff to support and they don't work for free."

"Don't worry Zee-Baby. You send the bill and we'll cover it." Her uncle assured her.

"I'll send the agent a formal response and set up a video call. After that, I'm not doing another piece of work on vacation."

"Yes, ma'am." Cisco quipped, earning himself side eye and a smirk from Zaria.

While she'd brought her laptop on the trip, she'd left it at the other house. So, after trying to start the process using only her phone, Zaria gave up and gathered the documents into a large envelope to take with her. Then, she went to let her aunt know she was leaving for a little while.

As was often the case around the holidays, her aunt was hanging out in the kitchen. To Zaria's surprise, Logan was with her. Zaria entered the room to see him leaning against the island, eating a petit four while Aunt Belinda looked on with a wide smile.

When he noticed her, he stood up straighter and hastily gulped the sweet treat.

"Ma'am. Do you need to go somewhere?" Logan's eyes pinged between the purse on Zaria's shoulder, to the package she held to her chest.

Giving him a lopsided smirk, Zaria waved a hand. "Logan, I've told you there's no need to be so formal. But, yes. I need to go back to the house for a little while."

Nodding briskly, Logan thanked her aunt for the snack, only to be presented with a to-go box and instructions to share with others. Zaria just shook her head and gestured for him to take the box. Aunt Belinda couldn't be stopped when she was determined to feed people. As soon as her security team decided on rotating coverage inside and outside, it was only a matter of time before they ended up being fed.

From the way Grace's eyes lit up when she saw the box in Logan's hands, she'd visited Aunt Belinda's kitchen as well. Climbing into the back seat, Zaria chuckled to herself.

Once they reached their destination, Zaria immediately went to the bedroom to grab her laptop. She'd been back long enough to find the appropriate form and send the correspondence to the agent to set up the meeting when Andrei stuck his head in the door. She was sitting in the window seat in front of the bay window. A wrinkle appeared between his brows as he walked into the room.

"I thought you were spending the day at your aunt and uncle's house."

Lifting her face to his for the quick peck he planted on her lips, Zaria grinned wryly. "I was. I just have to do this one thing for Cisco; then the laptop is being packed back up for the rest of the trip."

With his hands beneath her calves, Andrei scooped her legs up, draping them across his lap. Correctly reading into what she didn't say, Andrei's brow dipped. "What happened to Winstead? Is he refusing to work with Cisco?"

Rotating her finger between them, Zaria shook her head. "Flip that around. Cisco fired him."

"Fired him? Your cousin fired an attorney from Halsted, Markham and Blake?"

Zaria nodded. When Andrei recommended them, he'd given Zaria a portfolio with background information as well as client testimonials from the firm. Those testimonials and Andrei's recommendation were the reason she presented the firm to her family to begin with.

"Cisco said Winstead started being slow to respond to him among other things once he rejected the agent Winstead recommended."

More darkness fell over Andrei's features. Zaria closed the lid on her laptop and set it to one side. She was done with it anyway. Placing her hands on top of his, she stroked the backs.

"Hey, it's nothing for you to deal with. We'll work it out. I'm going to represent him temporarily for this one contract negotiation. Afterwards, we'll find him someone else."

Andrei's normally stoic expression didn't hide the thoughts Zaria was certain were running through his mind. He was a calculating person who didn't make a move without considering all angles. Which meant he was trying to figure out where he'd misjudged when he recommended the firm.

"Hey... This isn't on you."

"Still, I will make a call."

"Andrei, that's not necessary."

"No, Svet. It is."

"It's really not."

Andrei's eyes hardened, drawing a slight gasp from Zaria. "I will not argue about this, Svet. The books say stress is not good for you and the baby."

The set of his jaw and the unyielding expression on his face made Zaria's counter statement die in her throat. It wouldn't do any good. His mind was made up. Besides, it was kind of sweet that he was reading books on what to expect during pregnancy. Knowing arguing was a lost cause, Zaria decided to shift gears.

"Are you all done for the day, or do you have more to do?"

In understanding of her tactic, Andrei allowed her to guide the conversation in a different direction. Flipping his hands beneath hers, he squeezed her fingers before releasing them. Transferring his attention to her feet, he began massaging them one at a time. The almost perfect amount of pressure he used, drew an involuntary moan from Zaria's lips.

She watched as the storm clouds in his eyes receded and were replaced with a different emotion. It hadn't been her intention, but he started something when he pressed his thumb at the top of her arch just below the ball of her foot. Zaria could almost guarantee one of his books told him massaging there would aid in digestion or something involving helping her grow a human.

The unintended side effect was a zing to her core and a flood of warmth to her folds. Although she wasn't in the stage of pregnancy to expect an increase in her libido, her lady bits didn't get the memo. Either that, or Andrei had a special magic all of his own, causing her body to respond despite the tiredness that made its appearance. It's as if the symptoms of pregnancy were just lying in wait to descend on her when Dr. Kent gave her the test results.

While she had been fortunate to not have the sensitivity to smell and nausea—at least not yet—she'd needed more naps than usual in the past week. The bouts of tiredness were contrasted by energy bursts at various times of day. Those energy bursts had typically involved Andrei and his sex magic. She was now convinced he was a pussy genie.

Beneath her leg, she felt his cock thicken in response to the moans she couldn't control. With each caress of her feet, more throaty appreciation tumbled from her lips. Mentally, she added another thing to the list of ways Andrei had discovered to kick start her desire.

Zaria was momentarily weightless before her back made contact with the duvet cover. A portion of Andrei's bulk pressed against her as his lips connected with the hollow of her neck.

"What time does this, boy's night, typically begin, Svet?"

"Umm..." Zaria struggled to form coherent thoughts as he kissed a path to her ear. The scruff of his beard sent tingles skating across her skin, leaving goosebumps in their wake.

"Time, Svet."

"Umm..." Zaria tried. She really did, but she couldn't make sentences. Not with his fingers joining his lips in driving her into an erotic fog. Her tights were discarded along with her underwear.

Andrei's deep chuckle vibrated against her inner thigh. Warm puffs of air grazed her exposed mons before his lips made contact.

"It is okay, Svet. We will get there when we get there."

Zaria's thoughts scattered to the wind as Andrei latched onto the little bundle of nerves and he proceeded to toss her into her first orgasm.

Chapter Twenty-Two

WHO'S NEXT?

There were two additional cars parked in the circular driveway when they returned to the Truman home later that evening. After Andrei de-stressed his Svet, they took a short nap. Well, Zaria napped while he held her as he considered the best way to get to the bottom of the issues Cisco had with Winstead.

Sure, his woman had asked him to let her handle it, but he'd offered a solution to keep her from having to worry and she ended up worrying anyway. Andrei didn't like it. He'd have to maneuver the situation carefully. Because of Cisco's draft potential and Andrei being a team owner, he had to tread lightly to keep from affecting Cisco's eligibility. He also wanted to make certain he couldn't be fined for inappropriate contact.

Although, since he had a plausible reason due to family relationship, Andrei didn't see a potential issue. He just had to make certain Cisco understood that he couldn't tell anyone Andrei was involved in any way with his decisions surrounding his representation. If they were officially family, it wouldn't be a problem. But they weren't.

When he and Zaria entered the house, the atmosphere was more boisterous than in the previous days. Laughter filtered down the hallway into the foyer. After helping Zaria with her jacket, Andrei hung it on an available hook on the wall and followed her into the family room. There were four new faces—the likely owners of the extra vehicles in the driveway.

"Hey Zee!" A tall, slender woman called out as she came across the room with her arms spread wide.

"Hey Carmen! It's good to see you. Auntie said she didn't think you'd be able to get off work today and tomorrow."

Making a fist, Carmen released an obviously fake cough. "I'm sick. I couldn't make it." A few additional fake coughs were hidden behind her hand before the two dissolved into giggles.

"You're a mess!"

"Listen, you know I don't believe in letting no job steal my joy and my good time."

"Do you, girl."

Zaria's fingers laced with Andrei's as she pulled him into the conversation.

"Carmen, this is Andrei. Andrei, my cousin Carmen."

Andrei had to quickly adjust to the way the women in Zaria's family assessed him before and after introductions. He realized they weren't flirting; they simply had no issues letting someone know they were attractive. It explained parts of Zaria's personality and why she was so bold as to say what she did the first night they were together.

"Nice to meet you." Andrei nodded before extending his hand to Carmen, shaking hers briefly.

The introductions continued with the other occupants of the room before he and Zaria made their way into the kitchen where her aunt was holding court. Court is what Andrei called it in his mind. Belinda Truman was, without a doubt, the queen of her household. Andrei wondered how boy's night was supposed to work with the current co-ed situation in the house.

"Hey! You're back!"

Wiping her hands, Zaria's Aunt Belinda gave them both hugs as if she hadn't just seen them earlier. Andrei had been introduced to her Aunt Maryann and her partner earlier in the week. Maryann was currently perched on a stool at the kitchen island. Wiggling her fingers, she smiled at them.

"Hey you two. You're just in time. Neal was about to gather the rest of the guys and head to the basement."

Andrei noticed Zaria slipping an apron over her head and lifted a brow. This was new. In the time they'd been together, he'd done the majority of the cooking. His choice. However, seeing his Svet don an apron had a surprising effect on him. He'd never demand she conform, but he liked seeing the different facets of her being revealed during their visit.

Turning to him, she tapped his chest. Tilting his head in question, his eyes probed hers.

"I'll see you later. You should probably head to the basement before Uncle Neal comes looking for you."

"She's right."

Wiggling her fingers again, Maryann made a shooing motion. Andrei simply stared at her. Zaria's family had damn good genes. The women sported the same prominent cheekbones and lush frames. Even the ones who were slim were still generously curved.

Not moving from where he stood next to Zaria, Andrei's gaze roamed around the kitchen. Ingredients and foods in various stages of prep were on one section of the counter. There was only one pot on the stove, but the steam coming from the top carried a savory aroma with it.

The smell triggered grumbling in his stomach. They hadn't eaten earlier since Zaria assured him there would be plenty. From what he'd seen already, she was correct. His interest was piqued since his only experience with southern cuisine was at restaurants.

Zaria rubbed his chest, drawing his attention from the aromatic smorgasbord. Tipping her head toward the door, she reminded him that he was supposed to be leaving to join the men.

"If you don't want an apron and a pair of gloves before I put you to work, I suggest you hightail it on out of here." Her Aunt Belinda said as she smirked at him.

"Don't tempt him, Auntie. He likes to cook."

"He does?" The increased interest in Maryann's voice was noticeable.

"Yes. Andrei cooks for me all the time. He's great at it."

The pride filling his chest at Zaria's praise, caught Andrei off guard. He cooked for her because he enjoyed caring for her, but hearing her appreciate him in front of her family sent an unexpected rush of warmth through his chest.

"There he is." Neal's voice boomed in the kitchen. "The kids said Zee and her big boyfriend were here."

Andrei nodded at the other man's candor. It took him a moment to realize the kids being referenced were the adults Zaria introduced to him earlier. There wasn't anyone in the room under the age of twenty-one. He guessed to Neal, anyone less than forty years old was a kid.

Gesturing toward the door, Neal turned to leave. "Come on. The rest of the guys are already downstairs. Everything's all set up."

Andrei looked at Zaria, who returned his gaze with a slight smile. "Don't look at me. I'm all set here with the ladies." Lifting a shoulder, she looked from him to the doorway where her uncle stood.

Uncaring of the eyes chronicling their every move, Andrei pulled Zaria close, dropping a kiss onto her upturned lips.

"Do not overdo it. I will see you later, Svet."

Too quickly for her to thwart his efforts, he pressed a hand to her stomach, then released her.

"Lawd. You'd think y'all are going to be separated for days."

"Hush, Neal. You should take notes. My sister might not be so interested in what other folks are doing if you gave her something else to think about."

"Mind your business, Maryann." Belinda said in a warning tone.

"That's what I keep telling you, ma'am." Maryann quipped.

Andrei hid his smirk at their banter and made a quick exit behind Neal. As they walked out, three women walked in their direction, including Grace. He didn't say anything because he had no doubt she'd been ordered into the house by one of the elder Trumans.

When they were in Las Vegas, the team didn't constantly stay outdoors, but they tended to rotate outdoor duty when he traveled. However, the Trumans found it inhospitable for their security detail to remain outside—especially in the colder weather. Andrei didn't bother to tell them the mild temperatures they were experiencing weren't his definition of cold.

Glancing at Logan standing at the top of the stairs, Andrei assumed he'd find either Yeva or Dakota at the bottom. Walking past Yeva, they entered the basement. The television was set to a sports network channel while music pumped from speakers hidden around the room.

Toward the back, there was a pool table. A few men were standing around it with cues in their hands, while the rest were scattered on the sectional or at the bar. Between the pool table and the bar was a round gaming style table. Having studied casinos closely before going into the business, he recognized it.

It was a Spades table. They weren't seen often, since poker was more popular in casinos for betting reasons, but he was certain. Even if he'd had doubt, an emblem featuring the word as part of an ornate logo was at the center. An unopened deck of cards rested next to the logo atop the gleaming surface.

Neal's hand landed on Andrei's shoulder, drawing his eyes away from the gaming table.

"Antonov, I kinda like you. So, I'm gonna give you some advice. Stay away from that table. Come on over to the bar and I'll get you a drink. You have to fix your own plate, though. No women are allowed down here. You'll have to fend for yourself."

Ignoring Neal's dig about not being catered to, Andrei looked at the table again.

"Why would I avoid this table?"

"That there is for hard core Spades players. This is your first visit south. You don't have to do everything at once. Ease into it. Go on and get some food. I'll hook you up with a drink and we can kick back and relax."

Andrei squared his shoulders as he followed Neal to the food laid out on the bar. He was offended at the suggestion he should be afraid of a simple card game.

"I will accept the food and drink; however, you do not have to protect me from a card game."

"Oh yeah?" Neal stepped behind the bar and grabbed a glass from the shelf behind him. "Whatchu know about spades?"

"I have played before."

"Playing before and knowing how to play aren't the same thing." Neal waved a hand dismissively. "Don't worry about it. There's no rule saying you have to play. We won't hold it against you."

Andrei frowned at the implication while Neal moved on to the next item on his agenda. Drinks. Neal picked up an ice scoop from the bin beneath the counter.

"What are you drinking?"

"Vodka is fine. No ice."

No matter how many years he'd been in America, Andrei still preferred his drinks without ice. He'd accept chilled, but didn't want frozen water floating around in his alcohol diluting it.

"Coming right up."

Neal put the scoop back into the ice bin and selected a bottle of Belvedere from the upper shelf behind him. It wasn't Andrei's favorite, but it would work. With his drink in one hand, Andrei browsed the food selection.

He'd just finished loading a plate with delicious looking fare when Tim approached him. Nodding, Andrei kept his expression neutral. Zaria had told him how her Aunt Belinda was in a tizzy, as she called it, about Maryann bringing Tim without notice. Andrei listened to her thoughts on the situation without comment.

Tim greeted Andrei with a smile, relief obvious in his expression. When Maryann introduced them earlier, they hadn't spent any significant time talking. Andrei reserved a few hours each day to working. So, when he was at the Trumans with Zaria, there wasn't much one on one with any particular person. However, Andrei guessed Tim was happy to see another non-family member / significant other in the room. His demeanor made Andrei wonder if he was having a hard time meeting the family.

Andrei didn't spend much time speculating. Although her family never hinted race was an issue with them, at least Tim didn't have that concern. With his deep brown skin and close cropped, coarse hair, he visually fit in perfectly. Andrei's paler skin would definitely stand out in the family photos.

The other man must have taken Andrei's nod as encouragement because he glued himself to Andrei's side. Sitting next to him at the end of the bar, he commented intermittently about the game on the television or the one between the guys at the pool table. Occasionally, loud banter would break out among the pool players or there would be a shout from the sofa in front of the television.

When Brad, another of Zaria's cousins, moved toward the uninhabited Spades table, Tim sat up straighter at Andrei's side.

"Are we going to get a game going or what?" Brad looked around the room in expectation.

"Where's your partner?" Neal approached with a frosted beer mug in hand one.

"Are you putting me down, Unc? We've been partners for almost two years now." Brad turned a shocked expression on Neal.

"I didn't say all that. Just testing."

The exchange between Brad and Neal garnered attention. Cisco and a couple of the others came closer to the table. Grabbing the deck from the center, Neal opened it, removed the instructional pieces, then dumped the cards in the center, mixing them up.

"Who's playing?" He looked around at the men assembled. More than four hands went up. One of which was Tim's.

"Pick a card. Top two cards get first down." Neal instructed those who indicated they wanted to play.

Tim joined the others in selecting a card, then he stepped back. When Neal flipped his card over and placed it face down on the table, the others followed suit. Brad and Tim won with an Ace and a Queen, respectively.

The person with the third highest card called next down and Neal gathered the cards back into a neat deck.

"Who's your partner, Tim?"

Content to watch, Andrei pushed his empty plate away and picked up his drink. He wasn't prepared for Tim to point in his direction. Andrei almost looked over his shoulder, but he knew no one was behind him.

"You play, man?" Hope was painted across Tim's features.

With a curt nod, Andrei stood and approached the nearest empty seat. Quickly taking the one opposite him, Tim grinned broadly.

"Are you sure you wanna do this?" Brad asked, looking between Tim and Andrei.

"What? You think because he's white he can't play?"

Putting his hands up, Brad vigorously shook his head. "I didn't say that."

Tim looked at Andrei for a moment. "You play right?"

Andrei nodded, repeating what he'd said earlier to Neal. "I have played before."

Brad grinned broadly. "Alright. Since we don't have all day, we're playing best three out of five. A Boston is an automatic round win. Losers rise and fly."

Neal leaned forward on his forearms. "Do you need me to explain any of that, Antonov?"

"No. However, I do have questions."

"Oh Lord." Brad sat back in his seat. His body was limp, as if he was already exhausted.

"Don't mind him." Neal turned the cards face up and spread them out on the tabletop. Then, he gestured for Andrei to continue.

"How are we playing? Joker's high or are we using the deuces? If the deuces are in play, which one do you consider the higher of the two? Also, which do you consider the big joker, the one with the color or without?"

Neal's fingers faltered and hovered over the cards in front of him. Staring at Andrei, he said nothing for a full minute.

"I thought you said you didn't know how to play."

"No. I said I have played before. *You* said playing before and knowing how to play were not the same."

Andrei shrugged. Tim's face split into a wide smile. Extending his fist high across the table, he beamed at Andrei. "Give me some. I knew I made the right choice."

Bumping Tim's fist, Andrei looked at Neal, waiting for his response. Mumbling about smartasses and card sharks, Neal finally laid out the rules of play.

In many cases, it would be a safe bet that someone who looked like Andrei wouldn't know about the card game, but Andrei had made it a point to learn the rules and variations of every card game available. Back in the early days of their friendship, Denzel actually taught him to play spades. This was before Andrei purchased his first stake in a casino and long before he opened Anton's. It was a well-kept secret that there was a high stakes spades tournament running concurrently with poker tournaments held at Anton's. It was invitation only and the buy in started at six figures. It never ceased to amaze Andrei what people with money would pay to play a game.

After Neal took out the appropriate cards, the game began. Andrei and Tim lost the first two hands. While Brad and Neal crowed, Andrei and Tim remained silent. When Tim and Andrei evened the score, the grumbling started. Once they won the third straight, the comments were just shy of accusing them of cheating.

Andrei cut Brad a sideways glance. "Did you just call me a cheater?"

Quiet descended on the room. Even the guys at the pool table stopped talking. Andrei's voice was low and filled with gravel. A little of his accent bled through, making the sentence sound ominous. As if Brad answering in the affirmative could result in bodily harm. Andrei watched Brad's mental calculations as he determined how to respond.

They'd met less than an hour prior, so neither man knew what to expect from the other. While Neal and Brad had joked and bantered throughout the game, Tim and Andrei said very little.

Brad spread his fingers out on the tabletop and released a slow breath. "Nah, man. Nobody said you cheated. It's one of those things that goes with playing cards. We talk shit when we win. We talk shit when we lose."

Bobbing his head, Andrei looked at Tim with a twinkle in his eye before returning to Brad. "Oh. So, you were just being a little bitch about getting your ass whipped by a white boy and a desk jockey. I understand."

One side of Andrei's lips ticked up in a half smile when Brad's jaw dropped. Neal's chuckles joined the others as it became obvious Andrei wasn't seriously angry—only giving Brad shit for being a sore loser. The teasing increased when Andrei flicked his fingers at Brad and Neal, reminding them they'd lost, so they needed to vacate the seats.

"Who's next?"

Tim's question was as loud and bright as the smile he wore. Leaning over, he initiated another fist bump with Andrei. Tapping Tim's knuckles with his own, Andrei gathered the cards in preparation for the next game.

Chapter Twenty-Three

WHAT DID I SAY?

Zaria's eyes were glued to Andrei's back as he left the room behind her uncle. The big sneak had managed a belly rub before bolting. There was no way at least one of her aunts didn't notice. Honestly, everyone within the vicinity probably saw it. Ending her silent plotting to exact revenge, she went to the sink to wash her hands.

"Where do you want me, Auntie?"

Her Aunt Belinda opened, then snapped her lips closed. Her eyes darted to the others filing into the kitchen. Dominique was behind Carmen and Uncle Neal's youngest sister, Deirdre. Had Carmen and Deirdre not been there, Zaria was certain she would've heard an earful. Her aunt's pointed look carried the same effect as her speaking the words. She'd definitely put the pieces together.

Aunt Belinda's single raised eyebrow was enough. Zaria nodded in understanding. They'd have a talk in private. Honestly, Zaria was surprised it had taken her aunt this long. Belinda Truman's perceptive skills were off the charts. Zaria was thankful there weren't as many people as usual.

The gathering was scaled back more this year. She'd been informed in advance it would be smaller. Although the amount of food prep had been the same. The number of people invited had dwindled each year after

Dom's career really took off. Now, those in attendance were trusted to not bring strangers into the mix who wouldn't respect their family's privacy.

That was probably the other reason surrounding Aunt Belinda being bothered by Auntie Em not informing them in advance about bringing her new man. Tim seemed to be an okay guy, which took some of the sting away from no one knowing he was coming.

Waving her arm toward the ingredients laid out on one countertop, Zaria's aunt pointed her in that direction.

"I have all the stuff for you to mix up the dressing. When you're done, it can go in the fridge overnight and I'll put it in the oven in the morning. The turkey is already prepped for your uncle to fry. Everything else is done —including the desserts. The rest of this is just little things for us to munch on."

Sliding in front of the sink, when Zaria moved away, Dominique washed her hands. "I'm wondering why daddy and the other men haven't caught on yet."

"Caught on to what?" Carmen asked, popping a cocktail sausage into her mouth.

Dominique giggled. "This whole *boys' night* before Thanksgiving Day started as a way to keep the men and children busy and out of the way while the cooking was happening. Now that Mama preps in advance, there isn't very much going on the night before anymore. But, they still have their boys' night like clockwork."

"And we have our girls' night without them all up in our conversation." Adding to Dominique's explanation, Aunt Belinda opened the freezer section of the refrigerator and pulled out her special pre-mixed frozen daiquiri pouches.

Zaria's mouth watered and she groaned internally. Her aunt made *the best* daiquiris. She somehow managed to maintain the fruity flavor while using an obscene amount of alcohol. Anyone partaking was guaranteed to stay the night at the Trumans because they'd be too inebriated to drive themselves home.

Squeals of approval went up among the women as they made their selections. Zaria smiled and busied herself assembling the ingredients for her grandmother's cornbread dressing. The onions and celery were already chopped and sauteed. The roasted chicken was deboned and ready to go in as well.

Pulling on a pair of food safe gloves, Zaria plunged her fingers into the cornbread crumbles, breaking them into smaller pieces. Grabbing the opened container of chicken stock, she poured the contents over the bread. There were easier ways, but this was how her Grandma Lou taught her.

Dom bumped Zaria's shoulder. In her hand, she held the open container tipped so Zaria could see the remaining pouches inside. Smiling at her cousin, Zaria shook her head.

"No thanks. My hands are little full right now." Holding up her gloved digits, Zaria wiggled them before plunging them back into the pan.

"Since when has that stopped you?" Carmen quipped around the straw in her own pouch of holiday juice.

"Right?" Dom piled on. "You're normally halfway through with one before the rest of us even decide what we want."

"Well, this time I'm going to finish my assignment first. If you don't mind."

And pray there aren't any left by the time I get done. Zaria said to herself. She'd forgotten about that little part of their routine. Until now, gracefully avoiding alcohol hadn't been an issue. She and Andrei had eaten dinner together at the rental house. Her aunt and uncle didn't believe in drinking before five p.m.—outside of tropical island vacations. So, there wasn't a need to decline adult beverages during breakfast and lunch.

"Mmhmm..." Zaria looked over one shoulder at her Aunt Maryann.

"Mm-hmm, what Auntie Em?"

"Just Mmhmm." Her aunt responded with wide eyes. Slowly, she brought her own straw to her lips and took a deep draw from the fruity concoction.

Zaria lifted one eyebrow, then resumed her task, hoping no one latched on to what her aunt was putting down.

A frosted pouch landed on the countertop to her right. Zaria looked up into Dominique's smiling face.

"I know the kiwi-strawberry is your favorite. I'll just sit this here for when you're ready."

"Thanks, Dom." On the outside, Zaria was polite and appreciative.

On the inside, she was cursing her cousin for being her normal, thoughtful self. Who asked her to be so considerate? *Not me.*

Zaria fumed internally, then shook her head at herself. How could she be irritated with Dom for being nice? It wasn't like her cousin knew she was tempting a pregnant woman to consume alcohol.

"You're welcome!" Dominique responded brightly. "How can I help? That way we can speed up this process, since there's not any cooking happening tonight."

"You can cut the chicken into smaller pieces and drop it in."

"Cool."

The two worked side by side until they reached the point in the process requiring the addition of the final seasonings—which Zaria took care of. Dominique knew the basics of the recipe, but she hadn't graduated to that step in the process yet.

By the time they were finished, the others had moved from the kitchen island to the table. The finger foods had long since been relocated there, and the ladies followed the snacks.

"Zee, let Dom put that in the refrigerator. I forgot to clean off a low shelf. Only the higher one is available."

"Auntie, I'm not a member of the Lollipop Guild. I'm certain I can reach the shelf."

"What did I say?" Her aunt's tone catapulted Zaria to her youth in a flash. Those four words were dreaded in their household. If her aunt had to repeat herself, the results were seldom good.

"Yes, ma'am." Zaria secured the cover on top of the aluminum pan and walked to the refrigerator to hold the door open for Dominique.

Once everything was put away and the countertop cleaned, Zaria went back to the fridge. Grabbing a bottle of water, she let the door glide closed as she twisted off the cap. An involuntary sigh of appreciation escaped as she quenched her thirst.

"Do you two want to be alone?" Dom joked.

Opening eyes she hadn't realized were closed, Zaria looked at her cousin. Twisting her lips in a crooked smile, she shrugged.

"Whatever, Dom." Grabbing a paper towel, Zaria wiped condensation from the bottle as she went to the table to join the rest of the group.

"Zee, you forgot your kiwi-strawberry."

"That's okay. I'm good with this water. I didn't realize how thirsty I was."

Zaria snagged a piece of cheese from a nearby tray along with a cracker, popping the combo into her mouth. She munched contently until she recognized the conversation had come to a complete halt. Then she noticed all eyes were trained on her.

"What?" She finally asked.

"Are you pregnant?" Carmen blurted out, earning a light shove from Deirdre.

"Don't act like y'all weren't thinking it." Carmen scooted her chair farther away from Deirdre to avoid her next swat.

"Thinking it and saying it aren't the same thing." Deirdre leaned over, making sure to connect with Carmen's shoulder again.

"If she is, and she's not telling people. There's a reason." Turning those Truman light brown eyes onto Zaria, Deirdre asked, "right, Zee? If you are and you haven't said anything. You have a good reason, right?"

Zaria glanced away, trying to dodge the questioning looks directed at her. Warmth covered the back of her hand and Zaria followed it to her Aunt Belinda's face.

"Baby, you don't have to say it. I knew the moment I laid eyes on you Monday. I figured you'd tell us when you were ready. And you will. Correct?"

Words lodged in Zaria's throat and all she could do was nod. It had to be hormonal changes ushering in the tears she tried to blink away. Her normal quick-witted comebacks were conspicuously absent. Thankfully, no one challenged her aunt's statement. Zaria was given a few minutes to pull herself together before the conversation shifted, giving her a reprieve.

The house was buzzing with activity when Zaria and Andrei arrived the next day. They'd shared a light breakfast. Although Andrei insisted that she eat more, Zaria reminded him of the near gluttony in their future. Despite the smaller number of people attending, there would be enough food to feed everyone three times over.

A savory aroma hit her nose the moment the door opened. She was never more grateful to not suffer from sensitivity to smells, as some reported during similar stages of pregnancy. Instead of wanting to empty the contents of her stomach, she looked forward to sampling the holiday fare. The scents, sights, and sounds of home sent a slight pang to her heart, knowing they'd leave it all behind in far too few hours.

"Aat Aat!" Her aunt called out when Andrei went to close the door. Pausing mid-motion, he looked at her. Apparently, the sound was universal even to people who didn't grow up with a bossy southern auntie.

"Invite your people inside. This is a safe neighborhood. Tell them to come in so they can eat with the rest of us."

Andrei had obviously learned the futility of arguing with Belinda Truman because he simply stepped back through the doorway and gestured to the security team. Moments later, each walked into the house with huge grins plastered across their faces. Dakota stepped over the threshold with his head tilted back, inhaling deeply.

Not hiding her chuckles, Zaria led their small entourage farther into the house. She'd known it was going to happen—especially after the previous night, when Grace joined the ladies in the kitchen while Yeva and Logan went to the basement with the men.

All of them had attempted to do their normal routine and blend into the background, but her family had a way of pulling people in. While she hadn't said much, Grace was in the mix with the women, which meant Yeva and Logan probably had a similar experience in her uncle's man cave.

The Truman home overflowed with the festive fall decorations her aunt decided were a necessity this year. The centerpiece Zaria and Andrei made was on the table in the formal dining room. The smaller tables also held contributions from other family members. She was proud of their handiwork. Other than running into Vincent at the bargain store while searching for supplies, it was a pleasant bonding experience for the two of them.

Once they entered the family room, Andrei was immediately pulled into the festive chaos by Brad and Cisco. Zaria didn't key in on what they were saying to him as he listened to each intently. A chorus of greetings were called out as she made her way to the kitchen while he was entertained by her male cousins.

Andrei wasn't very forthcoming about the activities of boys' night other than to say it was fine. Judging by the way her cousins were jockeying for position near him, she'd say it went better than fine.

Meeting her uncle at the door leading onto the patio, Zaria held it for him while he brought in the turkey he'd just finished frying. The rest of the food was set up buffet style as was their normal during large family gatherings.

"Neal, put that right here, then you can go on upstairs. When you come back down, we'll be ready to eat." Her aunt pressed a kiss to her uncle's cheek and shooed him away.

While Zaria was setting out the serving utensils, Dominique sidled up next to her.

"Are you feeling okay?"

Eyebrows dipping, Zaria glanced at her cousin. "Of course, why wouldn't I?"

Speaking softly, Dom leaned closer. "I didn't know if you had morning sickness or if the different food scents would get to you."

"I'm fine, Dom. All the smells do is make me hungry."

Zaria hadn't confirmed her condition to her cousin. She hadn't denied it either. It was sweet that Dom was now trying to look out for Zaria the way she looked out for Dom.

Dinner was filled with laughter and conversation. Zaria soaked it up knowing it would probably be another year before she got a chance to gather with those present again. It was possible she'd see her aunt, uncle, Dom and Cisco before then, however the others she typically only saw once a year at Thanksgiving or Christmas. Since she'd come south for Thanksgiving, she wasn't likely to fly back for Christmas. It didn't matter that she now had access to Andrei's plane.

She was certain he'd agree if she suggested it, but she wouldn't. Zaria would continue with her established holiday routine. Andrei's moan drew her attention from her thoughts. Glancing at him, she saw his eyes closed as he slowly chewed whatever he'd just put into his mouth. When his eyelids lifted, he pinned her with a heated stare. It was almost accusatory.

"What?" For the briefest moment, she thought he was angry. His expression was a variation of the one he wore the day he showed up at her suite in Bali.

"Your aunt said you made this dish." Andrei's fork pointed to the cornbread dressing heaped onto his plate.

"I did..." Zaria spoke slowly, unsure of where the conversation was going.

"You have never cooked this dish for me. Why?"

"Because it's a holiday dish. It's not an everyday or middle of the week kind of thing. Besides, you do most of the cooking."

Andrei stared at her silently, then forked another portion of dressing into this mouth. Thinking they were done, Zaria went back to her own plate. Then, her attention was pulled away by Carmen. While she chatted with her cousin, Zaria picked up the thread of her Aunt Belinda's conversation. With Andrei.

"It does take a while, but if you have all the ingredients, it goes faster. Having cornbread already made is a huge time saver. Sometimes a box or two of stuffing mix helps as well. Because you really can't make dressing in small portions."

Andrei nodded in agreement. Looking at Zaria, he spoke to her as if he'd never started a second discussion with her aunt.

"Aunt says you know this recipe from memory. You can teach me. So, we can have this again at Christmas."

Zaria intentionally glazed over him referring to her auntie as 'aunt' and went right to him requesting specific foods for a date a month away.

"I'm sorry, what?"

"Aunt is going to show me how to make cornbread so I can help you make this dish for Christmas when they come to visit us."

Zaria folded her hands together in her lap. Her gaze pinged between Andrei and her aunt sitting to his left at the end of the long table. It dawned on her that the two of them had been sitting there making plans like it was normal.

Andrei had even said, '*when they come to visit us*', as if they shared a home. Zaria pushed away the technicality of them sleeping in the same bed every night. The majority of her belongings were still in her house in Coryville. So, they didn't officially live together. Therefore, saying her family was coming to visit *them* was a bit premature if you asked her.

Instead of addressing Andrei, Zaria looked at her aunt. "I didn't know y'all were thinking of coming to Vegas for Christmas. The last time we talked about it, you were saying something about going to Dom's place in Cali."

Her aunt waved a hand in Zaria's general direction and took a sip of her sweet tea.

"Yeah, your uncle and I reconsidered that idea. Last night, we were talking about how good it was to see you, and that we hadn't been out there in a couple of years. You either came here or we met in Cali. Dray said he has plenty of room and we can be assured privacy. So, we said why not?"

Zaria's eyes widened. So, not only was Andrei calling her Aunt Belinda *'aunt'*, he now apparently had a nickname.

"Close your mouth and eat your food, baby. We got this worked out."

Placing the back of her hand beneath her own chin, Aunt Belinda mimicked the mouth closing motion for Zaria.

Zaria was stunned. While she'd determined that Andrei had made a good impression on her family, she hadn't expected this level of acceptance. At least not so quickly. She didn't know how to process it. Andrei was still his same imposing, intimidating looking self, but managed to carve out a space for himself within their family unit.

When she looked at Andrei, his eyes sparkled with mischief she didn't recall ever seeing before. Returning his silent gloating with a raised eyebrow, she did as her aunt instructed. Zaria put her eyes on her own plate and returned to her meal.

She wouldn't begrudge Andrei the opportunity to connect with someone outside of herself. Vitaly had been his only family for almost two decades. Even their scaled back family dinner was larger than what he'd experienced even when his parents were alive.

Glancing back in his direction, she saw him point to the mound of collard greens on his plate.

"Collard greens? I have had this before in a soul food restaurant. They were good, but this is delicious."

Glowing under the praise, her Aunt Belinda launched into how she prepped the greens from selecting them, to cleaning, to cooking. She didn't miss a step. She loved passing on family recipes, and Andrei seemed genuinely interested to learn. Zaria wondered if it reminded him of times spent doing the same thing with his mother.

The way he got along so well with her family made her a little nervous about the next stop on their holiday tour. Their flight to New York was scheduled to leave mid-morning. Vitaly's game was during the day. They planned to have dinner together afterwards and stay the night before flying back to Las Vegas on Saturday. Vitaly would fly with them, giving the brothers a chance to extend their visit before he went back to Denver.

Returning to her conversation with Carmen, Zaria resolved to let tomorrow take care of itself. She planned to enjoy the time she had remaining with her loved ones.

Chapter Twenty-Four

DOES SHE KNOW WHO YOU ARE?

Andrei's phone buzzed in his pocket. He pulled it out, since he was expecting to hear from Vitaly. Andrei and Zaria arrived in New York with enough additional time for her to have a quick nap prior to them attending the matchup between the *Colorado Torrent* and the *New York Guardians.* He'd declined Vitaly's offer to get them tickets and secured a suite.

Brat: Finally done with my turn being a talking head. Are you still here?

Yes. We will pick you up at the players' entrance.

Looking up from his phone, Andrei instructed Logan on where to take them to retrieve Vitaly.

Brat: Be out in ten.

Ok.

Brat: Looking forward to meeting your lady friend.

Andrei rolled his eyes before tapping out his next message.

Try not to be so...you.

Brat: I'm a fucking joy to be around, brother.
She'll love me.

Huffing, Andrei stowed his phone in the inner pocket of his suit jacket. Zaria sat beside him with her gaze glued to the window. She hadn't even glanced over when his phone buzzed. Watching the area around the arena pass by the window seemed to have her entranced. It was more likely she was lost in her thoughts though.

Entwining their fingers, Andrei lifted her hand kissing the back of it. "Are you okay, Svet?"

Turning toward him, she offered a soft smile. "I'm fine. I find this view of The Garden interesting. I've only been here for concerts. Lyssa and I definitely didn't use the private entrance to come and go."

Nodding, Andrei squeezed her digits gently. "If you are tired, we can go back to the hotel and have the food delivered."

Snuggling into his side, she tapped his chest with her free hand. "I'm fine. The nap from earlier gave me an energy boost. Besides, didn't you say Vitaly was really looking forward to going out to dinner with us?"

"Vitaly would get over it, if you are not up to it."

Soft pats to his pectorals followed his statement. "We're going. It's bad enough you shot him down for his first choice."

Andrei grunted. He didn't feel an ounce of remorse for rejecting the first restaurant Vitaly suggested. It was a known hot spot in New York for spotting celebrities. That wasn't Andrei's issue with it. His issue dealt with being able to properly protect Zaria in such a place. Although his brother's second suggestion was only marginally better. It was still a place often frequented by the rich and famous.

The stretch SUV drew to a stop and the back passenger door was opened. Vitaly's bright blue eyes gleamed to match his smile as he ducked into the backseat sitting on the bench opposite Andrei and Zaria.

"Hello, Zaria. I have to say you are more beautiful than your pictures."

Andrei glared at his brother as he turned on the charm, lifting Zaria's free hand to kiss the back. Baring his teeth, Andrei narrowly suppressed the growl at the contact. Logically, he knew his brother wouldn't overtly try to steal his woman, but Andrei wasn't fond of other men touching her.

"Hey Vitaly. Nice to meet you." Zaria tugged her hand free, placing it in her lap once more.

Leaning into the plush leather of his seat, Vitaly stretched an arm along the top. "So, tell me. How did you and my brother meet? You are an attorney, correct?"

Leaning forward, interest put a sparkle in his eyes. "Did you sue him?"

"Why do you sound excited about the possibility, Brat?" Andrei stared at Vitaly in only partial disbelief.

"It makes for an interesting story. If she did sue you, you obviously came out of it the winner. In more ways than one."

Zaria giggled. Andrei was pleased their banter amused her. Especially since Vitaly was doing exactly what Andrei asked him not to do. He was being one hundred percent, full tilt, Vitaly 'gives no fucks' Antonov.

"I hate to burst your bubble, but it's nothing so dramatic." Zaria responded. "We met through mutual friends."

"Like boring grown-ups?" Vitaly wrinkled his nose distastefully.

"There is nothing wrong with being a grown up." Andrei huffed in offense. "You should try it sometime."

"I'll have you know, I'm a grown up at least eight hours every day." Vitaly puffed out his chest. He smoothed the vibrant blue tie against the stark white of his button-down shirt.

"Eight whole hours a day." Andrei replied in a dry tone.

Grinning triumphantly, Vitaly gripped his lapels. Straightening his suit jacket, he squared his shoulders.

Andrei shook his head while Zaria released more tinkling giggles at his brother's antics. The conversation shifted when Vitaly asked Andrei what he thought of the game. The *Torrent* squeaked by the *Guardians* with a narrow two to one victory. The game was a nailbiter going down to the last few seconds.

In Andrei's opinion, the *Guardians* had one of the most impressive line ups in the league. Their starting forwards were scoring machines who typically garnered at least one goal each per game. For Vitaly to hold them to the single goal was a feat within itself.

Andrei didn't have to tell him so. Zaria did it for him. Andrei watched as Vitaly seemed to sit taller with her praise of his abilities on the ice. She didn't gush like an over exuberant fan. By pointing out strengths and weaknesses, she earned his brother's respect on the drive from the arena to the restaurant on Thompson Street.

Friday night after a holiday, in New York City was guaranteed to draw a crowd—especially at a place known to be frequented by celebrities. Securing Zaria's coat and scarf, Andrei was thankful they visited before the snow. He would've been fine with the white stuff, but admittedly paranoid about Zaria injuring herself on slippery slush.

They stepped onto the sidewalk to an almost movie premiere atmosphere. Andrei wondered if he'd missed an event announcement when he'd made the reservation. There were paparazzi being held behind a velvet rope a few yards from the entrance.

Cries of "Vitaly! Vitaly, this way!" rang out as his brother put one loafered foot onto the pavement. While Vitaly smiled and waved, Andrei slipped an arm around Zaria, protectively guiding her toward the front doors. He didn't spare a glance in the direction of the clamoring shutterbugs.

Andrei didn't relax until they were securely inside the private room he reserved. He knew Vitaly wouldn't like being away from the action. However, Andrei didn't care. Spending much of his time at Anton's had spoiled him to having his privacy guarded. Being under the microscope of the public eye wasn't something he enjoyed.

His brother, on the other hand, seemed to thrive. It was almost like he drew energy and strength from the interactions. In Andrei's estimation, if Vitaly didn't enjoy it, he put on a helluva good act.

After dinner, they again walked the gauntlet of paparazzi and celebrity watchers. Zaria never complained about the extra attention. She simply followed Andrei's lead and didn't interact. Zaria's comment to Vitaly once they were ensconced inside the vehicle made Andrei look at his brother with new perspective.

"Thanks, Vitaly." She murmured softly.

"It's nothing."

"It was something to me. I don't like being in the spotlight that way. It's one thing to be the focus of attention while giving closing arguments in court. It's another to simply be out trying to live my life and having people documenting every step. No wonder Alyssa became even more of a hermit after she and Carver got together."

Nodding, Vitaly glanced at Andrei before looking out of the window at the passing scenery.

"Like I said, it was no big deal. I'm used to it."

Zaria focused her attention on the city scape outside their moving vehicle, dropping the subject, but Andrei stared at his younger sibling. Vitaly had always been more gregarious than him. So, to Andrei, it appeared Vitaly enjoyed the attention borne from his prowess on the ice.

Arguably the most difficult position in hockey was goalie. Despite the skill the position required, it wasn't as flashy as being a Center or Winger. So, Vitaly's popularity wasn't the norm. However, it was what Andrei expected based on his brother's personality.

Zaria's observation made Andrei wonder if he'd bought into the act he was certain his brother wasn't performing. Until she thanked him, Andrei hadn't considered Vitaly offering himself as a distraction. It allowed he and Zaria to avoid dealing with press or gawkers entering and leaving the restaurant.

Having it brought to his attention made Andrei wonder what else his brother craftily hid from him behind his wide smile and outgoing persona. Vitaly shot Andrei a questioning glance, to which Andrei simply nodded. It seemed his Svet was changing more in his life than he realized.

The trip to their hotel suites was made in relative silence. Their group parted ways in the hallway leading to their individual suites. After reminding Vitaly of the time for their departure the next day, Andrei led Zaria to their room. He was certain his brother would venture out again, since it was relatively early in the evening.

When they entered their suite, Zaria immediately began shedding her outer layers of clothing. Drawn into the moment, Andrei watched as she revealed more of her body without care. His mind immediately began conjuring images of how her body would look as it bloomed with their child growing in her womb. Until she'd given him the news, he'd had no idea how erotic he'd find the prospect of worshipping her form as it changed.

"I like your brother. He's sweet."

Zaria's statement snatched him out of his fantasy. *Vitaly? Sweet?*

"I am happy you like him, but I will admit I have heard no one, other than my mama, describe him that way."

Zaria paused with her blouse dangling from her fingertips. Andrei closed the distance between them to assist her with her bra. Although she hadn't asked.

"Really?" She tilted her head to the side. "He's super sweet. He's a whole mess and a half. Still... A total sweetheart."

Zaria was a pragmatic and astute person. If she said she thought his brother was sweet, Andrei wouldn't argue—even if he was certain her assessment was totally biased.

A soft mechanical hum along with an occasional click or rustle of movement were the only noises in the interior of the jet. Zaria was napping in the sleeping compartment, and Andrei was attempting to do some work when his phone buzzed. Looking at the message from Gregor, he sent a response.

Gregor didn't celebrate many American holidays, so he'd had no issue jumping into the assignments Andrei sent his way during his visit south with Zaria. His awareness of where she stood wouldn't stop Andrei from getting to the bottom of things. One thing he wouldn't have, was anyone fucking with his Svet or stressing her unnecessarily.

Faintly, he heard the snick of the lavatory door. As Vitaly approached from behind him, Andrei closed the message from Gregor and locked the cellphone screen. The photo of him and Zaria from the wedding appeared before the screen went dark.

"She is a very special woman, brother."

Vitaly walked past Andrei, taking the seat opposite him. A table rested between them. Andrei's laptop, along with a portfolio, rested atop it. Andrei was actually surprised Vitaly had waited so long to voice his opinion on Zaria. They'd been relatively alone during the flight, with Zaria being in the bedroom and their security detail toward the front of the plane.

Closing his laptop cover and putting his phone on top of it, Andrei lifted one eyebrow as he studied his brother.

"She is. Very Special."

"Does she know who you are?"

"Of course she does. We met in my casino."

Shaking his head, Vitaly leaned his forearms on the table between them.

"No. I'm not asking if she knows what you do. I'm asking if she knows who you are?"

Andrei's eyes narrowed. He assessed Vitaly's words, his posture, and his facial expression. Something was off. If Andrei wasn't mistaken, anger simmered beneath the surface of Vitaly's calm façade.

"What exactly do you mean, Vitaly? Speak plainly."

"Like you don't know."

"I do not. If I knew, I would not ask."

"Does she know you don't care what anyone else wants as long as things go your way? Or that you do what you think is best regardless of who it hurts? Or better yet, that you're the kind of man who will tell his only brother they have no other family, knowing full well it's a lie?"

The more Vitaly spoke, the harsher his facial expression became. His skin was tinted an angry red beneath his scowl. The ice-blue eyes they shared flashed at Andrei with barely contained rage. Andrei leaned forward, matching his brother's expression.

When Vitaly mentioned family, Andrei knew exactly where his accusations originated. Somehow, he'd learned their mother's younger brother, Ruslan, was still alive. He no longer saw the man as his uncle, so he wouldn't deign to give him the title—even in his mind.

Andrei had no guilt surrounding telling Vitaly that Ruslan suffered the same fate as their parents. To him, it was the truth. Ruslan was dead. He died the moment he gambled his sister's life fucking with the Bratva.

The fact that he was still breathing was Andrei's last gift to his mother. Sparing Ruslan's existence had nothing to do with preserving the life of the family he had remaining. Ruslan didn't deserve such kindness. But, Andrei's mama loved her brother.

Although she'd thought she was long away from death, she'd asked Andrei to look out for her him. She feared he'd never marry or have children of his own. They had no other family. Their parents were only children, born to only children. If Andrei's father had relatives, close or distant, he'd never mentioned them.

"We do not have any family other than each other."

Andrei stubbornly refused to acknowledge any part of Vitaly's accusations beyond his assertion that they had living blood relatives.

"You would sit here. In my face. And lie to me, Andrei? I ***know*** Uncle Ruslan is alive. I spoke to him last night."

The revelation explained Vitaly's quiet demeanor since they met in the hotel lobby. It was totally different from when they'd parted ways the night before.

"It is not a lie. Ruslan *is* dead to me."

"How can you say that? He's mama's brother. Her *only* brother. And he's been out there all this time and I didn't know it. Because of *you*."

Andrei's hands fisted on the tabletop. Angry wasn't a strong enough word to describe his feelings. The only way Vitaly would know about Ruslan still consuming oxygen would be if the man reached out to him in some way. Which also meant he was desperate again. He most likely owed someone he couldn't pay, and was trying to ease his way in with Vitaly.

Ruslan knew not to contact Andrei. It was crystal clear when they parted ways that if Ruslan found himself in dire straits again, Andrei would sooner pour the gasoline to watch him burn than to give him another ruble.

He didn't want to hear about Ruslan, but he now had a burning desire to see him again. It wouldn't be a happy reunion though. He simply wanted to complete the job Gavrill should have done instead of coming for Andrei's parents. Actually, the plan had been to only kill his mother. It was only because Andrei's father fought so hard to protect her that they both ended up dead.

What kind of man targeted a woman as retribution for a debt owed? Gavrill Morozov. The head of the Bratva family Ruslan thought he could con and use Andrei's money to repay. In the end, he did, but it was at a very heavy cost. One that Andrei had never told Vitaly about.

"There is much you do not know, Vitaly. You were only fourteen years old when our parents were taken from us. I was the one responsible for caring for you and making sure you were safe. Ruslan was and is a danger to you. To ***us***.

I did what I had to do to keep you alive. I will not apologize for it and I was not going to discuss it with a teenager who had no knowledge of how harsh and cruel the world could be. Losing Mama and Papa was enough."

"Why do you get to decide that for me? They were *my* parents too. He's my uncle, and it's *my* choice who to have in my life. Did you think of any of those things when you were being King Andrei, handing down decisions and crushing anyone who stood in your way? I bet you didn't. Saying anything to anyone else would mean they mattered to you, or you needed them. Can't have anyone thinking they have meaning in your life, can you?"

Andrei used every ounce of control he possessed to remain seated and not grab Vitaly. He had a rising compulsion to shake his brother until his brain cells began functioning correctly. His fingers unfurled and flexed on the tabletop. Instead of giving in to the urge, Andrei glared at him. Vitaly had no idea of the sacrifices Andrei made for him. Not just to afford him a good life, but to literally make sure he survived into adulthood.

"What? Nothing to say, big brother? Is the truth too much for you?" Vitaly's snide goading was the impetus breaking Andrei's silent battle to spare his brother potential heartbreak.

"You spoiled, ungrateful brat."

Vitaly's eyes widened in shock. With his finger pointing to his chest, he glared at Andrei. "Me? Spoiled and ungrateful? Why? Because I think I deserved to know we weren't alone in the world? How does that make me any of those things?"

"From the moment you were born, I have taken care of you. *I* am the one who put in countless hours working to be the best so that *you* could eat whatever you wanted without care. You had a nice safe, warm home, with your own bedroom to grow up in.

Unlike me, you didn't have to walk to a rundown school for education, you went to fancy private schools. Who paid for those schools, Vitaly? Me!" Andrei used his thumb to point at himself. "Could Papa have fed and clothed us? Yes, but could he have provided the life you lived from the moment Mama pushed you out? No. Your life of ease happened on ***my*** back with ***my*** sweat and hard work."

"I didn't ask you for any of that, Andrei."

Vitaly took the opportunity to speak when Andrei stopped to take a breath and try to calm himself. However, he wasn't done.

"You did not have to. You are my brother. My *family*. You think Ruslan sees you as family? As his nephew? I assure you, he does not. He sees you as an opportunity. A source of income he can leverage when he needs it. He does not care about you. He only cares about himself."

"Uncle said you wouldn't want me talking to him."

"He was right. Talking to Ruslan will only bring trouble and heartache."

"You keep saying that, but you won't tell me why. You call me a brat and say I'm ungrateful because I challenged you and I actually want you to talk ***to*** me for a change instead of talking ***at*** me and telling me what's best."

Breathing heavily, Vitaly sat back in his seat. His hands were braced against the table as if he was using it to hold himself together.

"I am not a fourteen-year-old boy anymore, Andrei. If you say Uncle Ruslan is a danger to us, you are going to have to tell me why. Tell me why I should pretend Mama's only sibling doesn't exist."

Andrei folded his arms. He stared at Vitaly without speaking as he considered what was best in the situation. It's possible he should've told his brother the full details long ago, except he'd honestly believed Ruslan wouldn't be stupid enough to try to contact either of them ever again.

Vitaly returned Andrei's stare, mimicking his pose. *Fuck!* The little shit was right. If Andrei wanted to protect him. He'd have to tell Vitaly the things he'd glossed over after their parents were killed.

"Ruslan is the reason Mama and Papa were murdered."

"What?"

Holding up a hand, Andrei silently asked for Vitaly to hold his questions. Andrei didn't want to have to repeat anything. Retelling the events of that awful night and the weeks which followed was a one-time deal.

"Ruslan owed money to the Bratva. A lot of money. He kept getting in deeper and deeper. They believed him when he said he could make good on his debts, because all he had to do was point to me. He told them how I was the highest paid defenseman in the American Hockey League. They let him get in so deep, he could not repay what he owed from the allowance I did not know Mama was giving him from the account I set up for her and Papa.

When he could not pay, Gavrill Morozov threatened Mama. I did not find out any of this until Ruslan called me to tell me they were dead. My first thought was to get to you and get you to safety. Gavrill had enough reach to get to me in Chicago, but it would have been much easier to get to you in Switzerland. Especially if he had Ruslan with him to simply walk you out of the front door."

Vitaly didn't say a word as Andrei recounted the horrible twenty-four hours following the death of their parents. The more Andrei spoke, he saw Vitaly's anger shift. There was still a portion directed at him, however each mention of Ruslan resulted in the clenching of his brother's jaw. By the time he was done, Vitaly's fists were clamped so tightly together, his knuckles were drained of color.

"Why didn't you tell me any of this?"

"You were too young."

"When I was old enough to hear it, you should have told me."

"Well, I did not think Ruslan was dumb enough to try to contact either or us. Not after the way I left things with him."

A few beats of silence stretched between them before Vitaly spoke again.

"So, that's why we lived in such a small condo when I first came here?" Vitaly scrubbed a hand over his face and exhaled deeply. Realization coated his features.

"It's also why you never wanted to go back to Russia. You said it was because of Mama and Papa's memory. But that's not it is it? You sold your house there. Sold the house you bought Mama and Papa. You did it to repay Uncle Ruslan's debt to the Bratva.

If you'd told me even some of this, I wouldn't have complained so much that first year. Especially not about wanting to go back to my school. I would've understood why it wasn't possible—that we couldn't afford it anymore."

"Again, you were too young. I did not want you burdened with financial worries. I figured it out."

"Yeah, but you shouldn't have had to do it alone."

"What were you going to do, Vitaly?"

"I don't know. Go to public school so you didn't spend the little money you had left trying to keep me in a certain lifestyle."

"You would not have been safe in public school. I was too well known. Even then. There may not have been danger from Gavrill, however there are people in this country who target children to get to their wealthy parents. Or in your case, sibling."

"Still, we could have figured something out." Laying his hands flat on the surface separating them, Vitaly pierced him with a look of regret. "I feel like the biggest asshole. Don't get me wrong, I'm still pissed at you for hiding things from me."

Andrei shrugged and turned his attention to the clouds as the plane cut through them. There was nothing he could do to make up for the past. There was no reason to belabor the point.

"So, when is the baby due?"

Andrei's head whipped back to Vitaly's smirking face.

"How did you know?"

"You're not very subtle, big brother. You can't keep your hands off your woman's belly."

Chapter Twenty-Five

DON'T BORROW TROUBLE

Zaria looked at her phone as if the image on the screen was going to change. It was the Saturday following their 'meet the family' tour, and she was sitting up in bed going through her normal routine—checking social media to see what she missed while she was trying to catch up on work during the week.

What she didn't expect was to see an image of herself. She liked watching Messytok. She wasn't supposed to be the topic of discussion. *What the hell?*

She'd never been more grateful Andrei was an early riser who liked to exercise to get the day started. Checking the clock, she noted that he should be downstairs in his gym for at least another thirty minutes. Minimizing the screen, her finger flew, swiping through screens to place a call. It took a few rings before Alyssa finally answered. Her voice was heavy with sleep.

"Lyssa!" Zaria whisper-screamed.

"What's up, Zee?" Alyssa said groggily.

"Lyss. Wake up!"

Zaria heard rustling with a grunt thrown in here and there before Alyssa's voice came over the line more clearly.

"What's wrong, Zee?"

"Why the hell do I see my face on Messytok? Look at this."

Zaria quickly sent Alyssa the link to the video. Giving her friend a chance to watch it, Zaria adjusted herself against the headboard. Andrei's scent hit her nose when she lifted a pillow to place behind her back, but she ignored the tingling it inspired. Now wasn't the time.

Since she'd been outed by Carmen during Thanksgiving, and Andrei informed her that Vitaly had figured it out, Zaria had expanded the circle of people who knew of her pregnancy to include her best friend. By extension, Carver was in the loop as well. So, she knew Alyssa wasn't shocked at the headline of the gossip Vlog which had made its way into Zaria's guilty pleasure video feed.

"Zee, that's not too bad. They're just speculating. On the plus side, they think you guys have been together longer than me and Carver."

Zaria adjusted the wireless earbuds in her ear. She couldn't have heard Alyssa correctly. It sounded like she was saying Zaria shouldn't be worried. Not the friend who had gone through a social media shit show when she and Carver first became an item.

"They're speculating ***with pictures***, Lyss. I watch the mess. Depending on the client, I clean up the mess. Being in the middle of the mess isn't what I do. Ever."

"Zee, it's not mess. Stop saying that. You are in a relationship with a man who's obviously crazy about you, and the two of you are having a baby. There's nothing messy about people knowing you're about to be parents."

"No. Not yet. Trust me. Now that the spotlight is shining in our direction, somebody is going to act a fool. I can feel it."

"Don't borrow trouble, Zee."

"I'm not. All I have to do is go to the comments on this video and I can see people have already started talking shit about stuff they know nothing about. They don't have a clue who I am, so their opinion doesn't matter. But if there are enough of them stirring the shit, the smell will eventually start to affect me."

Zaria tugged at a curl that escaped her hastily constructed pouf. Partially in frustration at the situation potentially spiraling out of control and partially to distract herself from going down the rabbit hole.

"I know what you're thinking, Zee."

"What am I thinking?" Zaria stopped tugging on her hair and stared at the phone in her lap.

"You're thinking about what happened to me when people found out I was with Carver. The way they came after me, and people from our past who climbed out of the woodwork to say really shitty things about me."

Zaria's response to Alyssa's assessment was silence. Her friend was one hundred percent correct. That wasn't all of it, but it was part of it.

"Zee, your situation isn't like mine. You and Andrei don't have a complicated past. There was no big viral scene where he damn near strangled a man in public. And I'm willing to bet Andrei already has a staff of people monitoring and managing social media for him. They'll find a way to spin this or make it a non-issue before you get to the office on Monday morning."

"I hope you're right." Zaria plucked at the soft duvet cover in lieu of returning to tugging on her hair.

"Trust me. The two of you are miles ahead of me and Carver when it comes to dealing with this stuff. That vlogger will regret jumping the gun on this."

Zaria didn't flinch at Alyssa's statement. Part of her hoped for something to make them understand the speculation and fact were not the same thing. In this case, part of what they said was true. The part about her being pregnant. No matter how much they used the word allegedly, it didn't make things better.

"I'm not one to go looking for revenge, but I don't appreciate them broadcasting my business at such a vulnerable point in my pregnancy. It was hard enough to keep Andrei from announcing it to everyone in our lives, and they've plastered it online for the world to see."

Zaria didn't vocalize her fear of having a miscarriage or some other complication arising during such a delicate time. She didn't have to. Alyssa had just gone through what she was experiencing in that regard. She hadn't even told Zaria about her own pregnancy until right before they were set to go to Bali for the wedding. It was literally the day the doctor gave them the okay to share the news.

It wasn't like Zaria had the intention of making some grand declaration. She simply didn't like having the option snatched from her this way. The invasiveness of it didn't sit right with her.

Although she was aware Andrei was essentially a household name, she hadn't expected any spotlight. He was very private. The way Anton's was locked down to protect the patron's privacy was the same way his life was locked down. The last thing Zaria would've predicted was that there would be a social media buzz about their impending parenthood.

She was partially consoled that none of her faves had jumped on the bandwagon trying to get in front of the wave spreading the news. Alyssa offered more encouragement and their conversation veered off to other things. Zaria's ears completely muted her friend when Andrei crossed the threshold into their bedroom.

Her gaze was locked onto him. He stopped in the doorway, mopping his face and hair with a towel. His white muscle tee was drenched in sweat. It hugged his pectorals while skimming his sides. Andrei was thick, yet his torso tapered nicely from his shoulders down to his waist.

Heat spread from Zaria's center as she watched the play of his muscles while he performed the rudimentary task. *Damn he was sexy.*

Dropping the towel, Andrei looked over at her. In her ear, Zaria faintly heard Alyssa say something. Her responding, "Mhm..." trailed off without any real understanding of what was said. She was too focused on Andrei's approach to concentrate on anything else.

When he neared the bed, his masculine scent came with him. Zaria wouldn't have ever said she was a fan of man-sweat or the way men smelled after a strenuous workout, but this was different. The aroma he carried made her want to lick him. Everywhere.

Giving her his, now familiar, not smile-smile, Andrei balanced himself on one hand as he leaned in to kiss her lips. Zaria unconsciously followed his retreat from the chaste peck and missed. He was too quick. He'd already lowered his head and moved the duvet down. Showering her stomach with the same attention, he stood up and whipped his shirt off.

"I am going to shower, Svet. Breakfast when I am done." He followed his statement with a hasty retreat into the bathroom.

Zaria didn't realize she was sitting there staring at the empty doorway until Alyssa yelled into her ear.

"Zee!"

"Huh?" Zaria jerked back into the moment. "Why are you yelling?"

"Because you completely zoned out on me. I called your name five times. The first time, I figured you were distracted. So, I tried again. By the third time, I was starting to get worried. Are you okay?"

"Hm?"

Zaria captured her bottom lip between her teeth and clenched her legs together. Her stare returned to the open door when she heard the faint sounds of water splashing against the tiles in the shower. Andrei was probably naked by now. He wasn't one to dawdle.

"Zee!"

"I'm sorry what?"

"Are you okay?"

"Yeah. I'm good. I'm...uh...just gonna get out of this bed and move around a bit."

She planned to move alright. Move right on into the next room to get Andrei to scratch this itch. He was wrong for strolling in looking like that and smelling like that and not giving her more than a little smooch. Zaria managed to say goodbye to her friend before disconnecting the call. Removing her earbuds, she placed them on the nightstand along with her cellphone. She wouldn't need those any time soon.

Shedding the oversized sleep shirt she'd thrown on when she'd first awakened, she let it fall to the carpeted floor as she single-mindedly continued toward her destination.

Picturing water cascading over the dips and plains of Andrei's large body had her quickening her steps in anticipation of relieving the ache in her center. Zaria approached the shower with purpose until she caught a glimpse of her reflection in the mirror. For a split second, she considered tossing responsible thoughts in the wind and getting into the shower without donning her shower turban.

From her peripheral vision, she saw Andrei turn beneath the waterfall spray of water and knew her tresses were destined to be drenched if she didn't cover them before she joined him. With far less care than she should've given the task, Zaria stuffed her hair beneath the colorful headwrap. The inside was lined like a traditional shower cap to keep her hair dry.

Task complete, she rotated toward the glass enclosure. Andrei now stood beneath the flowing water with his ice blue gaze pinned on her. Unbidden, her eyes traced every place the water touched, stopping at his shaft. As she watched, it hardened, thickening under her heated stare. Andrei didn't touch himself. Somehow, Zaria was able to stop gawking at his heavy cock and look up.

When she did, Andrei beckoned her forward. The heat at her core skated over her skin, leaving sweat beads on her brow. Her feet moved without conscious thought, taking her to him. Zaria couldn't explain how she'd gone from zero to *Fuck me* so quickly, but she didn't stop to think on it. Instead, she stepped into the tiled space.

Andrei tugged her against his hard frame almost as soon as her foot landed on the porcelain surface. He stroked one hand down her back, resting it on her ass and squeezing. With the other, he grabbed the back of her neck. Tilting her head up to meet his kiss, he crushed his lips to hers. Andrei swallowed Zaria's moan. The wetness dripping from her core couldn't be attributed to the shower spray. Her pussy throbbed with want.

Zaria's palms glided over Andrei's body, relishing in the feel of him. Her need wouldn't allow for lengthy foreplay—hell, *any* foreplay—as she encircled his length with both hands. His hips jerked slightly under her stroke, and a chuckle rumbled in his chest. Ending their kiss, his gaze bore into hers.

"You are eager this morning, Svet. Perhaps you need a different type of breakfast?"

"What I need is for you to bend me over that bench and fuck me."

Zaria returned Andrei's wide-eyed stare with a lifted eyebrow. "Now, Antonov."

"As you wish, Svet."

Andrei's reply was the only warning Zaria received before he lifted her, bodily placing her on the second step, in front of the aforementioned bench. There were two graduated stairs leading up to the bench, with the second being taller than the first.

The pressure from Andrei's hand between her shoulder blades sent Zaria leaning forward with her hands braced against the tiled surface. The porcelain gleamed so brightly, she could see their reflection almost as if it were a mirror.

Complying with her request to the letter, Andrei didn't put his face in her pussy to try to suck out her soul as he normally did. No. Instead, he notched the bulbous tip of his cock at her entrance. His first slight push made Zaria's breath hitch expectantly. The second, harder push caused her to release the breath with a moan. On the third, she felt his hips against her ass.

He was buried inside her to the hilt. Her eyes nearly crossed from the incomparable pleasure of having him within her walls. They had great sex. Fantastic lovemaking, but something was different about this moment. It was like she felt everything, everywhere, with her arousal heightened beyond anything she'd ever experienced.

Once he was fully ensconced in her dripping center, Andrei paused for the briefest of moments before he began working his hips in a rhythm that sent Zaria careening into an orgasm. Her shivers had nothing to do with the water pelting them from the multiple showerheads. The bliss produced goose pebbles on her skin, and made the soles of her feet tingle. *Damn...*

While Zaria worked her way through her first release, Andrei continued his erotic onslaught, taking her to the brink of another before tossing her into ecstasy and following her over the edge to his own muscle locking orgasm. His grunts and growls joined her moans and sighs as they came down from the explosive coupling.

She felt an immediate sense of loss when he withdrew from her depths. Andrei made sounds of comfort as he readjusted them until he was sitting on the wide bench and she was reclined in his lap with her head tucked under his chin.

"I don't care what anybody says. Sex genies are real, and you studied under a master."

Andrei's chuckle sounded like a low rumble beneath the ear Zaria had pressed against his chest. Despite him having thoroughly worked her pretty pocket and bringing her to a spine-tingling orgasm, her walls spasmed when she heard his amusement. It wasn't a joke. His sexual prowess wasn't the norm.

"If such a mentorship program existed, they would revoke my graduation credentials. You are far too coherent for a woman who was supposedly pleasured by a sex genie."

Zaria giggled. She delivered a soft tap before resuming her random pattern tracing on his chest.

"Do not abuse me, Svet. I am simply stating facts."

"Yeah, right...I think you actually have jokes of your own."

"I am a man of many talents."

Andrei spoke like someone putting on airs, drawing another light giggle from Zaria. Those giggles quickly turned to moans when Andrei's hands began their own random pattern drawing. They started on her hip, then moved down toward her knee before reversing course.

The pulsing in her core came back with ferocity. Whenever they were near one another, Andrei always had a hand on her in some way. So, Zaria was certain his intention wasn't to get her revved up for round two. But that's exactly what happened as his fingertips swirled on her skin without ever getting close to the place she wanted them most.

Zaria's skin felt stretched too tight. Fire seemed to emanate from within her core, reaching outward and sending flames along her skin everywhere his digits landed. Unable to stop them, her hips started a winding motion on his lap. Andrei's cock pulsed to life beneath her hip, giving Zaria all the encouragement she needed to continue. She didn't know where the intense bout of horniness came from, but she knew what would help assuage the ache.

"I need to ride your dick."

"Need, Svet?"

She couldn't explain it. Having him inside her again wasn't a want or a strong desire. Zaria felt like she'd literally climb out of her skin if she didn't feel him pulsing inside her walls within the next five seconds. His touch floated along her body as she took matters into her own hands.

Adjusting, she straddled his lap with his hard shaft pointed upwards. With no pre-amble, she lowered onto his thickness. A guttural moan escaped her lips as he filled every millimeter of available space in her channel.

"Fuck..." Zaria sighed. It was the only word she managed before Andrei's lips took hers.

His kiss was in contrast with the way his hands gripped her ass while he guided her on his turgid length. His tongue explored her mouth, mating with hers in a sensual dance which took her arousal up a level. She didn't think she could get much hotter. But she was wrong.

Even with her on top, Andrei orchestrated their movements like a skilled conductor. There wasn't a place requiring attention that he didn't kiss or caress. Zaria's breath hitched when he stroked her pearl in time with his thrusts into her slick walls, stimulating her externally and internally. His actions catapulted her into another explosive release.

The sounds of her completion bounced off the tiles, echoing throughout the space. Andrei's growling grunts joined in to round out their erotic symphony. His cock jerked inside her. Although she'd already found her release, Zaria's hips rotated, enjoying the feeling of knowing he flooded her walls with his essence.

That's what got your ass in trouble to begin with. Zaria shook off the voice in her head. What's done is done. She wouldn't change anything—even if it meant dealing with a potential media invasion into her private life.

Sighing against Andrei's chest, Zaria relaxed against his big body appreciating the comfort of his embrace. Her limbs were languid as she allowed him to support her. When he began the act of cleaning them both, she offered not one peep of objection. Participation from her was minimal. Andrei didn't seem to mind.

Twenty minutes after their shower, Zaria was seated once again on Andrei's lap, only their location was different. They were on the tufted lounger in the sunroom. A light brunch selection was spread out nearby and he was feeding her pieces of fruit between bites of pastry.

If someone had told her four months ago that this would be her life, she would've been ready to fight them in the face. Not because they were threatening her with pregnancy, but because the way Andrei took care of her was something she never dreamed would happen for her. Sure, they had a few rough spots in the beginning. And she was still working through her own personal issues.

The way Andrei made sure she was taken care of, in every aspect, was beyond addictive. Zaria loved it. Hell, she loved *him*. The thought brought a brief moment of tension before she quickly shoved it aside. Internally, she assured herself that loving someone didn't have to mean bad things would happen.

Love can be good. *Right?*

Chapter Twenty-Six

ARE THEY PAYING YOU?

Monday morning, Andrei left Zaria with as chaste a kiss as he could manage as he headed to his office at the casino. The weekend had been far from restful, but he had no regrets. The corner of his mouth tipped up as he remembered the way his Svet, and her supercharged libido, had jumped him repeatedly over the past two days.

Although she seemed slightly ahead of the curve with those particular hormones, according to the books, he was up for the challenge. Between their endless rounds of lovemaking, they talked. One topic of discussion was an article in an online gossip magazine.

While not all of their information was correct, they weren't too far off target. Zaria's concerns about being in the public eye were legitimate. Andrei was certain simple words wouldn't reassure her, so he sent the link to his social media director to get them working on a plan to address the speculation without acknowledging the truth of any part of the article.

He was confident they'd make certain those latching on to the story will be *encouraged* to set their sights elsewhere. If they know what's good for them, the budding entertainment reporters will take the advice. He was not above re-directing careers to relieve a source of stress from Zaria's life.

Frederick was standing next to his own desk when Andrei arrived at his office. In his hands were an electronic tablet and an insulated mug. The drink wasn't for Andrei, he'd drank his one cup of coffee before he left home. The caffeinated beverage was for Frederick. The younger man drank at least three cups of coffee before noon.

Andrei never asked, nor did he expect his assistant to perform those types of tasks for him. His legs worked. He could get his own coffee. For those rare occasions when he didn't have a cup before he left home, there was a station in his office—Jezve pot included.

As he came abreast of Frederick, the other man tapped the tablet with his thumb to wake it.

"Good morning, Andrei. I have a couple of things on your schedule I wanted to discuss with you. Based on the messages over the weekend, I'm guessing you want to meet with Rhoda and possibly Jeremiah."

"Good morning, Frederick." Walking past him, Andrei tilted his head toward the closed office door. "With me."

The two entered Andrei's office. Frederick selected one of the chairs in front of Andrei's desk and sat. Andrei placed his bag on the desk before sitting. He had his calendar open and was ready to start his day within seconds.

They spent the next ten minutes discussing Andrei's schedule and determining which meetings to cancel or move to different times. Frederick was correct. Andrei did want to speak to the social media manager and his personal attorney. It would be good to get Jeremiah in the loop—just in case.

Before they were done speaking, Andrei's screen refreshed with his updated schedule. He nodded in approval as Frederick stood. When his assistant finally decided he was done keeping Andrei's business life together and branched out, Andrei was going to have an extremely difficult time finding someone to fill his shoes.

Frederick did more than make calls and manage Andrei's calendar. Which was why Andrei was certain the other man would eventually want to put his skills to use, working to make his own dreams a reality. Honestly, whenever he did, Andrei would likely happily invest in whatever new venture Frederick conceived.

The moment the door snicked closed behind his assistant, Andrei's phone vibrated. Taking it from his pocket, he looked at the message on the screen. It was Gregor, asking if he had a moment to talk. As usual, the investigator had impeccable timing. Andrei's first meeting of the day didn't start for another hour.

Instead of replying to the message, he called. Gregor's heavy voice, with his slight Norwegian accent, greeted him after two rings.

"Hallo."

"What have you learned?" Andrei skipped the pleasantries and got right to the point.

"You know how I feel about giving out information over the phone, Antonov. I am in your lobby. I will be in your office in four minutes."

Neither bothered to say goodbye before disconnecting the call. Andrei wasn't concerned with Gregor's refusal to speak over the phone. The man's diligence could sometimes come across as paranoia. Considering he dealt in secrets and information, Andrei didn't fault him for being cautious.

Frederick knew not to block Gregor from entering unless Andrei specifically said to keep him waiting. So, he wasn't surprised, when exactly four minutes later, the investigator tapped his door while simultaneously pushing it open.

Once Gregor was settled into a chair, Andrei stared at him expectantly. Producing a file, Gregor slid it across the desk. Andrei didn't open it. With his hands folded on the gleaming wooden surface he waited.

"You were right to look into Winstead. He's trying to sabotage Halsted, Markham, and Blake. They don't have a clue. The other clients he's pulling his game on weren't as savvy as your little brother-in-law. They are still with the firm letting him string them along while tanking their careers."

Andrei ignored Gregor's reference to Cisco as his brother-in-law and focused on the actual information.

"Why would he do something so foolish?"

"My guess? There have been talks of adding a fourth managing partner to the firm and his name isn't even on the short list. Halsted, Markham and Blake is doing well, but there are other firms moving in on them. Those guys are nearing retirement, and their competition is looking for ways to capitalize on it. They're looking for inroads to take over the firm, absorb their client list, and become an unstoppable powerhouse in the industry."

"So what? Is Winstead hoping to speed the takeover along? To what end? He has to know that even if he puts the firm in a position where they are vulnerable to a buyout, he is tanking their reputation. At a minimum, he is damaging his own with his clients."

"Yes, but he is choosing very carefully who he mishandles. He's also not alone. According to my information, he has at least three of the junior partners working with him.

His problem now is that he misjudged Francisco and overplayed his hand. With it being months before the end of the season, it's likely he thought there was time to bring things around."

While Gregor's logic was sound, it didn't make sense to Andrei how Winstead was able to continue to get high-profile assignments while not performing his job.

"How is it that Winstead is doing this without at least one of the managing partners being aware?"

"Arrogance, age, take your pick. Those guys have been at the top of the food chain for a long time. Being so elevated tends to make some people lax. It is probably a good thing your brother changed representation a few years ago."

Andrei nodded in agreement. He'd never said anything to Vitaly about his choice, especially since his brother seemed satisfied with his current attorney. However, he'd wondered if the reason he wanted to change went beyond having attorneys with more style—as he'd put it at the time.

"Would you like them to be aware of the situation they have brewing?"

"Are they paying you?"

Gregor tossed up a hand of understanding.

"Is that all you have? Was there anything on the agent he was pushing on Cisco?"

"It's next on my list. You have to go through a few shell companies and silent partners, however eventually you'll learn the agent works for a subsidiary of the same firm which is looking to take over Halsted, Markham, and Blake."

"Well...they cannot be happy with him right now."

"I would think not. That is all I have at the moment. If you want me to keep an eye on the situation, I will."

Andrei shook his head. "No. I think it is best if I move to the next firm on my list. Before I recommend anyone else, I want you to do a deeper dive into the senior and managing partners. I will send you the list."

Gregor dipped his head slightly in acknowledgment. Unfolding his hands, he rested them on each arm of his chair.

"Now, on to the next thing you asked me to look into. Vincent Coleman."

Reversing their posture, Andrei clasped his hands tighter atop his desk.

"Continue."

"He lives modestly and has done so for quite some time."

"But?"

"But, he is not the polar opposite of his brother. It is obvious he likes people to think he and Lawrence are not identical in more than looks, but they are. He is simply better at hiding it, and he has not gotten caught."

"Yet." Andrei supplied.

"Yet." Gregor repeated Andrei as he lifted a questioning eyebrow. "Would you like for that to change?"

Andrei shook his head. "No. As long as he stays away from our family, we will continue to live like the other does not exist. If he does not..." He allowed the implication to land between them.

Gregor didn't need a painted picture, and Andrei didn't provide one. He'd given the investigator enough to know to keep his ears tuned to the situation, but not go any further. Gregor adjusted his posture, leaning forward slightly and bracing his hands on his knees. The new tension of his stance put Andrei on alert.

"Now, about the Ruslan issue." Gregor spit the man's name out like it was a bitter taste in his mouth.

Andrei understood the sentiment. Even thinking of his mother's sibling was a souring experience. He folded his hands on his desk and quirked an eyebrow, encouraging Gregor to continue.

"He managed to stay away from the gambling houses for a while. But it seems to be mainly due to lack of opportunity in the village he relocated to after..."

Gregor didn't say after what. They both knew the event he referenced. *After* Ruslan caused the death of his only sibling and her husband.

"The Morozovs banned him from all of their places because he is a bad risk who cannot pay. They at least took you at your word regarding any future debts Ruslan incurred. Knowing he has no way to cover his inevitable losses, he is not welcome in their establishments."

"So, what has changed?"

Andrei wasn't surprised the Bratva family didn't want to deal with a non-paying customer who they couldn't at least extort or leverage in some way. Ruslan had no money of his own. He hadn't pursued anything that could be considered a lucrative career track. And, he had no high connections that could be manipulated for the furtherance of the family's business interests.

What use was he to them? None. He was fortunate to still be alive. That was only due to Andrei paying his debt to Gavrill. Which Andrei did primarily to protect Vitaly and keep his promise to his mama. Were it not for the two of them, Ruslan would've long ceased to inhale and exhale.

"According to my sources, there is a new family trying to rise up in the area. It appears Ruslan saw it as an opportunity, since they didn't know about his dealings with the Morozovs."

It wasn't hard to conceive that there would be a disconnect even in the criminal underworld. As tight as those communities could be, Russia was a huge country in landmass, and the Morozovs were more prominent in the areas around Moscow. The last Andrei was aware, Ruslan lived in a small village which was closer to Saint Petersburg, in the northeastern part of the country. Their entire family had lived there before moving to Moscow to further Andrei's hockey career.

"Any idea who this family is?" Andrei didn't ask because he had intentions of saving Ruslan from himself. He simply liked having all the details.

"Kylmäveri is the name I was given. Believe it or not, they are based in Finland."

Andrei's brows lifted in surprise. Finland wasn't a country that immediately came to mind when one thought of crime syndicates. If memory served him, they had gangs, but not Bratva level criminal organizations. However, if they were Finnish, it would more than explain them not knowing about Ruslan's ties to the Morozovs.

While it was interesting, it didn't answer Andrei's most pressing question. How the hell had Ruslan made contact with Vitaly? It wasn't as if his brother had maintained the same phone number he had when he was a teen. He had someone else running his social media. So, sending him private messages was an improbable way to make contact as well.

"Were you able to find out how he managed to get in touch with Vitaly? Since he thought Ruslan was dead, my brother did not seek him out."

Andrei ignored the slight tick of Gregor's face at his mentioning of Vitaly's misinformation about Ruslan perishing with their parents. Gregor was never on board with keeping the truth from Vitaly. But he didn't go against Andrei's wishes.

"As unbelievable as it sounds, he reached out to him on social media."

Andrei frowned. "How? Vitaly has someone handling those accounts for him. I am sure they deal with numerous people claiming kinship or other things to get Vitaly's attention."

"Yes, however those people do not have pictures of themselves holding a young Vitaly's hand or with your mother."

Clenching his teeth so hard his jaw ached, Andrei glared. He should *not* be surprised Ruslan was willing to use their mother to get to Vitaly. Of course, Vitaly's people would pass those messages on when it appeared to be genuine. They wouldn't want to be fired for being the person who kept a legitimate family member away from their client. Especially when they had no knowledge of the danger that person posed.

Curses he couldn't seem to hold inside, tumbled from his lips aimed at Ruslan. His only consolation was knowing Vitaly was now aware of the coward's duplicitous nature, and would stay away from him. However, Andrei wouldn't leave that possibility to chance.

"Do you have someone who can pay Ruslan a visit? Remind him of why his sudden memory of having family is detrimental to his health?"

Gregor nodded. His lips stretched into a rare smile. He had no love for Ruslan. He was also one of the few people who was aware of everything Andrei went through to get himself and Vitaly out of Russia without being pressed into serving the Bratva indefinitely. He connected Andrei to the people he used to liquidate his Russian assets.

It was Andrei's former agent who introduced him to the people who had fast-tracked his application for citizenship. But, without Gregor's contacts, Andrei wouldn't have gotten to Vitaly in time, nor would he have made the right associations to get the Morozovs to accept his one-time offering to leave him and Vitaly out of Ruslan's dealings with them.

"Do you care *how* they encourage him?" Gregor scratched the stubble along his jawline as he asked the question.

"I do not. I simply want the message to be abundantly clear."

"I will take care of it."

"*Spasibo.*"

Gregor nodded in acknowledgement of Andrei's thanks. They didn't discuss payment since they had an understanding in that regard. Andrei's *thank you* was an indicator the discussion was over. However, Gregor remained seated in the chair across from him. Lifting an eyebrow, Andrei silently questioned him.

"I noticed there was chatter about you and your lady lawyer over the weekend."

Andrei simply stared, waiting for Gregor to make his point.

"It is pure speculation. Yes?"

Most didn't realize Gregor's curiosity went past normal inquisitiveness. He was what Zaria would call nosey. Gregor liked knowing things—especially about those in his circle. So, it didn't surprise Andrei that he was aware of what happened on gossip vlogs.

"Some of it." He finally responded. It would do no good to try to keep anything from Gregor. Besides, Andrei was not ashamed to have created a life with Zaria.

Gregor broaching the subject wasn't entirely unexpected. Considering he probably had an alert on the names of all his clients, he likely found out before Zaria ever mentioned it to Andrei.

"There is nothing for you to do there. At least not yet," Andrei assured Gregor. "I am meeting with my team this morning to discuss how to handle these so-called reporters. If our plans do not work, then I may contact you. As of now, I think you have enough to handle."

Gregor finally stood. Smoothing his hand down the front of his suit, he gave an almost imperceptible nod. "You will let me know if that changes."

"Of course."

Gregor paused with his hand on the door knob. He turned back toward Andrei, giving him a look Andrei couldn't quite place.

"Congratulations, my friend."

Andrei bobbed his head in reply. Barely a second later, he was once again alone in his office. He wondered if Zaria's day was off to a similar start as his. She'd told him about her plans to hire a new receptionist since the current one was taking another position within the firm.

It didn't shock Andrei to find out she, and at least one of her junior partners, was always involved in the last stages of the hiring process. She was far more hands on than attorneys with larger firms. That morning, she'd grumbled a little about the interview because it meant she couldn't work from home.

He'd held in a smile when she said it. Hearing her refer to his home as hers made him want to grin like a lunatic every time. He didn't. But he wanted to.

Looking at the time, he shifted his attention to the items on his agenda for the day. He'd reviewed the previous night's reports from the casino on his way into the office. There was a meeting later to solidify his plans to buy Van Cleef's stake in the Chevaliers. It was time for the man to go. And doing so would give Andrei seventy percent ownership of the team. As long as the others didn't follow in Van Cleef's footsteps, they could stay. There was no reason to invest more of his own money than he had to in order to make a profit.

Chapter Twenty-Seven

ZARIA MARIE'S LIFE

Zaria flipped through the resume Tika handed her when she entered her office. Printouts were a habit she'd picked up from her Uncle Neal. He was from the eighties and nineties era of management. He liked hard copies. Zaria saw his logic. Sometimes things seemed clearer when you held them in your hand versus reading them on a computer screen or electronic tablet.

They had three interviews lined up for the morning to fill Kendra's receptionist position. The plan was to get someone in who Kendra could train over the next few weeks. Then, that person could take over the job full-time after the first of the year. The office was typically closed beginning Christmas Eve and lasting through January second.

One of the benefits of Zaria being her own boss was the ability to build in off days for her and her staff around major celebrated holidays. It wasn't common—especially not in major firms that lived by clocking billable hours. However, not much would move in the branch of the judicial system they operated in during those times anyway.

It was a win-win in Zaria's opinion. Her employees got time off, and she didn't have people hanging around the office twiddling their thumbs because the judge or office they needed to contact was off for the holiday break.

The first applicant looked promising. Melinda, the Human Resources manager, thought so as well. She starred the young man's file as her first choice. Although, since he indicated he was in graduate school part time, it's possible they would only have him around for however long it took him to find a job in his field of study following graduation.

Zaria wouldn't allow the likelihood to be her deciding factor in her selections though. Some turnover was good. It let people know it was okay to seek other opportunities within and outside of the firm. Flipping to the next candidate, she skimmed the page. She glanced at the education section. Nothing spectacular there, however spectacular wasn't a requirement of being a good receptionist/office assistant.

Her eyes widened when they landed on the last place of employment. *That was interesting.* Normally, she didn't get into Andrei's business and she didn't invite him into hers. But Katelyn Norris listed Antonov Industries, specifically *The Rooftop* at Anton's, as her last place of employment.

Zaria's fingers itched to call Andrei to learn why Katelyn was no longer employed there, and to find out why she'd switch from being a hostess at an exclusive restaurant to a receptionist at a small law firm. Not that she couldn't decide to make a life change, except it was common knowledge that there wasn't a low paying position when you worked at Anton's. Being at *The Rooftop* meant she was also in a position to get tips from generous high rollers.

Zaria had almost made up her mind to satisfy her curiosity when she looked at her computer display and saw the time. The first interview was starting shortly, and she still needed to meet with Tanner, one of her junior partners. There wasn't time to call Andrei. Making a mental note to touch base with him later, she dialed Tanner's extension.

"Thank you, Miss Albright. We appreciate your time." Zaria thanked the older woman, their last interviewee.

When the door closed behind Melinda, she sank into the leather chair at the center of the conference table. A few moments later, Melinda came back into the room.

"Tell me again why I insisted on being a part of the hiring process?"

Zaria propped her head against her fisted hand. Her knuckles lightly massaged her temple.

"Because, and I quote, *I want to meet every person who comes through that door before I start signing paychecks. I can't have anyone coming in messing up the vibe."* Melinda replied.

Zaria didn't think the additional hand motions were necessary, but it was probably exactly the way she looked when she'd spoken those words to her HR manager. The woman had a steel-trap memory. So, there was no doubt in Zaria's mind she'd used those exact words.

Fuck being mature or professional. Zaria scrunched up her face and mouthed the words to Melinda, who laughed at Zaria's antics. Waving her off, Zaria sat up straight and lined the resumes up in front of her.

"Let's get this done." Tapping the first one, she looked from Tanner to Melinda. "Now that we've all met him, what are your thoughts on Marquan?"

"He's a perfect fit." Melinda stood behind her original assessment of the young man.

"Yeah... He's in grad school though. So, what would we get? Two, maybe three years before he moves on and we have to fill the post again?" Tanner added his thoughts.

Zaria nodded before contributing to the discussion. "True, but who honestly works a receptionist job for longer than a couple of years these days? Especially someone starting out in their professional life."

"That's a fair point." Tanner conceded.

Zaria jotted a few notes on the top of the paper before setting it aside and picking up the next application.

"This one is a 'no' for me." She offered her opinion upfront without any delay on Katelyn Norris. "Something about her seemed off."

Tanner lifted his eyebrows as he studied her face. "Really? She seemed qualified."

Of course Tanner would think Katelyn was a viable candidate. She was young, attractive, and seemed to defer to him during the entire interview process—despite knowing that it was Zaria's name on the door.

"I never said she wasn't qualified. Her vibe was off."

"In what way?"

Zaria didn't take offense to Tanner having questions. It was part of their process. Although he was a junior partner, she'd let them all know, in situations like this, she fully expected them to speak up without fear of reprisal.

"Honestly, it didn't seem like she really wanted the job. She appeared more interested in massaging your ego than selling herself as a valued addition to our team."

Nodding, Melinda chimed in. "I agree. She was personable in the initial interview, but today it was like Tanner was the only person in the room. The two of us could've been window dressing for all she cared."

Shrugging, Tanner shuffled the papers in front of him. Then, he leaned forward.

"You wouldn't happen to have any additional knowledge as to why she left *The Rooftop,* would you? I dated a girl once who worked at Anton's and I know they pay well. Much better than she'll make as a receptionist here—even though we pay slightly above industry standard for the position."

Zaria knew why he thought she should know more, but she decided she had time to mess with him just a little. Quirking an eyebrow, she folded her hands in front of her.

"Why would I know more than what she told us during her interview?"

A flush creeped up Tanner's neck. He sat back in his seat, flustered.

"Um...Well...I just thought since you and Mr. Antonov were a thing..."

"Since we were a thing, what?" Zaria leaned in, piercing him with a direct stare.

"I umm. Well..."

"Zaria, stop it." Melinda finally gave Tanner a break.

Zaria grinned at her human resource manager and settled back into her seat. She didn't answer Tanner's question, though. As laid back as their office environment was, she didn't encourage people digging into anyone else's personal business. If they volunteered the information, that was a different story. But you don't ask. Tanner was aware of the rules.

Melinda threw him a bone by picking up the conversation from the perspective of their standard policy with prospective new hires.

"As part of the background checks we do on potential employees, all we learned was the length of time she worked there. Any other details are being held confidential by Antonov Industries. Which is perfectly understandable."

"I figured as much."

Zaria had quickly scanned through the report before the interview. It made her want to see if she could find out more from Andrei, but she wouldn't tell Tanner that. She didn't want anyone getting the idea she'd use her relationship with Andrei to get inside information—even if she would.

"Moving on to our third candidate, Mrs. Albright." Zaria put her hand on the third resume. "She has tons of experience and she seems very personable. Melinda, how did she do with the skill set test modules?"

Not every person over fifty-five was inept when it came to computers. However, many of them had been in the workforce when there were paper ways around doing things, so they hadn't kept up with newer technology and applications.

"I only ask because I don't see it here with the rest of the information I was given on her." Zaria lifted the sheets in front of her.

"Her results were on par or better than Mr. Branson's. They both exceeded the other candidate's scores."

They didn't always go with the person who performed the best on those tests, but having the questionable Katelyn fall in the very last spot made Zaria feel better about not bringing her on board. The decision really was between Marquan Brandon and Tilde Albright.

"Do you want my opinion?" Melinda tapped the tabletop as she asked her question.

"Always." Zaria was quick to respond. Melinda was an excellent HR Manager who ran her small department well and kept the firm on the right side of employment issues.

"I say hire them both. Doesn't Christine need an assistant? Kendra's moving over to be Jared's assistant. The move would make Christine the only attorney on staff who doesn't have her own. This way, we can cover that base *and* get a new receptionist."

"I like that idea. Make contact with them and extend the offers. Since two out of three of us consider Mr. Branson to be the strongest candidate, offer him the job as Christine's personal assistant. Offer Mrs. Albright the receptionist position."

Gathering the papers together, Zaria stood from the table. She'd let Melinda handle the rest. She didn't envy her telling Christine about getting an assistant. The woman was determined she didn't need one. But, she regularly tapped Kendra to perform tasks which should be handled by her own assistant. That would end shortly.

Leaving the conference room, Zaria headed back to her office. It was near lunchtime and her stomach let her know it even if she hadn't seen the clock. Once she was seated behind her desk, she checked her phone for any missed calls or messages.

There was one from Andrei checking on her and wishing her a good day. Zaria could've melted into a puddle. Before they got together, no one would've been able to convince her the stern-looking casino owner could be such a loving partner. She didn't get the impression he mistreated people. Zaria simply never thought he was the kind of man who'd send check in texts asking about his woman's well-being.

There was another message from Cammy, the property management specialist she was using to list her house as a rental property. Zaria hadn't discussed it with Andrei, but he'd made it abundantly clear that he wanted them under the same roof every night.

There was no point in pretending it wasn't what she wanted as well. She'd basically been worried about the optics. At this point, who cared? Her mind drifted back to the conversation she had with her Aunt Belinda when they had a few moments to themselves.

"I really like your young man, Zee-Baby."

Her Aunt Belinda settled in next to her at the island in the kitchen. The house was quieter since almost everyone had either left or scattered. Cisco had cornered Andrei into watching game film with him in the basement.

"Thank you, Auntie. I think I'll keep him." Zaria chuckled lightly at her own joke.

"Is that what you tell yourself? ***You'll*** *keep* ***him****? Honey, you couldn't pry that man away from you with the jaws of life."*

They both laughed at her aunt's depiction of the situation. The way her aunt held her arms brought up the mental image of firefighters trying to insinuate the powerful oversized can opener between them as Andrei held onto Zaria tightly.

"He's not that bad, Auntie."

"Girl, the man's nose is wide open. He ain't going nowhere."

"Well, I guess it's good I don't want him to."

Rubbing her forearm lightly, Aunt Belinda stared into Zaria's eyes.

"What's bothering you, baby?"

"Nothing, Auntie."

Lifting one eyebrow, her aunt pinned her with **the look**. *It was one which said under no uncertain terms that Zaria needed to cough it up.*

"Really, Auntie. I'm fine. At first, I was nervous about if y'all would like Andrei. It turned out to be a non-issue."

Nodding, her aunt nudged her to continue.

"Well, I was also concerned about keeping my condition private until I was out of the danger zone."

"That's understandable. But since we know about it now, you don't have to call it your condition. You're having a baby." Aunt Belinda smiled; the softness in her expression tugged at Zaria. "Go on, Zee-baby. Tell me the rest."

"I can't."

"Of course you can. You can tell me anything."

It was the one thing Zaria had always known to be true. She could talk to her Aunt Belinda about anything. However, anything you said to Aunt Belinda, you said to Uncle Neal. Those two were tighter than tight. It was never possible to play one off the other. Their communication game was on point.

That being said, there were a few things which still weighed on Zaria. She was working through them with her therapist. Seeing Vincent opened old wounds. It made her worry about how deeply she was already in with Andrei.

Laughter drew Zaria's attention to the opening leading from the kitchen into the family room. She studied the empty space for a few moments. When no one appeared, she shifted her gaze back to her Aunt Belinda. Her aunt's expression said she was willing to wait however long it took Zaria to say what needed to be said. Releasing a sigh, Zaria let it all out. Starting with when she learned the news of her pregnancy to when she and Andrei encountered Vincent in the bargain store earlier in the week.

Once she was done, her aunt slid from her seat. Moving closer to Zaria, she gathered her into her arms. Zaria thought she'd worked things out enough with Dr. Fleming, but the relief she felt, after sharing with her aunt, told a different story. She'd been holding her breath and hadn't even known it.

Cupping the sides of her face, Aunt Belinda searched Zaria's eyes. A soft smile lifted her lips.

"You always did see too much and internalize it. You saw far more than most at far too young an age. Contrary to whatever is floating around in your head, you're doing life beautifully, Zee-Baby. I am proud of you. And I'm not just talking about your accomplishments. I'm proud of the human being you've grown to be.

You're ***not*** *Stacy. I wish I could take away the hurt and scars from seeing the things you were forced to watch. Foolishly, I'd hoped living with me and Neal—being nurtured by us—could wipe that away. But, I see it still has a hold."*

Placing a hand on Zaria's stomach, her aunt pierced her with a knowing expression.

"This child will be loved and protected. Not because of me or your uncle. Not even because of that big Russian. But because of you. You have the biggest heart, baby. You'll understand when you finally hold your little bundle against your chest and feel their soft breath on your cheek. It will be impossible for you to think of doing anything other than moving the earth to keep them safe."

"But—"

"But nothing. We're individuals for a reason. It means we make our own choices and decisions. It also means we're the only ones who get to lead our lives. You're not reliving Stacey's life. You're living Zaria Marie's life. And you're the only person who can do that."

With one last hug, her aunt retook her seat. Zaria gave herself a moment to mull over the sage advice she'd been given. She felt lighter about what she planned to do when she returned to the mansion she now considered her home.

Their silent exchange was interrupted by the arrival of Dom and

Carmen. Carmen had decided to stay the night instead of driving the hour and a half back to Jackson, Tennessee. Zaria smiled when she thought of how her cousin moved from one city named Jackson to another in a different state. Soon, the room was filled with laughter as they savored the last few hours they had before parting ways.

Once they returned from their trip, Zaria made contact with Cammy about listing her three-bedroom bungalow style home with her rental agency. A former client, Cammy was familiar to Zaria and she could be certain that her property would be handled with care.

Since Cammy's company also offered packing and relocation services, Zaria planned to use them to remove her personal belongings from the house. According to the message on Zaria's phone, there were already four applications submitted. One of them was ready to move in as early as the coming weekend. That sounded promising.

Tapping out a quick reply, Zaria pushed back from the desk and went into the ensuite to relieve herself. After she was done, she stopped at her desk to grab her purse from the bottom drawer. When she stepped out of her office, Bianca appeared at her side.

It never failed. Zaria didn't have to call the members of her security detail when she was ready to do anything. As quickly as they disappeared when she arrived at the office, they reappeared once she opened her door with the intention of leaving the building.

Only, today, she wasn't leaving the building. Just her office. She planned to have lunch at the restaurant on the first floor. The place had been open for about six months and was a welcome addition to the office building. The doors to the elevator opened, and she immediately smelled the savory scents coming from across the expansive lobby.

Giving the security guard a smile when he called out a hello, Zaria continued on her quest to quiet the rumbling of her belly. *Sapori d'Italia* was bustling without being overcrowded when Zaria entered the restaurant. They were immediately shown to a table, although only Bianca sat with her. Logan stood off to the side.

By the time the server arrived, Zaria had decided what she wanted. Ordering a Stromboli with Italian sausage, peppers and onions, she closed the menu and passed it to them. As the server walked away, Zaria's phone dinged with a notification.

It was another message from Andrei.

AAA: Svet, the article has been taken care of.
Enjoy your lunch.

I won't ask how. Thank you.

She was totally going to ask how, just not over the phone. She'd save that for later—once they were home.

BTW, one of your former employees came in today to interview for an opening I have at the firm.

AAA: ?

Katelyn Norris. Is the name familiar?

There was a brief wait before Andrei replied to her question.

AAA: Yes. Do not hire that woman. She cannot be trusted.

You know you're going to have to give me actual details later, right?

AAA: Da

With his confirmation, no new typing bubbles appeared, letting her know Andrei was done with their little chat. He left Zaria wondering why he was so adamant about Katelyn Norris that he'd broken one of his rules and made a demand on her regarding her business.

Chapter Twenty-Eight

IS THIS YOU?

Andrei shoved his phone into his pocket following his text exchange with Zaria. He was irritated. It couldn't be a coincidence that his former employee was trying to get hired at his woman's law firm. What it was, was suspicious. Since he had Gregor occupied, he called the other investigator he used on occasion.

Giving the man two sets of instructions, he lowered the phone. Continuing on with his day would happen after a quick lunch. Rather than go down to one of the restaurants, he had food delivered to his suite. Looking around the space, he tried to remember the last time he'd spent more than a couple of hours during the workday there.

After he and Zaria returned from their friend's wedding, they'd used the suite sparingly. Knowing she was home waiting for him gave him incentive to cut his extended days. Which meant he didn't keep hours so late that it made sense to stay in the suite instead of taking the long ride home.

He was in the middle of his lunch when his phone pinged with a new notification. Quickly reading the text, he picked up the remote. Andrei muted the financial analyst discussing the pros and cons of owning real estate in the current economic climate.

Selecting the phone icon on the device display, Andrei called the investigator. Fernando answered on the first ring.

"Good day to you, Antonov. Or at least it could be if you didn't have disgruntled employees trying to slide in next to your woman."

"Tell me." Andrei didn't acknowledge the informational carrot Fernando dangled. He didn't have the desire to indulge in the other man's game. Not when it came to Zaria.

"Oh. So, you're in one of those moods today."

"Ruiz."

"Fine. Let me get to it before you result to using my full name. No one except mi madre uses that and only when I'm in deep mierda."

Andrei heard light rustling noises before Fernando spoke again.

"I'm not one hundred percent certain what the Norris woman planned by trying to get on at Z. Coleman and Associates, but I have a pretty good guess.

Before she got bold, and sold pictures of Jamieson to the paparazzi outlets, it looks like she had a pretty good side hustle going on with letting them know where someone was going to be when they left Anton's. When you fired her, you cut into her money stream. If she hadn't fucked up and got greedy, she could've gotten away with it for years."

Andrei didn't like the sound of that. While he had no control of what happened outside the walls of his establishment, knowing someone inside was serving his patrons up to tabloid vultures got under his skin. The background checks they ran on each employee were extensive; however even the most thorough checks missed things. They'd obviously overlooked the part of Katelyn's past which would've clued him in to her being susceptible to such behavior.

He consoled himself with the fact that he at least cut off her avenue of exploitation at *The Rooftop*. Fernando continued to give him background, but Andrei was more concerned with what her future plans might be, rather than an explanation of how she'd come to be fired from Antonov Industries. They could get to the other stuff later.

"Why do you think she is seeking employment with Zaria's firm? For some sick revenge plot?"

"That's my first thought, but I think it goes deeper. I did a quick check of your woman's case history—those settled out of court as well as those she won by court decision."

"And?"

Andrei tired of the slow delivery of his assessment despite knowing Fernando getting back to him with *any* information in such a short amount of time was a large feat.

"Zaria Coleman is a quiet powerhouse in the legal field. Did you know that? She's won judgments against some companies with pretty deep pockets and much larger legal teams than she has at her disposal. Her office is not a bad place to get inside info on some of the Vegas elite.

If she were allowed a foothold there, the Norris woman would have access she wouldn't have as a hostess at *The Rooftop*. Depending on her level, how she did it and the outlet she used, Norris could cost your woman her license to practice on the low end of things."

As Fernando spoke, Andrei had a thought. He'd told Zaria not to hire Katelyn. What if the woman used his relationship with his Svet as ammunition to file a lawsuit in the event she didn't get hired? Stating that Zaria was allowing him to hinder future employment opportunities.

In the time since he'd gained his citizenship, and as a businessman, he'd learned there were people in America who were quick to file lawsuits —regardless of if it had any merit. He wouldn't have Zaria dragged into a situation simply because Katelyn Norris was angry, because she'd suffered the consequences of violating her employment contract.

Refocusing on his conversation with Fernando, Andrei asked a few more questions before they ended the call. He'd instructed the other man to continue digging. There was little doubt a full report would be in Andrei's hand inside of twenty-four hours.

Once he finished his lunch, he went back to his office. Frederick gave him a glance as he passed his desk, reminding Andrei with just a look that he only had a short time before he needed to leave for the Chevaliers headquarters. Nodding in understanding, he issued a quick instruction to his assistant.

"Get Clark on the phone."

Never breaking stride, Andrei continued to his office while Frederick called the head of casino security, as he'd directed. In less than five minutes, he was speaking to Jensen Clark via video chat.

"Clark, I need you to gather everything you collected on Katelyn Norris and take to Jeremiah's office personally."

Jensen nodded while giving Andrei an inquisitive look. "Is there an issue with Miss Norris? Do I need to make sure the guys are still looking out for her being on the premises?"

When they'd learned she'd sold photographs of Carver, Andrei had her banned from the casino. If she couldn't be trusted as an employee, she definitely couldn't be trusted as a customer who had no binding contract to keep them from doing whatever they wanted.

There were elegant signage and periodic messages letting anyone who entered Anton's know that patron privacy was highly valued. Photos and videos of others, without their express permission, were not allowed. Violators would be removed from the premises and banned.

"To my knowledge, she hasn't attempted to return here. It is a precaution in the event she needs to be reminded of the legal ramifications of breaking her contract with the company."

"Okay. I'll make copies of everything I have and take it down to him."

Andrei nodded and moved to end the call. Before he could, Jensen spoke up.

"If I believed in coincidence, I'd say it was one for you to ask for the information on Katelyn today. I got some info just a moment ago and I was going to try to get on your calendar to discuss it with you."

Andrei looked at the screen with a single raised brow. Nodding, Jensen continued.

"You'd asked me to look into Delancy to find out why she was so interested in Katelyn and trying to get her back on here. It took a little digging, because they're very careful. I found out those two have been an item on and off for years.

Before Delancy worked here, she worked for a company in Coryville as their Assistant Human Resources Manager. Katelyn didn't work with her then, but the two were living together at the time. When Delancy was hired here, that was the first time the two had worked at the same place at the same time. At least from what we could find out."

"So, this is a situation of one partner in a superior position trying to use their influence to help the other?" While it wasn't unheard of and

Antonov Industries didn't have a No Fraternization policy, it wasn't what Andrei expected to hear.

"That seems to be the case."

"Was she aware of what Katelyn was doing?"

"Doing? Was the incident with Mr. Jamieson not the first time?"

"No. It was not."

Taking a few moments, Andrei filled Jensen in on what he'd learned from Fernando. When he was done, the other man's teeth were clenched so hard Andrei could see the muscle working in his jaw. As he expected, Jensen took Katelyn's side business going undetected as a personal affront to his ability to do his job. Although he, like Andrei, had no way of knowing what people did when they left Anton's.

They didn't make a habit of following their employees. Present circumstances notwithstanding, they didn't do deep dives on people who were on active payroll. So, there was very little chance he could have caught on to what the woman was doing.

"Let me dig a little deeper. On the surface, it just looks like Delancy wanted to help Katelyn. If there's more, I'll find it."

Andrei ended his call with Jensen, gathered what he needed for his meeting with the other owners, and left his office. On the way out, he let Frederick know he wouldn't be back afterwards. If anything else needed his attention, he'd handle it from his home office.

Although he'd rarely used it prior to having Zaria there, his home office was equipped with everything he required to be connected to his business interests. Andrei had simply not been motivated to take advantage of not being obligated to show his face on a daily basis. Now he did. In the form of a feisty, curvy little lawyer who was carrying his progeny. That knowledge was plenty of incentive to utilize the option.

Despite him spending the majority of his time in the corporate wing of Anton's, Andrei also had his own office at the Chevaliers' headquarters. He kept his expression neutral as he entered; still, he felt the shift in the atmosphere when he stepped onto the executive floor. The conversational hum continued, but it was at a decidedly lower volume than when the elevator doors first opened.

Cynthia, the office manager, met him en route to the conference room.

"Good afternoon, Mr. Antonov. I have everything set up for you, and the others are starting to arrive."

"Thank you, Cynthia."

Andrei accepted the dossier she passed to him, and continued past the gawking senior staff. There was little doubt that word had gotten around as to the purpose of the meeting today. They were likely trying to gauge his demeanor to determine how much of a show they'd get to see when Van Cleef arrived.

There were twelve others who held small stakes in the team, excluding Van Cleef. Half of them were already in the room when Andrei arrived. Nodding in greeting, he went to his seat at the center of the conference table with the windows at his back.

Van Cleef arrived, with the remaining six stakeholders trailing behind him. The smug look on his face projected his confidence in having outmaneuvered Andrei in his attempt to force a buy-out. What he didn't know was, Andrei was fully aware of his machinations. They wouldn't yield the results Van Cleef anticipated.

"Now that everyone is here. Let us start." Andrei tapped the table, punctuating his statement.

"Yes. Why don't we start?" Van Cleef's snide voice matched his self-righteous expression.

"Thank you all for gathering on short notice." Andrei made eye contact with each person at the table before looking toward the door where Cynthia stood. With his nod, she began passing out the additional dossiers he'd had her make.

As the folios landed in front of them, the others immediately flipped them open and began looking at the information. Everyone except Bertrand Van Cleef. Following a brief silence, Andrei once again redirected everyone's attention to him.

"As each of you know, in order to buy into the team, we agreed to follow a strict set of rules. They are stipulated in the contracts we signed. At any time, should we break any one of those rules, the body retains the right to compel the offender to relinquish their shares at fair market value."

People began shifting in their seats. The first few pages in everyone's folio were copies of the document Andrei referenced. While he was positive he had legal grounds for what he was doing, he didn't want any after-the-meeting blow back because the information was explicitly reiterated to everyone present.

"That being said, Bertrand, your shares in the Chevaliers are now forfeit."

"Under who's authority? The last time I checked, you're only one person out of fourteen of us with partial ownership of this team."

Andrei's face and voice were void of emotion as he stared at the older man coolly.

"While it is true, the others hold shares. It is also true that I am majority and managing owner of this team. My sixty-five percent holdings mean my vote carries more weight than the thirteen of you combined."

Some of Van Cleef's coolness started to wane. It obviously hadn't occurred to him that he and the others couldn't overrule Andrei's decision. Not without Andrei himself breaking the clauses stipulated in the owner's contract.

"Even if you have more shares, you can't just arbitrarily pressure one of us to sell those shares to you or anyone else."

Van Cleef looked around the conference room. He'd seated himself at the head of the table as some type of power play, but he didn't understand the concept of where the most powerful person in the room was actually positioned. It wasn't at the end of the long table.

"That is where you are wrong."

Andrei picked up the remote to his left and clicked the button to turn on the display screen.

"I have had the size of the image increased to allow everyone to see it clearly."

Using the laser pointer, he circled the blown-up section of the owner's contract to emphasize his point.

"Like the players, we have a morality clause in our contracts. The provisions placed on owners are not the same as the athletes, but we are held to a standard. You, Bertrand, have flouted the conditions of your contract. You are doing damage to our brand. So, you must go."

"That's a lie! I haven't done anything others in this room haven't done."

Andrei swept his gaze around the room before directing his stare toward Van Cleef. Clicking through images on the screen, he asked, "Is this you?"

Breaking eye contact briefly, he looked at the screen. He took in the image of Bertrand huddled together with the owner of another team, passing a document between them.

"Yes, it is definitely you. What exactly did you need to give Mr. Reuben which required the two of you to meet in secret? Why couldn't it have been done publicly?"

A tremor worked its way through Van Cleef, causing his head to appear as if it were vibrating.

"You've got this all wrong. Reuben and I have known each other for years. That picture proves nothing except we were in the same place at the same time."

"I thought you might say that."

Andrei proceeded to move through a series of images, each one more damaging than the last. When he reached the final one, there was an audible grumbling from the other owners, specifically those who'd trailed into the meeting behind Van Cleef in a show of outward support.

Bertrand Van Cleef had committed a cardinal sin in sports. He'd bet on and against his own team—on multiple occasions. In addition to the betting, he'd provided inside information to competitors. They could and should report him to the league, but Andrei wanted him gone before he dropped the hammer.

"Is there any objection to the only item on the agenda today?" Andrei looked around the room once more. "Would anyone like to speak in support of Bertrand before we vote?"

No one responded. They didn't so much as blink when Andrei made eye contact with them.

"Good." Without any further discussion, Andrei put the formal vote on the table. It was a unanimous decision.

"You can't do this!"

Van Cleef's mask slipped completely at the conclusion of the vote. Red splotches invaded his jowls and his hand shook as he pointed at Andrei.

"You! You have a vendetta against me. And I know why!" Jumping to his feet surprisingly quick, Van Cleef yelled at Andrei.

Andrei shook his head at Yeva, who stepped forward when the other man stood. He determined that Van Cleef would only dig himself deeper with his outburst.

As it turned out, he should've allowed Yeva to remove him before he opened his mouth and caused Andrei to reconsider not burying him somewhere in the desert.

"You've always had it in for me. You with your new money, buying your way into rooms with people like me. People with family names and lineage not tied to drafty shacks in Siberia."

Andrei was unbothered by Van Cleef's assumption he'd grown up impoverished. He wasn't the first and wouldn't be the last person born into wealth who presumed their financial status made them better than others.

"I was willing to look past your new money stench. I didn't even hold it against you for trying to drive us all into the poor house by saying we should pay the players more. They're fucking millionaires! How much more do they need anyway?

Then, you've been seen publicly with that ambulance chasing lawyer. Turning your back on good whi—" Van Cleef cut off the word, but it was clear what he was going to say. "You threatened an upstanding member of this community over a piece of black p—"

"That is enough!"

Andrei's voice boomed over Van Cleef's. If he allowed him to continue talking, he would violate not just the terms of his contract but the law by making sure Bertrand Van Cleef breathed his last breath.

He hadn't even realized he'd stood until Yeva placed himself between Andrei and the now shrinking older man. While Yeva protected Andrei from himself, building security escorted the blubbering Van Cleef from the conference room.

Turning away from Yeva and the others, Andrei stared out the window at the city below. He didn't need the full ten minutes in the penalty box. He took a solid ninety seconds to get himself together before turning back to the table. Once he was re-seated, he continued the meeting as if it hadn't just been interrupted by racist rantings.

Chapter Twenty-Nine

DON'T ACT BRAND NEW

Zaria ended her workday on a somewhat pleasant note. For a Monday, it wasn't too bad. She didn't have anything against the start of the week, because she loved her career. But something about Mondays seemed to bring out the irritable in the rest of the working world.

It was when the most complaints came in about the most asinine things. By Tuesday morning, everyone had usually cooled their tits and wasn't biting off people's heads because they hadn't gotten their way the day before. As she was leaving, she encountered Melinda, who informed her that both candidates had been contacted to let them know they would receive an official offer letter tomorrow.

It was very old school, but Melinda held fast to the tradition of sending formal offer letters to potential employees. Zaria didn't balk at it, since she considered it a nice touch as well. A prospective employee's first introduction to the company should be welcoming enough for them to expect their work environment to reflect the same.

During the drive home, Zaria considered if she wanted to tell Andrei about her plans for her house. Or if she should hold it until she officially had a tenant. She didn't anticipate any pushback from him. Actually, once she told him, she'd be surprised if he didn't want to immediately make plans to move the rest of her things to the mansion. As it was, a large chunk of her wardrobe was there—along with some items he thought she didn't know he'd added.

When Logan opened the door for her, she stepped out of the vehicle to see Andrei standing in the doorway. *That would never get old.* Whenever he arrived before her, he was usually waiting for her on the doorstep.

Meeting her on the walkway, he took her bag, dropped a kiss on her lips, and pulled her into a hug.

"Mmm... This is nice. Hey, to you too," Zaria murmured against his lips.

Andrei guided her into the house with a hand at the small of her back. Without thought, she leaned into his warmth. Her gaze swept around the entryway. It occurred to her that, while lovely, the home didn't look the least bit festive. A slight furrow painted her brow.

"What is wrong, Svet?"

"Hm?" Zaria lifted her eyes to his. His concerned expression had her shaking her head. "Nothing's wrong, I just had a thought."

"About?"

"Do you not decorate for the holidays?"

Shrugging, Andrei looked around the foyer. "Mrs. Keith normally handles that. The decorators will probably start next week."

"Christmas is two weeks away, and they aren't going to start until next week?"

When she said the words, the reality of it hit her. *Christmas was two weeks away!* And her family would be coming here. With her. And Andrei. At ***this*** house. ***Shit!***

Through her processing, Zaria felt the weight of Andrei's stare. The pressure against her back increased until she was moving through the opening leading to the front living room. By the time she realized what was happening, she was seated across his lap with his large hands stroking her back and legs.

"Would you like for Mrs. Keith to arrange for them to come earlier? It is not a big deal for me. I have not held onto many traditions. In my family, we celebrated Christmas on January seventh."

"Really? I didn't know that. Is it a common practice in Russia?"

"Yes. My mother was very religious. It is one of the few things she insisted on. Although, she would allow us to put up a Christmas tree on the more popular Christmas Eve date. Then, we would take it down on January eighth."

Zaria made a mental note to learn more about her man's culture and traditions. He'd been wonderful about respecting hers. It was only right to extend him the same support.

"You don't have to rush Mrs. Keith. If she already has the decorator's set up. We can just follow her plan."

Although Andrei had told her more than once that she could make any changes she desired, Zaria didn't feel right coming in trying to make the household conform to her.

"It is not a problem, Svet."

Running her hand over his pectoral, she rested it on the curve of his shoulder. The muscle twitched beneath her touch.

"No. It's okay. I won't ask her to alter her schedule. I'm sure she has it down to a science by now."

Some part of her told Zaria he wouldn't listen, however she held out hope. Snuggling into his embrace, she tried to imagine what the room would look like decked out in holiday trimmings. The place in front of the large window would be perfect for a tree.

With the high ceilings, and the space, she'd guess they could fit one on the scale of those only seen in major department stores or the mall. Not quite the fifty footers, but taller than the twelve-foot tree her aunt usually put up at home.

The rumbling of her stomach broke through the silence shrouding them. With two taps on her hip, Andrei encouraged her to abandon her cozy position.

"Come, Svet. We will get you something to nibble on until dinner is ready. Chef is cooking Chicken Marsala tonight."

"That sounds amazing. But let's not forget you have tea you're supposed to be spilling, Mr. Antonov."

Zaria felt him stiffen beneath her. There were times when she tripped one of his sexual triggers purposely. There were others...like now...when she was simply speaking and not trying to rile him up for an Incredible Fucking Russian performance. Andrei didn't differentiate between the two.

Had it not been for her heightened libido, she would've tapped out with the way he responded to her repeated use of *sir* during their trip south. Ninety percent of the time, it wasn't even directed at him. He. Did. Not. Care. The only thing that saved her was the repeat performance of her stomach's objection to being empty.

"We will address your hunger first. The rest...later." His scorching gaze raked over her with his words.

Unsure if she was happy for the reprieve, Zaria accepted his assistance standing from his lap. Her pretty pocket was shameless these days. It only took the slightest hint for her core to make preparations to be invaded. She had very little control when it came to yielding to those urges. And Andrei was complicit, so he wouldn't be trying to dissuade her from any sexual shenanigans.

With a quick pit stop for hand washing, they continued to the kitchen. Once they entered, the smells and sounds of the meal being prepared engulfed her. The watering of her mouth joined the rumbling of her belly. As if he had some sort of intuition, Chef turned away from the cutting counter and slid an artfully arranged charcuterie board onto the marbled surface in front of her.

"Thank you, Chef."

Zaria reached for a small cube of cheese, popping it into her mouth. The flavors burst on her tongue and she closed her eyes briefly to savor them. When she lifted her lids, Andrei had the board in his hand. His gaze was glued to her face. The heat of his stare washed over her, coalescing at her core.

Averting her eyes, she tried to get herself under control. Thanking the Chef again, she grasped Andrei's free hand, tangling their fingers together. Zaria had quickly learned the sunroom was one of Andrei's favorite places to take his meals whether it was morning or night. Once they were settled onto a lounger, she snagged a slice of cured meat. Humming around the bite, she looked at Andrei. When he continued to simply stare at her, she lifted one eyebrow.

"Come on, Antonov. Don't act brand new. Spill. Why shouldn't I hire Katelyn Norris? Who is she, and what made you say she was untrustworthy?"

Zaria settled against the cushions after snagging a piece of crusty bread, topping it with spreadable cheese. She watched Andrei with expectation.

"She is a former employee who broke the terms of her contract. She was a hostess at *The Rooftop*."

"Which terms?"

At his responding brow raise, she mimicked his expression.

"You're the one who gave *me* instructions on how to proceed with a potential employee. I know you didn't expect me to defer blindly."

Zaria felt a small twinge of guilt for her statement, but she squashed it. He had no idea they'd already come to a decision. So, she was in no danger of adding a dishonest person to her staff.

"She is the person who leaked the photos of Carver taken inside the Casino."

Zaria froze with her hand midway to her mouth with another bite. "You mean the photos which were all over social media trying to make it look like Carver was cheating on Alyssa with his real estate agent? Those pictures?"

"Yes."

"And that bitch had the audacity to show her face in ***my*** office? What kind of crazy shit is she on?"

Zaria went from mildly curious to flaming mad in a split second. If Carver and Alyssa's relationship had been the least bit unstable, she could've caused serious damage. As it was, Katelyn put her friend through unnecessary angst. And for what? To get in with a tabloid? Make a few bucks?

Andrei's large, warm hand landed on her thigh, rubbing in soothing circles.

"Svet, I would prefer if you did not get yourself worked up about this."

"Yeah, and I would prefer that trifling heifers, who try to cause trouble in my friend's relationship, wouldn't sashay their ass into my place of business trying to get a job."

Shifting, she moved to stand. Andrei's hands were on her hips immediately. Zaria couldn't tell if he was trying to help her or stop her.

"Where are you going?" Andrei's normally fierce expression was tinted with concern answering her unspoken question.

"I'm going to get my phone. I left it in my bag. I need to send Melinda a message. The word needs to go out about that trick, and my HR manager knows the right ears to drop a bug in about her. Her ass won't be working for anyone who cares about their reputation."

Instead of releasing her, Andrei tugged her between his legs. Resting her hands on his shoulders, Zaria gave him a nudge. His response was to shake his head and tighten his grip.

"Do not worry about it, Svet. When you mentioned her name, I put someone to work to find out what she was up to. I will handle it."

Part of Zaria wanted to object to him taking over. After all, it was her business Katelyn was trying to infiltrate. And it was Zaria's best friend whom the other woman caused emotional harm. Then, there was the other part of her brain which wasn't operating in reactionary mode. It reminded her that the woman was a former employee of Antonov Industries for the reasons Andrei had just laid out not five minutes ago.

In essence, Katelyn Norris was his mess to clean up. Zaria softened her stance and stopped trying to get out of Andrei's embrace.

"Fine... You handle it, because if I have to handle it, she'll have to move several states away to one where I don't have family and friends in order to get anything resembling gainful employment."

Andrei's chuckle sounded like a half-grunt. He was amused. In contrast, Zaria was very serious. She might not be mega wealthy, but she had connections of her own. Katelyn had better take her bullshit somewhere else. Zaria still fully intended to tell Melinda about the woman when she got into the office the next day.

Accepting the bite of bread slathered with creamy cheese from Andrei, she cuddled into his chest.

"So, what else do I need to know about?" Looking over her shoulder, she peered up into his face.

Popping the remainder of the bread into his mouth, he chewed on it. One eyebrow lifted in question as he assessed her. Finishing her bite, she held up a hand to decline another.

"Don't give me that look. You think you're the only one who knows how to read people? You're holding back on me. And before you say you don't want me to worry or get worked up, consider this. If you don't tell me, my mind is going to come to its own conclusions.

Those conclusions may or may not cause me to be upset or angry. Because, we both know, when someone goes off on a mental tangent, it isn't to a happy place. It's always the worst-case scenario."

Zaria's gaze was glued to Andrei's face. He was probably an excellent poker player. He gave very little away. But, she was an avid student of the school of Andrei Antonov; she saw something behind his eyes and he wasn't going to get away with leaving her in the dark.

Folding her arms, she resolved herself to wait him out. Her stomach rumbled, prompting her to reach for a new selection from the charcuterie board. She ignored his side eye from her feeding herself instead of accepting his offering. He needed to dispense information, not snacks. After a solid minute with nothing except the sounds of them breathing and her chewing, Andrei released a resigned huff.

"Fine, Svet. I know you did not want me to try to fix it..."

Zaria pursed her lips. After which Andrei rushed to continue, "And I have not. I simply asked someone to look into the reasoning behind Winstead's treatment of Francisco. It did not sit well with me to know I had recommended a firm that treated him poorly."

Zaria relaxed her posture. Even as she'd told him not to do anything, she had a feeling he wouldn't let it go. Andrei was protective, almost to the extreme, of those he cared about. Although he didn't know Cisco well, it wasn't hard to see he considered her cousin an extension of her. Therefore, by Andrei-logic, hurting Cisco hurt Zaria.

Even if she hadn't experienced such before, Zaria was able to draw a direct line between the cause and the action. So, she couldn't even be mad at him about it. At least not until she found out how far he'd taken his *Save The Day* routine.

"And, what did they find out?"

Zaria listened without interruption as Andrei laid out what he'd learned through a person he referred to as a business associate. She didn't dispute his word. The confidence with which he relayed the information said his relationship with the person was more than business. Andrei liked to play things close to the vest. Even with her. Instead of dwelling on what he didn't say, Zaria focused on what he did say.

"So, given what's going on with the heavy hitters, maybe I should tell Cisco we need to broaden the search to include smaller firms. Something similar to mine, with really great attorneys, but more client focused. It might be better for him than a corporate machine like Halsted, Markham, and Blake."

Andrei nodded with a contemplative expression. "It may be best to exclude the bigger firms. Now that I have met your family, I do not think those large firms will give Francisco the kind of attention he deserves. Perhaps..."

When he trailed off, Zaria waited a beat before she prompted him. "Perhaps what?"

"I was thinking perhaps we should make contact with Vitaly's attorney. He was instrumental in helping him sign with the agent he is with currently. She negotiated an excellent contract for him with the *Torrent*."

"She?" Zaria was intrigued. There were not many recognizable, successful female sports agents of whom she was aware. She loved the idea of a woman succeeding in a male-dominated field.

"Yes. She. Jamie Shannon. From what I have noticed, she is very hands on."

"Color me intrigued. But, before we jump into anything, I told my aunt and uncle I'd represent Cisco at one meeting with an agent who's expressed interest."

When Andrei opened his mouth, she put a finger on his lips.

"I know. He can't officially sign with anyone right now. I'm simply allowing them to talk. He can't commit and he won't be present. It'll keep them from trying to use his coach to get to him, which already has me giving them side eye."

"Good. I would not want anyone to move too quickly and damage his eligibility."

"Thank you for your concern." Zaria cupped Andrei's cheek, giving his lips a light peck.

Andrei nodded in agreement, but didn't comment further. A few moments later, Chef called them in for dinner. Despite snacking liberally on the meat, cheese and bread, Zaria was ready to dig into the delectable smelling meal he'd prepared. Conversation was lighter as they ate, with Andrei reminding her of their cornbread making lessons. He was serious about being prepared to make dressing for Christmas.

Once she was done eating, Zaria placed her silverware on her nearly empty plate. As delicious as it was, there was no way she could finish the portion she was given.

Having finished before her, Andrei sipped his after-dinner drink and watched her. She wondered if she'd ever get used to the intensity of his stare. After he finished his drink, they took their dirty dishes into the kitchen. Other than the items they'd used, the space was spotless. Placing his empty plate into the sink, Andrei reached for hers after she dumped the remainder in the trash compactor.

She loved that he didn't think twice about traditional gender roles. While he had staff to take care of most things, he had no problems cleaning behind himself and doing small tasks like washing dishes when he was done with them. Although it was tempting to slack off with someone there to handle it, Zaria did her share of dishes and other small household chores.

Zaria could've gone upstairs to have her bath and change out of her work clothes, but she didn't. Instead, she propped herself next to the sink to watch Andrei in his domestic glory. The man still hadn't gotten the hang of lounge clothes. He wore a white button down and slacks. It wasn't the business suit he'd sported when he left that morning, so he'd attempted to dress down.

What should've looked stiff and uncomfortable, on Andrei, simply made Zaria's mouth water. When she realized she was licking her lips, watching the play of his muscles as he cleaned the dishes, she blinked hard and cleared her throat. Andrei's eyes searched hers and Zaria asked the first question to pop into her head.

"Is Vitaly going to come here for Christmas?"

Chapter Thirty

YOUR BROTHER NEEDS YOU

Andrei knew exactly what Zaria was doing when she blurted out her question, yet he'd let her get away with it—for now. At least she hadn't attempted to restart their previous conversation, where she wanted to know what else he wasn't telling her. He'd let her in on what was going on with Francisco, but there was no way in hell he was going to tell her he was looking into Vincent. Nor would he burden her with what was going on with Ruslan.

It was non-negotiable. There was no need to stress her unnecessarily. Gregor would find out the details, and the situation would be handled. Now that Vitaly was aware of the depths of Ruslan's betrayal, Andrei was certain he didn't have to worry about his brother falling prey to whatever sob story Ruslan concocted.

"I do not know."

"What do you mean you don't know? Don't you two spend at least one holiday together?"

Drying his hands, Andrei matched her pose, leaning against the edge of the countertop.

"Between our schedules, we have not always been able to do more than share a meal or phone call for quite some time. I do not recall the last time we spent Christmas together."

Taking the towel from his hands, Zaria placed it on the rack next to the sink before putting herself in his arms. She would get no complaints from him. That is exactly where he liked for her to be—with her luscious curves pressed against him.

"Baby, you and your brother need to stay connected. You're the only family the other has. Why don't you invite him for Christmas? I think he'll enjoy it. You know it'll be loud and slightly chaotic, but I'm positive it'll be better than him sitting in his condo alone.

I already checked the schedule and I know there are no games between the twenty-third and the twenty-seventh. Depending on when he has to get back for practice, that means he could at least be here for two days. Maybe even three."

Andrei stared into Zaria's expressive eyes. Before she finished her explanation, he already knew he was going to fold. He was turning into a *neudacha*. At least where his Svet was concerned, he was unapologetically a pushover.

"I will ask him." Zaria squeezed herself closer to him in a hug, and he relished having her softness against his hardness. "I cannot make any promises, Svet. He may have plans."

"He won't. He's been waiting for you to reach out to him."

Frowning, he held her away as he searched her eyes. "You have spoken to him?"

"No. Not since New York." Rubbing his chest, she went up onto her tiptoes with her lips puckered. Closing the distance between them, Andrei accepted the light kiss.

"I told you, Sir. You aren't the only one who can read people. Your brother needs you. He's just waiting for you to realize you need him too."

Normally, when his Svet called him *sir* or *Mr. Antonov,* it turned him feral with a desire to do nothing more than plant himself deep inside her heat. This time, the words following it doused his flame. Not her saying she was observant. He was well aware of her keen observation skills. No, it was her saying Vitaly needed him and he needed Vitaly.

"My brother has me." Andrei's words were stiff, even to his own ears.

"Yes. It is obvious to me that you love and support him. Even if your nickname for him is Brat and you act put out when he jokes around." Zaria shrugged. "It was just something I picked up on when we were all together in New York. He was positively giddy you came to his game and wanted to go to dinner after. You would've thought it was pee-wee hockey and his big brother had come home from college early to see him play. He acted cool, but he was about to jump out of his skin."

Andrei's gaze was on Zaria, but he was in his head, replaying their recent visit with his brother. Vitaly was important in his life. Since Andrei was starting a new phase of living with Zaria, it was imperative the two meet as she was his Svet. It dawned on him that he was in full protective mode when they were out, so he hadn't focused on Vitaly one on one until their conversation on the plane.

He hadn't noted any difference in the way his brother behaved the previous evening. Vitaly was being Vitaly. At least that was what he thought. And what did she mean by his brother was waiting for Andrei to realize he needed him as well?

Zaria stroked his hair away from his forehead and slid her fingers into his short locks. "I can tell you're replaying everything in your head trying to figure out what you missed. He never said anything. It's something I'm sensitive to; so, I noticed. The desire for family closeness is one I know well."

Andrei wasn't sure how to proceed. Having the words to respond to anything thrown at him wasn't usually a problem. However, he'd also never been with a woman like Zaria. She wasn't just observant. She was open, and she called him on his shit. From the very beginning, Zaria was straight forward and bold in their interactions. It was one of the qualities which drew him to her.

When she stepped out of his arms, he missed her immediately. Tangling their fingers together, she tugged until he followed her up the side stairs to the second level and the bedroom suite they shared. Instead of stripping out of her clothes as he hoped she would, she led him to the sitting area. With both hands in the center of his chest, she pushed until he sat on the sofa.

Then, she climbed into this lap with her thick thighs straddling his. She seemed unbothered by the way her skirt rode up her thighs, while he found the exposed expanse of skin distracting. Andrei's fingers were magnetically drawn to their silky softness. Beneath the edge of the skirt, he traced a path up toward her hips, only to be stopped by Zaria's hands on his.

"That's not why we're here. At least not yet." The seriousness of her expression didn't completely hide the passion banked behind her eyes. But, Andrei stopped his exploration—for the moment.

"Why are we here, Svet?"

"To talk. When I told you downstairs that you and your brother needed each other, the gears in your head started to grind to the point I could see them turning. So, talk to me."

"I do not know what it is you want me to say."

"Whatever you think. Whatever you feel. There are no guidelines for this, Andrei—except for you to be honest. With me and yourself."

Andrei's fingers squeezed reflexively, anchoring himself with the feel of her in his hands and on his lap. Feelings. Expressing his feelings wasn't a luxury he'd had for a very long time. His mama was an affectionate parent, but his papa was...not. In contrast, he was stoic. Gruff. Mainly concerned with providing food and shelter for his family.

Zaria watched him with eyes filled with empathy. Although he hadn't spoken a word yet, she was already with him emotionally. So, Andrei did something he'd never done. With anyone aside from his brother. He talked. About his childhood. His parents. His life before he came to the United States to play hockey.

"I have not told you much about the way I grew up. I am fourteen years older than Vitaly. So, it was almost like we were raised by two different sets of parents. My mama was very affectionate. She gave praise, hugs, and kisses. My papa...he was...different. It was not that he did not care. He was simply focused on being a provider for his family.

By the time Vitaly was born, I was doing really well at hockey. There were private and government sponsors; so, money was better. We left the little village outside of St. Petersburg and moved to Moscow.

We all doted on Vitaly. Protected him. I was never jealous of the way Papa played with him. But I will admit, I did not recognize my papa as the same man from when I was that age."

Andrei stopped speaking as he considered if he was being completely honest. He didn't recall ever being jealous of Vitaly having access to both of their parents. If anything, he was complicit in the sheltering of his younger brother.

Zaria snuggled into his embrace, tucking her head beneath his chin. He paused for a beat to appreciate how perfectly she fit in his arms. Then, he picked up his retelling where he left off.

What he didn't anticipate was the emotions elicited by some of the memories he recounted. Some happy. Others not so much. When he was done Zaria squeezed him in her arms, then sat up so she could look into his face. Andrei closed his eyes briefly at the feel of her soft fingertips against his skin as she stroked his beard.

Andrei felt a sense of relief and understanding once he was done speaking. Yes, Vitaly had the opportunity to be loved differently by their parents. However, they'd been brutally taken away during a time in his life when he needed them most.

With only the example of his papa, Andrei took over caring for his brother in much the same fashion as he'd been reared. Having the dual role of sibling and parent had placed a barrier between them. Until Vitaly went to college, Andrei had worked to keep some normalcy—at least with celebrating the Christmas holiday and Vitaly's birthday.

Once he was at university, they both had hectic schedules. Vitaly played college sports while getting his degree. Andrei was building his wealth and establishing himself in the business world. They didn't carve out time to celebrate. There was always something which needed to be handled. It caused their time to be cut short. It was just the two of them, so there wouldn't have been large, boisterous get togethers like the ones Zaria's family had. But they could've done better. ***He*** could've done better.

"Hey. Look at me."

Although Zaria spoke her demand softly, it was definitely a demand. One Andrei didn't fully understand. He *was* looking at her. He never stopped. He lifted both brows in silent question of her command.

"I'm not saying you failed your brother. Please don't think that. I just wanted you to consider the possibility there could be more to your relationship. You took a lot on yourself after the two of you lost your parents. More than I realized.

From what you just said, you didn't even really allow yourself time to properly grieve. You made it your mission to build a life for you and Vitaly. One where the two of you could thrive. Congratulations, baby. You achieved your goal. Ten—hell—twenty-fold. Now, you can take some time to just enjoy being siblings.

You're his brother. Not his father. Maybe take the opportunity to nurture your fraternal relationship. Dom and Cisco are the closest thing I have to siblings, and I wouldn't change a minute of those times when they come to me as their big sister or when we can talk and reminisce about our childhoods."

"That is nice, Svet. But, Vitaly and I were never children together."

"Let's keep it real. You weren't a child when you were a child, baby. So, that's not an apples-to-apples comparison. I was a senior in high school when Cisco was born. We still have shared memories with my aunt and uncle."

"Yes, however Francisco's memories, which include you, are from the perspective of a child. It is the same for me and Vitaly. By the time he was old enough to form lasting memories, I was away playing hockey full time. Until he came to live with me in Chicago, I only saw him when I went home for visits."

Zaria shifted on his lap, reminding him of their current position and the thin scraps of clothing separating them from skin-to-skin contact. Andrei shoved his baser impulse away to focus on their conversation.

"Okay... I'm not expecting you to have the same relationship I have with Dom and Cisco. There is no cookie cutter format to these things. What I am saying is, maybe consider that your relationship with your brother deserves the opportunity to grow to match the different places the two of you are in your lives."

Zaria's observation was a healthy one. A thought, he wouldn't dare voice out loud, flit across his mind. He considered her healthy outlook was likely the result of the hard work she'd done with her therapist.

Andrei didn't think it would be insulting to say it aloud, but he wasn't certain he could put voice to it without it sounding as if he was poking fun at her quest to be her best self. Also, she was simply trying to help him and his brother have a better relationship. For that, she endeared herself to him even more.

"Thank you, Svet. I will call Vitaly in the morning and invite him to spend his Christmas downtime here with us."

"Tomorrow?" Zaria's brow wrinkled. "Why not tonight? It's not late."

Andrei's fingers resumed their previous trek beneath her skirt.

"Because… I will be too busy. In the morning would be better."

"Busy doing what?" Her head tilted slightly to one side and her bottom lip protruded.

Andrei took the protrusion as an offering, nipping the plump gift.

"You, Svet. I will be too busy doing you."

"Is that so?" Zaria's lashes lowered, partially covering her eyes from him, giving her a coquettish appearance.

Andrei's fingers found the rounded curve of her ass, squeezing the plush cheeks.

"Da."

His one-word reply was followed by him taking her sassy mouth in a heated kiss. The cloth separating them didn't stop Andrei from pumping his hips upward, stimulating her as much as he could with the barriers in place. His grip tightened as he tugged her forward in rhythm with his movements.

Zaria broke their kiss, trailing her lips along his jawline, leaving scorching pecks down to the crook of his neck.

"Ummm… Shit… Why am I so fucking horny?" Her breathy question was accompanied by the rocking of her hips. "The way I want you to fuck me all the time is insane. I wasn't even thinking about sex two minutes ago."

"It's the hormones, Svet. Your body is changing."

Dropping kisses along any exposed part of her skin he could reach, Andrei's digits searched out the clasp to her skirt. They needed to be naked. Now. Apparently, Zaria was on board with the quest for nakedness. She attacked the buttons of his shirt with precision, amid tiny grunts of frustration.

The amount of time it took to get them undressed made Andrei briefly consider the merit of wearing the type of clothing Zaria mentioned was *real* loungewear. His shirt, and hers, had entirely too many buttons to navigate. A tearing sound was followed by a light gasp when Andrei tired of trying to undress her the normal way and opted for ripping at the material separating them.

He'd buy her another outfit. The one now hanging from her body had spent its last day as part of her wardrobe. Andrei's cock throbbed to be inside Zaria. His mouth watered to taste her delicious cream, and his ears hungered for her appreciative moans.

Standing from the sofa with Zaria wrapped around him, Andrei stalked into the bathroom. In seconds, he had them both naked and standing inside the glass and tiled enclosure. He was never happier for the large bench along the back of the shower.

Turning Zaria to face it, he peppered kisses down her back as he dropped to his knees behind her. When her delectable ass was eye level, he cupped the rounded globes with both hands. Bites and soothing kisses were placed on each cheek as he simultaneously punished and paid homage to his woman. Zaria's sharp inhales were followed by aroused sighs.

She'd called him *sir* earlier. He hadn't forgotten. Now, she'd be reminded of what using that word earned her. Tonight, it would earn her the rough fucking she obviously needed.

With one hand against her shoulders, he gently but forcefully encouraged her to lean forward. Without being told, she grabbed the bar attached to the wall to anchor herself. She'd need the support.

As soon as the puffy lips of her pussy were visible, he latched onto them, dipping his tongue between the folds, seeking her pearl. The moment her clit peeked out of its hood, Andrei latched onto the little bundle of nerves with erotic brutality. Zaria's strangled cries rang out against the porcelain walls, spurring him on.

Her hips rocked back, pressing her core into his face. A firm smack to one plush cheek had her walls clamping tightly around his tongue.

"Do not try to fuck me, Svet. I am fucking you." Another smack was delivered to the other cheek. "Now, take your punishment like a good girl."

A gush of her cream had him closing his eyes to savor the flavor. It was too much. His desire was riding too close to the edge. He had to get inside her silken heat. With a growl, he tore himself away from dining on her pretty pussy. Getting to his feet, he guided his thickness into her velvet center, surging inside in one firm stroke.

"Aw shit!"

Andrei's lips tipped up in a feral grin at Zaria's exclamation. He loved hearing her pleasure. Withdrawing, he surged inside again with a swiveling tilt to his thrust. His fingertips gripped her hips, pulling her to him as he plunged into her depths.

Zaria's back arched, presenting him with the most beautifully erotic view of his woman. *Fuck.* She was amazing. Delivering unrelenting blows to her slick channel, Andrei didn't relent until her tunnel clamped down tightly around his shaft and her screams bounced off the wall, announcing her orgasm.

When her channel began to pulse, massaging his shaft, he was tossed into his release, igniting her aftershocks. One hand held onto Zaria, keeping her ass pressed against his pelvis, while the other was braced against the wall above her head. His cock jerked inside her, releasing his seed. If she wasn't already pregnant, he was certain he'd come hard enough to give his soldiers an excellent chance to find their target.

Once he was spent, he reluctantly withdrew. Gently lifting her, he turned her around. Grabbing a washcloth and body wash, he cleansed her body. Zaria limply allowed him to maneuver her until the task was complete. Normally, he would prepare a bath for her, but she looked spent.

Andrei wasn't worried. With her new heightened sex drive, he was assured she'd be revived and ready soon. After their shower, they were tucked into bed with the television playing softly in the background. Zaria snuggled into his side.

"What *is* your deal with the 's' word?" Although she sounded slightly groggy, her words were easily understood.

She'd grumbled about his response to her use of the word *sir* in the past. This was the first time Zaria had directly asked about his response to her use of it. Andrei didn't have an explanation that he thought she would see as reasonable. It simply did something to him when she said it. It brought out his dominant nature—even though he didn't practice a Dom-Sub lifestyle.

Shrugging, he ran one hand along the smoothness of her leg while hugging her to him with the other. Zaria sighed under his touch and stroked his chest.

"It is not hearing the word. It is hearing *you* say it. I cannot accurately explain it. Just know you should not use it if you are not prepared to be fucked."

"Andrei!" Zaria's protest and tap to his chest were half-hearted at best. "You're a mess."

"Yes. But I am your mess, Svet."

"Yes. Yes, you are."

That was the end of their conversation as Zaria drifted off to sleep. Shortly after he was certain she was out, Andrei turned off the television. As he went to replace the remote on the nightstand, his cellphone display lit up.

Quickly swiping it to access the alert, he saw a message from Gregor.

Gregor: Your birdie has decided to sing. How would you like to proceed?

Come to my office in the morning. Six a.m.

He didn't wait for a reply. Andrei placed the phone face down on the surface, wrapped both arms around his woman, and willed himself to fall asleep. He'd deal with their songbird tomorrow.

Chapter Thirty-One

UNTHINK THAT THOUGHT

Zaria awoke the next morning to an empty place where Andrei normally lay. It wasn't surprising, since he typically woke before her to work out. What did surprise her was the sheets didn't hold any warmth from where his body had been. It meant he'd risen earlier than usual.

Levering herself up from the bed, Zaria saw her phone face up on the nightstand. It wasn't where she'd left it. The screen brightened when she picked it up and she saw the message notification. It was from Andrei. The time stamp had him sending it at six-thirty a.m. It was seven thirty.

Zaria had slightly overslept. Andrei had become her alarm clock, so she was usually up by seven. It didn't matter that she'd slept late. She was working from home today to enable her to also coordinate with Cammy about final tenant selections.

AAA: Svet. I have a long day today. I will not be home for dinner. Do not wait up for me.

Zaria frowned, looking at the screen. That wasn't like Andrei. It was common for him to work late, but not to the point for him to tell her not to bother to wait up for him. Whatever it was, he'd probably tell her about it later. Although, he didn't go into specifics about his business, he'd begun to open up more.

Not starting her day with an orgasm had her slightly salty, but she went on with the rest of her morning routine. Once she was showered and dressed, she went down to the kitchen. Mrs. Keith was standing at the sink rinsing a coffee cup when Zaria entered the room.

"Good morning, Mrs. Keith."

"Good morning, Mrs. Antono—I mean Ms Coleman! How are you feeling?"

Regarding the house manager with a side eye glance, Zaria walked over to the refrigerator, reached inside, and pulled out the pitcher of orange juice. She hadn't missed the woman's near slip, calling her Mrs. Antonov. There wasn't a need to make a fuss about it. However, her expression told Mrs. Keith that her mistake had been noted.

"I'm doing well, thank you. How are you?"

Mrs. Keith's cheeks pinkened under her lightly bronzed complexion as she busied herself drying the mug and placing it in the cupboard.

"I'm doing quite well. Thank you for asking." Turning to face Zaria, she ran her hands along her slate grey pants before clasping them together in front of her. As Zaria poured a glass of juice, Mrs. Keith's eyes tracked her movements.

"Is there something you needed, Mrs. Keith?"

"Oh. No, ma'am. I was going to ask if there is anything I can do for you. Chef doesn't get in for another hour or so, but I can take care of breakfast for you, if you'd like."

Holding up one hand, Zaria took a sip of the sweet citrus. *That's gotta be fresh squeezed.* "Don't trouble yourself. I'm not very hungry. I'm just going to have a bowl of oatmeal with some fruit and walnuts."

As she spoke, Mrs. Keith's head began a slow side-to-side wag. Zaria paused with the glass part-way to her lips.

"What? Why are you shaking your head no?"

"I can't let you simply eat oatmeal, fruit, and nuts. That's not enough nourishment. Chef baked some fresh bread before he left. I'll just whip you up some toast, eggs and some of Chef's custom apple sausage. It's delicious. If you still want oatmeal. I can put a little bowl on the side."

"Mrs. Keith. Really, I'm not hungry enough to eat all that." Zaria tried again to dissuade the older woman. But...her body was a traitor. Her stomach picked that moment to grumble. Loudly.

With a light giggle of chagrin, she took another sip of her orange juice. "Okay. Maybe I *could* eat a little more than oatmeal."

"Excellent!" Mrs. Keith clapped her hands, smiling broadly. As she tied an apron around her waist, she tipped her head toward the entrance to the sunroom. "You go on in and wait. I'll have your food ready in no time. You have a big day ahead of you."

"Thank you. You're right. I do have a busy day planned." When Zaria made it to the threshold between the rooms, she stopped. Turning back toward the house manager, she assessed her.

"Mrs. Keith?"

"Yes, Ms Coleman?"

"Call me Zaria."

"If you insist, but you must call me Peggy." Peggy smiled broadly, showing even, white, teeth.

"Okay, Peggy. Why did you say I have a big day ahead of me?" Zaria didn't recall sharing her schedule with anyone outside of her office. She didn't even tell Andrei everything she'd do—only that she intended to work from home today.

Peggy continued to move around the kitchen, taking out ingredients after she washed her hands.

"Oh. I got a message from Mr. Antonov. He moved up the schedule for the decorators. They'll be in around ten a.m. to get started. He said you'd want to have input on the overall theme."

Zaria clamped her lips together to keep from blurting out the words zipping through her head. She'd specifically told Andrei it wasn't necessary to move up the plans for decorating. And at no time did she imply she wanted to assist or oversee any part of the process.

She held her tongue, because what she had to say didn't involve the other woman. Peggy was simply doing her job. Oblivious to Zaria's silent fuming, the house manager continued to move around preparing the food.

"I'm actually kind of glad you said something to him. It didn't seem right to me to wait so close to Christmas to actually decorate. The only time we've done it even this far in advance was when he hosted a party for his executives and business associates once. It was a one-time thing. After that year, the event was held in one of the ballrooms in the casino."

Instead of going into the sunroom, Zaria perched on a tall stool at the island counter. She watched Peggy cook her breakfast and listened to the recounting of the bachelor Antonov household being contrasted to the household after she arrived. It was enlightening.

As she predicted, Peggy placed a hot meal in front of Zaria in no time at all. It smelled as delicious as it looked. The only interruption to Peggy's illuminating conversation had been when one of the cleaning staff had a question. Answering, then seamlessly picking up the thread of their chat, Peggy continued.

By the time she'd finished setting the kitchen back to rights, Zaria was only one quarter of the way through her meal. Taking a bite of the sausage, she closed her eyes and hummed. She'd almost wrinkled her nose when Peggy mentioned apple sausage. But, having now tasted Chef's creation, she wanted to wrap the man in a bear hug.

Somehow, she thought Andrei may take exception to her showing appreciation in such a manner. So, Zaria simply made a mental note to compliment Chef the next time she saw him. The meat was so good, she seriously pouted when she went to spear another bite and there was none left to be had.

"Would you like some more? It's no problem for me to slide a few more into a skillet."

Declining the offer, Zaria finished the rest of her food while chatting amicably with Peggy. When she was done, the house manager insisted on taking care of the dishes while she shooed Zaria off to her office with an insulated water bottle in her hand.

Zaria walked out of the kitchen and down the wide hallway to reach her home office. She'd been surprised when Andrei first showed her the room. He'd given no indication he'd been planning anything. While it hadn't been a secret that he wanted her with him every night, he hadn't said a word about making space for her work there as well.

He'd even set up monitors and a docking station on the desk. Large windows flanked the garden doors leading out onto a poolside patio and made her wonder about the function of the room before Andrei converted it into her office. Walking behind her desk, Zaria picked up a remote. Pressing a button, she adjusted the polarity of the glass to allow more light into the room.

It was winter in southern Nevada. While the temps could get as low as thirty degrees Fahrenheit, they'd hovered in the mid-forties for the past week. A little sunshine felt good pouring through the glass.

Once she was settled, she considered sending Andrei a message about his high-handed, hard-headed behavior. But, she decided against it. In the end, she knew he did it to please her. He probably also hoped that having a distraction would soften the blow of him not making it home at a reasonable hour.

Instead of working up a head of steam, Zaria placed her laptop on the docking station, powered it up, and got to work. She still had things to do before she could step away to talk to Lacey. Apparently, she also had Christmas decorating to supervise.

Zaria was just finishing her final review of the Settlement documents for the Thompson Industries case when her cellphone pinged. She'd forgotten to put it on vibrate earlier. Checking the time, she noted she'd been working continuously for the past hour and a half. It wouldn't hurt to take a break.

Thompson Industries had attempted to drag their feet with requests for continuances. They finally had to concede to discuss a settlement with her client. They didn't have a leg to stand on, and their attorneys had obviously succeeded in making the CEO and Board of Directors see the futility of taking the case to court.

Zaria was happy to have it resolved without court intervention, but she'd been ready. It was possible she could've won a larger payout than what was stipulated in the Settlement, however her client wasn't vindictive. She simply wanted to be fairly compensated for the lost earnings, damage to her reputation, and, of course, legal fees.

The case hadn't been pro-bono, but Zaria had only accepted a portion of her normal retainer to begin working on it. The bulk of the fees her firm accrued would be paid by Thompson Industries. She'd made the arrangement with the client because Zaria was that confident in their case.

She typed the last few words to correct a statement in the document; then saved it to the secure cloud service. Tapping out a quick message to Tika, she let her know she could move forward with getting everything ready for the wrap up meeting scheduled for later in the week. With her work done for the time being, Zaria picked up her phone to check the notifications.

Although Andrei told her he had the gossip vlog situation under control, Zaria still set up an alert on her name with a few other criteria to keep from getting excess notifications. With the settings she used, she was able to weed out little mentions and only got reports when the same thing appeared from multiple sources. It was a trick her investigator friend taught her a while back.

When she unlocked her phone to look at the information, there was a series of links beneath similar headings. Even though the headings made her stomach clench, she selected the first one anyway. It was an article from a small newspaper in Mississippi.

Mississippi native and powerhouse Las Vegas Attorney, Zaria M. Coleman, Esq. refuses to help her father overturn wrongful murder conviction.

Zaria bit down on the inside of her cheek to hold in the curses. *Why couldn't those bastards just leave her alone?* It'd been more than thirty years. A big part of her didn't want to. But Zaria read the article, which included quotes primarily from Vincent and Lawrence, as well as a few of their other family members.

The delusional assholes made it seem like the Greens and Trumans had coached Zaria in her original testimony. They also heavily implied her aunt and uncle had knowledge of the drugs and other criminal elements uncovered when Lawrence was arrested. That they bore some responsibility for the additional time added to his sentence.

As she read, Zaria was surprised they didn't blame her and her other family members for Lawrence committing more crimes while he was behind bars getting his sentence extended. It would be par for the course with them. As much as she wanted to close the app and forget she'd ever seen the bullshit, Zaria reviewed the other links as well.

When she'd seen enough, she opened up her contacts looking for the information for one of her law school classmates. She'd come too far in her healing and growth to let Vincent, Lawrence, and the rest of their enabling kin keep fucking with her simply because she wouldn't help an abusive murderer be released from prison.

Once she found the name she was looking for, she put her earphones in and dialed the number. While the phone rang, she continued clicking her mouse around opening applications. The call connected on the third ring.

"Spooner and Associates, how may I help you?"

"Hello, this is Zaria Coleman. Is Attorney Spooner available?"

"Hold on one moment, please. I'll check."

Zaria listened to the hold music as her fingers continued to click at her mouse and tap on her keyboard. It didn't take long before the smooth jazz was cut and her classmate's husky voice came through.

"Hey Zee-Baby! Long time no hear from!"

Lavo's chipper greeting prompted Zaria's lips to stretch into a wide smile, despite her irritation.

"Hey Spoon. How are you?"

"I'm doing okay. I can't complain." There was a slight pause before Lavo broke the silence. "So, what's going on? I know we don't talk often, but you don't usually call me during business hours."

Zaria leaned back in her chair and picked up a pen, rolling it between her fingers.

"I called during business hours because I need to discuss business."

"Oh! Okay."

The surprised note in Lavo's voice was expected. Zaria rarely asked for her legal expertise, although her classmate was top-notch. It had shocked everyone when she decided to move back to Mississippi to set up her practice after law school. She'd received offers from some top firms in California. But, Lavo had said the people in her home state needed more good attorneys of color, and she wanted to help change things.

"So, what can I help you with, Ms Coleman?" Lavo's tone was all business.

“I’d like to issue Cease and Desist Orders to the parent companies of the news outlets in the email I just sent you. If you’ll check your account, you’ll see that I’ve also paid your required retainer.”

“Okay...” Zaria heard light tapping and waited for Lavo to open the correspondence and review the information.

“These are serious news outlets, not gossip rags. I can send the order. They’ll probably claim freedom of speech though.”

“I understand they’re supposedly serious and respectable news sources, but they’re running straight up lies about me. Gossip columnists and vlogs can get away with more because they can claim it as rumors. These people are printing bullshit without even bothering to fact check. Here, let me show you.”

Zaria forwarded the links to the articles she’d read earlier. She sat quietly as Lavo reviewed them. Zaria was quiet as her friend kept up a mumbled commentary which grew more hostile the longer she perused the articles.

“They must not care about being sued? Have they switched to being tabloid news now? Because this is tabloid shit, and even they aren’t immune to lawsuits. Hell yeah, I’ll get my paralegal started on drafting those Orders right now. For your mental health, I want them to stop this shit, but part of me hopes I get the chance to sue their asses into the poor house. They’re going to retract this crap. And they’re going to do it on the front freaking page by the time I’m done with them.”

The remainder of Lavo’s rant was mumbled curse words before she cut off to speak to her paralegal over the intercom, asking her to pull up their standard Cease and Desist template and come into her office.

Relief washed over Zaria that she was able to set a plan in motion to keep Vincent and Lawrence from harassing her through the media. It was their only option since she’d gone no contact to the point they couldn’t call, text, email, or reach out to her on social media.

“I have a question.” Apparently done with her rant, Lavo spoke more calmly.

“Shoot.”

“Why do you think these people started this mess up again?” Having grown up in Mississippi, Lavo was aware of what Lawrence had done. It was a big enough deal that even children, during the time period, were aware of it. She and Zaria didn't know one another until law school, and it took a while for Lavo to put it together. They didn't have long discussions about it. They simply acknowledged that it happened and moved on. It worked best for Zaria, as she hadn't started doing the real work to heal at the time.

"I visited my family during Thanksgiving, and I ran into Vincent in a store. He said something about me going to see Lawrence, and I re-iterated I would never go to see Lawrence in prison again."

"So, he ran to the papers? It has to be more than that."

Zaria nodded, although she knew Lavo couldn't see her. "I was with my boyfriend at the time."

"Hold up. Boyfriend? No ma'am. I'm not living under a rock. I've seen the pictures. What you have is a man. Now, continue."

A chuckle escaped before Zaria could stop it. Lavo was the breath of fresh air she needed at the moment.

"Anyway. If you've seen the pictures, you know there were a couple of gossip vlogs speculating about our relationship. They listed his business holdings, along with the casino and his ownership in the Chevaliers."

"So, it's possible they saw your proximity to mega-money as an opportunity to try to force you into helping Lawrence Coleman get his sentence overturned? Why would they think you'd be on board with their plan?"

"I don't know, but they can unthink that thought. I never want to see Lawrence again, and I'm damn sure not helping him get out of prison. He earned his spot."

"You know they're playing on how drug charges were being disproportionally sentenced among black men, right? Saying he served his time for the murder charges, but the sentences he was given for subsequent charges were unfairly extended because of his race?"

"I saw." Zaria flipped the pen from her fingertips to the desk. She didn't need anything in her hands at the moment. She might throw it.

"It pisses me off, because there are so many young black men who are falsely arrested or over charged for crimes who deserve the extra effort and attention to help them fight the system.

Lawrence was a criminal before he went to Parchman, and he didn't stop just because he was behind bars. He isn't deserving of people campaigning and fighting the system for his release."

Not having any personal connection to Zaria's sperm donor, Lavo didn't comment. The two talked strategy for a few more minutes before wrapping up the call. Zaria closed out of her computer and left her office in search of Peggy. She now felt the burning urge to be productive making something pretty to counteract this ugliness.

Chapter Thirty-Two

THIS MUTHAFUCKA

Andrei stepped off the plane at the private air strip adjusting his suit jacket. He hadn't bothered with a coat despite the temperature being several degrees lower than when he'd left Las Vegas. After sending Zaria a quick text message letting her know he'd be home late, he boarded one of his smaller jets with Gregor and Yeva.

This wasn't an overnight trip and his Svet wasn't with him, so there wasn't a need for the larger security detail. Besides, the fewer people involved, the better. Striding toward the large black SUV, Andrei's lips almost stretched into a smile when he saw the driver through the glass. Opening the door, Neal stepped out onto the tarmac.

"It took you long enough."

The older man closed the remaining distance between them with his hand extended. Andrei accepted the shake and the half hug from Zaria's uncle.

"It has been less than four hours since we spoke."

"Yeah, well I thought these fancy jets were faster than regular planes. Direct flights don't usually take as long especially when you're not flying commercial."

"That is true, but even I cannot bend the laws of physics. It takes as long as it takes."

They'd actually arrived more quickly than the projected three hours and twenty minutes. So, even considering the change in time zones, it wasn't noon yet.

"Yeah, yeah. Well, come on. We got shit to do."

Neal turned to walk toward the vehicle and Andrei wondered if Zaria had ever met this side of her uncle. This wasn't the man who gave her hugs and encouraged her to do her best. No. This was a much harder man with a glint of viciousness in his eyes. That was good. They would utilize his fierceness very soon.

By the time Neal reached the driver's side door, Yeva was there. Silently stretching out his arm, he offered to open the rear door.

"What's this?" Neal pulled up short staring from Yeva to Andrei.

"Yeva will drive us."

"I drove this beast here just fine."

"And I appreciate it. However, driving is part of Yeva's job. So, we will allow him to do it."

It wasn't a request, but Neal's demeanor didn't hint at further offense and he conceded, getting into the back seat after Yeva opened the door. Andrei walked around to the other side; then settled into the back seat as well. Once Gregor was settled in the front passenger seat, they left the airstrip.

"While I waited for y'all to show up, I made some discreet inquiries. I didn't find out anything definite. I have a place to start though."

Neal drummed his fingers on his knee as he looked out the window. Andrei had no doubt that had Neal been able to uncover more concrete information, they'd be having a totally different conversation right now. Honestly, he wouldn't blame the man. They had a mutual goal—protecting his Svet.

Gregor turned in his seat looking between Andrei and Neal. "It is okay. We know where to go."

"Oh really?" Neal cocked one eyebrow looking at Gregor. "How did you manage that?"

"I have a contact in the area."

Gregor faced forward and went silent after giving his brief explanation. Andrei knew it was all he'd be willing to say. He wouldn't reveal his sources, and it didn't matter to Andrei—so long as the information was reliable.

"Tell me this?" Neal leaned forward with his hands braced on his knees. "How is it a man, who from his accent I can tell doesn't call this place his home, has a connection in Southhaven, Mississippi?"

Looking over his shoulder, Gregor's gaze flicked between Andrei and Neal. Andrei gave a barely perceptible shrug.

"I do not have connections in Southhaven. But I do know people in Memphis, Tennessee. Those people know people who were able to get the information we needed."

"So, how do you know they can be trusted?"

At Neal's question, Gregor rotated as far as the seat belt would allow. "They do not want to...what is it people say these days?...Fuck around and find out. That is it. They do not want to fuck around and find out what happens if they lie to me."

Neal silently assessed Gregor before nodding curtly. "Good to know, because I warned that muthafucka what would happen if he didn't leave my child alone. If your connect gets me closer to reminding him than mine, it works for me."

Andrei watched the entire exchange without saying a word. He didn't allow himself to consider how Zaria might respond to him involving her sixty-plus-year-old uncle in his plans. She wouldn't like it; but he'd made the man a promise. He intended to honor it. There was no need to bring his Svet in on private conversations between him and her uncle.

As the somehow still green landscape passed by the window, Andrei listened to Neal's intermittent questions to Gregor. Once he'd gotten over Gregor having better contacts than him in his own area of the country, he was curious about what the person had uncovered. What he learned seemed to confirm what he'd been thinking for years.

When they turned off onto a barely recognizable side rode, Neal ceased his questioning as he took in their surroundings.

"Now how the fuck did you even know this road was here?" He directed the question to Yeva who simply tapped his temple and replied that he had a great memory for maps.

Bringing the vehicle to a stop on the back side of an old weathered barn, Yeva cut the engine. Andrei placed a hand on Neal's arm to stop him from immediately exiting the vehicle. However, he said nothing to Gregor when he joined Yeva in sweeping the area.

"They will make certain there are no surprises first."

Gregor may have put the fear of the almighty in his contact, but it never hurt to be safe. Neal nodded in agreement before sitting back against the leather seat. Gregor and Yeva returned a few minutes later opening either of the back doors for Andrei and Neal to exit.

When they entered the building, Andrei's sense of smell was assaulted by the dank aroma of the space. It was clear the barn had been used to house livestock at some point and hadn't been cleaned when it was abandoned. At the center, with open stalls on three sides, was a man with greying hair seated in a wooden chair which appeared to barely hold his weight.

Vincent Coleman looked like he'd had a rough morning. Not one drop of sympathy would be mustered for his haggard condition. He'd been warned and chosen to ignore it.

When Neal stalked over to him and kicked at the side of the chair causing it to tip over, Vincent let out a moaning screech and threw up his hands ineffectively. He wasn't tied to the chair. So, in theory, he could've caught himself before landing on the hard, hay-strewn ground.

Andrei was certain not many people got to see this side of Neal Truman. The man was a retired airline executive; that meant nothing in this moment. In front of them, was a man who defied his sixty-plus years on earth. The way he lifted Vincent from the floor and planted his fist in the other man's face was the feat of a very fit person. Anyone thinking his former cushy job, age, or lifestyle meant he couldn't hold his own would be sadly mistaken.

Gregor gave Andrei a questioning glance. Andrei simply shook his head. He could wait his turn. In fact, Neal was doing a good enough job Andrei may not have to do much when it was all said and done. Strangely, he didn't feel cheated of possibly dispensing retribution.

"Wha?! Man, stop!"

Vincent attempted to push Neal away, but he'd already been roughed up before they arrived. Neal was noticeably stronger, and filled with far more rage. So, Andrei determined he'd stop when he was ready and not a second sooner. When Vincent managed to land a punch, Neal growled at them to keep their distance. If Andrei had considered intervening, the directive was clear. This fight was a long time coming.

However, calling it a fight was generous. It was more of a *reznya*—a slaughter. Finally, Andrei felt Neal had effectively made his point. Besides, he didn't want to explain to Belinda Truman why her husband's swollen knuckles had nothing to do with arthritis.

Knowing better than to put himself between Neal and the target of his aggression, Andrei called out to him until the other man finally heard him. When Neal stood up straight, breathing heavily, Andrei stepped closer. He stopped when he was shoulder to shoulder with Neal standing over Vincent who cowered against the upright post leading into one of the stalls.

"Do you remember me?" Andrei slipped his hands into his pants pockets as he waited for Vincent to answer.

The other man assessed him behind eyes which were quickly swelling closed. *Who knew Neal could throw powerful punches with both hands?*

Wiping his bloody lip, Vincent looked at him warily. "Yeah. You're the white dude I saw with Zaria Marie a few weeks ago."

"Come now. We both know I am more than just *some white dude*. You know exactly who I am."

Vincent looked around as if he hoped someone would come save him, but it was an exercise in futility. No one present was sympathetic to his plight. Even if Gregor's associate had some thought about it, it wouldn't matter. The man had left the moment they arrived.

Andrei had noticed him in the woods when they drove in. During Yeva and Gregor's sweep of the area, Gregor had handled his arrangement with the other man, and he'd departed soon after. So, there wasn't another living soul around who remotely cared about Vincent's pain.

"Yeah...I know you. Rich white dude making my niece think she's too good for her family now."

"Apparently, you need your ass kicked a little more." Neal bristled next to Andrei putting him on alert. "I told you years ago that if you didn't leave Zaria the fuck alone I'd make you regret learning how to talk."

Neal moved toward Vincent only to have Andrei block his approach. "Nah, Dray. Move. He's still talking too much shit. He hasn't learned."

"Just give me a moment."

Andrei came as close as he would to asking for permission. By rights, they both had grounds to make Vincent Coleman suffer. However, he recognized Neal had more history with the man. Taking a step closer to Vincent, Andrei pinned him with a pointed look.

"As I was saying, you know exactly who I am, which means you remember as well as I do that Zaria stated she wants nothing to do with your brother."

Vincent's eyes widened as much as they could under the rapid swelling. It had finally dawned on him that his current situation was the result of him running his mouth to news outlets trying to guilt or shame Zaria into helping Lawrence get out of prison.

"We're family. She's some hot shot lawyer with money and won't even help her own daddy. It ain't right."

"This muthafucka." Neal growled and tried to step around Andrei, but Andrei was too quick.

In a flash, he had Vincent lifted from the floor and pinned to the post with fingers clamped around his neck. Vincent's hands swatted at Andrei's arms with no effect as he gasped for oxygen.

"Choke his ass out." Neal offered his gruesome advice with a gleeful lilt to his voice.

"I told you before. I do not like repeating myself. Zaria is an extension of me. She has told you she wants nothing to do with you. Yet you think the best answer is to run to the newspapers with her name in your mouth. We cannot have that. Since you are obviously a slow learner, a stronger lesson is in order."

The swats against Andrei's forearm weakened and he lowered Vincent to allow him a modicum of air. He didn't intend to kill him. At least not today. It would put more negative spotlight on his Svet and Andrei wouldn't allow for any adverse attention on her. By the time he lowered Vincent, the other man was out cold.

"What are you doing? I said choke his ass out. Move. I'll do it if you don't have the balls."

Neal tapped against Andrei's shoulder. *Who knew airline exes were so blood thirsty?* Shaking his head, Andrei shrugged him off.

"Killing him would draw unnecessary attention to Zaria. I have a better idea. A way for he and his brother to be together the way he obviously wants."

Mentioning the possible negative impact on Zaria appeared to be the magic phrase to get Neal to stop advocating for murder. However, it didn't stop him from kicking Vincent to make sure he was actually unconscious.

"So, if we aren't burying his ass in one of these fields, what are we doing?"

Andrei stood from the slumped over Vincent and backed away, taking Neal with him. Stepping outside the rank barn, he didn't stop until they were standing next to the SUV.

"People like Vincent, who are pretending to be law abiding citizens, are hurt most when their mask is ripped away—exposing them. At this moment, the layers of Vincent's double life are being peeled back and those he has counted on to maintain his public image are learning exactly what kind of person they have aligned themselves with."

"That's not enough." Neal pushed the words out like gravel was lodged against his vocal cords.

"That is not all." Andrei then proceeded to let him know all of the ways Vincent's life will be picked apart.

"What's going to stop him from telling people about today? How's he going to explain his busted ass face? I'm also pretty sure I cracked a couple of his ribs just now."

Placing one large hand on Neal's shoulder, Andrei gave it a squeeze. "Do you actually think he will be able to speak or even hold a pencil once we leave here today? I need you to have more faith in me, Uncle."

Neal's face stretched in a bright smile belying the darkness of Andrei's assurances. Trying not to read too much into the look of approval, Andrei gave them a few minutes before they went back inside. True to his word, once they were done, Vincent's jaw was broken along with six of his fingers—including both thumbs.

When the duo stepped back out into the overcast day, Andrei was dusting off his jacket and Neal was inspecting his shirt.

"Shit. I have blood on me. How am I gonna explain this to Belinda? She's gonna kick my ass."

Casting a sidelong glance at the other man, Andrei took note of the blood spatter on the light blue button down. He was also missing a button. He squelched the comment on the tip of his tongue regarding the folly of wearing such a light color on a day like this. Instead, Andrei started mentally working out a solution.

"Are you wearing an undershirt?"

Neal's quizzical expression projected his thoughts on the insanity of Andrei's question.

"Of course I'm wearing an undershirt."

"Good. We'll get rid of this one and replace it."

"And you think my wife won't notice a brand-new shirt?"

"She absolutely will. Your wife is very observant."

Neal's frown said Andrei's statement was redundant. Anyone who spent more than three minutes in Belinda Truman's presence learned as much about her.

"Tell her you spilled something on it at lunch."

"Then she'll ask me where I went for lunch, and why didn't I ask her if she wanted to go. Nope. Just when I'd started thinking you were smart..." Neal shook his head, giving Andrei a side eye glance.

Instead of arguing with him, Andrei got into the back seat of the SUV and encouraged Neal to remove the shirt. Taking it from him the moment he removed it, Andrei snapped a picture of the tag inside. Then, he draped it over the back of the seat in front of him and took a photo. Once he was done, he tapped out a message to Frederick.

"What do you plan on doing with those pictures?" Neal removed the shirt from the seat and rolled it into a ball.

"I sent them to my assistant. He'll have another, appropriately aged, shirt ready by the time we're done with lunch."

Locking his phone, Andrei slid it into his pocket. Listening to Neal with one ear, he looked out of window at the vehicle approaching. He wasn't worried about being seen. The tint on the windows was dark enough to completely obscure their presence unless one was standing directly outside of the SUV.

"Who's that?" Neal leaned over trying to get a better look at the non-descript van rolling to a stop thirty yards from where they were parked. From their position, they could see the front plates and part of the driver, although the person in the van wouldn't be able to see anything behind the tail end of the SUV.

"Clean up."

As Andrei spoke, the side door on the barn opened. Gregor and Yeva stepped out and immediately joined him and Neal in the vehicle. Driving around the building in the opposite direction, Yeva took another barely discernable road leading away from the barn.

After driving for approximately thirty minutes, Yeva turned into the driveway of a home on the outskirts of Memphis. From the way Neal was looking around, Andrei assumed he wasn't familiar with the area.

"Come. Let us have lunch."

So...that is how Neal, Andrei, Gregor and Yeva ended up having lunch at a rental home being served by the executive chef from one of the nearby casinos. Over their meal, Andrei lobbed suggestions to Neal on what he could tell his wife to keep them both out of trouble. He had a sinking suspicion Neal was going to fold like a deck of cards the moment his wife looked at him for too long.

Which meant, Andrei would need to prepare himself for potentially dealing with his own woman's wrath. He'd had ample opportunity to let her know what was going on, but he felt no guilt at keeping the day's unpleasantness away from her. With that thought in mind, he approached his conversation with Neal from a new angle.

They had much in common. Zaria's happiness with the absence of undue stress was at the top of the list. By the time they made it to their next stop, Andrei felt better about Neal's ability to keep their secret. It helped that Frederick had an exact replica of Neal's shirt waiting for them.

Waving away his questions as to how it was possible, Andrei stepped out of the vehicle with Yeva at his side. Once Gregor drove away to drop Neal off at his car, Andrei and Yeva entered the glass doors of an office building. Shaking hands with the man waiting for him, he continued through the lobby to the bank of elevators.

Chapter Thirty-Three

PLEASE STOP TRYING TO LEAVE ME

Zaria awakened slowly. She came to consciousness in a room devoid of the morning sounds she'd become accustomed to when she started sharing space with Andrei. After spending the better part of the day working with the designer and decorators, she was in bed long before he slipped in behind her. Until he'd done so, she'd been in and out of sleep. She'd only been able to drift into a deeper rest when he wrapped an arm around her, tugging her into his side.

The lack of shower noises, or any noise for that matter, meant he'd once again started his day so early he didn't want to wake her. Andrei's absence made Zaria wonder if he'd grown comfortable in knowing she'd be there, and was slipping back into his previous routine of late nights and early mornings working.

Checking the time, she was happy at least she hadn't overslept. She went about her morning routine in a bit of a funk, since this was the second morning in a row, followed by a night, sans an orgasm from her man. *This shit was for the birds*. And it made for a cranky Zaria.

Logically, she knew it wasn't the end of the world, prior to her first hook up with Andrei, it had been longer than she wanted to admit since she'd experienced a big 'O' which wasn't self-induced. He'd gotten her used to his sex genie act. Now, she craved him like an addict.

Shaking off the feelings of want, Zaria went about getting dressed before going down to breakfast. She had a conference call set up for the afternoon with the agents who'd been aggressively pursuing Cisco. There was work to be done on her own cases before she entertained them.

When she finally checked her phone, she saw another message Andrei had left her. This time, he was assuring her he'd be home at a reasonable hour instead of saying the opposite. Maybe her earlier fears were unfounded. The healing side of her said she still needed to deal with her feelings, and talk to him before it festered.

But the old Zaria was in her ear saying, *"Fuck that shit! He's a grown ass man. He knows he can't ignore his woman and expect everything to be okay."*

Healing Zaria managed to calm the other side down enough for her to have a pleasant conversation with Peggy before heading out to her office. She even managed to send Andrei a text without throwing an ounce of shade about not seeing his face for a solid twenty-four hours.

Zaria's morning was jam packed with one court appearance and a couple of meetings. It was to the point she didn't even have a free moment to respond to Lavo's message asking her to call. Zaria hadn't expected to hear back from her classmate so quickly. So, she wondered what Lavo could have to report. Unfortunately, whatever it was would have to wait. When she did get time to call around lunch, Lavo was out of the office.

By mid-afternoon, Zaria was ready for a nap. Yet another thing that would have to wait since Kendra had just called to say everything was set to go in the conference room. Tapping Falana on her way past the paralegal's desk, Zaria continued to the small conference room where the virtual meeting was set to begin.

Once they were seated with the necessary documents spread in front of them, Zaria logged into the system and started the call. Prime Performance Agency, if nothing else, was punctual. Two representatives appeared in the rectangular boxes on screen mere moments after she pressed the button to begin. It's too bad they worked for leeches. Zaria typically admired people who respected other's time and showed a good work ethic.

"Good afternoon." Zaria tilted her head politely. The man and woman occupying separate rectangles on the monitor returned the greeting. Gesturing to Falana, she introduced her.

"Thank you both for taking the time to meet with me today. For clarity, all parties recognize this meeting is informal and no commitments have been or will be made on behalf of Francisco Truman. However, I am here to represent his best interests, and can listen on his behalf."

Zaria waited patiently for both to agree before moving forward. Apparently, they'd simply been anticipating an opening to begin their sales pitch. As expected, they trotted out the list of clients they represented. Professional hockey players as well as football, soccer, Olympic athletes, and baseball players. That was the short list. Many of the names were quite impressive and Zaria told them so.

"Your client list is very impressive." She studied them as they preened under the compliment. "However, I do have a question."

"We're happy to answer any questions you have." Ryan Adams leaned forward as if he were eager to accommodate. Lauren Sullivan simply waited watchfully with her hands folded on top of the desk in front of her.

"Is it standard practice for your agency to claim percentages of income from your clients when you weren't responsible for the existence of the income stream?"

"What do you mean?" The overly bright smile on Adams' face slipped slightly.

"What I mean is this section of the standard contract you sent to Mr. Truman by way of his coach. And we'll discuss that little nugget shortly." Flipping open the folder in front of her, Zaria pointed to the document inside.

"You should have a copy of the document dated, November sixteenth of this year, correct?"

Both nodded in agreement. "Good. If you could flip to the third page midway down where it delineates compensation to the agency. Section 5., subsection d."

Pausing for a moment, she waited for them to join her in the correct location. At her side, Falana opened her document as well, although she was probably more versed in the contents than Zaria was at this point. She'd researched standard sports and entertainment contracts prior to the meeting. Zaria wanted to make certain there hadn't been any major changes she wasn't aware of.

"Are we all there?" After their nods of agreement, she read the subsection in its entirety. Once she was done she looked up at them.

"Please do correct me, if I'm wrong, but this reads as if you're expecting Mr. Truman to pay you a portion of endorsements he garnered on his own without assistance from you. And at a higher percentage than is normally expected. Are you asking Carson Cooper or Megan Parker for twenty-five percent, when we all know the top end of endorsements is twenty?"

Adams' face flushed red while Sullivan's lips tightened into a thin line. Reading their body language, Zaria deduced that Adams' response was due to embarrassment at being caught and Sullivan was pissed to learn what Zaria pointed out. It became clear exactly who had been involved with the final details before they sent out the document.

"Well, Miss Coleman..."

"Attorney." Zaria corrected him simply because she didn't like the way he said *Miss*.

"Attorney Coleman." He cleared his throat before continuing. "It's my understanding that, while you're a contract attorney, sports and entertainment aren't your specialty."

"What's your point?" Zaria leaned away from the table, resting her palms on the arms of her chair.

"My point is, the contract is standard. Maybe it seems unfamiliar to you because you don't typically work in this arena."

Zaria allowed his attempted slight to roll off her back as she stared at his image on the monitor.

"Regardless of my unfamiliarity with sports and entertainment law, I'm well versed with contracts." Pointing at the papers on the table she tapped them. "And this. Is an insult."

"Excuse me?" Ryan Adams sat up straighter, his embarrassment sliding into something else at this point.

"I'm sure you've heard the phrase, 'you eat what you kill'." Not waiting for him to answer, Zaria continued.

"It's old school, and possibly a little archaic, however it fits this situation. If you're so confident in your agency's ability to negotiate not just a great contract with a good team, but bring in endorsements for your athletes, why are you holding your hand out for a piece of a pie you didn't cook?"

"As I said, you don't know how things work. Even if the athlete brings the endorsement deal to us, we still have to negotiate terms. Do you expect us to work for free?"

Zaria shook her head, then picked up a pen twirling it between her fingers.

"Absolutely not, but what you aren't going to do is take a bigger piece than you've earned. We all know it won't be hard to sell a company on using Francisco Truman to endorse their products. You've seen him.

He's handsome, intelligent, and desirable to many. Just standing there existing, he's going to generate revenue. Put a product in his hand and he's going to keep thousands employed to keep up with the demand.

And you think you deserve a piece of what you didn't bring to him? No. Absolutely not. If you don't bring it in, you don't get a cut. Period."

The color in Adams' face settled into his neck, and a large protruding vein pulsed there.

"You're not an agent. Heck, you aren't even a sports attorney. If Mr. Truman wants to be represented by the best, then he'll agree to the terms of this *standard* contract."

Zaria stopped twirling the pen. Closing the folder on the document, she placed the pen on top.

"You're right. I'm not an agent. I'm a contract attorney. A damn good one. Which means, you can't pull that, this is how things are crap on me, when I can read and understand every word of this document. Francisco Truman is going to have a very long, very lucrative, career. If you want a piece, you have to do your part."

Ryan Adams stared at her with a dumbfounded expression. "What exactly are you saying?"

Zaria leaned forward, resting her elbows on the table. "I've already said what I mean, but maybe you need to hear it again. ***You eat what you kill.*** If you don't bring the endorsement to the table, you don't even get a nibble. You want to eat? ***Hunt.***"

Adams took a breath like he was prepared to speak. Jumping in before he could, Lauren Sullivan spoke for the first time.

"Thank you for your time, Attorney Coleman. We appreciate you reviewing your concerns with us, and we will take it all into consideration."

"You're welcome. Thank you as well. One more thing before we go." Zaria spoke lightly. Lauren Sullivan's gaze was clear and expectant, while her colleague looked ready to jump through the computer screen and strangle Zaria.

"There are to be no more attempts to contact Mr. Truman. I'm sure you're aware of the rules. He will hear proposals for services once the season is over. Please let your people know not to try to make inroads with his coaches to skirt the system."

Once they wrapped up the virtual meeting, Zaria gave Falana a quick reminder to log her time working on Cisco's account, and went back to her office to sort out what remained of her day. She wasn't playing around when she said he'd have to pay for using her firm. Of course, she wouldn't charge him full value for her time, but Falana and anyone else who worked on the account would be compensated fairly.

Settling behind her desk, she opened her middle drawer pulling out her cellphone. Another missed call from Lavo on her mobile number. Whatever she wanted to discuss must be a doozy. Quickly noting the time, Zaria took a chance, and returned the call. Lavo answered on the second ring.

"Girl! You are a hard woman to pin down."

Smiling Zaria leaned against the buttery soft leather of her executive chair. "I've had a very busy day. What's up?"

"I feel you there. Hold on a second, let me close my door." Zaria heard the retreat and return of Lavo's footsteps against hardwood floors.

"Okay. I'm back. So, you know I immediately got to work on the Cease-and-Desist Orders after we talked yesterday morning."

"M-hm."

"Well, we drafted letters first because it could take a week or more to get in front of a judge to file the Orders."

Zaria nodded. She understood Lavo's reasoning. Depending on one's relationship with judges, it was hit or miss to get on their calendars for civil matters like that.

"Well, when I had the courier deliver the letters this morning, my office was immediately inundated with calls and emails."

"Really? Why?"

"It turns out, as of five p.m. yesterday afternoon, they were bought out. I was assured the new ownership did not condone such behavior from their reporting staff and editors, and a formal retraction would be on the front-page tomorrow morning.

When I tell you the language from all four of those outlets was identical. They were verbatim. That ma'am brings me to my question. What the hell did you do?"

Zaria sat up straighter placing the call on speaker and laying the device on her desk. Her jaw worked as her mind raced.

"What did I do?" Zaria's fingers pressed into the space between her breasts despite knowing Lavo couldn't see her. "I didn't do anything except call you. I didn't tell anyone other than you that I'd seen anything at all. Why would I have anything to do with—Andrei..."

The thought hit Zaria's mind with the weight of a two-ton hammer. Her eyes closed at the implications. It didn't matter that she hadn't confided in him about the newspaper articles. She hadn't had a chance. He had been gone all day the previous day and he was gone again when she woke up this morning. Taking everything into consideration, she was still one hundred percent certain his hand was in it somehow.

"Andrei what?" Lavo prompted. "You think your man is behind this sudden change of tune? I know he's rich, but is he buy multiple businesses in less than twenty-four hours kind of rich?"

Zaria clamped her lips together. She no longer wanted to talk to Lavo. About anything. No. She needed to talk to Andrei.

"Lavo, thank you for calling me with an update. I really need to go."

"Zee-baby, don't leave me hanging. Are you saying your man's answer to someone running their mouth about you is to go buy them out, and shut them up?"

"No. That's not what I'm saying...I just...I really need to go. Bill me for your time, and whatever costs you incurred. Thank you."

Zaria didn't wait for a response. She disconnected the call. Reaching in the drawer for her purse, she packed up her laptop and stood to leave her office. Looking neither right nor left, she powerwalked down the aisle separating the cubicles. By the time she reached the door to the reception area, Grace was there to open it. When they walked through the sliding glass doors leading from the building, Dakota pulled up in the car. Today, she didn't marvel at their ability to know what she needed before she needed it. She simply accepted it. Sliding into the back seat, she put on her seat belt.

"Do either of you know where Andrei is right now?"

She didn't miss the quick, but silent exchange between the two. "Please don't do that. I'm not in the mood. Take me to him."

Without a word, Dakota guided the vehicle into traffic. Zaria sat in the rear fuming. Not only had he taken it upon himself to solve an issue, he'd also done it without consulting her. *How did he even know she'd be okay with him throwing his money around to defend her?* Because she wasn't. At least not on this scale. What the hell did he know about running media outlets? And didn't he have plenty of other shit to do?

Not once did Zaria consider calling Andrei to make certain he was even available to see her. She didn't trust herself to talk to him on the phone. Besides, if he was going to lie to her, she wanted to look into his face while he tried it.

When the car rolled to a stop and Grace stepped out to open the door, Zaria refocused on her surroundings. They were in the underground garage at Andrei's private entry to the casino. She'd been so busy stewing in her own juices she hadn't paid attention to where she was being driven.

The ride up on the elevator was done in silence. None of her security detail were verbose, but they were especially quiet on that particular journey. When the doors opened, Zaria stepped off first although she hadn't a clue which direction to take. She'd never been to Andrei's office before.

It didn't matter, he was walking toward her. His brow was knit in what looked like concern as he approached her. Once he was in front of her, he stroked her arms as he stared into her face.

"Is something wrong, Svet?"

Shaking her head Zaria stepped back. "I need to talk to you."

"Of course. Come with me."

The warmth of his large hand on the small of her back chipped away at a little of her anger, but she reminded herself of why she was there. Stiffening her posture, she walked with him past the young man seated at a desk in his outer office. Closing the door behind them, Andrei led her to the plush leather couch on the wall opposite the floor to ceiling windows.

The moment he sat beside her, the words pushed their way out of her mouth.

"What were you thinking, Andrei?"

Brow dipped in confusion, Andrei stared at her.

"Don't give me that look. You know what I'm talking about."

"I sincerely do not, Svet. What was I thinking when? I have many thoughts multiple times a day."

Zaria sucked her teeth and rocked her head back on her shoulders.

"I know I'm cute, but it doesn't mean I'm dumb. What did you do? And before you say nothing, remember that I know you. I know you did something, because the newspapers I was serving with Cease-and-Desist Orders were suddenly bought out and they've now had a change of heart about running negative articles about me."

"I did what I had to, Svet. That is all you need to know."

"That's all I need to know?" Zaria hopped up from the sofa so quickly, she was halfway across the room before she realized it. Pacing back and forth, she cut him a hard glance.

"I'm not a child, Andrei. I don't need you acting like your friend, running around ruining people because they hurt my feelings. And for the record, they didn't hurt my feelings. They pissed me off, and I was handling it."

She rotated to pace in the other direction only to come face to chest with Andrei. Before she could sidestep him, he wrapped his arms around her holding her firmly enough to keep her near, but not tight enough to be uncomfortable.

"Svet... I will not apologize for using my resources to keep you protected."

"Andrei... I was handling it. I'd already contacted a lawyer to get them to print a retraction, and stop running unfounded rumors about me."

Shaking his head, Andrei squeezed her closer. "Nyet. Legal proceedings would take too long. My way is better. There will be a retraction printed on the front page tomorrow."

"And you don't think that could've happened without you throwing your money at it?"

A look flit across his face. It was quick. Zaria still caught it. "That's where you were yesterday isn't it? You went down there personally throwing more than just your money around, didn't you?"

When he continued to stare at her mutely, she wiggled in his embrace.

"Svet. Please stop trying to leave me."

His choice of words stopped her squirming immediately. Looking up at him, she read the concern laced with determination in his expression. Releasing a huffing sigh, she placed both hands on his chest maintaining eye contact.

"I'm not trying to leave you, Andrei. But, I am very upset with you taking matters into your own hands, and closing me out. If I hadn't found out about any of this on my own, would you have told me?"

Zaria watched Andrei looking for any indication of what he was thinking. He hadn't said a word in response to her question. Probably because she was one hundred percent correct. Still. He needed to say something.

"Talk to me, Antonov. Were you ever intending to tell me what you did yesterday? Or were you simply hoping none of it ever came to my attention at all?"

Chapter Thirty-Four

WHO FUCKED UP?

Thoughts swirled in Andrei's head as he tried to determine how to deescalate this situation while keeping everything he and Zaria had on track. After over twenty years living and working in English-speaking spaces, he was rarely at a loss for how to express himself properly in the English language. However, just now, when Zaria twisted and turned, attempting to release herself from his embrace, all he could think of was she was trying to leave him. He couldn't allow it. Even if that hadn't actually been her goal; it was how it felt. It was the word in his head.

In truth, he'd never planned to tell her anything he thought might cause her to worry. Looking into her eyes, he knew his truth wasn't what she wanted to hear. She wanted to hear him deny it. She wanted him to tell her he was simply waiting for the right time. He wasn't.

But, he knew telling her that wouldn't end well for him. Having limited experience with long-term relationships had reared its ugly head and collided with his naturally protective nature. Zaria wasn't a person who dealt in half-truths or secrecy.

She released another huffing sigh before she began moving her hands in massaging circles on his chest.

"I don't understand why you seem to think you can't talk to me about this. When you handled the article from the gossip vlog, you had no issue letting me know you'd taken care of it."

That was true. He simply didn't give her the details of how he handled it. Besides, this was different. He'd done far more than put a few vloggers and wannabe influencers on a different career path. However, her question let him know she was simply asking about the newspapers.

He battled between feeling relief that she was only concerned about what he was willing to discuss regarding the buyouts, and she wasn't delving into the other activities he'd been involved in the previous day. Should he tell her he had also paid her birth father a visit in prison? Would she want to know he'd looked into the eyes of the man who fathered her and made very thorough promises as to what would happen if Lawrence didn't stop indulging his brother and his family in their campaign to get him released?

"Andrei...Don't do this. Don't shut down on me. If you can't talk to me about things you do *for me*, how can we build a relationship together? Because I have to tell you, I'm not signing up for a lifetime of only being told what you think I can handle. That's not a partnership."

Andrei felt his brows come together as he processed her words. His chest tightened with unfamiliar dread. It sounded suspiciously like she was saying they couldn't be together because he hadn't confided in her about the decisions he made to protect her. That couldn't be right.

"What are you saying, Svet? Are you saying if I do not talk to you now, tell you everything I have done over the last forty-eight hours, you will leave me?"

Zaria's eyes drifted closed and her head fell forward, landing on his sternum, just below his pecs.

"That is not what I'm saying, Andrei." Her voice was muffled, but tinted with more than simply frustration. "How can I get you to actually hear me?"

"I hear you just fine when you are not speaking into my shirt."

"You aren't acting like you hear me. You're closed off, and in your head again. I need you here with me, not trying to think five moves ahead."

Lifting her head, she returned her gaze to his. It offered him no comfort to see the tortured look on her face. *Fuck!* What was worse?

Telling her and having her be disappointed in him for taking things too far in her eyes? Or, not telling her and having her make things up in her mind, causing her anxiety?

"Come, Svet. Let us sit."

Andrei took some solace in her allowing him to guide her back to the sofa and taking a seat. Unlike the last time they shared a similar piece of furniture, she didn't sit on his lap. However, she didn't pull away when he captured her hand in his.

"Yes, Svet. That is where I was yesterday. I went to Mississippi to speak to people personally about their unethical behavior. When I did not get the responses I was comfortable with, I took the next step and bought them out."

"I don't want a newspaper, Andrei."

Raising one eyebrow, he looked at her. "I was not planning to give you one."

"Fine. I didn't know if you were taking a page out of your lil friend Carver's book and buying companies to give them to your woman."

The tightness in his chest dissipated slightly at her calling herself his woman. Rationally, he knew she wasn't trying to end their relationship this very moment, however the emotions he'd experienced since the first night he touched Zaria had rendered him far from rational on his best days.

"I did not think you had an interest in running a media outlet. This is totally different, Svet."

Her pursed lips said he was being delusional, but he would accept the expression over the ones she'd directed toward him since she exited the elevator. At least this one didn't make his heart feel as if it had forgotten how to perform its duties.

"Anyway." She leaned back against the cushions and twirled her fingers, motioning for him to continue.

His Svet had no intention of allowing him to hold back on her. Yet, he still hesitated to tell her more. When she folded her arms beneath her breasts, he knew he didn't have a way out. Besides, it was likely Neal had already spilled what he knew to his wife, who would probably be calling soon.

"I did not trust that Vincent would accept your decision, so I had my associate gather information about him. My associate contacted me to inform me of what he and some others had done. So, while I was there, Vincent and I had a chat as well."

"A chat?"

"Yes."

"Are you serious right now? You expect me to believe you took the time to dig up info on Vincent and all you did was talk to him?"

"Well. That is not all I did. There will also be some pertinent details about his activities which the public will be made aware of in the retraction the papers publish tomorrow morning."

"That's all?" The look Zaria leveled at him gave Andrei a glimpse of their children's future. It was one which was destined to draw out many confessions of wrong doing.

"No..." Scooting a little closer to her, he captured both of her hands in his. "He required...encouragement to understand why it was in his best interest to stop his crusade to get Lawrence released by smearing your name."

"What kind of encouragement? Are you saying you roughed up an old man?"

"First, he is not elderly. Second, I technically did not *rough him up*. Your uncle did."

"What!? You brought my Uncle Neal in on your vendetta?"

"I had to, Svet. I made him a promise."

"You promised him that if you had to tune Vincent up you would let him do the honors? Is that it?"

"Not exactly. I cannot give you the details. That is between me and him."

She tugged at her hands, trying to detangle their fingers. Andrei wouldn't allow it.

"No, Svet. Do not pull away. Some things stay between me and the person to whom I gave my word."

"I bet Uncle Neal told Aunt Bee."

"That is between the two of them. This is between us."

The small pout of her lips made him want to kiss them, but he wasn't sure of his reception. Moreover, he wasn't done with his revelations. The last of which was likely to upset her more.

"Svet, there is one other thing."

Zaria narrowed her eyes, yet her fingers tightened around his instead of pulling away. It was as if she needed to hold on for fear of falling from the force of what he said next.

"Before I came home, I paid Lawrence a visit."

"You did what?!" Her words were barely more than a whispered croak. "Why? How? There's a whole process to visiting inmates. You can't just show up."

"Of course you can. If you know the correct people and offer the right incentive."

Zaria stared at him with her mouth slightly ajar, shaking her head slowly. "Unbelievable. So, what did you expect to come out of seeing Lawrence face-to-face?"

What she left unsaid, but he clearly read in her tone, was that he wouldn't have the access to Lawrence to *encourage* him the way he had Vincent. Andrei chose to let her believe he didn't have enough freedom at the prison to put his hands on the man. She had enough to think about. What Andrei had learned as a wealthy man in America was, money opened many doors which were normally closed. And for him, it was money well spent.

"I expect that he now fully understands his problems are his own, and you are not a part of them. You are not his ticket to freedom. He is also well aware of the consequences to himself and his family if they do not leave your name out of any of their endeavors."

"What kind of consequences, Andrei?"

"The kind you do not have to worry about, Svet."

Zaria's grip on his fingers increased marginally. "Andrei, I don't think it's a good idea to go around threatening people. Their petty games can't hurt me. Like I said, the articles didn't hurt my feelings."

Unable to take even their miniscule separation any longer, Andrei scooped her into his lap with her legs draped across his.

"Svet, there is something you need to understand. You are mine to protect—in *all* ways. My methods may not align with what you think should happen, but they are effective. I refuse to allow anyone to think it is acceptable to fuck with you—no matter if you consider them a mild annoyance. I do not. They should find another way to occupy their time and thoughts."

Andrei nearly closed his eyes in bliss when her soft palm caressed the side of his face as she stared into his eyes.

"What am I going to do with you?" Her brow furrowed slightly with the question.

Shrugging, Andrei's lips cracked in a lopsided grin. "I believe you will just have to keep me, Svet."

The heavens opened up when Zaria returned his smile. The angels sang when her lips met his in a tender kiss. When she pulled back, an involuntary growl rumbled in his throat.

"You are such a cave man." Zaria chuckled, shaking her head.

Over the next week, Andrei and Zaria fell into a rhythm. After a few concessions were made. He promised no last-minute trips or large purchases on her behalf without at least letting her know. And she promised not to push for details on how he protected his family. It was a hard-won concession that required the intense application of his *softer* skills to bring her around to his school of thought.

They'd awakened the morning following their intense conversation in his office, to retractions from the newspapers along with articles about Vincent. In the circles that mattered, there was a buzz regarding his illegal activities. Links of his likeness to his brother extending beyond looks gave way to the swift crumbling of his reputation. Anyone who spoke in his defense was quickly added in with his unlawful dealings and placed under the microscope with him.

As far as Andrei was concerned, it couldn't happen to a better guy. What was absent from the reports was any mention of Vincent's stint in the hospital or the extent of his injuries. He had several broken bones, and a jaw wired shut. His physical condition wasn't the focus of any of the reports. So, Andrei didn't have to have any further discussion with Zaria about his and her uncle's actions that day.

In the meantime, Andrei noticed the changes at the mansion beyond simply hanging festive decorations. The place had begun to feel like a real home. Andrei couldn't recall the last time he actually considered staying the night at his suite in Vegas. Other than the short trip he took to Mississippi, he was home every day before six p.m. Considering the drive from the city, it meant he ended each day no later than four p.m.

As he'd promised Zaria, he'd made more of an effort to keep in contact with Vitaly. He would admit it was a little awkward in the beginning, as his brother normally initiated the calls simply to chat. Andrei's calls usually had a purpose other than hearing Vitaly's voice. Once he understood that, it was easier to carve out a few minutes, usually on the drive home to connect with him.

Yet another thing Zaria was right about was Vitaly waiting for an invitation to come to visit for Christmas.

Last week

"I didn't do it."

Vitaly answered the phone with the denial ready. Since he answered in Russian, Andrei continued the conversation in the language. It was a habit they'd started once he brought Vitaly to the U.S. to live full time. Before that, he'd been insistent on them speaking English to sharpen both of their skills with the language. Now, conversing in Russian was their way of staying connected to their homeland.

"You did not do what, Brat?"

"Whatever it is you called to get into my ass about. I didn't do it. I've been a good boy."

Andrei tapped his thigh as he looked at the image of Vitaly on his cellphone screen.

"I did not call to get into your ass. I called to ask if you had plans for Christmas."

"Christmas as in December twenty-fifth, Christmas?"

"Yes."

The bright blue eyes they inherited from their mother stared back at him as his brother silently assessed him.

"I haven't made any firm plans. I was invited to a few dinners and parties, but I didn't commit to any of them. Why?"

Vitaly drew the last word out slowly. Andrei wasn't sure how he felt about his little brother being suspicious of his motives for asking such a simple question.

"Zaria's family is coming to visit for the holiday, and I thought maybe it would be good if you came as well. You are my family."

The scrutinizing gaze which met Andrei's statement was a resounding whistle indicating a problem on the play. Had he really been so hard on Vitaly that a simple invitation to spend the holiday together was met with stark disbelief? After another moment, Vitaly finally spoke again.

"Let me check the practice schedule one more time. I may only be able to be there for Christmas Eve and Christmas day."

"You do that. Let me know. Your room will be ready either way."

Although Vitaly had never lived with Andrei in his new home, he still had a room set aside for his younger brother. He always would. Wherever he called home would include a space for Vitaly. Andrei was happy Zaria not only understood, she encouraged it.

Andrei was pulled away from his thoughts by a tapping on his door. Knowing it could be no one but Frederick, Andrei called out to him.

"Yes, Frederick. Come in."

"This was just delivered."

Andrei accepted the sealed document sized envelope from his assistant. Without saying a word, he prompted Frederick for an explanation. Hand delivery of correspondence wasn't Frederick's norm.

"It's from Fernando. I went down to the first floor to check on some things when I ran into him. If I remember correctly, he's on your calendar. He got a call that seemed to be very important. He shoved this package into my hands and left in a rush."

A frown creased Andrei's brow. It wasn't like Fernando to miss an appointment. At least he had the presence of mind not to walk around with sensitive information unsealed and he didn't pass it to just anyone. He gave it to Frederick.

"Thank you, Frederick." Running his finger along the top of the package, he looked back at his assistant. "No interruptions."

Nodding, Frederick exited. Using the hockey stick shaped letter opener, Andrei broke the seal on the envelope. As he looked through the photos and information, he shook his head. The lengths some people went to in the name of hubris was astounding. Once he was done reviewing Fernando's notes and conclusions, Andrei checked the time. Then, he picked up his cellphone.

He didn't bother wondering about not getting a response. If he didn't get an answer, he knew the call would be returned.

Picking up on the third ring, the next thing Andrei heard was the voice of one of the few people he called friend.

"Triple A, to what do I owe the honor of this midafternoon call?"

Andrei rolled his eyes. Denzel seemed to always have a snappy quip whenever they spoke. Ignoring the attempt to goad him about the rarity of him initiating phone conversations, Andrei got to the point.

"Are you still looking to diversify getting into solar energy more?"

"Give me just a second." Denzel's voice was muffled as he said something to another person before he came back to the call with Andrei.

"Okay, now I can really talk. To answer your question, yes. I've been looking at a few companies I was considering buying shares in. Why? Do you have a lead on something?"

"Actually, I do." Andrei leaned into the high back of the executive chair custom made to fit his large frame. When he realized he was swiveling side to side almost gleefully, he planted his feet. The motion was slight, but it was enough to make him take note.

Without delay, he launched into the information on the company he thought Denzel would be interested in, only not to purchase a few shares. No, he'd want to purchase enough to gain controlling interest.

Denzel may seem flip and outrageous to some people, but he was a savvy businessman. The gregarious, joking persona had some people fooled. Not Andrei. Denzel was giving the former NBA star Shaquille O'Neal a run for his money when it came to having his hand in various business ventures. Many times, whatever Denzel invested in grew. Whether he publicly made his involvement known or not.

"Are you thinking of getting in on this too?" Denzel's question wasn't unexpected. Typically, when Andrei told him about an opportunity, he'd already invested or was contemplating doing so.

"I've considered it until I recalled you mentioning added diversity to your holdings."

"Okay. I'll look into it." Denzel was quiet for a few short seconds before he asked another question. "Real quick though, before I hang up and get back to doing my other job. Who fucked up?"

"What do you mean?"

"Don't try to play me, Antonov. I ain't that guy. Spill."

As compartmentalized as Andrei kept pieces of himself and his life, this side his closest friends knew well. Hell—if Zaria was correct—they shared it to some degree.

"The CEO. Hiriam Baxter."

"Oh yeah? Wait. Is he the guy who pissed his adult diaper in the Owner's lounge at the Chevaliers' game?"

"How do you know about that?"

"You know CJ is messy. He couldn't wait to tell me about it the next day."

Shaking his head at their antics, Andrei gave Denzel the shortened version of what Hiriam Baxter had done in some bid to retaliate against him and Zaria for embarrassing the other man in two arenas of his life. The man was behind the appearance of Katelyn Norris at Zaria's law firm. According to Fernando's notes, Katelyn had been happy to go along, because she felt she'd been unfairly terminated for what she considered a small infraction.

"Damn, man. I swear y'all stay pissing people off by living. You should consider being more like me."

"And do what? Pine for a woman who will not talk to you while you are publicly seen chasing under skirts all over the city of Atlanta?"

"You know what? Fuck you. That was low. I'm not chasing skirts. People think every time they see me with someone, I must be banging them. Nothing is farther from the truth.

But since you brought her up. Has your lady said anything to you about her cousin? Although no one will confirm it, I've heard rumors she might be moving down here.."

Andrei allowed his amusement to rumble in his chest at the quick turn of Denzel's question and demeanor. He must be going soft, because instead of returning Denzel's inquiry with silence, Andrei offered him advice.

"If you are seriously interested in Dominique, you need to put a stop to even the appearance of having a playboy image."

"Nobody says playboy anymore."

"Playboy. Fuck boy. Whatever you would like to call it, it has to stop if you have a genuine interest in Dominique Truman. Do you not think she has seen enough of it from the men she meets as an actress?"

Denzel's silence said he was considering Andrei's words.

"Besides, there is something else you should be concerned with."

"And what's that?"

"Dominique is the closest thing Zaria has to a sister. Therefore, hurting Dominique, in any way, hurts Zaria. I do not like it when Zaria is hurt."

Andrei allowed the rest to hang in the air between them. It didn't require an explanation.

"Yeah, man. I hear you. You're on your big brother shit, and I respect it. But, know that it won't stop me should I decide to make her mine."

"I hear you as well."

Andrei's response was short, and he allowed that portion of the conversation to drop as they spent the rest of the time recapping the business discussion before ending the call. He almost looked forward to what Zaria would have to say about Denzel's pursuit of her cousin/little sister.

Chapter Thirty-Five
HE IS AN ANTONOV

Zaria's gaze swept around the room just off the foyer, taking in every inch of the transformed area. The decorator had been amazing and very flexible with the suggestions Zaria made regarding the theme this Christmas. It seemed the only person to offer any guidance previously had been the house manager, Peggy, and she hadn't strayed too far away from traditional American décor, which would be a pleasant backdrop for any unexpected guests or business associates Andrei had over.

Today, Zaria was anxiously awaiting the arrival of the first of her family members. She expected her Aunt Belinda, Uncle Neal, and Cisco to arrive any moment now. Two members of the security detail were sent to pick them up from the private airstrip Andrei used to house his planes. It was only after their trip for Thanksgiving that Zaria learned he had more than the two planes she'd flown in with him.

A tingling series of notes alerted her to the front door opening. Running her hands down the front of her clothes, she went toward the foyer. Dressed in a light-weight, bright red sweater reaching the tops of her thighs and the black tights she practically lived in when home, she was prepared for the slight rush of cold air. She heard them before she reached the threshold.

"Oh! This is niiice! It looks so festive!"

Her aunt's voice reached her first, followed closely by her uncle's.

"This is a big ass house. No wonder Dray said everyone could stay here with no problem."

"Neal, stop it. We have a lot of people at our house, too."

"Yeah, but we don't have a separate house in the backyard for security and I'm positive that one building back there is a hockey rink."

"There's a hockey rink?" Cisco's eager comment made Zaria smile around the tears which suddenly welled in her eyes. Rounding the corner, she tried to blink them away. A wide smile stretched across her face when she saw her family standing there.

Although she'd just seen them less than a month ago, having them there made her emotional. Knowing they'd altered their original plans to come to her for the holiday touched her heart. She refused to blame it on hormones, although it was likely the tricky chemicals her body was producing were once again fucking with her.

"Hey, y'all." Zaria's voice was shaky, and she cleared her throat in an attempt to get it together.

"Zee-Baby!"

In two steps Zaria was swept into a hug by Aunt Belinda before her uncle nudged his wife to the side to embrace her as well. Her hug from Cisco was brief as he was going back and forth between the house and the car, helping to bring in their luggage along with some large boxes.

"What's all this?"

Zaria walked to the door to watch Cisco and a couple of the guys as they went to the lifted trunk of the SUV parked outside.

"Blame, Bee." Her uncle groused. "I think if I hadn't put my foot down, she would've tried to ship half the house here."

Her aunt swatted his arm as she shushed him. "You be quiet. You'll be the first one asking me for something you forgot—just watch."

"I resent that, woman. I'm a grown man. I know how to pack for a trip."

"Mhmm. Whatever you say." Her aunt looped one arm through Zaria's. "Do we have time for you to show me around, or do you want to wait for Dray to come home?"

"I can show you around, but honestly, you'd get a better tour from Andrei. I still haven't completely learned my way around. Other than this area near the door, I know how to get to the ice rink, my office and my bedroom."

"Mmhmm... I bet you learned how to get to that bedroom real fast." Her aunt teased low enough for only Zaria to hear.

"Auntie!"

"What? You don't think I know how babies are made? Speaking of, how have you been feeling? Any morning sickness?"

"I'm doing okay, Auntie. So far, it's been pretty mild, and doesn't last all day."

"That's good."

"Hey Zee, where can we put this stuff?" Cisco came back into the house carrying what Zaria hoped was the last box.

"Um..." Thankfully, Peggy took that moment to appear. Taking a moment to introduce her, Zaria was happy to hear their rooms were ready.

Aunt Belinda looked on with a neutral expression as a couple of staff entered and began taking their luggage and the boxes.

"The boxes stay down here." Her aunt interjected before the staff could take them to the rooms that had been prepared for them.

"Okay, well, you can put those in here." Zaria pointed to a corner of the living room.

She watched as people moved around in an almost choreographed synchronicity. The organized chaos, along with the sounds of chatter and laughter, did something to her insides. A smile lifted the corner of her lips as she studied her aunt and Peggy becoming embroiled in conversation even as both were giving directions to the men jumping to accommodate their requests.

Zaria followed behind her aunt and Peggy as the house manager showed her family to the rooms which had been prepared for them. While they were near one another, they were on the opposite side of the mansion from where Zaria and Andrei slept. Thank goodness.

She didn't relish the possibility of them overhearing the two of them in the throes of passion. There was also no need for her to learn if her aunt and uncle were still active in the sex department. Zaria was good not having that bit of information.

By the time Peggy showed them their rooms and the staff had brought up their luggage and stored the boxes, Andrei was home. It was the most natural thing ever for Zaria to walk into his arms, giving him a kiss. To have him receive the same treatment she had from her aunt and uncle made her heart swell.

If anyone had told her a year ago this would be her life, she would've checked their head for fever and other symptoms of illness. Yet here she was, standing in the foyer of a grand house decorated resplendently for the Christmas holiday, surrounded by family and the man she loved as she carried their child in her womb. She still hadn't said the words aloud to him, but she'd tried to show him in as many ways as she could. Her reasons for not telling him weren't a mystery. She was still a work in progress. Part of that work was letting go of the last bit of fear keeping her from fully expressing herself to him.

The nagging inner voice, the one she managed to ignore most of the time, reminded her that he hadn't said those words to her either. Shoving it to the back of her mind, Zaria was determined not to give doubt a foothold. The words were meaningless without action. Andrei's actions conveyed his feelings far more than spouting flowery phrases and platitudes.

However, she couldn't stop herself from watching the interactions between Andrei and her Uncle Neal and wondering if her aunt was aware of what the two of them had gotten up to with Vincent. Finding out her sperm donor's brother was just as deserving of being locked away as him wasn't a huge surprise. Zaria was shrewd enough to know one of Andrei's many contacts had something to do with the information coming to light and his subsequent arrest.

Now, instead of people throwing shade online, there were crickets from Zaria's critics. The few times it was brought up, it was by influencers calling out the hypocrites who'd attempted to attack her for not letting the past go and helping Lawrence. *Funny how that happened.*

"Zee-baby. Zee. Zaria!" Her aunt's voice tugged Zaria from the place inside she'd unknowingly retreated to.

"Yes, Ma'am?"

"Are you okay?"

Pulling up a smile, Zaria rushed to reassure her while actively avoiding Andrei's assessing gaze.

"I'm sorry. I kinda zoned out. What were you saying?"

"I was saying we only have a couple of days until Christmas. How much prep have you done? Do you need some help?"

"Thank you, Auntie. But, you don't have to do anything if you don't want to. Between me, Andrei, and Chef, we have it all worked out."

Her aunt's face scrunched slightly. It wasn't total disapproval. Still, Zaria fully expected the questions that followed.

"Chef? What kind of chef?" Aunt Belinda's side eye game was legendary, and her expression said the things she didn't voice.

"Don't worry, Auntie. He's a really good chef. I'm handling the staples we're accustomed to having during the holidays. We have a good system worked out. He's just assisting with prep. The staff has Christmas Eve and Christmas day off, so he won't be here cooking the meal."

"Mhm. We'll see."

Her aunt's folded arms told her this wasn't the last of the conversation. So, Zaria decided to nip it in the bud. Grasping her aunt's hand, they left the men hanging out in the media room to head to the kitchen, where she introduced her Aunt Belinda to Chef Paolo Marchetti.

Within five minutes, Chef had her aunt blushing as he let her taste the baked ravioli he'd just removed from the oven. The entire time, they discussed cooking methods. Her normal interrogation was done with a much softer touch, and plentiful smiles.

When Chef turned back to the stove, Zaria gently bumped her aunt with her shoulder. "I'm telling Uncle Neal on you."

"You hush your mouth, little girl. You're not telling your uncle anything."

"What's she not gonna tell me, Bee?"

Both Zaria and her aunt jumped at the sudden appearance of her uncle interrupting their conversation. With hands pressed against their breasts, they turned to look at him.

Swatting at him, her Aunt Belinda chastised him for sneaking up on them, but stopped mid-sentence when her gaze landed on something just past him.

"My baby!" Nudging her husband out of the way, Aunt Belinda flew across the kitchen toward Dominique, who met her halfway.

"Yeah, I was gonna tell you Dom was here. She brought somebody with her."

Waiting behind her aunt for her chance to hug Dom, Zaria looked over her shoulder at her uncle.

"Brought someone with her?"

"Daddy, stop. I told you we simply arrived at the airstrip at the same time. Vitaly isn't *with* me."

"You wound me, Starlet-Mine. I thought we had a connection."

Vitaly entered the kitchen with one hand laid over his heart. Andrei followed behind silently. His gaze pinging between his brother, Dominique, and Zaria. Reading the question in his ice-blue stare, Zaria shrugged. She had no idea what was going on. As far as she knew, Dom and Vitaly had never met.

Poking Vitaly's shoulder, Dom sucked her teeth and pursed her lips. "Stop playing before these folks think you're serious."

Dom wasn't a short woman, but she still had to look up to visually connect with Vitaly to give him the stink eye. In turn, Vitaly sent her a lovesick, forlorn expression. After a few beats, Dom poked him again.

"Ooo! I can't stand you!" Her laughter and the broad smile on her face belied her words. When Vitaly joined in, it was obvious the game was done.

"You have to admit, I had them going for a little while." Vitaly wrapped one arm around Dom's shoulders, hugging her to his side briefly before releasing her.

"When you're done playing hockey, you should get an acting coach. You could make a killing. Just don't let them typecast you in action roles as a Viking or some sh—stuff like that."

Zaria smirked at Dom quickly catching herself so as not to curse in front of her parents. Wrapping her fingers around Vitaly's bicep, Dominique turned to introduce him to Aunt Belinda.

Although it should have been Andrei's or Zaria's task, neither said a word. Slipping her hand into Andrei's, Zaria leaned into his side, watching the show. Her Uncle Neal still regarded the two of them as if he didn't quite believe it was all an act.

He remained that way for the rest of the evening. He participated in conversation, but he kept his eye on Vitaly's interactions with Dom—despite most of Vitaly's attention being taken by Cisco with his million and one questions. It amazed Zaria how her cousin could be considered a star athlete in his own right, yet he transformed into a ten-year-old when he met a prominent professional in the sport he loved.

Later, as they were getting ready for bed, Zaria couldn't resist asking Andrei his thoughts about Vitaly and Dom.

"Even if Vitaly has an interest in Dominique. I do not think the feeling is mutual."

"How do you know?"

Grasping her around the waist, Andrei pulled her closer until she was tucked into his side in the bed.

"Your cousin is simply a friendly person. Polite. Besides. Vitaly... He is an Antonov. If he was genuinely interested, he would not have taken his eyes off her all night. He only looked in her direction when she spoke to him. Otherwise, he was focused on whomever he was conversing with."

Tracing one finger along Andrei's chest, Zaria considered what he'd said. She knew for a fact Dom thought Vitaly was cute. Except finding someone attractive didn't really mean anything. One could find another person appealing without wanting to get with them.

"Maybe you're right."

"Of course I am."

Zaria delivered a light tap to his chest. "You don't have to be so smug about it."

"I am not being smug, Svet. I am simply confident in my observations. Besides, Dominique is already spoken for. Vitaly knows this."

Shooting upright, Zari whipped her head around to look into Andrei's face. "Excuse me? Spoken for? By whom? And since when is this 1895 where women are *spoken for* by men?"

Andrei's large, warm hands rubbed soothing circles on Zaria's back, tracing over her hip to her legs.

"I am aware it is not 1895. But, men still have a code among friends. As such, Vitaly is aware that Dominique is off limits to him."

"On who's authority? They can't just tell my cousin who she can and cannot date."

Zaria's brow dipped and Andrei pressed a kiss to the frown. She was helpless to maintain the expression under the gentle caress.

"Svet, this is not our business. It is between them. Why are we arguing about people who are not even thinking of being in a relationship with one another? Dominique has no interest in Vitaly and vice versa. So, the point is moot."

"Uh-uh, Antonov. You don't get to drop something on me like that and not give me the rest of the goods."

"Are you sure, Svet?"

Andrei's hands made a quick trip back up to latch onto her breasts, tweaking her nipples through the thin barrier of the sheet before tugging it away to expose the turgid peaks to his hungry gaze. Her breasts were very sensitive, and Andrei took advantage of his knowledge of that fact, swooping down to take one swollen nipple between his lips.

Zaria's back bowed the second his mouth made contact with her flesh. Whatever thoughts rattling about in her head tipped out of her ear when she tilted it to the side, moaning in appreciation of the attention Andrei lavished on her. It was a distraction. She knew it, but couldn't bring herself to fight it.

What would be the point? Deny her body the orgasms she'd craved to continue discussing...What was it again? It didn't matter. At that moment, Andrei tossed the cover aside completely. Maneuvering her until she straddled his lap, he stroked one long, thick digit between her folds. The slickness already leaking from her core was spread to the sensitive little nubbin he coaxed from its hood.

"Mmm!" The moan was ripped from her throat.

"I agree, Svet. We have other things requiring our attention."

With his statement, Andrei lifted her hands, placing them on the headboard on either side of him. His intention for her to hold on was clear, although unspoken. In a move she didn't anticipate, he lifted her while sliding down onto his back. When he was done, she was on her knees with her dripping pussy directly in line with his waiting mouth.

Zaria's gasp morphed into a keening wail as Andrei grasped her ass, jerking until she was seated with her wet folds directly on his face. His nose became an instrument he used to strum her pearl as his tongue delved into her channel.

Not needing his reminder to sit and not hover, Zaria wound her hips, uncaring of how much or little air was available to him in this position. The vulnerability and trust involved had her tipping over into bliss in no time, bathing Andrei's beard with her juices as he lapped feverishly at her pretty pocket. It was like he was trying to capture every single drop of her essence.

The aftershocks of her release caused quivering in Zaria's legs. Taking pity on her, Andrei rolled them until she was on her back sideways across the bed. His head remained between her thighs with his tongue, lavishing attention on her pulsating flower. Peeking down at him through her eyelashes, Zaria's stomach fluttered and tensed as he placed parting kisses on her folds before sitting up on his knees.

His thickness stood at attention like a battering ram between them. A pearlescent drop of pre-cum hovered at the tip of his length. Licking her lips, Zaria reached for him, only to have him block her attempt, and grab her legs at the bend of her knee.

Holding them up and out, he wasted no time feeding his hardness into her channel. His icy-blue gaze was molten as he watched himself disappear inside her. The visual of him being entranced by their coupling was so erotic, Zaria's muscles contracted on the verge of yet another orgasm.

Watching him while he fucked his length into her weeping core became too much. But closing her eyes heightened her other senses, putting her into sensory overload. Just when she thought she couldn't take any more, Andrei threw one of her legs onto his shoulder, straddled the other and began a pounding rhythm that catapulted her into an orgasm so intense stars burst behind her eyelids.

Unknowingly, her fingers gripped his leg and arm, leaving tracks of red in the wake of her nails scoring his skin. Above her, Andrei's grunts and growls were the sexiest soundtrack as he followed her over the cliff. His cock jerked within her walls, filling her with his hot seed.

In the aftermath, as Andrei carried her into the bathroom for a quick shower, Zaria was never more grateful for the vastness of the mansion. There was no way she wasn't loud enough to be heard by anyone within earshot of their suite of rooms.

A warm kiss pressed to her forehead awakened Zaria a few scant hours later. When she opened her eyes, Andrei was leaning over her with an unreadable expression on his face. Pushing herself up to a seated position, Zaria cupped his face.

"Hey. What's wrong?"

"I must go, Svet."

Trying to shake the sleep out of her eyes, Zaria peered into Andrei's face.

"Go? Go where?"

After a pregnant pause, he released a huffing breath. "Russia."

"Excuse me? What?"

"I wish I had time to explain it all, Svet. But I am already two hours behind him."

"Behind who?"

"Vitaly." Andrei's eyes vacillated between sorrow and anger. "It is my mother's brother Ruslan. That is all I know for now. Vitaly has gone to him. I have to go."

As much as she tried not to do it, tears welled in her eyes, blurring her vision. Vitaly was Andrei's family. Of course, he had to help him if he was in a possibly dangerous situation. Part of her wished he would just send someone and not go himself.

It was supposed to be their first Christmas together. Yet, he was sitting before her, in the pre-dawn hours of the morning, less than two days before the day telling her he needed to leave. Undoubtedly, whatever he planned to do would put him in danger.

Crashing through her internal turmoil, Andrei pulled her into his arms, hugging her close to his chest. She felt pressure from the kiss he placed against the top of her bonnet covered head.

"I must go, Svet. I will return as soon as I can."

Mutely nodding, Zaria struggled to release the hold she had on his shirt when he tried to stand. She managed to relax her digits before he had to peel them away. With one parting glance at the door, Andrei slipped out, leaving her in semi-darkness. Alone.

Chapter Thirty-Six

WE ARE DONE HERE

Wind whistled past the windows of the vehicle Gregor's contact secured for them once they landed in Helsinki. Although he flew in on one of his jets, Andrei didn't risk flying directly into Russia. There was still bad blood with some Russian officials who considered his bid for U.S. citizenship, all those years ago, to be a defection from the mother country. Technically, it was, but they took his protection of himself and his brother from their corruption personally.

Therefore, Andrei had the pilot land at an obscure private airstrip in Helsinki, Finland. From there, they took ambiguous, unmonitored roads to drive across the border into Russia to the small village outside of St. Petersburg where Ruslan had taken up residence. The flight took twelve hours. The lengthy time wasn't enough for Andrei's anger to cool. *What the hell was Vitaly thinking? Why would he come here to meet with that worthless liar?*

Questions whirled in his head as Andrei considered all the options. He searched for any reason his brother would go back on what they'd agreed to when Andrei had finally told Vitaly everything that happened surrounding their parents' deaths. Knowing the truth, Vitaly had cut off the tenuous contact he had with Ruslan. Or at least it's what Andrei thought.

Andrei's gaze swept the landscape as they passed the occasional landmark—looking but not really seeing. Although they traveled under the cover of darkness, from what Andrei could make out, things had not changed much from what he remembered as a child growing up in the area.

His attention snapped from the landscape when Yeva turned from the paved road, following the lead vehicle onto a narrow path barely wide enough for automobiles. Either side of it was lined with towering trees. Snow blanketed anything within eyesight. After a few more minutes, both vehicles rolled off the trail into the dense snow-covered foliage, cutting the lights and engines.

The only sound in the interior of the SUV was the soft electronic beeps being emitted by the device in Gregor's hand. His longtime associate was the reason Andrei knew of his brother's late-night departure from his home. While he'd tried to pull back to let Vitaly live his life without interference, old habits were hard to break.

When Vitaly and his detail left Andrei's property, he wasn't notified. However, when the impromptu flight was scheduled from the private airfield, he received an alert which triggered a phone call. That is how he found himself saying goodbye to his Svet before dawn, two days before they were set to spend their first Christmas together.

Recalling the confusion and hurt in her expression added another knot to the ball of anger growing in his stomach. She'd valiantly tried to hide it, but he'd seen it. He cursed himself for not doing more to make her feel secure in knowing he'd always do whatever was necessary to return to her.

"The signal has not moved for twenty minutes." Gregor's deep voice held a grumbling rasp. "On foot, we are twelve minutes away at a swift walk. Eight if we jog."

Tugging on an ultra-knit cap and gloves suitable for the harsh Russian weather, Andrei nodded. They'd discussed their plan of action. There was no point in further conversation. All four doors of both vehicles opened and the men who'd volunteered to accompany him stepped out alongside Andrei.

All of whom were similarly attired in black; they stood waiting for orders. Nodding to Gregor, Andrei began a light jog. Gregor fell in step with him, guiding the group through the brush to their destination. They arrived at the edge of the woods near the small cabin in exactly eight minutes. Taking a moment, they assessed the area before they spread out —each man aware of his assignment.

Obviously, whomever was in charge of the secluded meeting Vitaly was attending had no fear of being interrupted, as there was only one man outside the cabin guarding the perimeter. Saying he was guarding it was a severe overstatement. The young man was obviously enthralled by something on his phone. Or at least he was until the signal blocker Gregor used knocked out all service.

Then he was aggressively tapping the device, trying to get it to respond. He never saw the impromptu nap coming. Pulling him to the darkest side of the cabin, they leaned him against the wall—trussed up like the spoils of a hunt.

In a coordinated move, the team Andrei assembled entered the small structure through each of the three available entrances. They converged on the largest room at the same time, coming upon a scene which was a surprising mix for Andrei.

"I told you he would come."

Andrei looked, from his brother's irritated expression, to face the person who'd spoken. The man, who matched Vitaly in height, had traditionally Nordic features. Andrei didn't recognize him. However, it was obvious he was in charge. The face of the Finnish mafia he'd heard about.

"Brother, why did you come? I had it handled." Vitaly groused, voicing the frustration painted across his expression.

"Why did I come? You deliver yourself as a lamb in a lion's den and you would ask me why I am here?" Andrei swept the room, trying to come to terms with what his eyes told him in contrast to what he'd believed he'd find.

"Pardon me. But now that you see your brother is unharmed, could you ask them to lower their weapons?"

The other man's request was so congenial, it was tempting to forget he was standing over the bound and gagged body of their mother's only brother. Despite his position and condition, Andrei couldn't drum up even a modicum of sympathy for Ruslan. The bruising on his face and the state of his clothing said his torment had been going on for some time.

"It's okay, Andrei. They're not a threat to us. This is about Ruslan."

Staring at Vitaly incredulously, Andrei gave one stilted shake of his head. Easily slipping into Russian, he spoke to his younger brother.

"Just because this is about Ruslan does not mean you are safe, Vitaly. What happens if they do not get what they want from him? Whatever reasons he used to bring you here are not going to go away simply because he cannot pay them. Did you forget what happened to Mama and Papa?"

"I haven't forgotten. Why would you ask me that?"

"Because we are here! Just like they tried to rescue him, you are here and someone will have to pay. You should have told me what was going on. You should have stayed as far away from Ruslan's poison as you could get. Saving his miserable life is not worth yours or you putting yourself in danger."

Vitaly's eyes blazed with indignation as he stepped closer to Andrei, invading his space.

"Of course it's not worth it to save *him*, but what about if it were to save Zaria? Or the baby? Would you say it wasn't worth the trip if they were at stake?"

Andrei's gaze whipped from Vitaly to Ruslan to the silent Finnish mafia front man standing over him.

"What the fuck do you mean? They threatened my family?" Andrei's pulse roared in his ears so loudly it was difficult to hear anything else.

Vitaly touching his shoulder grounded him in the moment. Slightly. Andrei scanned the room, looking into the face of every man present, designating everyone not with him to be an enemy. Even the two members of Vitaly's security detail weren't exempt from scrutiny. After all, they'd escorted him into a dangerous situation.

"I did not threaten your family. We do not look to women and children to clear the debts of men."

The man's Russian was flawless as he interjected himself into the conversation between the brothers. Andrei regarded him as he stood in the same spot. He hadn't moved since Andrei and the others had gained entry into the small cabin. Signaling Gregor and the others, Andrei silently ordered them to lower their guns. With his eyes trained on the unknown man, Andrei continued his discussion with Vitaly.

"Explain."

Dropping his hand away from Andrei, Vitaly released a huffing breath.

"The message I received implied that, if Ruslan was unable to pay his debt, your family could and would be harmed. It leaned heavily on us being held responsible for him as his only living relatives."

"The fuck we are." Andrei growled, turning his attention back to the huddled lump on the dusty wooden floor.

"I know, brother. Also, I didn't disregard what you told me about him. So, I decided to face the situation head on. I contacted Mikael directly to determine the best solution to this issue."

Andrei returned his stare to Vitaly. The darkness in his expression was tinged with disbelief.

"How?"

"You are not the only Antonov with connections." Vitaly's normal smirk appeared briefly before his expression hardened. "I didn't know for certain the message was a lie until I was halfway around the world."

"Then why did you not turn around? Come home?"

"Because...This has to end. Now that he knows there's a way to get to you, to us, he's not going to stop. The Kylmäveri family may not look to women and children to pay debts. Who's to say the next people Ruslan owes will have the same view? No, Andrei. I had to come here. For once, I will protect *you* and *our* family."

Andrei's words lodged in his throat. He didn't know what to say. The verbiage to explain to his brother his potential sacrifice was appreciated, but unnecessary was locked behind his teeth. If the situation hadn't worked out with the Kylmäveri Mafia, he could be bound right alongside Ruslan.

"Do you understand the risk you took by coming here, Vitaly?"

"Yes. Did you understand the risk you took by leaving him alive the first time?"

Andrei searched Vitaly's face for a few beats. At the time, he thought there was no way for Ruslan to be a threat to them in the future—not after the way Andrei had cut ties. As it turned out, he was wrong.

"I thought I did. But, I guess I did not."

"Why? Why did you leave him alive when he's responsible for our parents' deaths?"

Softening his gaze, Andrei looked at his brother. "He's Mama's only brother. I promised her I would look out for him."

Vitaly's expression darkened even further. He looked from Andrei to the prone figure that used to be their uncle.

"Yeah? Well, I didn't."

Turning to Mikael, he pointed to Ruslan. "His debt is his own. If he can't pay it, then his life is forfeited. Whether you take it or I do it, me nor my brother are responsible for his actions."

Andrei looked from Vitaly to the Kylmäveri boss wondering if Ruslan's pitiful life would be enough for them to consider the bill cleared. It hadn't been for the Morozovs. To protect his family, Andrei would pay again. Only this time, he would insist on ending Ruslan's life with his own hands to be certain he never resurfaced with veiled threats looking for handouts.

Knowing when to remain silent was a skill Andrei had perfected many years ago. So, he didn't utter any of his internal thoughts surrounding the payment of Ruslan's debt. In a blink, guns were drawn again when Mikael reached into his jacket.

"Relax, gentlemen. I'm simply honoring Mr. Antonov's request." Tilting his head to the side, he gave a small, crooked smile. "Younger Mr. Antonov that is."

Slowly, he unsnapped the strap on his holster and pulled out a pistol. Pointing it at Ruslan, he pressed the trigger, shooting him in the thigh. Muffled wails rent the air as Ruslan came to consciousness painfully. Wild, tear-filled eyes searched around the room before landing on Andrei.

When he saw him, Ruslan's muted cries became even more plaintive. Ruslan shared their mother's bright blue eyes, but not her kind spirit. So, the tears that escaped them didn't move Andrei in the slightest. The years hadn't been kind to their mother's brother. His once brawny build was now gaunt, and the whites of his eyes were tinged with yellow. It was a clear indication he was in ill health.

Even if he hadn't manufactured lies to lead to his own death, his remaining days were short. Andrei wondered if killing him would be merciful. Mercy wasn't something Ruslan deserved. He'd earned a painful death.

When Mikael extended the gun, butt first to Vitaly, Andrei shook his head.

"Brother..." Vitaly protested, giving Andrei an expression of disbelief.

Instead of a verbal answer, Andrei passed Vitaly the gun holstered to his left leg before drawing the one strapped to his right. If his brother insisted on having a hand in this, he would do it with a weapon Andrei knew and trusted. He would not be leaving his fingerprints on a gun to be left in the possession of a mafia boss that neither of them knew.

Wrapping his fingers around the grip, Vitaly took the forty-five-caliber pistol designed specifically for those with larger hands. Mikael stepped back, holstering the gun he'd offered Vitaly.

As Andrei and Vitaly approached Ruslan, he squirmed on the floor. His hands, which were bound in front of him, alternated between gripping his bleeding leg and reaching out to them in supplication. No one attempted to remove the tape covering his mouth. It didn't matter what he had to say.

Without planning or a conscious countdown, the brothers aimed and fired simultaneously. They'd never know which of them inflicted the kill shot as one bullet entered the center of Ruslan's forehead, while the other entered his heart. His cries were abruptly cut off as the sound of the shots reverberated off the walls.

Andrei didn't so much as wince from the noise that was certain to cause ringing in his ears for the next few hours. Re-holstering the pistol, he held out his hand, accepting the other from Vitaly. Once he was finished storing both weapons, he regarded Mikael.

"We are done here." Andrei wanted to be certain there wouldn't be any reason to attempt to contact them further. He gestured to Yeva, who stepped forward, detaching two tight bundles from the black tactical vest he wore.

"This should be enough to compensate you for your trouble."

There was a brief hesitation before one of Mikael's silent companions came forward to accept the packages.

"Can your man turn off his signal blocker now? We will need a cleaner."

"No, we will not." Andrei nodded at one of his men, who immediately stepped forward. He motioned to everyone else to follow him from the small house.

"I would suggest you retrieve your ineffective guard dog and move your vehicles."

The other man bristled, likely from being given orders. Andrei didn't flinch. If Mikael wanted to lose his property, leaving evidence and a man behind, it was up to him. With a jerk of his head, Mikael sent one of his men in search of their missing comrade while the others moved the two vehicles they'd driven to the cabin.

Less than ten minutes later, they all stood at the edge of the woods, watching Ruslan's last resting place go up in flames. It was possibly blasphemous, but Andrei prayed he roasted slowly over a spit in hell for the rest of eternity. Uncaring about the frigid temperatures, he watched from the cover of the trees until he could be certain nothing linking them to Ruslan's timely demise would survive.

He probably would've stayed until the place was nothing except ash if Gregor hadn't prodded him.

"We have to get moving. This place is isolated; however, the smoke will still get attention. We have several hours to sunrise, but we do not want to risk being seen out here."

Mutely agreeing, Andrei threw one arm around Vitaly's shoulders and turned away from the last unwanted piece of his past. The brothers were silent as they retraced the path Andrei and the others had taken previously. Light snowfall got heavier the closer they got to the vehicles. Soon, their tracks were completely obscured, and it was like they were never there.

The drive to the airstrip in Helsinki was done with minimal talking. Andrei didn't have anything to say until they were on his plane together. Yes, Vitaly had his own jet fueled and ready, but Andrei's unspoken demand was issued on the tarmac. So, the group split with Gregor and a couple of the others taking Vitaly's plane.

On Andrei's larger aircraft, there was more than one sleeping cabin. So, they were able to shower and change, removing all traces of where they'd been and what they'd done. When Andrei exited the compartment, Vitaly was semi-sprawled in the seating area near the hallway with a bottle of water in his hand.

The members of their security details, who weren't on the plane with Gregor, were at the very front in the regular seats. Far enough away that Andrei and Vitaly were insulated from being overheard.

"Why did you give Mikael money? You didn't have to pay Ruslan's debt."

"I did not pay for Ruslan. I paid for us. For us to not be dragged into a war with the Kylmäveri Syndicate. Whatever that coward owed them was peanuts in comparison to what they could try to extort from us, given the right incentive. At least with these people, there don't appear to be any government ties."

Vitaly nodded. His gaze turned to the water bottle in his hand, studying the contents as if the answers to all of life's secrets lie in the clear liquid inside. Andrei pulled out his phone, powering it back on. They'd been in the air for almost an hour. He'd transferred his communications to a burner, but he figured it was now safe to use his primary phone again.

"Why did you come, Andrei?"

"You are my brother, Vitaly. What did you expect?"

"I expected you to stay home. I am a grown man. I knew what I was doing. You have a family now. Dropping everything to come to protect me isn't your life. At least it shouldn't be."

Andrei placed the phone face down on the seat next to him. Vitaly's statement felt like an accusation. Like he was saying Andrei failed Zaria and their child by putting someone else before them. Even as anger flared to life inside him, he knew directing it at Vitaly wasn't the correct place. His brother was simply speaking to the battle within Andrei from the moment he'd been alerted to Vitaly's movements.

"Big brother...You've spent more than half your life looking out for and taking care of me. So, I know it feels like second nature to you. This time...I was going to look out for you. Protect you and *your* family."

"You are my family, Brat."

"Yes, but you have a woman and a child on the way."

"I do not need to be reminded of my woman and child."

"Apparently you do." Vitaly held up a hand. "I didn't say it to start an argument with you. But it needs to be said."

Leaning closer, Vitaly put a hand on Andrei's shoulder. "It is okay for someone to look out for you for a change, Bro. What I didn't say earlier was, the message I received had pictures attached. Pictures of the three of us when we were in New York.

Of you with your hand on Zaria's belly. The circle drawn around that area of the photo made the threat crystal clear to me."

Hearing the blatant threat to his family made Andrei want to turn the plane around and kill Ruslan a dozen more times. That the other man had such a putrid lack of character in comparison to their mother would forever be a source of wonder to him. Andrei was glad Ruslan no longer drew breath. He felt no regret in the way he'd chosen to keep his promise to his mother.

She'd asked him to look after her brother. Andrei had done what he could when he spared Ruslan's life the first time. Hearing that his Svet and their *businka* were threatened, even indirectly, meant the best way to look out for Ruslan was to sever his ties to the living world. He was dangerous and had no sense of kinship or blood loyalty. Andrei was certain his mother would not want him to put his family in further danger to honor her request.

Tapping Vitaly's shoulder, Andrei bobbed his head. "Thank you, Brat. However, should you get the urge to get on a plane to travel around the world to protect me again... Do not. Talk to me. Let us work together to keep our family safe. Da?"

"Da." Vitaly's agreement was followed by a one-armed hug. After the brief embrace, Vitaly nudged Andrei. "You should get some sleep. If we can keep our flight schedule, we'll land with just barely enough time to make it home for Christmas dinner. And you, brother, have some heavy groveling to do."

Andrei pierced Vitaly with a half-hearted, fierce expression. "If I am to grovel, you will be beside me on your knees. I would be home with my Svet making corn bread dressing if I did not have to get on a plane to come save your ass."

The two slipped into a light-hearted banter as they went back down the hallway to the cabins they'd used to shower. Bumping forearms with his brother before they entered separate compartments, Andrei's spirits were lifted somewhat. However, he knew he wouldn't be one hundred percent until he had Zaria back in his arms.

How he was going to navigate their reunion weighed heavily on his mind as he lay in bed alone. While comfortable, the mattress failed to lull him to sleep. Without Zaria pressed against his side, he only managed a light doze.

Chapter Thirty-Seven

IT MAKES YOU A HUMAN

When Andrei walked out of their bedroom during the pre-dawn hours of the morning, Zaria tried to go back to sleep. She tried not to worry about where he was going, what could be happening, and if he was safe. She also tried, and didn't quite succeed, to not be angry that he'd chosen to chase his brother. Instead of staying there. With her. And the family they were creating together.

Those thoughts made her feel even worse, because she knew if it were Dom or Cisco, he would've had to physically restrain her to keep her from hopping a flight to get to them. She really couldn't expect anything less from Andrei. Not when a huge part of his character resided in his protective nature. The turmoil she watched play out on his face was enough for her to know he hadn't come to his decision lightly.

After lying there staring into the darkness for almost an hour, Zaria got out of bed. Showering, dressing, even taking extra time on her hair, only took forty-five minutes. So, she silently padded into the darkened kitchen in search of something to occupy her hands, if not her mind. Flipping on the light switch, she immediately went to the refrigerator, removing eggs and butter, placing them in the open area at the center of the range top.

Using a trick her Grandma Lou taught her, she turned on the oven to help bring them up to room temperature more quickly. Next, she went into the adjacent pantry and started pulling out the other ingredients. With her hands filled, she turned to exit. A squeaking gasp caught in Zaria's throat when she saw her Aunt Belinda leaning in the doorway between the kitchen and the pantry.

"Goodness! Aunt B, you startled me."

"Mhmm. I wouldn't have, if you hadn't been so preoccupied you didn't hear me calling your name." Her aunt's expression didn't match the slight sting of her words. The dark brown eyes, which mirrored her own, were soft. Concern swam in their depths, belying the censure in her statement.

"I'm sorry. I guess I'm more in my head than I realized." Keeping her eyes trained in front of her, Zaria tried to maintain an even tone. "What are you doing up so early? I didn't expect to see anyone for at least another two hours."

Stepping past her aunt, Zaria put the cake flour, dry vanilla and other ingredients on the countertop. Following her into the room, her aunt stopped next to her. Zaria closed her eyes briefly when the weight of her aunt's arm draped across her shoulders.

"What's going on? Why are *you* up at five a.m. looking like you're about to try to bake a cake?"

"What do you mean, try, Auntie? I can bake cakes."

"No. You can bake *a cake*. Not cakes." Her aunt paused to peruse the ingredients Zaria gathered.

Zaria couldn't really dispute Aunt Belinda's statement. She wasn't much of a baker. The only cake she'd buckled down and learned to make from scratch was Red Velvet. Mainly because it was her favorite. She only made it at Christmas time using the recipe passed down to her by her grandma. Her mother's mother. She had nothing from Lawrence's mother—which she'd long ago come to terms with.

"Okay, fine, Auntie. I can bake *a cake*. Cisco asked about it yesterday, and I promised I'd have one for tomorrow."

Without her consent, her breath hitched on the word tomorrow, because it hit her once again that it was Christmas Eve. It was the day before what was to be her and Andrei's first major holiday as hosts, and he wasn't there. He was on a plane going God knows where in Russia, following his brother.

Zaria didn't protest when she was steered away from the kitchen counter, through the doorway, and into the sunroom. Unlike most times when she was in the room, there were no rays of sunlight streaming through the windows into the space. Using the dimmer switch, her aunt turned on the lights just enough for them to see their way around. Stopping at one of the window seats, Zaria was encouraged to sit.

"Okay. Talk to me. What's going on? We've visited you for the holidays before. And even when you were doing most of the cooking and prep yourself, you didn't get up doing things at this time of morning."

Zaria stared at her aunt. For a moment, she considered brushing it off. After all, what was between her and Andrei should stay that way. *Right?* Her aunt had forty years of marriage under her belt. Those years came with experience. Experience Zaria could definitely benefit from. Still...she hesitated.

"Auntie, I'll figure it out. I just need a little while."

"I have no doubt you can figure out whatever you put your mind to. But, Zee-Baby. You don't have to do things alone." Her aunt's gaze essentially pleaded with Zaria to trust her.

"Have you talked to Andrei about whatever is bothering you?"

At the mention of Andrei's name, a sob ripped from Zaria's throat. She couldn't contain the tears streaking her cheeks, leaving wet rivulets on her face.

"Oh! Oh... Baby... Come here."

Scooting closer, her aunt wrapped her arms around Zaria, resting her chin atop Zaria's curly poof. In the security of her aunt's embrace, Zaria allowed herself a moment to feel her feelings. After a little while, her crying tapered off to sniffles. Using the cloth napkin her aunt pressed into her hand, Zaria wiped at tears, then her runny nose as she sat up straight.

"I'm sorry, Auntie."

"You don't have to apologize to me for having emotions and allowing yourself to feel them."

The softness and sincerity in her aunt's voice almost started another round of sobbing. Zaria's emotions were all over the place. Nodding, she swiped at the last of the wetness and sat up as tall as the tufted seat permitted. Twisting the napkin between her fingers, she searched for the right place to begin. She knew saying nothing after her crying jag wasn't an option.

"Andrei is gone. So, I can't talk to him right now."

"Gone? What do you mean, gone?"

"He left a couple of hours ago."

"Left?" Her aunt's brow dipped. "Zaria Marie, I'm trying not to jump to conclusions, but I'm gonna need you to fill in these blanks a little more quickly."

"Sorry. Andrei woke me up to let me know he had an emergency situation with his brother, and he had to leave. I don't know exactly where he went. Only that he went to Russia. I don't really even know the full reason why. And I don't know when he'll be back. He simply said he *would* be back. Not when."

Warmth covered Zaria's fingers when her aunt laid her hand over them.

"So, he's helping Vitaly? The same Vitaly who was here with us cracking jokes just twelve hours ago?"

Zaria bit back the rest of the details she knew about Andrei's family and the root of her concern. It was his story to tell, and she wouldn't break his confidence.

"Yes, ma'am. It's his brother. I wouldn't hesitate if Dom or Cisco needed me. So, I get it. It's just...I feel like a terrible person for being upset with him for doing something I would've insisted he do if he'd tried to stay here and not help.

What kind of person does that make me? I'm upset with him for not choosing me first, when I know if he'd tried to make any other decision, I would've pushed him to go."

"It makes you a human. That's what kind of person it makes you."

Even understanding her aunt's assessment, Zaria's head shook in denial. Aunt Bee wouldn't have it though.

"No. Don't do that. You're entitled to have feelings—even conflicting ones."

Sliding farther back onto the window seat, her aunt tugged her into her side with an arm draped across her shoulders.

"Zee-Baby... Do you know how many times I wanted to call CPS on my own sister whenever she walked out of my door with you on her hip?"

Zaria's lips parted as she stared into her aunt's face in disbelief. Aunt Bee met her gaze with a grave expression.

"It's true. Stacey may have given birth to you, but you were always my baby. At least in my heart. I know she was the one who carried you for nine and a half months and spent fourteen hours in labor. Despite knowing what she went through to bring you into the world, I felt some kind of way about it whenever she came to get you."

"Auntie...I don't know if that's the same. I'm sure you were concerned about the environment we were in because of Lawrence."

Rubbing Zaria's arm, her aunt nodded in agreement.

"That was part of it, just not all of it. A bigger part was I didn't want you to go—with her or anyone else. However, I knew had the tables been reversed, I would've fought tooth and nail to keep the child I birthed with me. So, I couldn't fault Stacey whenever she felt she'd been away from you too long. Even if it tore at my heart to watch her walk away, knowing there was no guarantee it wouldn't be the time she decided you needed to live with her permanently."

Cuddled next to her aunt on the bench seat, reminiscent of when she was a small child, Zaria listened while Aunt Belinda revealed things she'd never spoken of before. As far as Zaria knew, after Stacey's death, her aunt and uncle took her in because they were the most stable. She had some memories of being with them a lot prior to being there full time. She hadn't realized to what extent until now.

"So, Zee-Baby. I get it. You want to be first with him, but you also recognize you don't want to stand in the way of him being the man you fell in love with."

Sitting up, lines appeared between Zaria's eyebrows as she looked at her aunt.

"I didn't say anything about being in love with Andrei."

Tilting her head down, her aunt's lips tipped into a wry grin.

"Did you forget who you were talking to? You don't have to tell me you love that man's dirty draws. I have two eyes. I can see."

Zaria shifted her gaze away from her aunt's knowing expression. She felt exposed. Vulnerable.

"Don't worry, Baby. He loves you just as much, if not more."

Surprise brought her eyes back to her aunt's.

"What makes you say that?"

Pointing to her own face, her aunt's lips twisted.

"Really? Did you forget about the eyes? They're more than half a century old, but they still work really well. Besides, the man's name for you is *Light*. Who calls someone their light without being completely in love with them?"

Zaria's face scrunched. She'd long ago looked up Andrei's pet name for her and hadn't come to the same conclusion as her aunt. Reading her expression, Aunt Belinda squeezed her arm.

"Don't tell me it never occurred to you? You're too smart for that."

Shrugging, Zaria allowed her gaze to sweep the room before coming back to her aunt's face.

"The Russian version of my name, Zorya, means *light*. Literally. In the beginning, he called me that before he moved to Svet. Since it's a literal translation, I didn't think anything of it. It was just another way to say Zaria."

Hugging her once more, her aunt clicked her tongue.

"Zee-Baby, if it was one thing I wish you would do, is give yourself more credit. I know between what you saw in your formative years and the shit show relationships you've watched from the sidelines, it might seem like real love is an anomaly. Even seeing me and Neal make it all these years might seem like an exception instead of the rule.

None of it means it can't happen for you. That it isn't happening for you right at this moment. No matter where he is, or his reasons for going. Andrei loves you like it's necessary for his survival. And you deserve to be loved that way. So, don't try to downplay it or minimize it."

Being smacked in the face with the truth of her aunt's words, all Zaria could do was nod in agreement. Absorbing her declarations also meant evaluating her relationship with Andrei. Regardless of him being absent at the moment, it didn't diminish what her aunt said. In countless ways, almost from the moment he first touched her, Andrei had shown her how he felt about her—even if he hadn't said those three words so many people craved.

Being completely honest with herself, Zaria admitted to longing to hear them as well. But, who said he had to say them first? She could put on her big girl panties and take the leap instead of waiting for him to jump. There were no rules saying he had to be the one to initiate the exchange.

Of that, she was certain. However, with him currently absent, there wasn't much she could do except wait. In the meantime, she had to trust he was going to keep his word. He *would* come back to her. When he did, she wouldn't keep the words locked behind her teeth anymore. Without worrying if he'd reciprocate, she'd tell him how she felt, and let the chips fall where they may.

Gentle pats to her shoulder brought Zaria back from inside her head. Her aunt's gaze was soft and understanding as she encouraged Zaria to stand. When they were back in the kitchen, Aunt Belinda started moving around getting familiar with where things were while Zaria went to wash up. Soon, they fell into the holiday routine they'd developed once Zaria was old enough to stand at her aunt's side, contributing to the meal preparation.

It wasn't long before the smell of Chef's apple sausage, bacon and other breakfast offerings filled the space. Zaria's stomach rumbled in appreciation of the savory scents. As if on cue, Dominique, Cisco and Uncle Neal entered with their appetites ready to be filled. For a little while, Zaria was able to take her mind off Andrei, where he was, and what he might be doing.

Knowing she couldn't do anything about it, she focused on the family who were present. Although, occasionally, her gaze drifted to the clock. A quick internet search gave her the approximate flight time from the airstrip outside of Las Vegas to the nearest large city in Russia. She hadn't received so much as a text from Andrei. Zaria itched to reach out, but something told her it would be best for her to wait for him to make contact.

Trying to keep things as normal as possible, she spent the day hanging out with her family. They even went out to the ice rink, although Cisco and Dominique were the only ones who ventured onto the frozen surface. Zaria wasn't surprised to see Andrei had planned in advance. So, everyone's size was on hand. Her skates were suspiciously absent though.

Participating in the joking around with the others helped the time go by without her constantly checking her phone. However, when night fell, she had to face the bed she and Andrei shared.

"Who the hell have you turned into, Zaria Marie?"

Zaria whispered to herself as she stared at the huge, empty bed. Dread surrounding sleeping there alone settled over her. She stood just inside the room with the door closed behind her.

"Shut up, trick. I can miss my man without your salty commentary."

Contemplating another night alone was plenty to deal with. She didn't need snarky comments adding to the mix. Even if they came from her inner voice.

Walking past the bed, she went to the bathroom to prepare for her night. Zaria's concern for Andrei and Vitaly had ebbed somewhat. Finally, during their light dinner, she received a message from Andrei letting her know they were safe. There was no additional context, only the reassurance that he would return as soon as he could.

The early morning talk with her aunt had helped tremendously. Having her feelings validated went a long way. Also, hearing her aunt admit to having her own feelings of selfishness surrounding a loved one helped put things into perspective. Zaria's head reeled for a little while after hearing her aunt's assessment of hers and Andrei's feelings for one another.

All things taken into consideration, when she opened her eyes from a restless night of sleep, she still experienced a slight twinge of disappointment when she rolled to her side and the place Andrei normally slept lay untouched. One look at her phone denoted no missed calls or texts, only the date and time blared at her from the bright display.

It was Christmas day. Her first in her new home, hosting her family. She tried really hard not to allow the sadness to become overwhelming. Andrei had promised to return. He had yet to break his word to her. Exclude some things... Maybe. But once he made a promise, he kept it.

Determined to face the day with a positive outlook, Zaria left the warmth of the bed coverings, heading to the bathroom to get ready.

Excited voices greeted her at the landing before the last few stairs. Her heart rate picked up as she rounded the corner into the kitchen.

Keeping the smile on her face from slipping when she only saw her aunt, uncle, and Dominique was some of Zaria's finest work. Part of her had hoped their cheerful banter meant Andrei was back, and they were filling him in on their exploits the previous day. No, it was simply them enjoying being together for the limited time they had before Dom hopped on a plane to get back to the set of whatever movie or show she was working on.

"Merry Christmas, Zee-Baby!" Aunt Belinda was the first to break away from the discussion to acknowledge her presence.

"Merry Christmas, Aunt Bee. Merry Christmas, everyone."

The rumbling of her stomach had her moving closer to the stove where her aunt stood. Dom was moving around while Uncle Neal sat at the island with a steaming cup of coffee in front of him.

"Want some coffee?" He held up the mug, tilting it in her direction.

Wrinkling her nose, Zaria put up a hand while shaking her head vigorously. Smelling coffee too close to the source caused her stomach to roil like it wanted to reject its contents. As long as she didn't get too close to it, she could handle it.

"No thank you, Uncle Neal."

"Are you sure? I can make you some." He moved to stand, only to be waved back to his seat.

"I'm sure. I can't with the coffee right now."

It took a couple of seconds, but understanding dawned on her uncle's face.

"Oh... Sorry, Zee-Baby. I can pour this out if it bothers you too much."

Moving to the other side of the room, Zaria shook her head.

"That's not necessary. I'm okay. I just have to keep a few feet between me and coffee."

She wasn't a normal coffee drinker even before it was placed on the No-No list by her OB-GYN. Zaria gave her uncle a pass for even offering it since it had been many years since he'd had to deal with a pregnancy in the family. Smiling at him indulgently, Zaria went about setting the table in the kitchen for their breakfast.

Part of their family tradition was to eat breakfast early, then open gifts. After which, there would be a few hours where they'd part ways and come back together for a late lunch/early dinner. If they'd been in Mississippi, the time between breakfast and lunch would've been when they'd go out and visit nearby relatives.

As much as she enjoyed hanging with her family, opening presents and making a fuss over the gifts, Zaria had to work to stay in good spirits. She tried not to let on how much it bothered her to see the presents under the tree which couldn't or wouldn't be opened until Andrei returned. Some had her name on them. From him. While others had his name on them.

Zaria wanted to see his face when he saw that her family had purchased gifts for him. A man with Andrei's wealth didn't want for much. However, she felt he'd appreciate knowing someone thought enough of him to get him something—no matter how large or small.

If she had to say so herself, Zaria did an excellent job of holding it together, and not allowing the other joyous moments to slip by. It wasn't until it was time to sit for dinner that her mask slipped. Without conscious thought, her eyes roamed the room before gluing themselves to the empty seat where Andrei should've been seated.

"Hey, Zee. You good?"

Quickly trying to clear her expression, Zaria smiled at Cisco, who was staring at her with concern.

"Yeah. I'm good. I was just thinking we were missing something."

Thankfully, when her gaze swept the table, she did see there were something missing. She was actually surprised her uncle hadn't spoken up about it. Aunt Belinda, knowing some things wouldn't be as easy to find in Las Vegas, had brought the purple hull peas that her uncle loved, along with a couple of jars of homemade Chow-Chow relish. The peas were on the table in a serving dish, but the relish wasn't.

With the perfect excuse to step away to get herself together, Zaria hopped up from the table.

"We forgot the Chow-Chow, y'all. I'll be right back."

Not giving anyone a chance to say anything, she shot from the formal dining room. Once she crossed the threshold into the kitchen, her steps slowed. Making sure to keep her word, she went into the pantry to retrieve the jar her aunt had stored there when they arrived.

Taking a moment to herself, she inhaled deeply before releasing it slowly. She could do this. It wasn't the end of the world. It was just one day. She and Andrei had many holidays to look forward to in their future.

Nodding in agreement to her silent pep-talk, Zaria turned to exit the pantry. Numb fingers let the mason jar slip on a trajectory to hit the tiled floor, only to be saved by the quick reflexes of Andrei Antonov. *He was back.*

Chapter Thirty-Eight

ANDREI ARTYOM ANTONOV

"Careful, Svet."

Andrei placed the jar Zaria dropped onto a nearby shelf as he stepped closer to his woman. Her face was frozen in a surprised expression, which had her lips slightly ajar and her eyes wide. Her parted lips were a perfect invitation that he didn't decline.

Slipping his arms around her, he lifted her to meet the kiss he placed on their pillowy softness before delving his tongue into her mouth. Her legs automatically encircled his waist with her center pressed against his stomach. It had been less than two days, however it felt like an eternity since the last time he'd tasted her.

He and Vitaly had landed not even an hour ago. It hadn't been necessary to encourage Yeva to get him home as quickly as possible. The head of his personal security didn't let little things like speed limits deter him from delivering them home in less than half the normal time.

Feeling Zaria's softness pressed against him, her fingers gliding into his hair, and her taste on his tongue was all Andrei needed at this moment. No purchased gift could compare to having the woman he loved in his arms again. Especially after what he'd learned from Vitaly.

"Hey, Zee. Mama sent me to check—oh. I see why."

Cisco's voice penetrated their bubble, but Andrei couldn't bring himself to release Zaria just yet.

"If I can just scooch by you..." Vaguely, Andrei noted Cisco moving around them into the pantry.

"I'll just...Never mind." The young man trailed off as he exited the kitchen.

After he'd reacquainted himself with as much of his Svet's sweetness as he could, considering they had family waiting for them, Andrei lowered Zaria, placing her back on her sock covered feet.

"Hey."

Her voice was raspy. It reflected the emotions swirling in her eyes. Some of it was clearly lust. Some was relief. But, there was something else there as well. Andrei ate her up with his gaze, not trying to figure out the other element—simply enjoying being back with her, knowing she was safe.

"I apologize for being late, Svet. The wind worked against us."

Although he'd lowered her to stand on her own, he kept her inside the circle of his arms. Tangible proof was required for him to believe he was actually home with her once more. That this wasn't a dream.

Andrei's eyelids slid closed when her soft fingertips stroked his face, then his beard. He took a moment to just appreciate the experience of being with her again. It helped calm the beast inside him. The vengeful creature who wanted to return to Russia, revive Ruslan, and kill him again. Only more slowly, and far more painfully than the first time.

"It's okay. You're here now."

Her sweet acceptance did very little to appease his guilt at having left her the way he had. He didn't regret going after his brother. He simply wished it hadn't been necessary to do it so close to a day that was special to her.

Growing up in his family, the more western world style Christmas celebration hadn't been held in his household. They observed more Russian traditions in which celebrating didn't start until January 1st of the new year. Except, Zaria wasn't Russian. She was very much a product of the American south. Christmas was an important holiday for her and her family.

He was supposed to be here with them. That was where his guilt stemmed from. Not from anything he did to assure the current and future safety of her and their child. Instead of being present to be certain she was calm and enjoying an anxiety-free holiday experience, he was on the other side of the world dealing with a problem which should've been taken care of years ago.

So, in the place of the relaxing, celebratory atmosphere he wanted for her, she was worried about him, what he was doing and if he was okay. Zaria hadn't said any of those things aloud. However, the way she embraced him, the way her eyes held the sheen of unshed tears, told him everything he needed to know.

"It is far from okay, Svet. But, I will make it up to you. I promise."

Shaking her head, she cupped his face with both hands. "I don't want promises, Antonov. I just want you."

"You have me. Always, Svet."

"That's good, because I'm not doing this life thing without you."

Although very little space separated them, Andrei closed the gap until there was none. Dropping a kiss on her nose, he pressed one hand against her abdomen and the other at her back, keeping her close.

"Did you actually think doing it alone was an option?"

Zaria's hand landed atop his on her stomach, and she laced their fingers together. Andrei finally recognized the other element in her expression when she looked up at him again. *Love.* The moment it hit him, his knees almost buckled from the weight of understanding. He didn't have a second to wrap his mind around it before she responded to his question.

"No, Andrei. The way I love you doesn't allow me to even consider having another day without you in it."

Lifting her until they were eye-level, Andrei searched her smiling face. He'd heard what she said, yet he sought confirmation.

"You love me, Svet?"

"Yes. I love you, Andrei."

With hands braced on his shoulders, she leaned forward and connected their lips. Between pecks, she continued to affirm her words.

"I love you." Kiss. "I love your overprotective." Kiss. "Always have to be in charge." Kiss. "Hand in everything, self." Kiss.

Growling, Andrei walked them into the pantry, closing the door with his foot and turning to press her back against it. With the last kiss she placed on his lips, he slipped his tongue inside her mouth to deepen it.

Hearing her acknowledge her feelings had him ready to forget the guests in their home and mark the occasion by joining them together. *Immediately.*

Instead, he kissed her until he was hanging on by the thinnest of threads. Then, he delivered parting pecks as he basked in the glow of having the woman he loved profess her love to him.

Caressing his shoulders in a motion which felt like she was smoothing out invisible wrinkles in his shirt, Zaria stared at him. Another emotion slowly crept into her gaze.

"What is it, Svet?"

"Don't you have something to say to me?"

"Of course. But I thought I would tell you what happened in Russia later."

"Not that." A crease formed between her eyebrows. "Well, I wanna know about that too. I wasn't asking about what you and Vitaly got into on the other side of the world. At least not yet."

Andrei replayed the past few minutes, trying to figure out what he missed. The longer it took for him to respond, the more the hint of sadness and uncertainty stole into Zaria's eyes. The moment it dawned on him, he dropped his forehead to hers.

"I love you, Svet." Pressing his lips to hers, he held back from deepening the kiss. "I have told you so many times, I thought you already knew."

Zaria's expression shifted to confusion as she stared at him from beneath her lashes.

"You've told me many times? When might those times have been?"

Andrei started to question if she really didn't know, but stopped himself. His Svet wasn't a game player. The only time she asked questions she already knew the answer to was when she was in court. Tilting his head toward her, he dipped the fingers of one hand into the curly coils at her nape.

"The first time I told you I loved you was the night we spent together at your other house after we returned from the island."

With her face scrunched, the cutest wrinkle appeared on her nose while he watched her physically go through calling up the memory. A smile hovered at the corner of his mouth when her lips formed a pout before she let him have it.

"Andrei Artyom Antonov. Did you have the audacity to tell me you loved me in a language you know I don't speak?"

"What do you mean, Svet? I have spoken Russian to you before and you have responded."

Swatting his chest, Zaria's face maintained a pout. "You know good and well that I speak and comprehend maybe twenty words in Russian. Definitely not enough to understand a string of words while I'm in the midst of having an orgasm."

The last part of her sentence was delivered through clenched teeth as she tapped his chest with each one. Neither carried a sting, but Andrei captured her lips to squelch the rest of her rant. When he finally released her mouth, she was ready with her next question.

"What else did I miss? You said you've told me many times. Were they all during sex? That's when you speak the most Russian, other than when you're talking to your brother. If it was, I need to tell you, Antonov, your delivery system could use some work. That's if your goal was to get your message across clearly."

Zaria's face held a tinge of mirth, however Andrei returned a serious expression. He could never deny her anything—not even words he wasn't sure how to express.

"Each time I refer to you as Svet, I am expressing my love for you. Did you truly not know?"

Andrei didn't wait for a response. Instead, he pressed on.

"You are my Svet. My Light. Your given name is perfect for you. You shine so brightly, it's impossible for my life not to be brightened with you in it. You sashayed into my casino and lifted the cloud of darkness I did not even know surrounded me. You shifted my existence to living. Svet. You are my way. My hope. My future.

Since the first moment I touched you, I have felt nothing but honor to stand in the glow you emit while simply occupying the same space. Of course I love you, Svet. My life would be forever night without your sun to illuminate it."

Gently, Andrei used his thumb to swipe away the tears now streaming down Zaria's cheeks. Resting his forehead against hers, he whispered the words again. Affirming his feelings in a way which couldn't be mistaken. Raining kisses on her face, he held her close.

They probably would have stayed that way indefinitely had there not been a knock on the pantry door.

"Hey! I don't know what you're doing in there. And I don't want to know. Dinner is getting cold. So, can you wrap it up?"

Zaria's face morphed into embarrassment before she buried it in the crook of Andrei's neck.

"We'll be right there, Uncle Neal."

Although her words were partially muffled, they were apparently loud enough for her uncle to hear.

"Uh-huh. Don't make me come back in here."

Andrei listened to the muted sounds of his retreating footsteps. Once they were gone, he lowered Zaria to her feet once more and opened the door to the pantry. Clasping her hand in his, he led them to the formal dining room where their family waited.

Andrei didn't think he could be any happier. Seated next to his woman, having holiday dinner in their home, surrounded by their loved ones, he sincerely believed he couldn't get better. That is until Zaria tugged him to the room she referred to as the front living room. Presents were still wrapped under the tree, and she informed him they were mostly for him.

He wasn't able to contain his shocked expression. There were a few he recognized by the wrapping as things he'd bought for her and the others, but there were more than a few boxes surrounding the base of the large pre-lit fir. His gaze went from the collection to Zaria, then to her family, who all sat around the room grinning at him.

Pushing against his chest, Zaria encouraged him to sit while she went to the tree to retrieve his gifts. Dominique and Cisco hopped up to help with the distribution.

Andrei was accustomed to the spotlight. Considering his previous and current occupations, being watched was a part of the package. However, it felt odd to tear away the colorful wrapping paper while they watched him expectantly. Lifting one set of the athletic wear from the box, he looked to Zaria's aunt and uncle, giving them a nod and word of thanks.

He didn't have to wonder why they'd decided on such a present. Zaria wasn't the only one who'd made mention of his lack of what she considered casual clothing. The Trumans had made it their mission to rectify the situation. It didn't matter that Andrei could more than afford those items for himself; it touched him that they'd gone out of their way to purchase them in the first place. The offerings from Dominique included jeans and golf-style polo shirts which she said were originals from a fashion designer friend of hers.

Not enjoying being the center of attention, Andrei was relieved when Zaria placed packages in front of Vitaly before sitting on Andrei's left with a rectangular box on her lap. From the way she handled it, the box wasn't very heavy. Andrei knew exactly what was in it. It was one of his gifts to her. Pausing from opening another package, he was laser focused on her progress.

Instead of ripping into the paper as he and Vitaly had done, Zaria removed the bow around the box and carefully tugged at the tape. It was a big departure from what one would expect from a person with such a vibrant personality. When she lifted the cover, Andrei's breathing became shallow.

"What is it, Zee-Baby? It's taking you a long time to open that one little box."

Her aunt's question and comment snapped Zaria's attention from the object inside the box to Andrei's waiting eyes. Reaching inside, she removed the small building replica. Then, the bundle of paper beneath it.

"Andrei...what is this?"

"What does it look like, Svet?"

While he appeared cool, Andrei wasn't as confident as he seemed. His pulse quickened as he watched her set the little building on a side table and unfold the papers. The chatter in the room dropped to a low hum. The longer it took Zaria to scan the papers she held, the more the thumping of his heart drowned out the other sounds in the room. He had no explanation for his sudden case of nerves.

Finally, she raised her eyes from the paper, looking up at him through her thick lashes.

"Andrei...you bought the building?"

"What building?" Cisco's outburst was immediately quieted by his mother.

"You said you did not want a newspaper. But you did not say owning real estate was not an option."

"Andrei..." Zaria's head moved side to side in obvious disbelief.

"If you will notice, it is completely in your name. You can expand your office space to other floors if you like, or continue to rent them to other businesses."

When she fingered the small model building and placed it back in the box, Andrei began shaking his own head. Shifting the item in his lap to the floor next to him, he wrapped an arm around her pulling her into his side. It was pointless to try to keep their conversation private, however he attempted by speaking lowly, directly into her ear.

"Do not, Svet. Do not even think of refusing this gift."

Her dark eyes searched his, while he regarded her with fierce determination.

"Andrei...it's too much."

"There is no such thing when it comes to you."

"But—"

"No buts, Svet. You deserve the security of owning the space you do business in without being subjected to someone else's mandates and whims surrounding that space."

Zaria's brows shot up her forehead. She stared at him incredulously. His lips tilted up into a full smile. She hadn't uttered one word to him about the previous building owner, and how the older man was considering retirement. She didn't have to. Everything Zaria Marie Coleman related, Andrei considered his business to know.

Once the elder Nevins retired, ownership of the building would change hands going to his only child. A son who'd made no secret that he'd institute significant changes when he was at the helm.

One of the changes he planned was a drastic increase in the amount required to lease space. The area around the building had undergone a revitalization. The agreement Zaria worked out with the father for the two floors her firm occupied would expire within the next year, allowing for the son to implement his new, market-comparable agenda when it came to the tenants.

The way Zaria stared at him gave the impression she was going to continue to deny his gift. However, she surprised him by launching herself at him, wrapping her arms around his neck, and planting kisses on his face. Between pecks, she thanked Andrei, making him realize she'd been more concerned about the changes than she'd ever wanted to admit.

"Wait... So, Dray bought Zee a whole building? In Las Vegas?"

Cisco's questions came at the end of Zaria's exuberant appreciation. She settled into his side, apparently unphased that neither of them had finished opening presents. Andrei looked at Cisco, who stared at him with an awe-filled expression.

"Is this what life is like when you have money-money? Is that the bar? I'm gonna have to get hella endorsements to do stuff like that for my lady."

"First of all, watch your mouth." His mother swatted at him. "Secondly, what lady are you talking about? You said you didn't have a girlfriend."

Smoothing his hands down the front of his shirt, Cisco sat back in his seat on the sofa.

"Sorry, Ma. I don't have a girlfriend, but a man's gotta think ahead. Right, Pops?"

His father nodded in agreement, but he never took his eyes off Andrei and Zaria. Andrei returned the older man's stare until he received the barest of nods from Neal Truman. Zaria stirred at his side, wiggling from beneath his arm to grab the box he'd set aside when she started opening hers. The box was large and had a little weight to it, so he took over, putting it back in his lap. When he moved to resume opening it, she put her hand on his.

"Wait. Open this one first." She placed a flat rectangular box on top of the larger one.

Wasting no time, Andrei ripped into the small box. His brow dipped as he examined the contents. First, he looked at the photo showing what looked like a mobile storage box that he'd seen in television commercials. Beneath the photo were folded papers. His gaze shot to Zaria before he picked them up, quickly unfolding them.

"This is a rental agreement, Svet."

"I'm aware." The apples of Zaria's cheeks were more pronounced when she smiled at him broadly.

"It is for the home you own in Coryville."

"Yes it is. I figured, if I was going to be living here with you, there was no point in that property sitting empty. So, I rented it out. The new tenant moved in last week."

The tips of Andrei's fingers went numb, and the papers slipped from his digits. She'd expressed her love for him earlier, however hearing that she was making plans to be with him permanently set off an explosion inside of him. His normally steady hands shook slightly as he cupped her face in his. She'd risen to her knees on the cushion beside him. He leaned in to capture her lips in a grateful kiss. His heart was full beyond measure with the events of the day. To think he'd almost missed out on such a precious gift tugged at him internally.

When Zaria ended their kiss with parting pecks, Andrei was tempted to follow her, but she placed a hand on his chest, keeping him in place.

"You still have one more gift to open, remember?"

"As do you." Andrei tilted his head toward the two neatly wrapped boxes next to the sofa they occupied.

"You first." Zaria sat back on her heels with her hands clasped in front of her.

Eyeing her speculatively, Andrei resumed tearing away the wrapping on the large package. When he finally had it open, he simply stared at the contents for a moment. Excitement vibrated off Zaria to the point she was slightly bouncing in her seat.

From the depth of the box, Andrei knew there were other items below the racing suit. Confusion knit his brow as he tried to understand the reasoning for such a gift. The other clothing, he understood. This... This didn't make sense.

When he lifted the garment, an envelope fell, drawing his attention. Lowering the suit, he looked inside it. When he was done reading, he glanced at Zaria, who wore a stunning smile.

"You like it?"

"I love it, Svet. Thank you."

"You're welcome." Zaria leaned forward, once again pressing her lips to his.

"Umm... Excuse us, but do the rest of us get to know what it is or is it a couple thing?" Andrei looked at his brother, who held up one hand as if he were in a classroom asking a question.

"It's not a secret." Zaria supplied. "It's an adventure box."

"What's an adventure box?"

Zaria rubbed her hand along Andrei's forearm while she explained the present to Vitaly. Andrei kissed the back of his Svet's hand, then tangled their fingers together. This day was turning out to be much more emotional than he would've ever imagined.

"I thought it would be nice for Andrei to have time where he just gets to have fun. So, I put together some activities that allow him to just have a good time without any worries. The racing suit is for when he hits the track with a few professional drivers."

A chorus of "*Holy shit!*" "*Are you serious?*" and "*That's awesome!*" came from around the room. While Andrei thought it would be an interesting experience to get to drive alongside professionals, he was happy about it solely because it seemed to bring Zaria joy to provide the experience for him.

In honesty, it was something he wouldn't have arranged for himself. Neither was the zip lining in Hawaii, nor the jet boating and rafting in New Zealand. He actually couldn't recall the last time he'd taken a real vacation prior to their time in Bali. In true Zaria fashion, she'd put a time limit on him partaking in the activities. With the exception of the race car driving, they all had to be done within the next three months, before she reached the stage of pregnancy where travel wouldn't be recommended.

Vitaly drew Andrei's attention from Zaria's smiling face. Leaning closer, he tipped the box in his direction.

"Is there just one of these, brother? Are you sure there isn't one for me? You'll need a companion."

The chuckle rumbling from Andrei's chest surprised even him.

"I already have a companion, Brat. But, if you are good. I will see what I can do."

Zaria's fingers squeezed his in approval as she assured Vitaly she'd taken him into consideration, which had him scrambling to open his last box that contained a similar racing suit as the one she gifted Andrei. He wouldn't be with them on every adventure, however his Svet had given him and his brother this one experience to share.

Chapter Thirty-Nine

PAPA

Zaria's cheeks hurt from the amount of smiling she'd done since Andrei appeared in their pantry several hours ago. Following the opening of presents, they'd drifted to the media room. Andrei had added some items; so the set up contained more than just the theater style seats and projection screen.

While not as loud and boisterous as their normal family gatherings, the evening was still filled with laughter, games, and decadent desserts. Like her, her family had waited for Andrei to return to open his gifts to them. They were equally pleased with his over-the-top offerings.

It was well after midnight before she and Andrei climbed into bed, following a heated joining in the shower. Her pretty pocket was thoroughly pleased with his efforts to make up for his absence.

Once they were settled, Zaria curled into his side with her head on his chest. Andrei absently stroked his fingers from her hip up to her shoulder, then back down to begin the process again.

"Okay, Antonov. You've had plenty of time, and I've allowed your distraction tactics. It's time to come clean. Tell me what happened."

"I was not trying to distract you, Svet. I missed you."

Sweet talk was not going to work. Raising her head, she pinned him with an expression that had him nodding and cuddling her close.

"Okay, Svet. I will tell you everything. But, first you need to understand that you and our baby are safe."

Andrei squeezed her in his embrace following the immediate stiffening of Zaria's posture. Heading off any questions with a soft shushing noise, he quickly continued.

"I told you about my childhood and the things I did to support my family. You also know about my parents' untimely deaths. The full details surrounding their deaths involve my mother's younger brother. It was his debt to the Bratva which brought collectors to my parents' doorstep. Supposedly, they were there to send a message and force me to cover Ruslan's debts with interest. However, according to what I learned later, my father did not like his wife being threatened and he fought them. The end result was both of their deaths."

Zaria's heart hurt for Andrei as she listened to his recounting of how he lost his parents. How his uncle was the catalyst that brought the Grimm Reaper to their door and put his brother in danger. Hearing how he called in favors to get a private flight to Switzerland to retrieve Vitaly before he could be swept up in the Morozov family's vengeance had her jaw clenching.

She couldn't contain the tears when she learned he'd essentially had to pay for his and his brother's freedom. Because, unbeknownst to him, his uncle had made deals with corrupt government officials who didn't like having one of their income streams taken away from them. Payment included large sums of money and all the property he owned in his homeland. Listening to him made Zaria wish for Ruslan to cease to exist. He didn't deserve oxygen, let alone life.

Her wish became a mandate when Andrei reached the point in his story regarding why he'd left to chase after Vitaly. Bolting upright, she stared down at him.

"He did what?!"

"Please, Svet. Do not upset yourself. He will never get a chance to touch you or our child."

"That was some ratchet ass, low down shit. From what you just told me, I have no doubt he wouldn't give two shits about serving anyone you cared about up to the wolves, as long as it saved his sorry ass."

Andrei's large hand cupped her face as he wrapped his other arm around her to pull her back down to his chest. Zaria allowed him to gather her close once more, but she was fuming.

"Calm, Svet. It is over. He will never hurt us, or anyone else, again."

The finality with which he assured her told her what he hadn't yet said. Ruslan was dead. Andrei didn't have to tell her how or who'd made it happen. She was certain of it. It was a good thing. She hoped the human waste was being tortured in his own special room in hell for the way he'd treated those who had done nothing except love and support him.

When her breathing was more even, Andrei finished his retelling. She was positive she received the severely edited version of the events prior to him and Vitaly boarding a flight to return home.

"So, let me make sure I heard this right. Vitaly flew all the way to Russia, made contact with a Finnish mob boss. And we'll come back to that little nugget. I didn't even know there was a such thing as Finnish Mafia."

Zaria stared at him with one lifted eyebrow before she continued.

"He then proceeds to strike a deal with the Finnish mob boss who scooped up your uncle.—"

"Ruslan is my mother's sibling, but he is ***not*** my uncle."

"Sorry, baby." Zaria rubbed soothing circles on Andrei's chest.

"Vitaly strikes a deal with the Finnish mob boss. They scoop Ruslan up and give him the business. When you get there, the two of you make it clear no one will be paying Ruslan's debt. And the Finnish mob just takes you at your word? That's it? No more Ruslan and no more mafia debt? Do I have that right?"

Zaria couldn't explain it, but part of her needed to hear all of it. There was no way for her to see it, however she needed to hear from Andrei's mouth that Ruslan was no longer among the living.

"Yes, Svet. That is it. It is handled. We will not be hearing from anyone about Ruslan and his gambling debts again. Any promises he made died with him."

Unexplainable relief washed over Zaria when Andrei confirmed her belief. It wasn't in her nature to celebrate the death of another human being. However, Ruslan had been at the center of too much heartache and trauma. From everything she'd deduced, he would've never stopped on his own.

They lay there in silence for a little while, but Zaria was too keyed up to sleep. Apparently, Andrei wasn't sleepy either. He absently stroked various parts of her body. His touch wasn't sexual. It was more geared toward lulling her into the sleep which eluded her for the moment.

"You know what I was thinking?"

Andrei's stroking stopped, and he hugged her to him, as if what she planned to say might cause her to fly away. Smiling, she patted his arm.

"It's nothing bad. I was just thinking about how you've been such a good sport about celebrating the holidays with me and my family according to our traditions and culture. We should celebrate yours as well."

"I do not have traditions, Svet."

"I thought you said your family used to observe Noby God?"

"Novy God. And yes. When my parents were alive, my mother was very big on participating in Novy God. She decorated the house and made sure we had time to spend together. When I started playing hockey here in the U.S., it was more difficult. It was not possible for me to be there for the entire two weeks following the New Year."

Zaria walked her fingers up his chest, then tapped him on the chin.

"Well, now you're in a different place in your life. You have the means to set your own schedule. So, we could restart the tradition. You can teach me the things you learned. And when our baby comes, we'll teach her or him about both of our cultures and traditions. How about that?"

Resting her chin on his chest, she regarded him with expectation. Andrei gazed at her with an expression identical to the one he'd worn when she told him she'd turned her house into a rental property and made plans to live with him permanently. His hold on her shifted, and she suddenly found herself sitting up, straddling his torso.

"What is it you are trying to do, Svet?"

Tipping her head to one side, her brow dipped in confusion.

"What do you mean?" Zaria thought she'd been pretty clear with her suggestion. "Do you not like the idea?"

The warmth of Andrei's hands landed on her thighs, giving them a gentle squeeze.

"It is a very nice idea, Svet. Although unnecessary. It is still nice of you to think of combining family traditions."

Laying her hands on top of his, she tangled their fingers together.

"That's what couples do. Right? When they're sharing their lives, they combine traditions. I don't expect us to always do things the way me and my family have done them."

Taking his hands, she placed them on her abdomen.

"The little person in there deserves to learn about their father's culture as well as their mother's."

"Papa." Andrei splayed his fingers on her stomach as he spoke. His attention was solidly on her midsection. He swore it was more rounded, even though she was just entering her second trimester.

"I am her papa."

"Ok, papa. It's your job to teach them. Tell them stories about their Grandma and Grandpa Antonov."

"Her babushka and dedushka."

"See. I didn't know either of those words. So, if we start now, next year, when Baby Antonov is with us, we'll already have a routine established."

"Da. We will." There was so much context in those three words Andrei didn't need to say more.

Zaria was so focused on being happy he agreed, she didn't pay attention to the way his demeanor had shifted. It wasn't until his fingers went from caressing her stomach to cupping her breasts that she noticed.

"Oh!"

"Yes, Svet. Oh."

Meeting her lips with his, he delved between them to mate their tongues. Zaria felt him harden beneath her, and her core clenched in anticipation. The short amount of time since they'd last come together in the shower didn't matter. Her pretty pocket was reporting for duty.

It wasn't even a thought in her mind to object to another round of lovemaking. Andrei was a master at fucking her to sleep. Zaria wouldn't complain for even a second.

New Year's Eve presented Zaria with her first opportunity to appear with Andrei at an official event as his significant other. They attended the

Annual New Year's Eve bash held at Anton's. She'd heard about it, but hadn't ever gone. She usually rang in the new year with family other than the one time she and Alyssa went to New York to see the ball drop. She wouldn't do that shit again. It was too cold in New York in January for those kinds of shenanigans.

To her surprise, Andrei had the decorator duplicate the decorations from the house in his suite at the casino. They spent the night there after the party and attended the Chevaliers game the next day before going home.

From Zaria's perspective, both the event and the game were a success. The party was fun. Completely drama-free. At the game, there were a couple of people noticeably absent from the last time she attended. So, there were no incidents of Andrei putting hands on anyone.

Now, she was back in their home looking at the additions the designer added to the décor once Andrei was on board with extending their holiday season. Nodding appreciatively at the way they'd managed to blend the elements Zaria was accustomed to with things Andrei and Vitaly would find familiar, she touched a cone-shaped ornament. It held a painted image of the Russian version of Santa Clause. The pointed top, with a golden string looped through keeping it dangling from the branch, was of course the top of his festive hat.

One look at the companion nesting dolls, and Zaria had to have them as well. They weren't hanging from the tree. Instead, two sets were nestled in the greenery placed along the mantle. Each night, since it's completion, she became a child again marveling at the additional lights on the tree as well as those woven into the garland above the mantle and wound along the stairway. It was the best night light ever.

Andrei tried to play it cool, but Zaria was on to him. He enjoyed the new festive décor as well. They spent more time in front of the fireplace than they had previously. The room had become a gathering place before or after dinner. He had been teaching her the family traditions they'd observed with each corresponding day.

The party at Anton's was used as the kick-off. Since they'd attended the hockey match on the first, they combined the day one and day two activities. Andrei explained that usually, the house would be cleaned from top to bottom on the first day of the year. Zaria was happy to mark that one off the list when he suggested it. It wasn't feasible with the size of the mansion. However, they did clean their suite of rooms themselves, since the staff didn't start back until the third.

To help her, he'd made a list to correspond to each day. Zaria had also done a little internet sleuthing as well. Andrei's list appeared to be missing one of the first day activities, but had all of the others. Walking into the kitchen where he stood next to the range top preparing their dinner, she held out the notepad he'd given her.

"Hey, I have a question."

Putting the lid on the pot of savory goodness he'd been stirring, he accepted the pad.

"Yes?"

"I'm just checking to see if you left something off on purpose or was it something your mama didn't press y'all to do?"

Andrei folded his arms across his chest and lifted one eyebrow. From his stance, Zaria was certain he knew exactly what she was talking about. Yet, she continued anyway.

"The information I found online said part of the cleansing process for the New Year was forgiving those who've wronged you. Did you leave it off on purpose?"

"I did." Andrei spoke so matter-of-factly; Zaria considered letting the matter drop.

"Okay. I can't say I don't understand. We've both had our fair share of people fucking with us this past year. I'm not even sure that, if I were to try to say the words, I could be sincere."

Stepping into his space, she pulled his arms loose and wrapped them around her back.

"Aunt Belinda has told me for years that forgiveness isn't for the person who harmed you. It's for you. So you can let go of the hurt and harm and be free to move forward."

Rising on her tiptoes, she puckered her lips for a kiss. Andrei met her partway with a gentle peck.

"Auntie is a very wise woman. But, I will decline her offer. I do not need to set aside time to forgive anyone. I am perfectly content to not think of them ever again."

Zaria was beginning to speak fluent Andrei, because she heard what he didn't say. So long as the person or people who tried him didn't pop back up, they didn't have to fuck around and find out what happened when they attempted to hurt him or anyone he loved. His facial expression was resolute.

Opting not to press him, she decided to let the subject drop. Heck, she wasn't sure she was ready to verbalize forgiveness for those who endeavored to injure her emotionally or financially. It was something she'd have to work through in her next therapy session.

"Okay. If that's how you feel, I'll keep that one on the back burner. However, I do think it would be something we don't want to drop from the tradition in the future. Especially if it was important enough to your mama to make sure she included it."

She was playing a little dirty. Zaria knew it, and it couldn't be helped. Being able to let go was part of being a healthy adult and she wanted a healthy father for her child. Physically and emotionally. They just had to figure out what healthy meant for Andrei. Baby steps.

"We shall see, Svet." With a light tap to her butt, he set her away from him. "Dinner is ready. Have you finished setting the table?"

"Of course." She grinned, adding a little extra sway to her hips as she walked away to grab the serving dishes from the island to transfer the food.

Over dinner, Zaria processed the events of the next week aloud. Andrei indulged her by occasionally chiming in. She appreciated it, since she was more hyper focused than she was with Christmas. Mainly, she attributed her increased attention to detail to the surprise she'd planned for him on the seventh.

Understanding that the Christmas holiday wasn't the be-all-end-all it was among the American population, she still wanted it to be special. It was another first. The next few days went by more quickly than Zaria planned. Since they hadn't fully prepared to be absent the first two weeks of the new year, they both had to do some schedule juggling and partial days to make it work.

So, by the time the fifth of January arrived, Zaria was ready for the weekend and the activities she planned for the seventh. While Andrei was privy to most things, she had a trick or two up her sleeve. As hard as it was to keep it a secret, she managed. The moment the door chimed with the arrival of their first guests, she felt a gush of relief.

She entered the foyer to the sight of her Aunt Belinda hugging Andrei while her Uncle Neal and Cisco stood behind her surrounded by their luggage. Despite them only planning to stay the weekend, not all of the spinner style suitcases were carry-on size. But Andrei had spoiled them with the private flights, so her aunt no longer had to worry about over-packing.

And, bless her heart, her Aunt Belinda was wearing a sweater so bright it almost hurt to look at her. Gaudy was possibly too tame a word for the electric red sweater with what looked like tinsel garland around the neck, cuffs and bottom. Upon closer inspection, Zaria realized the Christmas tree on the front had actual lights on it.

After she'd taken her turn being squeezed by her aunt, Zaria stared at the garment with a slightly dropped jaw.

"Auntie, are those lights real?"

"Of course they are. Watch!"

With unbridled joy, her aunt lifted the bottom edge of her sweater and flipped a switch. Not only did the lights illuminate, and flicker, a jaunty holiday tune began to play. Zaria's jaw dropped completely.

"Auntie, where in the world did you get this?"

"The Flea Market. You know you can find anything at the Flea Market. I bought this from that lady who sells the Christmas stuff all year round."

Spinning around as if she were modeling a couture design. Her aunt beamed.

"You like it?"

"It's...very festive."

It was the best Zaria could come up with, but she added a bright smile which seemed to satisfy her aunt.

"See, Neal. I told you this was cute. I'm glad you like it, Zee-Baby. I got one for you and Dom. We can take pictures in front of the tree since we didn't do it when we were all together a couple of weeks ago. When is my baby getting here anyway?"

Her aunt kept up the stream of questions and conversation while walking into the front living room, leaving the rest of them to follow her.

Zaria's stricken expression had Cisco hastily grabbing up the luggage heading toward the stairs.

"Let me help you." Andrei dropped a quick kiss on Zaria's cheek; then, quickly grabbed up the larger of the suitcases.

When Zaria turned to her uncle, he threw up his hands.

"Don't look at me. You know I can't tell Bee what to do."

Zaria folded her arms across her chest, staring at her uncle assessingly.

"You know what I find suspicious, Uncle Neal? She just said she got one for me and Dom. What about you? What about Cisco, Andrei, Vitaly?" Making sure to keep her voice low, she practically hissed.

When she started tapping her foot, her uncle dipped his head, rubbing the back of his neck.

"I might have said something about how long it's been since you three had something that was just for the girls."

"Uncle Neal!" Zaria folded her fingers because she wanted to pinch him like she'd seen her Grandma Lou do when one of the boys got *fresh*—as she called it.

Backing away toward the stairs, her uncle's face was set with a wry smile.

"A man's gotta do what a man's gotta do. I'm gonna go help Dray and Cisco with those bags."

With that he turned around and took the stairs two at a time to get away from her.

"Where'd everybody go?"

Zaria whirled around to see her aunt standing in the doorway on the other side of the foyer. Pasting a smile on her face, she walked toward her.

"They went to put your luggage away."

"Oh, good." Looping her arm through Zaria's, her aunt tugged her toward the stairs. "I can get your sweater. I got a text from Dominique. Her plane just landed. She'll be here in about thirty minutes. This is gonna be so cute!"

Zaria had nothing to add as she allowed herself to be led to the second floor. Things could be so much worse than being loved with such ferocity. So, ugly sweater and all, she'd take it.

Chapter Forty

MY LIGHT

Andrei looked around his home with new eyes as he regarded the people his Svet had gathered together without ever hinting at her plan. He wasn't sure if he should thank Frederick for helping her, or fire him for keeping the man who paid his salary in the dark.

Shaking his head, Andrei dismissed the thought. If Zaria caught a sniff of him considering punishing his assistant, she'd have some choice words for him. She'd likely remind him that he didn't ***have*** to know every detail of everything ***all*** the time. He didn't necessarily agree, but he wouldn't argue with her about it.

Gregor stood to his left sipping the vodka and Kahlua laced eggnog one of the women pressed into his hand when he entered. Although he didn't comment, Andrei noticed Gregor made the one glass last for the past thirty minutes. Nor did he mention to them that alcohol typically wasn't a part of the celebration. Especially considering what he, and the rest of the men had gotten into the previous evening while the ladies were having their night.

Last Night

Andrei looked at Zaria over his shoulder as she shooed him, Carver, Cisco, Uncle Neal, Denzel and Vitaly from the kitchen. As they had done during Thanksgiving, the men had activities separately from the ladies.

Seeing it as a melding of traditions, Andrei didn't push back or mention that there wasn't anything left to prepare for the next day.

Instead, he led the group to the media room where a buffet of party foods had been laid out for them, and a hockey matchup played on the projection screen. Cisco immediately fixed a plate and glued himself to one of the theater seats to watch the game.

Once the rest of them were settled around a table with food in front of them, Uncle Neal placed a bottle of bourbon at the center along with five tumblers. Andrei watched him pour each man a generous portion and pass them out.

Vitaly was the first to pick up his glass. Looking at the amber liquid, he tipped the bottle to inspect the label more closely.

"This is the good stuff."

"What did you expect?" Uncle Neal leaned forward with his elbows on the table.

"I didn't expect swill, but this bottle says more than 'let's get drunk'." Vitaly swirled the bourbon then took a sip.

"You're smart for a guy who takes biscuits to the head."

"I'll have you know that only happened twice."

Vitaly's rebuttal to the crack about him being hit with pucks set off a round of laughter lasting only a few moments before silence reigned once again. Andrei suspected what the topic of discussion might be, however he let the older man broach the subject.

He didn't have to wait long. With one deep draw on the drink in his glass, the man who'd accepted him and his brother as family got straight to the point.

"Since, you're a man of your word, I know whatever reason you ran off on Christmas Eve must've been critical. However, you also know how I feel about my children being hurt. She didn't say anything to me and she didn't have to. I know my child.

Everybody was all smiles and happy when the two of you showed back up, but don't get it twisted. One of you need to tell me what was so important you risked breaking my baby girl's heart."

"It's my fault, Uncle."

Andrei shot Vitaly a glance. When had he started referring to Zaria's uncle that way?

"I do not need you to speak for me, Brat."

"I'm not. I'm speaking for me. You wouldn't have done what you did if it wasn't for what I'd done."

The two lapsed into Russian, but their conversation was swiftly interrupted by Uncle.

"Uh-uh. Whatever you have to say, say it in English."

Andrei ignored Denzel and Carver muttering their agreement. They didn't jump into the conversation. They also didn't disguise their eagerness to hear everything. To this point, he hadn't discussed it with them, nevertheless he was mostly certain the best friend grapevine was to thank for neither man looking surprised. His Svet had obviously spoken to Alyssa at some point.

Scanning the table, Andrei made eye contact with each man. Checking to be certain Cisco remained engrossed in the hockey match, he finally spoke.

"I believe it goes without saying that what is said here is not to be repeated. Not even to your wives."

His last statement was directed specifically toward Uncle Neal and Carver. Any slip from the two of them would immediately get back to Zaria. While he'd told her most of what happened, he knew the leeway she'd given him to omit certain parts was unlikely to be extended by her uncle.

"We're grown ass men. We know how to hold our water."

"What he said."

Andrei wasn't completely familiar with the term the older man used, but he picked up on the context clues. From the way Carver immediately agreed, he recognized the phrase. Glancing at his brother, Andrei started by giving them a brief background, then Vitaly jumped in to explain his part.

Other than the occasional, 'That's fucked up', or 'Damn, that's cold', the other men didn't comment until the brothers were done. As with Zaria, Andrei didn't go into details about how Ruslan's life was ended. With a quick glance over his shoulder at his son, Uncle Neal looked at Carver and Denzel.

Apparently seeing what he needed to see in their expressions, he turned blazing eyes to Andrei.

"I feel like you skipped some shit. Did you kill him? And if you did, was it slow or fast? I know he was technically your family—"

"Nyet. He was not our family." Andrei cut across his sentence. He couldn't stomach hearing anyone say he shared blood with Ruslan.

"Fine. Not your family. I'm just asking if it was slow? Because it sounds like a quick death was too good for him."

"He was already dying slowly, Uncle." Vitaly interjected. "His liver was failing."

Narrowing his eyes, the older man stared at Andrei. "Did you at least shoot him in the face?"

"Damn..." Denzel muttered. Andrei didn't spare him a glance, but he understood his friend's sentiment. It was hard to believe a man who appeared as mild mannered as Neal Truman would be quite so blood thirsty.

"Da." Andrei's one word answer seemed to placate him. So, he saw no need to specify it was a shot to the forehead.

Tapping two fingers on the table Uncle Neal stared between Andrei and Vitaly.

"I don't appreciate you running off without telling me anything."

While he respected the man, Andrei refused to apologize for acting to protect his family. Sitting quietly, he allowed his new uncle to vent his frustration at not being given the opportunity to assist.

"Next time, one of you better tell me something."

A look passed between Andrei and Vitaly before they both answered, "Yes, Uncle."

Nodding as if the matter was settled, Uncle Neal dug into his food, immediately declared it too cold, then left to warm it in the microwave. While he was gone, Denzel tapped Andrei on the arm.

"Hey. He looked like he was dead-ass when he said he wanted to go next time."

"He was." Andrei's prompt reply was met with lifted eyebrows followed by a look of acceptance.

Bobbing his head, Denzel picked up his own plate of food.

"Bet." Standing he walked across the room to the microwave as well.

Carver hadn't said much the entire time. He drank the last of his bourbon, then reached for the bottle to refill it.

"Den's in for a ride isn't he?" Carver looked at Andrei, offering to refill his tumbler.

"Absolutely." Andrei responded.

Vitaly's chuckle drew their attention. "What are you giggling about, Brat?"

"Me?" Vitaly attempted to look innocent. "I'm just happy, brother."

Not totally believing his brother, Andrei opted to let it slide. The rest of the evening was spent polishing off the bottle of bourbon along with a bottle of special reserve of Wither's Rye. By the time he climbed into bed, Andrei was the very definition of shit-faced drunk. Although, no one was the wiser since he'd still been upright and coherent when his friends were driven away in their cars and he showered with his Svet.

Present

Andrei winced slightly at the volume of the laughter reaching him from the other side of the sunroom. No matter the season, the space remained his favorite place to have meals. Holiday cheer had spilled into the area from the other parts of the house with the windows draped in garland and a smaller Christmas tree in one corner. He and Zaria had decorated that one together earlier in the week.

The headache, courtesy of his overindulgence and failure to hydrate, had been his companion when he first awakened. It was mostly gone, yet he remained somewhat sensitive to sound and Dominique's giggles hit the exact right octave to remind him of that fact.

"How long do you think it will take your friend to realize your brother is simply fucking with his head, and isn't actually interested in the lovely actress?"

Gregor's question drew Andrei's gaze from roaming the room to settle on Vitaly standing with one arm draped across Dominque's shoulders and the other around Zaria's. Several feet away from where Andrei and Gregor stood, Denzel sat in an overstuffed chair with Carver on his left. His posture was relaxed, but his stare was firmly fixed on the conversation across the room.

"He is aware. It is simply taking a moment for him to get the knowledge to transfer to his brain completely."

Andrei could understand. He wasn't the most rational himself when it came to Zaria. No matter the man's intent, he wasn't fond of anyone being so familiar with her who wasn't a blood relative. It was very cave man. He didn't care.

Although it was impossible Denzel heard them over the other chatter in the room, his head swiveled to where they stood. Carver was engrossed in a conversation with Ryker Stephens, and Denzel didn't spare them a glance as he left their small grouping.

When he reached them, Denzel didn't mask the attention he was giving the group on the other side of the room. Zaria had moved away and was now in a huddle with Ryker's fiancé, Ensley. However, Alyssa still stood on the other side of Dominique.

"Did you come over to simply stare at her from a different angle?" Surprising even himself, Andrei allowed the internal question to leave his thoughts.

"Fuck you, Dray." When Andrei shot him a glare, Denzel lifted one eyebrow and his trademark smirk appeared.

"What? I can't call you Dray? It took you over forty years to get a decent nickname and only certain people can use it?"

Saying nothing, Andrei just stared at him. Denzel bumped a forearm to his shoulder, while shaking his own head.

"Whatever, man. No, I didn't come over here to stare at anyone from a different angle. I remembered we didn't talk about that tip you gave me in December. My team and I finalized everything yesterday when I got into town."

Andrei nodded in response. When he'd called Denzel about the possibility of him purchasing controlling shares of CleanSun, the solar power company, he'd known his friend would run with the suggestion. For Andrei, it handled a situation without him getting directly involved. Baxter would be tossed out on his ass, which was the least he deserved for trying to use one of Andrei's former employees to get back at Zaria.

As far as Katelyn Norris and her girlfriend Delancy were concerned, they'd been having an endless run of bad luck. Jensen had uncovered enough surrounding Delancy's involvement in Katelyn's breach of company policy that she was terminated.

Andrei would lose no sleep in knowing she'd been forced to move back in with her parents in Wisconsin. They lived in a tiny town more than an hour west of Milwaukee. It was a desolate, desperate place. Even with the poor prospects, she should consider herself lucky. It could've been worse, but she hadn't been involved with Katelyn and Baxter's plans surrounding Zaria, only the attempts to cover up Katelyn's side business at Anton's.

Her girlfriend didn't fare as well. Katelyn didn't have loving parents to take her in, so she was currently living out of a rundown motel in a dust bowl town in Kansas, waiting tables in a truck stop diner. It was the only place she could get a job. Again, Andrei would lose no sleep about it.

"I guess I'll be seeing more of this city than usual."

Andrei lifted a questioning eyebrow, and Denzel continued.

"Until I feel out the board, and get someone better at the helm. I'll probably have to be here a few times a month to keep an eye on things."

Nodding in understanding, Andrei sipped his own drink and allowed his gaze to seek out his woman. Zaria's smile was bright as she gestured with her hands recounting something to Ensley which appeared to amuse them both. Her happiness seemed to spill over onto everyone around her. The atmosphere in the room was a reflection of that.

She'd brought together people who were important in both of their lives. With all the years Andrei spent as a professional athlete, and the time he put into building himself as a businessman, he'd purposely kept his circle small. He had many acquaintances and business associates, however very few got to see him the way the people in this room had.

Denzel wandered away, and Gregor drifted off to stand next to Yeva. Andrei's head bodyguard was having difficulty adjusting to being present as a guest and not being on duty. So, he stood with the wall at his back next to the door leading outside.

The emotions welling inside Andrei were foreign and familiar at the same time. From the moment Zaria entered his life, things had begun to shift. He was still Andrei Artyom Antonov, but he'd also changed in some ways. And his Svet was the catalyst.

Seeming to feel his eyes on her, Zaria stopped talking mid-sentence. Staring at him, she tilted her head to the side. Her silent question was clear. *"Are you okay?"*

A barely perceptible dip of his chin was Andrei's response. When her expression shifted, he tilted his head toward the doorway leading into the kitchen. Placing a hand on Ensley's arm, Zaria left their conversation with a quick word.

Exiting the room behind her, Andrei caught Uncle Neal's expression, and noted him leaning over to whisper into his wife's ear. Undeterred, Andrei followed the sway of Zaria's hips. When she stopped in front of the island in the kitchen, he slipped an arm around her waist guiding her through to the hallway. They walked until they were in the family room standing before the fireplace.

Behind the protective grating, a fire crackled giving the room a soft glow enhanced by the twinkling lights on the Christmas tree. Once they stopped, Zaria turned to him, placing her hands on his chest and searching his face. Andrei wrapped his arms around her and schooled his features, giving her no clue as to why he'd brought her so far away from the others.

"Are you okay, big guy?"

Clasping one of her hands in his, he brought it to his lips. The kiss he placed on her palm was gentle. Reverent. Her response to the affection was to caress his beard with her other hand.

"I am fine, Svet. More than fine."

"Okay...So, why are we in here instead of with our family and friends?"

Pressing a peck to her forehead Andrei fingered the sun shaped pendant attached to the necklace hanging from her neck. It rested just above her bosom with the gemstones reflecting the light, twinkling like a star in the sky. This wasn't the moment he'd planned, but Andrei couldn't wait a second longer.

"Svet, when I gave you this necklace for your birthday, I knew you didn't understand why. To you, it was simply a pretty bauble. You accepted it graciously and indulge me by wearing it every day."

Both of Zaria's soft hands cupped his face. Her dark brown eyes seemed to peer directly into his soul.

"I'm not indulging you. I love this necklace. Not just because it's beautiful. Because you gave it to me. But, please tell me. What did it mean to you?"

Andrei's fingers flexed at her back before he guided her to the chair nearest the hearth. Gently encouraging her to sit, he dropped to his knee in front of her. Taking both of her hands in his, he rubbed his thumbs along the backs up to her wrist.

"To me, Svet. It was part of a promise as well as a symbol of who you are to me."

Zaria's expression softened and her eyes projected her love as clearly as if she'd spoken the words aloud. Turning her hands beneath his, she tangled their fingers. Andrei looked down at them admiring the contrast. Her softness. His hardness. Her small slender digits where his were long and thick. They complimented one another beautifully.

Gazing into her face, Andrei reached into his pocket removing the velvet covered box which looked tiny in his hand. Lifting the lid, he revealed the custom-made ring. One five carat diamond positioned at the center surrounded by yellow sapphires all set in a platinum band. It perfectly matched the pendant resting against her chest.

Zaria's cupped hands covered the lower part of her face. Eyes brimming with tears, probed Andrei's.

"Svet, I love you. You are my light. The center of my universe. Your rays brighten everything around you bathing it in your warmth. Would you do me the honor of being my wife?"

Her nod preceded her launching herself into his arms.

"Whoa, Svet! Careful."

Andrei chided gently as he quickly adjusted to having both arms full of his woman. Shifting until he was seated on the floor with Zaria in his lap, he returned her tight hug resting his chin on top of her head, nestled amongst her springy curls. After a few moments, Andrei pulled back to look into her face.

"Should I take your response as a *yes*, Svet?"

Swatting his chest, Zaria swiped at her eyes. "So, now you've got jokes?"

Maneuvering until she straddled his lap, Zaria stretched up to kiss his lips. Ending with parting pecks, she murmured, "Yes, Andrei Artyom Antonov. I will be your wife."

While her initial reaction was a good indicator of her acceptance, actually hearing her say the words released a flood of emotions, causing Andrei's normally steady hands to tremble slightly when he removed the ring from its pillowy home. Sliding it onto her finger, he kissed the back then front of her hand before capturing her lips once again.

Taking care not to squeeze her too tightly, Andrei pulled his Svet as close as humanly possible as he whispered words of appreciation and love in her ear. This. This was the moment he'd contemplated as he stared at her from behind the bar the night of her best friend's engagement party. Having her in his arms, carrying his child and soon to be his wife. It was the life he'd never dreamed he'd have, but one he'd cherish until he could no longer draw breath.

Zaria Marie Coleman would soon become Zaria Marie Antonov. She revived and was keeping his mama's traditions alive, had helped him breach the gap with Vitaly and had given him a new family. Everything was right in his world.

Epilogue

Three Months Later

Andrei bolted from the vehicle as soon as it rolled to a stop. Yeva said something to him, but he couldn't hear anything above the pounding of his heart. Taking long strides through the automatic doors of the hospital, he was almost frantic in his search for signage telling him where to go.

Turning in response to a hard tap on his shoulder, Andrei glared at the offender. Yeva tilted his head to the right and pointed.

"This way."

Those two words were all Andrei needed. Everyone not his Svet was ignored as he traversed the hallway until he finally saw the sign indicating the direction to the private birthing rooms. He'd researched hospitals and had contemplated purchasing property to be near what was arguably the best maternity hospital in the world.

His Svet wouldn't hear of it. She conceded to the private hospital north of Las Vegas and more than a half hour away from their home. The time now seemed like entirely too long of a trip.

Pacing impatiently in front of the doors, he considered shouldering his way through. But they opened, allowing him entry. When he rounded the corner he stopped so suddenly, someone bumped into his back. Not bothering to look behind him. Andrei advanced on Zaria who was seated next to Carol Jamieson on a plush two-person sofa. Carver's father was seated in the chair. His stare was fixed on the door to the right of the seating area.

"Svet?" Andrei's chest heaved as his thoughts attempted to catch up with what his eyes told him. Zaria looked from Andrei to just past him. When she went to stand, he hurried to her side.

Now nearing the end of her second trimester, she'd complained of having difficulty doing normal things—like standing up after being seated on a particularly comfortable piece of furniture.

"Do not try to stand, Svet. Are you okay? When Frederick said you called. That you were in the hospital."

Zaria rubbed his facial hair and shook her head. "No. I called and said I was ***at*** the hospital, not ***in*** the hospital. I'm fine. Alyssa's in labor."

"Alyssa?" It was taking longer than it should for the information to filter past Andrei's anxiety, but her statement finally penetrated the wall.

"Yes, big guy. Alyssa is in labor. Carver is in with her now. We stepped out when Yeva texted saying you were on your way."

At the mention of his name, Andrei looked over his shoulder at the other man. Yeva simply shrugged.

"I tried to tell you. Multiple times. You were not listening to me."

Zaria drew his attention back to her with two fingers on his chin guiding his gaze back to hers. Taking his hand in hers, she placed it on her protruding belly.

"I'm fine. Your daughter is fine as well. She's kicking me like she's trying out for a professional soccer team and standing on my bladder. Business as usual."

The rapid thumping of his heart finally slowed as he focused on where his fingers were spread across her middle. Right on cue, his little angel performed her trick causing a bump to appear beneath two of his splayed fingers.

"Look at her. Always showing off for her papa."

Zaria often said their daughter was more active when she heard his voice. So, he talked to her often.

Now assured of the safety of his family, Andrei sat back on his heels. The door to their right opened and Carver stepped through wearing hospital scrubs. Ripping away the cap covering his hair, he stepped into the room wearing the biggest smile Andrei had ever seen on his friend's face.

Andrei got to his feet then helped Zaria stand. The Jamieson's shot across the room to embrace their son.

"She's so beautiful. Wait til y'all see her." Carver hugged his parents.

Andrei slipped an arm around Zaria's waist, tugging her into his side with a hand resting on their child's first home. Her fingers tangled with his on her stomach and he dropped a kiss onto her forehead.

Soon, this would be them. It would be him walking out to let their family know their little *businka* had arrived. And he couldn't imagine anything he wanted more than to welcome his daughter into the world surrounded by everyone who was ready to love and protect her. It was going to be a beautiful day.

The End

Sneak Peek

DRAFT PICK SEASON III: DENZEL

Denzel stared at the monitor in his home office as his attorney went over the final details surrounding his acquisition of controlling shares of CleanSun, the solar energy company. Wendy was seated to his left with her laptop open in front of her. His personal business manager was always checking and double checking, no matter who dispensed the information.

According to Derek, everything was in place and a meeting with the board had been arranged for the next week. Two days after Christmas, people were typically still in holiday mode. It was impressive that the team had managed to keep this moving forward so quickly. But, money was a great motivator.

When Denzel received the call from Andrei about the company, he'd joked that someone must have fucked up to get on the big Russian's radar. He was right, but the recommendation had been sound. With better leadership at the helm, CleanSun could more than double their profits and help the environment in the process.

The meeting was just wrapping up when Denzel's phone rang. Looking at the screen, a smile spread across his face. Waving to Wendy, he stood from the table.

"What's up, CJ? Did you miss me? We just video chatted two days ago."

Denzel plopped into the chair behind his desk and moved the mouse around to wake the computer. He was slightly exaggerating about the last time they'd spoken. It had been more than a week since he'd had to talk his friend down from going overboard with the buying for his and Alyssa's yet to be born child. Not that he totally succeeded, but at least he kept him from buying anything the baby wouldn't be able to use until age three.

"Miss you? You call me every other day. I could be just making sure your ass was still alive."

"Whatever, man. I know you're all broken up inside."

"Anyway..." Carver dragged out the word, letting it be known he was done with the joking segment of their conversation.

"I was checking to see when you're coming in for the thing at Andrei's place."

"Funny you should ask. I have some business in Vegas next week, so I was planning to stay over since the festivities kick off on Saturday. Why? What's up?"

Denzel heard shuffling in the background and the closing of a door before Carver spoke again.

"I heard through the grapevine that the queen might be coming in early. I didn't know if you knew."

Denzel's pulse kicked up at Carver's revelation. He'd hoped, but it hadn't been confirmed that Dominique would be in attendance at the Russian Holiday/Christmas celebration Andrei and his lady were having at his place. Since they were cousins, there was a high probability Zaria would invite Dominique. But until now, he hadn't been certain.

He would've gone regardless. But knowing she'd be there was the ice cream, cherry, and chocolate fudge on his sundae. Pumping a fist in the air, he sat up straighter in his seat.

"See. That's what real friends are supposed to do. Let a brotha know what's going on, so he can be ready."

"You're welcome." Carver's tone carried a cocky edge, but Denzel wouldn't let the razzing dampen his excitement. This time when he saw Dominique Truman, things would be different. He'd grown tired of their current dynamic. It was time to stop playing around.

"Question." Carver broke into Denzel's mental planning.

"What?"

"Do you plan to actually talk to her this time?"

"Fuck off. You act like all I do is stare at her whenever I see her."

"That's because you do, creeper." Carver quipped wryly, prompting Denzel to flip him off. It didn't matter if his friend couldn't see him. That part was irrelevant.

~

Denzel worked to keep his fingers from tapping out a beat on the arm of the chair. He was seated in the festively decorated sunroom at Andrei's. And Fuck Carver Jamieson. He ***was*** staring at the beautiful Dominique Truman.

The urge to tap was to squelch the desire to stalk across the room and rip off Vitaly Antonov's arm. His logical mind said the little shit was fucking with him by deigning to touch her, but logic didn't apply to this situation. Knowing he was Andrei's younger brother was saving the goalie from the consequences of being so forward.

Denzel had heard all the rah-rah about them being a family now that Andrei was with Zaria, but he called bullshit. The guy was clearly flirting with Dominique, and she was eating it up. Every time she giggled, Denzel wanted to knock out one of Vitaly's teeth. Let's see him smile pretty with big ass gaps where his incisors were supposed to be.

The conversational hum in the room was background noise to the thoughts in Denzel's head. Knowing Vitaly was doing this shit on purpose wasn't doing much to keep him from wanting to walk over there and tell him to get his hands off his fucking woman.

The problem was, if Denzel gave in to that urge, it would definitely set him back with Dominique. Not to mention what would happen with her parents being in the room. Hell, he'd just listened to her father rip into Andrei and Vitaly the night before because they hadn't included him in their little venture to eliminate a threat to Zaria.

The man had been dead ass serious when he told them not to do it again without telling him. While Denzel appreciated Neal Truman's protectiveness, he wasn't interested in being on the man's bad side before he'd had a chance to truly win Dominique.

Acknowledgments

First, a huge Thank You to everyone who has supported me and this series. From what began as a thought I had in passing, we are now on the second published novel and the third Vella in the Draft Pick series. I am more than grateful for the readers who continue to purchase tokens, leave thumbs up and give feedback. It is invaluable. For the ladies who give me a serotonin boost every time a new episode releases, you are the absolute best! Angela, Cindy, Kimberly, Raquel, Shavon, Stacey. You are amazing and I can't thank you enough for rocking with me.

I couldn't have done any of this without the support of the best writing partners in the world. Brianna and Niccoyan, thank you for reading everything I write first and giving me your honest feedback. They say 'Iron sharpens iron', and it's never more true with the two of you. You keep me striving to improve.

A special thank you to Authors Cereza and Ancelli. You both gave me to push to try something different with my writing platforms and you changed my world. I can't express how much it means to me.

About the Author

Darie McCoy is an independent author of contemporary, interracial, romantic suspense, and paranormal/shifter romance books. A reader first, she enjoys reading books across many genres although romance holds a special place in her heart. Her experience working in a STEM field offers her a unique perspective which she uses in each story she pens.

When she doesn't have her nose in a book or her fingers on the keyboard, Darie enjoys working in her vegetable garden. A serial hobbyist, she also enjoys knitting, sewing, baking and canning. One of her favorite treats to make is salted caramel popcorn. Amongst her friends, she's known to transport the sweet treat in large quantities to share whenever they get together.

Born and raised in the south, Darie stands by the staunchly held southern sentiments that the best tea is sweet tea and college football is life.

Also by Darie McCoy

Central Valley Pack Series

Chosen

Healed

Frost Family Series

For Real

Sano's Queen (A Novella)

Christmas Candy

Draft Pick Series

Draft Pick Season I: Carver

Draft Pick Season III: Denzel (Kindle Vella)

Other books/stories

Involuntary

Just Kiss Me (Part of Cupid's Kiss Anthology)

Toad: Sin City MC Oakland

Controlled Desire: Fall of Desire

www.ingramcontent.com/pod-product-compliance
Lightning Source LLC
LaVergne TN
LVHW010630110826
845149LV00014B/2816
9781961999114